Three Spiritualist Novels

Three Spiritualist Novels
by
Elizabeth Stuart Phelps

The Gates Ajar (1868)
Beyond the Gates (1883)
and
The Gates Between (1887)

Introduction by
Nina Baym

UNIVERSITY OF ILLINOIS PRESS
URBANA AND CHICAGO

Introduction © 2000 by the Board of Trustees
of the University of Illinois
All rights reserved
Manufactured in the United States of America
♾ This book is printed on acid-free paper.

This compilation of three late-nineteenth-century novels
by Elizabeth Stuart Phelps retains the spelling, capitalization,
punctuation, and grammar of the originals.

Library of Congress Cataloging-in-Publication Data
Phelps, Elizabeth Stuart, 1844–1911.
[Novels. Selections]
Three spiritualist novels / by Elizabeth Stuart Phelps;
introduction by Nina Baym.
p.   cm.
Includes bibliographical references.
Contents: The gates ajar—Beyond the gates—
The gates between.
ISBN 0-252-02597-0 (alk. paper)—
ISBN 0-252-06907-2 (pbk.: alk. paper)
1. Future life—Fiction. 2. Spiritualism—Fiction.
3. Christian fiction, American.
I. Title: 3 spiritualist novels. II. Title.
PS3142.A6   2000
812'.4—DC21   00-023420

1 2 3 4 5 C P 5 4 3 2 1

Contents

❋

Introduction

Nina Baym

When *The Gates Ajar* appeared in 1868, Elizabeth Stuart Phelps was just twenty-four years old. She started writing it when she was twenty, took two years to complete it, and then revised it "so many times that I could have said it by heart."[1] Published by the prestigious Boston firm of Ticknor and Fields, the book made her a literary celebrity. Its description of an afterlife where the dead retained their physical shapes, their personalities, and their love for those left behind made a powerful impression on readers who had lost sons and brothers to the Civil War. They wrote thousands of agonized, grieving letters to this young writer who argued so persuasively that ideas of a material heaven did not contradict the Bible's teachings.

In her long, successful career, Phelps published more than fifty-five books—novels, stories, poems, children's tales, essays, biographies, an autobiography, and religious fiction. She is among the most important of a generation of literary women active from the 1870s to the end of the nineteenth century. Nostalgic for antebellum ideals of Christian domesticity and homogeneous community life, pushed ineluctably into confrontation with a deracinated, heterogeneous modernity, they struggled to situate women like themselves—white, Anglo, genteel, idealistic, socially conscious—in a world constantly outrunning their efforts to grasp it. The work of these women, including Mary E. W. Freeman, Sarah Orne Jewett, Louisa May Alcott, Rose Terry Cooke, Celia Thaxter, Rebecca Harding Davis, even

Harriet Beecher Stowe, has been especially difficult for contemporary critics to appreciate on its own terms.

Fifteen years after *The Gates Ajar,* Phelps returned to its premise with *Beyond the Gates* (1883) and, four years after that, with *The Gates Between* (1887). Although the three books share no characters or plots, their allusive titles construct them as a series. The gates represent the barrier between this world and the next. Insisting that they are open just enough for mortals to catch glimpses of the beyond, each book describes the next world in loving detail. God, says *The Gates Ajar,* "has obviously not *opened* the gates which bar heaven from our sight, but he has as obviously not *shut* them" (133).

The careful specificity of each *Gates* book conveys the same notion of the spiritual world as a perfected, beautified version of the world we live in. Except for the absence of sin, death, and defect, the next world is recognizably our own, with landscapes, towns, homes, people. It is the world as one would wish it to be. In that they correct all the shortcomings of our current existence, these are by definition Utopian books.[2] But they lack the Utopian thrust toward realizable social reform. On the contrary, they rise from the conviction that life in this world falls so far short of human needs and desires that only a compensatory afterlife can rectify its tragedies. As Phelps put it powerfully in her autobiography, "Unless He created this world from sheer extravagance in the infliction of purposeless pain, there must be another life to justify, to heal, to comfort, to offer happiness, to develop holiness. If there be another world, and such a one, it will be no theologic drama, but a sensible, wholesome scene" (*Chapters* 129).

Phelps's goal in all three books was to depict a "sensible, wholesome" afterlife whose attributes might reconcile human beings to earthly loss and sorrow. Although a devout Christian, she rejected the orthodoxy that after death the saved became disembodied entities devoted entirely and eternally to worshiping the godhead. Raised as a Calvinist, she nonetheless discarded the central Calvinist tenet that almost everybody had been damned either by predestination or by their own free will and would therefore spend eternity in Hell. Surely, she reasoned, a loving God would allow continued progress toward perfection after death. In an afterlife available to all, what has been taken away in this world will be restored, what has not been given in this world will be granted.

Most twentieth-century critics of *The Gates Ajar* assumed that Phelps's materially specific afterlife was her own invention. This is not so; rather, the details came directly from prior Spiritualist writings. A widespread, informal Spiritualist movement had emerged in the United States in the late 1840s. In 1855 the Boston-based *North American Review* said there were at least two million American Spiritualists; in 1869 Harriet Beecher Stowe urged her publishers to advertise her *Oldtown Folks* in the Spiritualist weekly *The Banner of Light* because its visionary episodes would appeal to the four or five million Spiritualists in the nation; in 1870 the Spiritualist historian Emma Hardinge claimed that American Spiritualists numbered about eleven million.[3] Even if Stowe's number was closer to the truth than Hardinge's it seems clear that there were millions of Spiritualists; and if one grants Hardinge's claim that Spiritualism was a religion despite its lack of organized church and formal creed, then it must be seen as one of the largest "denominations" in the United States in the second half of the nineteenth century.

The great surge in Spiritualist numbers came after the Civil War, in connection with the war's horrible death toll. Bereaved people took comfort in the Spiritualist vision of a friendly, familiar, material heaven populated by recognizable, embodied, sociable spirits busily perfecting themselves, on the one hand, and trying to communicate with those they had left behind, on the other. What Phelps did uniquely, however—what, as the daughter of one of the nation's foremost Calvinist theologians, she was especially well positioned to do—was assure people that Spiritualist ideas about the afterlife comported with Holy Writ. This made Spiritualist consolation available to many who would otherwise have dismissed it as unscriptural if not downright sacrilegious. *The Gates Ajar* clearly said something that mattered: it sold at least eighty thousand copies in the United States before the end of the century, sold more than that number in England, was translated into at least four languages, and remained constantly in print in the United States until early in the twentieth century.

Phelps's biographers think *The Gates Ajar* emerged from a personal crisis: the young man Phelps had expected to marry was killed in the Civil War.[4] In her reticent autobiography, *Chapters from a Life,* she herself located its origins in a more impersonal and benevolent, yet passionately felt, motive: she wanted to comfort "some few—I did not think at all about comforting many, not daring to suppose that incredible privilege possible—of the women whose misery crowded the land" (97). She never anticipated the book's enormous success (neither did her publishers) and had no plans to follow it with other *Gates* books. By the time she returned to the concept fifteen years later, she had published (among many other works) four important novels struggling to make a place for women in the postbellum world: *Hedged In* (1870), about unwed motherhood and the underclass; *The Silent Partner* (1871), about the working class and industrialization; *The Story of Avis* (1877), about the conflict between a woman's artistic ambitions and her life as wife and mother; and *Doctor Zay* (1882), about a woman physician.

These four novels, like *The Gates Ajar,* were written for women; unlike it, they are secular works. They feature middle-class heroines for whom bourgeois domesticity—the great ideal of antebellum women's fiction—is a trap. Moral duty to other women, or ethical duty to one's own abilities, strains the boundaries of the domestic. In *Hedged In* a genteel woman takes in the working-class fallen mother; in *The Silent Partner* the daughter of a factory owner involves herself in the workers' lives. Avis is an artistic genius but also—fatally for her talent—a professor's daughter and a faculty wife. Dr. Zay is a homeopathic physician driven by the desire to ease the physical and social suffering of rural women, as likely to force an errant man into marriage as to deliver the child he has fathered with an innocent woman whose fault was loving too deeply. These stories start where antebellum fictions had ended, asking, What should a privileged woman's work be on this earth? Phelps's narratives give equal weight to the liberal idea that women have the same right as men to fulfill themselves individually and to the conservative idea that women naturally fulfill themselves through useful, devoted service to others. In *Avis* and *Dr. Zay* as well, the theme develops partly in relation to invalid men who need noble, self-sacrificing women to care for them. This particular focus, which might have reflected the fact of her father's protracted invalidism, strongly emphasizes the competing ideologies of womanhood that Phelps and other women writers in her generation tried so hard to reconcile.

The 1883 and 1887 *Gates* books responded to events in Phelps's life rather than to a cultural crisis. (Perhaps this is why she does not mention either of them in *Chapters from a Life*.) In 1883 her much-loved younger brother, Moses, tripped over his loaded gun and accidentally shot himself to death. Increasingly incapacitated by chronic insomnia, she thought her career was over. And, at the age of thirty-nine, she had not yet married. Despite the marital misery of *Avis*—today her best-known heroine—Phelps's work overall demonstrates an intense belief in romantic, heterosexual love as essential to any woman's full development. How to reconcile the struggle for individual integrity with the drive to surrender oneself to romantic passion formed a subtext in all four novels named above. The second and third *Gates* books, like the first, merge the motifs of love lost and love not experienced. They again evoke an afterlife both restorative and compensatory.

As strongly as *The Gates Ajar* had done in 1868, the two *Gates* books of the 1880s direct attention away from the real present toward an imaginary future. Like most of Phelps's books, they care more about the desires and losses of women than of men. It is not that she thought men suffer less, however; it is that she thought women are more needy. Once again publicizing her consolatory vision, Phelps modeled the kind of woman's work she thought women like herself—genteel women of some means, with influence, with access to the public sphere—ought to do: helping the less fortunate of her own kind. Claiming the right to sermonize, to promulgate a countergospel to that enunciated by the conservative churches, Phelps continued to work at the boundaries of women's permissible speech.

The womanly focus in these books comes through most strongly in their vision of the afterlife as profoundly domestic—therefore, profoundly feminine. (Whether it is feminist or not is a matter for debate.) Phelps saw the human spirit as fundamentally relational, which is why even in heaven it needs a body. She saw the highest relation as the domestic, heterosexual couple. She theorized that whereas only the best men are domestically inclined, even quite ordinary women are domestic by nature. This does not mean that all women like to do housework; rather, it means they are most fulfilled when they occupy a protected home space. The *Gates* books never overturn the domestic model; instead, they perfect it.

※

Elizabeth Stuart Phelps's commitment to domesticity accorded with the shape of her own life, most of which she spent in the state of Massachusetts—in fact, in the college town of Andover, to which she moved at the age of four. Because both her parents were writers with a sense of moral mission, she saw authorship as a form of social activism. Baptized Mary Gray, she assumed her mother's name when she became a literary professional, as a gesture of filial piety. The mother's brief authorial career, cut short by early death, was to be continued in her daughter's work.

Phelps's mother was born in 1815; her father, Austin Phelps, in 1820. Her mother was a daughter of Moses Stuart, a professor of sacred literature at Andover Theological Seminary, a resolutely Calvinist college. Her father, a minister's son, was a young pastor in Boston when her parents met. The two married in 1842 and their first child, Mary, arrived on August 31, 1844. In 1848 her father became a professor of sacred rhetoric and homiletics at Andover. Her mother began to write after moving back to her natal home. *Sunny Side; or, The*

Country Minister's Wife appeared in 1851 to considerable acclaim, selling 100,000 copies by the end of the year. She followed this in 1852 with *A Peep at "Number Five"; or, A Chapter in the Life of a City Pastor.* Both books told about the pains and pleasures of ministerial life from the back side of the tapestry, as a wife would experience it. In her daughter's words, these were "simple home stories" that took "a hold upon the popular heart" (*Chapters* 12).

Phelps's mother survived the birth of her third child, Amos Lawrence, for only three months. (Moses had been born in 1849.) Her death in November 1852 at the age of thirty-seven elevated her to sainthood in the memory of her eight-year-old daughter. Much later, the adult writer limned a striking picture of a New England woman driving herself to death through perfectionist overwork. In her memorial biography of her father, Phelps said that in the early years of marriage her mother had given herself "utterly to the sweet ingenuities of love." Marriage, she continued, "under such conditions becomes no idle or leisurely dream. To the usual struggle, to the common human battle, is added a fine, high fever of aspiration, a silent determination to achieve a supreme result, to 'be what woman never was before,' and to do 'what love has never done.' Under the movement of a nature like hers a woman may make a man divinely happy. But she may die in trying to do so."[5]

In short, looking back on the event, Phelps suggested that even had she never become a writer her mother might well have killed herself by overinvesting in her domestic roles. But this was not all: "genius was in her, and would out. . . . [A] wife, a mother, a housekeeper, a hostess, in delicate health, on an academic salary, undertakes a deadly load when she starts upon a literary career. She lifted it to her frail shoulders, and she fell beneath it" (*Austin Phelps* 87). Whether this story of her mother's doubly caused death corresponds to the now unrecoverable facts, it captures for later readers Phelps's sense that womanhood, rightly performed, meant martyrdom. *Chapters from a Life* puts it tersely: "Her last book and her last baby came together, and killed her. . . . She lived one of those rich and piteous lives such as only gifted women know; torn by the civil war of the dual nature which can be given to women only" (12).

As for herself: "It was as natural for her daughter to write as to breathe" (*Chapters* 12); but a few pages later she revises this statement in a crucial way: "I said it was impossible to be her daughter and not to write. Rather, I should say, impossible to be their daughter and not to have something to say, and a pen to say it" (15). For Austin Phelps was also a writer, and a writing instructor as well. His work as a professor of rhetoric was teaching students to write sermons. He contributed often to theological journals; among his several books, one on prayer—*The Still Hour* (1860)—may have sold 200,000 copies, twice as many as *The Sunny Side*. "He was my climate," Phelps wrote. "His appreciation of the uses and graces of language very early descended like a mantle upon me. I learned to read and to love reading, not because I was made to, but because I could not help it. It was the atmosphere I breathed" (*Chapters* 17).

Thus the daughter imagined her parents as equal contributors to a domestic and artistic whole. Even before chronic insomnia forced her father's early retirement from Andover, he worked much at home; after his wife's death, though he married twice more and started a second family, as his own father had done, he assumed many maternal duties; and after retirement his constant poor health looked much like the sort of invalidism stereotypically associated with nineteenth-century women. Phelps's writing merged her mother's domestic fiction with her father's polemical sermonizing. Her domestic ideal, on earth or in heaven, fantasized a home enclosing two differently gendered people who were nevertheless much the same: equally womanly and manly in the best senses of both words.

Although the *Gates* books depart radically from her father's Calvinism, although the books may be thought of as quite openly rejecting his particular theological worldview, Phelps nevertheless insisted that her deepest idea of what God ought to be (and therefore had to be) came directly from her father's feminized example: he "represented everything that was tender, unselfish, pure, and noble, to my mind," sustaining "the ideal of a fatherhood which gave me the best conception I shall ever get, in this world, of the Fatherhood of God" (*Chapters* 53). Phelps dedicated *The Gates Ajar* to her father even though she meant it especially for women in a time when grief hung over the land "like a material miasma" (97). It seemed to her that women needed a comforting message more than men because they had fewer resources for coping with grief and because "even the best and kindest forms of our prevailing beliefs had nothing to say to an afflicted women that could help her much. Creeds and commentaries and sermons were made by men" (98).

The year after publishing *The Gates Between,* Phelps married twenty-seven-year-old Herbert Dickinson Ward. Ward was an aspiring journalist whom she met through family friends. The two collaborated on three biblical romances, none a commercial success. From the start Phelps was acutely conscious of the age difference between them. Both were in poor health, and after a while they wintered separately, he in Florida and she in Massachusetts. Phelps died of heart failure in 1911 at the age of sixty-six. She published up to the year of her death, with her last novels focusing increasingly on the twinned, autobiographical themes of sickness and caretaking. Her literary interest in the spiritual afterlife continued to find expression: in essays collected in an 1889 volume, *The Struggle for Immortality,* and in a closet-drama version of *The Gates Between* published in 1901 under the title *Within the Gates.* Essays in *The Struggle for Immortality* express hope that science would authenticate at least some of the claims to psychic experience swirling about in the fin-de-siècle atmosphere of intensified Spiritualism, New Thought, Theosophy, and other occult movements. It is clear that she "believed" in spiritualist phenomena even though she herself never experienced them directly.

❊

Phelps's beliefs in spiritualist phenomena partly derived from spiritualist events in her family. To remind readers of these events, both her memoir of her father and her autobiography start by noting that the famous "Stratford poltergeist" was a family visitation. For seven months in 1850, the home of her grandfather Eliakim Phelps (at that time a minister in Stratford, Connecticut) was invaded by a rampaging spirit. The spirit moved furniture, tossed dishes around the table, bent spoons, and performed other acts typical of house-possession. Eliakim Phelps never doubted that the events were genuine or that they were demonic in origin. Austin Phelps, married and living in Andover, supported his father: "That the facts were real, a thousand witnesses testified," he said. "That they were inexplicable by any known principles of science was equally clear to all who saw and heard them, who were qualified to judge. Experts in science went to Stratford in triumphant expectation, and came away in dogged silence, convinced of nothing, yet solving nothing" (*Austin Phelps* 8). Skeptics connected the occurrences to a teenage son, especially when the phenomena followed him to boarding school.

The events had a strong impact on Phelps herself. She says in *Chapters from a Life* that as a child, "Night upon night I have crept gasping to bed, and shivered for hours with my head under the clothes, after an evening spent in listening to this authentic and fantastic family tale. How the candlesticks walked out into the air from the mantelpiece and back again . . . how the dishes at the table leaped, and the silver forks were bent by unseen hands" (6–7). A story, "The Day of My Death," published in *Harper's Monthly* in October 1868— shortly before *The Gates Ajar* appeared—and in her tellingly titled collection *Men, Women, and Ghosts* (1869), repeats the much-publicized details. Though, as she admits, "not a candlestick ever walked an inch for me" (*Chapters* 9), she was inclined to believe in the authenticity of these phenomena—one might say she *wanted* to believe in them—and hoped they might "be tamed and yoked, and made to work for human happiness" (9).

The Stratford home invasion occurred shortly after wide press coverage of the "Rochester rappings" effectively made Spiritualism into a popular religion.[6] The theoretical basis for the movement, merging Mesmerism's idea of an occult magnetic fluid with views

of the afterlife drawn from the Swedish mystic Emanuel Swedenborg, was already in place. Those who know Swedenborg only as a
major influence on Ralph Waldo Emerson will be surprised to learn
that Swedenborg claimed to have visited the afterworld frequently,
touring it with a spirit guide. His *Heaven and Hell* showed up on many
an American bookshelf and is cited in *The Gates Ajar*. An indigenous
account resembling Swedenborg's was dictated to a scribe by An-
drew Jackson Davis, a shoemaker's apprentice from Poughkeepsie,
New York. Davis publicized his regular visits to what he influential-
ly called the "summerland" in many books that appeared from the
late 1840s into the 1860s.

In 1848, in the hamlet of Hydesville, just outside Rochester, New
York, an older farm couple and their two young children—Kate and
Margaret (whose ages vary in diverse accounts from early teens to
just eight and six)—heard mysterious knocks and rappings in the
night. Neighbors came to hear them. Word got out. Through an
evolving, unstructured series of events participated in by many people,
the rappings came to be interpreted as signals from the spirit of a
murdered peddler buried in the basement. The sisters—young, innocent, female—came to be seen as unwitting mediums for this spirit
communication. Apparently spirits could not yet directly cross the
barrier between worlds; they could communicate only through what
was called—in specific reference to the telegraph, invented four years
earlier by Samuel F. B. Morse—spiritual telegraphy. Since few understood what electricity consisted of, the presumption that spirits
might communicate through the mysterious ethereal fluid perme-
ating the universe, a fluid also transporting magnetism, electricity, and
light—a fluid not to be disposed of until Einstein's theories made it
superfluous—seemed reasonable not only to the uninstructed but also
to the educated.

Hydesville became the focus of a media circus as crowds arrived
to witness the raps, which were never heard unless one of the sisters
was present. Somebody suggested the spirit might answer questions
by rapping out numbers corresponding to letters in the alphabet (one

rap for A, two for B, and so on); another proposed that one rap for yes and two for no would be much more efficient. This spirit—and, soon, others like it—obliged. Inevitably, people began trying to contact their beloved dead. The Fox sisters, helped by a much older sister with managerial ability, began holding public seances for pay, traveling to such large cities as Boston, Philadelphia, and New York. Throughout the nation, dozens, hundreds, perhaps thousands of professional mediums followed in their wake. The spirits sent messages through them by rappings, lights, bells, tipping tables; by trance or automatic writing; by entranced speech. Untold numbers of people tried to reach the spirits privately.

If one defines an educated person as someone who rejects the possibility of spirit communication, then by definition no educated person was a Spiritualist. It seems, however, that the movement did attract diverse kinds of educated persons, as that phrase might be more capaciously interpreted. Idealistic, anticonformist optimists distrustful of organized religion but inclined toward belief rather than skepticism, who thought of spirits making contact with mortals as a great step forward toward the millennium, became Spiritualists. Radical Quakers, Unitarians, and especially Universalists—with their belief in immediate salvation for all—were especially drawn to Spiritualism. Kind-hearted, pious people uncomfortable with the wanton cruelty of an all-powerful God who would wrap up a life of earthly torture by sending one to Hell also adopted Spiritualism. Orthodox people trying to understand what St. Paul meant by saying the dead would rise as spiritual bodies, not disembodied essence, thought perhaps Spiritualism had the answer. Utopianists and communitarians of all kinds, including socialists, found the progressive Spiritualist afterlife attractive. Advocates for women's rights and abolitionists were often Spiritualists.

Less abstractly, Spiritualism spoke to people in dire and immediate need. Bereaved parents and spouses turned to Spiritualism to contact a lost loved one, to hear that the dead child or wife or husband was happy and looking forward to reunion. The idea, too, that the living would eventually enter a world without death, sin, crime, sadness, injustice, need, poverty, illness, loneliness, inequality—a world in which, in short, one lived happily ever after—was tremendously appealing to people from all walks of life whose own lives had disappointed them. It is easy to discount the rationality of these believers, but it would be facile to discount their grief. This, in fact, was exactly Phelps's point in all three of her *Gates* books.

There was inevitably a vast amount of fraud connected with Spiritualism. This constituted less of a deterrent than might have been expected. Some Spiritualists were themselves eager to expose tricksters, although their will to believe kept them from performing this task very well. Most of the better-known mediums of the era were eventually discredited—as sleight-of-hand experts, charlatans who gathered information on their subjects beforehand, or persons especially good at interpreting body language—but the belief that at least some mediums were genuine continued to hold sway. Some well-known scientists in the United States (Robert Hare) and England (William Crookes) signed on as Spiritualists. When, in 1888, Margaret Fox publicly recanted and gave a demonstration of how the rappings had been accomplished, many chose not to believe her.

While it was, specifically, the belief in spirit communication that made Spiritualism abhorrent to many believing Protestants, in times of great grief even they found comfort in the Spiritualist view. Phelps's father, for example, saw Spiritualism as a pure "evil": "The whole business of seeking to unveil the future by means of 'familiar spirits' is forbidden as a sin. The curiosity which prompts it is a sin. Good people have a clear a warning in the Bible to avoid it as they have to avoid lying or profaneness" (*Austin Phelps* 189). Yet, when he lost his son, this man could not forbear from speculating about what he said his creed forbade: "I do often pray to God that He will send some messenger to my boy, to tell him what is in my heart. . . . Every year drops a link in the shortening chain that holds me here, and soon I shall see the boy again" (278).

In the *Gates* books Phelps equivocates on the issue of spirit communication. *The Gates Ajar* contains one carefully placed incident of possible spirit appearance—but whether it was real or just the hallucination of a dying woman is left for readers to decide. *Beyond the Gates* ultimately makes its depiction of the summerland into a fever-caused fantasy—but this does not mean the experience was unreal, only that the narrator, not yet dead, was required to return to earth. *The Gates Between,* the most daring of the three, depicts several episodes of spirit crossings, not least the spirit-written narrative itself. Yet because the author is obviously Elizabeth Stuart Phelps, not a spirit, readers must take the first-person narration as a literary device—thus, Phelps has her cake and eats it too. Overall, and quite unlike the Spiritualists whose belief rested on a material occurrence whose authenticity they accepted, Phelps argues not only for the particularities of her vision but for the requirement that it remain a matter of faith. From her profoundly orthodox, Protestant perspective, the occurrence of a persuasive material phenomenon makes faith unnecessary. Contrariwise, a belief in Spiritualist phenomena on the part of one who has never experienced them firsthand represents a spiritualizing of Spiritualism itself and, through such spiritualizing, an innovation on Spiritualist belief designed to make it acceptable to those who balked at claims of direct, material manifestations.

✳

It remains to say something briefly about the narrative form of the *Gates* books. Each loving description of the afterlife is folded into a novelistic romance. All three are told in the first person. *The Gates Ajar* is written as a series of journal entries by Mary Cabot, whose beloved brother has recently been killed in the Civil War. Mary comes to accept this loss through the counsel of her visiting aunt Winifred, a widow. Mary is disconsolate at first, both because she misses her brother and because she cannot imagine any kind of afterworld in which he might be there, caring about her. Her recovery begins when Winifred suggests that the brother knows very well what is going on in Mary's mind and cares for her as he did when alive. This is to imply that he is still alive in some human sense.

Winifred then talks to Mary about a different kind of heaven from what she has been taught to believe in. Soon, Winifred extends her ministrations to the entire town. She argues differently with each interlocutor, from the simplest kind of assurance that in heaven there will be pianos, or at least their spiritual equivalent, to sophisticated biblical exegesis. The discussion becomes increasingly abstract, amounting ultimately to an extended demonstration that belief in the afterlife as she describes it is nowhere contradicted, and is sometimes authorized, by Scripture.[7] The reader comes to see in time that Winifred's faith is inspired by her own loss: she needs to believe in the possibility of a personal, individual reunion with her husband after death. The specific details of Winifred's vision, as she freely admits, correspond to what she is capable of imagining. The reality may be quite different, she concedes, but whatever it is, it will correspond to unmet earthly need or desire. The heavenly piano may not be anything like the earthly one—but it will do a piano's work for the longing soul.

Beyond the Gates is narrated by a desperately ill woman after her apparent death. Her adventures begin when her beloved dead father comes to collect her, and we then follow her activities in the spirit land as she learns to live there. Lacking the polemical edge of *The Gates Ajar,* this book is chiefly descriptive, amounting to a sort of tourist visit to an exotic land heavily dependent on Swedenborg and Davis. Its motives, as I have suggested, are not Utopian; heavenly arrangements have no chance of being adopted on earth because they are essentially spiritual. As in *The Gates Ajar,* the book's emotional energy derives from a disrupted love story. The protagonist has never been married, and even in heaven, living in her father's house, she feels the continued emptiness of her solitary state. She knows that her father, much as he loves her, is waiting for her mother—who does, indeed, arrive before the narrative ends. She feels lonely, superfluous; evidences of the great good she has done in her earthly life do not console her.

Ultimately, she meets the spirit of an early love who married some-body else. The marriage was not happy, and his wife, still living, has made a good second marriage. In this narrative turn Phelps approaches the question of spirit affinities, of heavenly recouplings according to affective, not juridical, principles. This was a much-debated question among Spiritualists, the most radical of whom became associated with Free Love advocacy. Phelps hints at this position but evades the issue by returning her protagonist to earth.

In *The Gates Between,* the protagonist is Dr. Esmerald Thorne, who has been killed in a carriage accident. The narrative is presented as a written communication from his spirit; its focus divides once again between a romantic emphasis and the delineation of the afterlife. Dr. Thorne was a good doctor and a well-meaning man but a very im-perfect one. He wooed and married a superlative wife and then neglected her. Happily for him, he is given the otherworldly task of raising his young son, who has also died. Learning to be a nurturing parent, he becomes worthy of the wife he has left behind. His reha-bilitation requires an interim period and an interim space, so that Phelps presents an afterlife not specifically identified with "heaven" but rather with intermediate worlds scattered across the galaxy. *The Gates Between,* unlike the other books, has an unambiguously happy ending, as the long-awaited wife arrives and the domestic family is reunited. Here Spiritualism, far from being an enemy of Christian-ity or even a belief compatible with it, becomes Christianity's high-est expression.

What to make of these three books is up to each reader. That they picked up on numerous emotional and theoretical issues agitating the culture in the years following their publication cannot be doubt-ed. They merge with Phelps's larger woman-centered project in var-ious ways and connect to the work of many other postbellum women (and men) writers whose work, partly energized by religious mo-tives, registered increasing difficulties in accepting conventional or-thodoxy. One leaves the *Gates* books—or, rather, they leave the read-er—with a strong impression of Phelps's tragic sense of life. She was not prepared to reject the religious foundations that so many of her contemporaries were abandoning. But her resolution of the dilemmas of earthly existence—at least as it manifests itself in these three books—is to define death as God's great gift to his human creatures.

Notes

1. Elizabeth Stuart Phelps, *Chapters from a Life* (Boston: Houghton Mifflin, 1897), 100. Subsequent references to this work appear parenthetically in the text.

2. Phelps scholars Carol Farley Kessler, in *Elizabeth Stuart Phelps* (Boston: Twayne, 1982), and Lori Duin Kelly, in *The Life and Works of Elizabeth Stuart Phelps, Victorian Feminist Writer* (Troy, N.Y.: Whitston Publishing Co., 1983), both call the works Utopian.

3. "Modern Necromancy," *North American Review* 80 (1855): 512–27; Joan D. Hedrick, *Harriet Beecher Stowe: A Life* (New York: Oxford University Press, 1994), 346; Emma Hardinge, *Modern American Spiritualism* (1870; rpt., New Hyde Park, N.Y.: University Books, 1970), passim.

4. See "Ward, Elizabeth Stuart Phelps," in *Notable American Women,* ed. Edward T. James (Cambridge, Mass.: Harvard University Press, 1971), 3:539; Kessler, *Elizabeth Stuart Phelps,* 30.

5. Elizabeth Stuart Phelps, *Austin Phelps: A Memoir* (New York: Charles Scribner's Sons, 1892), 53. Subsequent references to this book appear parenthetically in the text.

6. For the summary that follows I draw chiefly on Slater Brown, *The Heyday of Spiritualism* (New York: Hawthorn Books, 1970); R. Lawrence Moore, *In Search of White Crows: Spiritualism, Parapsychology, and American Culture* (New York: Oxford University Press, 1977); Anne Braude, *Radical Spirits: Spiritualism and Women's Rights in Nineteenth-Century America* (Boston: Beacon Press, 1989); Bret E. Carroll, *Spiritualism in Antebellum America* (Bloomington: Indiana University Press, 1997).

7. For a splendid discussion of Winifred's (and Phelps's) interpretive strategies, see Gail V. Smith, "The Popularization of Hermeneutics in *The Gates Ajar,*" *Arizona Quarterly* 54 (1998): 99–133.

The Gates Ajar

Splendor! Immensity! Eternity! Grand words!
Great things! A little definite happiness would be
more to the purpose.

—Madame De Gasparin

To my father, whose life, like a perfume from beyond
the Gates, penetrates every life which approaches it,
the readers of this little book will owe whatever
pleasant thing they may find within its pages.

—E.S.P.

Andover, October 22, 1868

❦ 1 ❧

One week; only one week to-day, this twenty-first of February.

I have been sitting here in the dark and thinking about it, till it seems so horribly long and so horribly short; it has been such a week to live through, and it is such a small part of the weeks that must be lived through, that I could think no longer, but lighted my lamp and opened my desk to find something to do.

I was tossing my paper about,—only my own: the packages in the yellow envelopes I have not been quite brave enough to open yet,— when I came across this poor little book in which I used to keep memoranda of the weather, and my lovers, when I was a school-girl. I turned the leaves, smiling to see how many blank pages were left, and took up my pen, and now I am not smiling any more.

If it had not come exactly as it did, it seems to me as if I could bear it better. They tell me that it should not have been such a shock. "Your brother had been in the army so long that you should have been prepared for anything. Everybody knows by what a hair a sol- dier's life is always hanging," and a great deal more that I am afraid I have not listened to. I suppose it is all true; but that never makes it any easier.

The house feels like a prison. I walk up and down and wonder that I ever called it home. Something is the matter with the sunsets; they come and go, and I do not notice them. Something ails the voices of the children, snowballing down the street; all the music has gone out of them, and they hurt me like knives. The harmless, happy children!—and Roy loved the little children.

Why, it seems to me as if the world were spinning around in the light and wind and laughter, and God just stretched down His hand one morning and put it out.

It was such a dear, pleasant world to be put out!

It was never dearer or more pleasant than it was on that morning. I had not been as happy for weeks. I came up from the Post-Office singing to myself. His letter was so bright and full of mischief! I had not had one like it all the winter. I have laid it away by itself, filled with his jokes and pet names, "Mamie" or "Queen Mamie" every other line, and signed

"Until next time, your happy

"Roy."

I wonder if all brothers and sisters keep up the baby-names as we did. I wonder if I shall ever become used to living without them.

I read the letter over a great many times, and stopped to tell Mrs. Bland the news in it, and wondered what had kept it so long on the way, and wondered if it could be true that he would have furlough in May. It seemed too good to be true. If I had been fourteen instead of twenty-four, I should have jumped up and down and clapped my hands there in the street. The sky was so bright that I could scarcely turn up my eyes to look at it. The sunshine was shivered into little lances all over the glaring white crust. There was a snow-bird chirping and pecking on the maple-tree as I came in.

I went up and opened my window; sat down by it and drew a long breath, and began to count the days till May. I must have sat there as much as half an hour. I was so happy counting the days that I did not hear the front gate, and when I looked down a man stood there,—a great, rough man,—who shouted up that he was in a hurry, and wanted seventy-five cents for a telegram that he had brought over from East Homer. I believe I went down and paid him, sent him away, came up here and locked the door before I read it.

4

Phoebe found me here at dinner-time.

If I could have gone to him, could have busied myself with packing and journeying, could have been forced to think and plan, could have had the shadow of a hope of one more look, one word, I suppose I should have taken it differently. These two words—"shot dead"—shut me up and walled me in, as I think people must feel shut up and walled in, in Hell. I write the words most solemnly, for I know that there has been Hell in my heart.

It is all over now. He came back, and they brought him up the steps, and I listened to their feet,—so many feet; he used to come bounding in. They let me see him for a minute, and there was a funeral, and Mrs. Bland came over, and she and Phoebe attended to everything, I suppose. I did not notice nor think until we had left him out there in the cold and had come back. The windows of his room were opened, and the bitter wind swept in. The house was still and damp. Nobody was there to welcome me. Nobody would ever be . . .

Poor old Phoebe! I had forgotten her. She was waiting at the kitchen window in her black bonnet; she took off my things and made me a cup of tea, and kept at work near me for a little while, wiping her eyes. She came in just now, when I had left my unfinished sentence to dry, sitting here with my face in my hands.

"Laws now, Miss Mary, my dear!" This won't never do,—a rebellin' agin Providence, and singein' your hair on the lamp chimney this way! The dining-room fire's goin' beautiful, and the salmon is toasted to a brown. Put away them papers and come right along!"

Who originated that most exquisite of inquisitions, the condolence system?

A solid blow has in itself the elements of hit rebound; it arouses the antagonism of the life on which it falls; its relief is the relief of a combat.

But a hundred little needles pricking at us,—what is to be done with them? The hands hang down, the knees are feeble. We cannot so much as gasp, because they *are* little needles.

I know that there are those who like these calls; but why, in the name of all sweet pity, must we endure them without respect of persons, as we would endure a wedding reception or make a party-call?

Perhaps I write excitedly and hardly. I feel excited and hard.

I am sure I do not mean to be ungrateful for real sorrowful sympathy, however imperfectly it may be shown, or that near friends (if one has them), cannot give, in such a time as this, actual strength, even if they fail of comfort, by look and tone and love. But it is not near friends who are apt to wound, nor real sympathy which sharpens the worst of the needles. It is the fact that all your chance acquaintances feel called upon to bring their curious eyes and jarring words right into the silence of your first astonishment; taking you in a round of morning calls with kid gloves and parasol, and the liberty to turn your heart about and cut into it at pleasure. You may quiver at every touch, but there is not escape, because it is "the thing."

For instance: Meta Tripp came in this afternoon,—I have refused myself to everybody but Mrs. Bland, before, but Meta caught me in the parlor, and there was no escape. She had come, it was plain enough, because she must, and she had come early, because, she too having lost a brother in the war, she was expected to be very sorry for me. Very likely she was, and very likely she did the best she knew how, but she was—not as uncomfortable as I, but as uncomfortable as she could be, and was evidently glad when it was over. She observed, as she went out, that I shouldn't feel so sad by and by. She felt very sad at first when Jack died, but everybody got over that after a time. The girls were going to sew for the Fair next week at Mr. Quirk's, and she hoped I would exert myself and come.

Ah, well:—

"First learn to love one living man,
Then mayst thou think upon the dead."

It is not that the child is to be blamed for not knowing enough to stay away; but her coming here has made me wonder whether I am different from other women; why Roy was so much more to me than many brothers are to many sisters. I think it must be that there never *was* another like Roy. Then we have lived together so long, we two alone, since father died, that he had grown to me, heart of my heart, and life of my life. It did not seem as if he *could* be taken, and I be left.

Besides, I suppose most young women of my age have their dreams, and a future probable or possible, which makes the very incompleteness of life sweet, because of the symmetry which is waiting somewhere. But that was settled so long ago for me that it makes it very different. Roy was all there was.

February 26th.

Death and Heaven could not seem very different to a Pagan from what they seem to me.

I say this deliberately. It has been deliberately forced upon me. That of which I had a faint consciousness in the first shock takes shape now. I do not see how one with such thoughts in her heart as I have had can possibly be "regenerate," or stand any chance of ever becoming "one of the redeemed." And here I am, what I have been for six years, a member of an Evangelical church, in good and regular standing!

The bare, blank sense of physical repulsion from death, which was all the idea I had of anything when they first brought him home, has not gone yet. It is horrible. It was cruel. Roy, all I had in the wide world,—Roy, with the flash in his eyes, with his smile that lighted the house all up; with his pretty soft hair that I used to curl and kiss about my finger, his bounding step, his strong arms that folded me in and cared for me,—Roy snatched away in an instant by a dreadful God, and laid out there in the wet and snow,—in the hideous wet and snow,—never to kiss him, never to see him any more! . . .

7

He was a good boy. Roy was a good boy. He must have gone to Heaven. But I know nothing about Heaven. It is very far off. In my best and happiest days, I never liked to think of it. If I were to go there, it could do me no good, for I should not see Roy. Or if by chance I should see him standing up among the grand, white angels, he would not be the old dear Roy. I should grow so tired of singing! Should long and fret for one little talk,—for I never said good by, and—

I will stop this.

A scrap from the German of Bürger, which I came across to-day, shall be copied here.

"Be calm, my child, forget thy woe,
And think of God and Heaven;
Christ thy Redeemer hath to thee
Himself for comfort given.

"O mother, mother, what is Heaven?
O mother, what is Hell?
To be with Wilhelm,—that's my Heaven;
Without him,—that's my Hell."

February 27th.

Miss Meta Tripp, in the ignorance of her little silly heart, has done me a great mischief.

Phoebe prepared me for it, by observing, when she came up yesterday to dust my room, that "folks was all sayin' that Mary Cabot"—(Homer is not an aristocratic town, and Phoebe doffs and dons my title at her own sweet will)—"that Mary Cabot was dreadful low sence Royal died, and hadn't ought to stay shut up by herself, day in and day out. It was behaving con-trary to the will of Providence, and very bad for her health, too." Moreover, Mrs. Bland, who called this morning with her three babies,—she never is able to stir out of the house without those children, poor thing!—lingered awkwardly on the door-steps as she went away, and hoped that Mary my dear wouldn't

[handwritten marginalia: confusion over Christian faith]

take it unkindly, but she did wish that I would exert myself more to see my friends and receive comfort in my affliction. She didn't want to interfere, or bother me, or—but—people would talk, and—

My good little minister's wife broke down all in a blush, at this point in her "porochial duties" (I more than suspect that her husband had a hand in the matter), so I took pity on her embarrassment, and said smiling that I would think about it.

I see just how the leaven has spread. Miss Meta, a little overwhelmed and a good deal mystified by her call here, pronounces "poor Mary Cabot *so* sad; she wouldn't talk about Royal; and you couldn't persuade her to come to the Fair; and she was so *sober!*—why, it was dreadful!"

Therefore, Homer has made up its mind that I shall become resigned in an arithmetical manner, and comforted according to the Rule of Three.

I wish I could go away! I wish I could go away and creep into the ground and die! If nobody need ever speak any more words to me! If anybody only knew *what* to say!

Little Mrs. Bland has been very kind, and I thank her with all my heart. But she does not know. She does not understand. Her happy heart is bound up in her little live children. She never laid anybody away under the snow without a chance to say good by.

As for the minister, he came, of course, as it was proper that he should, before the funeral, and once after. He is a very good man, but I am afraid of him, and I am glad that he has not come again.

Night.

I can only repeat and re-echo what I wrote this noon. If anybody knew *what* to say!

Just after supper I heard the door-bell, and, looking out of the window, I caught a glimpse of Deacon Quirk's old drab felt hat, on the upper step. My heart sank, but there was no help for me. I waited for Phoebe to bring up his name, desperately listening to her heavy steps, and letting her knock three times before I answered. I confess to having taken my hair down twice, washed my hands to a most unnecessary extent, and been a long time brushing my dress; also to forgetting my handkerchief, and having to go back for it after I was down stairs. Deacon Quirk looked tired of waiting. I hope he was.

O, what an ill-natured thing to say! What is coming over me? What would Roy think? What could he?

"Good evening, Mary," said the Deacon, severely, when I went in. Probably he did not mean to speak severely, but the truth is, I think he was a little vexed that I had kept him waiting. I said good evening, and apologized for my delay, and sat down as far from him as I conveniently could. There was an awful silence.

"I came in this evening," said the Deacon, breaking it with a cough, "I came—hem!—to confer with you—"

I looked up. "I thought somebody had ought to come," continued the Deacon, "to confer with you as a Christian brother on your spiritooal condition."

I opened my eyes.

"To confer with you on your spiritooal condition," repeated my visitor. "I understand that you have had some unfortoonate exercises of mind under your affliction, and I observed that you absented yourself from the Communion Table last Sunday."

"I did."

"Intentionally?"

"Intentionally."

He seemed to expect me to say something more; and, seeing that there was no help for it, I answered.

"I did not feel fit to go. I should not have dared to go. God does not seem to me just now what He used to. He has dealt very bitterly with me. But, however wicked I may be, I will not mock Him. I think, Deacon Quirk, that I did right to stay away."

"Well," said the Deacon, twirling his hat with a puzzled look, "perhaps you did. But I don't see the excuse for any such feelings as would make it necessary. I think it my duty to tell you, Mary, that I am sorry to see you in such a rebellious state of mind."

I made no reply.

"Afflictions come from God," he observed, looking at me as impressively as if he supposed that I had never heard the statement before. "Afflictions come from God, and, however afflictin' or however crushin' they may be, it is our duty to submit to them. Glory in triboolation, St. Paul says; glory in triboolation."

I continued silent.

"I sympathize with you in this sad dispensation," he proceeded. "Of course you was very fond of Royal; it's natural you should be, quite natural—" He stopped, perplexed, I suppose, by something in my face. "Yes, it's very natural; poor human nature sets a great deal by earthly props and affections. But it's your duty, as a Christian and a church-member, to be resigned."

I tapped the floor with my foot. I began to think that I could not bear much more.

"To be resigned, my dear young friend. To say 'Abba, Father,' and pray that the will of the Lord be done."

"Deacon Quirk!" said I, "I am *not* resigned. I pray the dear Lord with all my heart to make me so, but I will not say that I am, until I am,—if ever that time comes. As for those words about the Lord's will, I would no more take them on my lips than I would blasphemy, unless I could speak them honestly,—and that I cannot do. We had better talk of something else now, had we not?"

Deacon Quirk looked at me. It struck me that he would look very much so at a Mormon or a Hottentot, and I wondered whether he were going to excommunicate me on the spot.

As soon as he began to speak, however, I saw that he was only bewildered,—honestly bewildered, and honestly shocked: I do not doubt that I had said bewildering and shocking things.

"My friend," he said solemnly, "I shall pray for you and leave you in the hands of God. Your brother, whom He has removed from this earthly life for His own wise—"

"We will not talk any more about Roy, if you please," I interrupted; "*he* is happy and safe."

"Hem!—I hope so," he replied, moving uneasily in his chair; "I believe he never made a profession of religion, but there is no limit to the mercy of God. It is very unsafe for the young to think that they can rely on a death-bed repentance, but our God is a covenant-keeping God, and Royal's mother was a pious woman. If you cannot say with certainty that he is numbered among the redeemed, you are justified, perhaps, in hoping so."

I turned sharply on him, but words died on my lips. How could I tell the man of that short, dear letter than came to me in December,—that Roy's was no death-bed repentance, but the quiet, natural growth of a life that had always been the life of the pure in heart; of his manly beliefs and unselfish motives; of that dawning sense of friendship with Christ of which he used to speak so modestly, dreading lest he should not be honest with himself? "Perhaps I ought not to call myself a Christian," he wrote,—I learned the words by heart,— "and I shall make no profession to be such, till I am sure of it, but my life has not seemed to me for a long time to be my own. 'Bought with a price' just expresses it. I can point to no time at which I was conscious by any revolution of feeling of 'experiencing a change of heart,' but it seems to me that a man's heart might be changed for all that. I do not know that it is necessary for us to be able to watch every footprint of God. The *way* is all that concerns us,—to see that we follow it and Him. This I am sure of; and knocking about in this army life only convinces me of what I felt in a certain way before,— that it is the only way, and He the only guide *to* follow."

But how could I say anything of this to Deacon Quirk?—this my sealed and sacred treasure, of all that Roy left me the dearest. At any rate I did not. It seemed both obstinate and cruel in him to come there and say what he had been saying. He might have known that I would not say that Roy had gone to Heaven, if—why, if there had been the breath of a doubt. It is a possibility of which I cannot rationally conceive, but I suppose that his name would never have passed my lips.

So I turned away from Deacon Quirk, and shut my mouth, and waited for him to finish. Whether the idea began to struggle into his mind that he *might* not have been making a very comforting remark, I cannot say; but he started very soon to go.

"Supposing you are right, and Royal was saved at the eleventh hour," he said at parting, with one of his stolid efforts to be consolatory, that are worse than his rebukes, "if he is singing the song of Moses and the Lamb (he pointed with his big, dingy thumb at the ceiling), *he* doesn't rebel against the doings of Providence. All *his* affections are subdued to God,—merged, as you might say,—merged in worshipping before the great White Throne. He doesn't think this miser'ble earthly spere of any importance, compared with that eternal and exceeding weight of glory. In the appropriate words of the poet,—

> 'O, not to one created thing
>   Shall our embrace be given,
> But all our joy shall be in God,
>   For only god is Heaven.'

Those are very spiritooal and scripteral lines, and it's very proper to reflect how true they are."

I saw him go out, and came up here and locked myself in, and have been walking round and round the room. I must have walked a good while, for I feel as weak as a baby.

Can the man in any state of existence be made to comprehend that he has been holding me on the rack this whole evening?

Yet he came under a strict sense of duty, and in the kindness of all the heart he has! I know, or I ought to know, that he is a good man,— far better in the sight of God to-night, I do not doubt, than I am.

But it hurts,—it cuts,—that thing which he said as he went out; because I suppose it must be true; because it seems to be greater than I can bear to have it true.

Roy, away in that dreadful Heaven, can have no thought of me,

(handwritten in left margin: God consumes our lives)

cannot remember how I loved him, how he left me all alone. The singing and the worshipping must take up all his time. God wants it all. He is a "Jealous God." I am nothing any more to Roy.

March 2.

And once I was much,—very much to him!

His Mamie, his poor Queen Mamie,—dearer, he used to say, than all the world to him,—I don't see how he can like it so well up there as to forget her. Though Roy was a very good boy. But this poor, wicked little Mamie,—why, I fall to pitying her as if she were some one else, and wish that some one would cry over her a little. I can't cry.

Roy used to say a thing,—I have not the words, but it was like this,—that one must be either very young or very ungenerous, if one could find time to pity one's self.

I have lain for two nights, with my eyes open all night long. I thought that perhaps I might see him. I have been praying for a touch, a sign, only for something to break the silence into which he has gone. But there is no answer, none. The light burns blue, and I see at last that it is morning, and go down stairs alone, and so the day begins.

Something of Mrs. Browning's has been keeping a dull mechanical time in my brain all day.

> "God keeps a niche
> In Heaven to hold our idols: . . . . albeit
> He brake them to our faces, and denied
> That our close kisses should impair their white."

But why must He take them? And why should He keep them there? Shall we ever see them framed in their glorious gloom? Will He let us touch them *then*? Or must we stand like a poor worshipper at a Cathedral, looking up at his pictured saint afar off upon the other side?

Has everything stopped just here? Our talks together in the twilight, our planning and hoping and dreaming together; our walks and rides and laughing; our reading and singing and loving,—these then are all gone out forever?

God forgive the words! but Heaven will never be Heaven to me without them.

March 4.

Perhaps I had better not write any more here after this.

On looking over the leaves, I see that the little green book has become an outlet for the shallower part of pain.

Meta Tripp and Deacon Quirk, gossip and sympathy that have buzzed into my trouble and annoyed me like wasps (we are apt to make more fuss over a wasp-sting than a sabre-cut), just that proportion of suffering which alone can ever be put into words,—the surface.

I begin to understand what I never understood till now,—what people mean by the luxury of grief. No, I am sure that I never understood it, because my pride suffered as much as any part of me in that other time. I would no more have spent two consecutive hours drifting at the mercy of my thoughts than I would have put my hand into the furnace fire. The right to mourn makes everything different. Then, as to mother, I was very young when she died, and father, though I loved him, was never to me what Roy has been.

This luxury of grief, like all luxuries, is pleasurable. Though, as I was saying, it is only the shallow part of one's heart—I imagine that the deepest hearts have their shallows—which can be filled by it, still it brings a shallow relief.

Let it be confessed to this honest book, that, driven to it by desperation, I found in it a wretched sort of content.

Being a little stronger now physically, I shall try to be a little braver; it will do no harm to try. So I seem to see that it was the content of poison,—salt-water poured between shipwrecked lips.

At any rate, I mean to put the book away and lock it up. Roy used to say that he did not believe in journals. I begin to see why.

15

❧ 3 ❧

March 7.

I have taken out my book, and am going to write again. But there is an excellent reason. I have something else than myself to write about.

This morning Phoebe persuaded me to walk down to the office, "To keep up my spirits and get some salt pork."

She brought my things and put them on me while I was hesitating; tied my victorine and buttoned my gloves; warmed my boots, and fussed about me as if I had been a baby. It did me good to be taken care of, and I thanked her softly; a little more softly than I am apt to speak to Phoebe.

"Bless your soul, my dear!" she said, winking briskly, "I don't want no thanks. It's thanks enough jest to see one of your old looks comin' over you for a spell, since—"

She knocked over a chair with her broom, and left her sentence unfinished. Phoebe has always had a queer, clinging, superior sort of love for us both. She dandled us on her knees, and made all our rag-dolls, and carried us through measles and mumps and the rest. Then mother's early death threw all the care upon her. I believe that in her secret heart she considers me more her child than her mistress. It cost a great many battles to become established as "Miss Mary."

"I should like to know," she would say, throwing back her great, square shoulders and towering up in front of me,—"I should like to know if you s'pose I'm a goin' to 'Miss' anybody that I've trotted to Bamberry Cross as many times as I have you, Mary Cabot! Catch me!"

I remember how she would insist on calling me "her baby" after I was in long dresses, and that it mortified me cruelly once when Meta Tripp was here to tea with some Boston cousins. Poor, good Phoebe! Her rough love seems worth more to me, now that it is all I have left me in the world. It occurs to me that I may not have taken no-

16

tice enough of her lately. She has done her honest best to comfort me, and she loved Roy, too.

But about the letter. I wrapped my face up closely in the *crêpe,* so that, if I met Deacon Quirk, he should not recognize me, and, thinking that the air was pleasant as I walked, came home with the pork for Phoebe and a letter for myself. I did not open it; in fact, I forgot all about it, till I had been at home for half an hour. I cannot bear to open a letter since that morning when the lances of light fell on the snow. They have written to me from everywhere,—uncles and cousins and old school-friends; well-meaning people; saying each the same thing in the same way,—no, not that exactly, and very likely I should feel hurt and lonely if they did not write; but sometimes I wish it did not all have to be read.

So I did not notice much about my letter this morning, till presently it occurred to me that what must be done had better be done quickly; so I drew up my chair to the desk, prepared to read and answer on the spot. Something about the writing and the signature rather pleased me: it was dated from Kansas, and was signed with the name of my mother's youngest sister, Winifred Forceythe. I will lay the letter in between these two leaves, for it seems to suit the pleasant, spring-like day; besides, I took out the green book again on account of it.

Lawrence, Kansas, February 21.

My Dear Child,—I have been thinking how happy you will be by and by because Roy is happy.

And yet I know—I understand—

You have been in all my thoughts, and they have been such pitiful, tender thoughts, that I cannot help letting you know that somebody is sorry for you. For the rest, the heart knoweth its own, and I am, after all, too much of a stranger to my sister's child to intermeddle.

So my letter dies upon my pen. You cannot bear words yet. How should I dare to fret you with them? I can only reach you by my silence, and leave you with the Heart that bled and broke for you and Roy.

Your Aunt,

Winifred Forceythe.

Postscript, February 23.

I open my letter to add, that I am thinking of coming to New England with Faith,—you know Faith and I have nobody but each other now. Indeed, I may be on my way by the time this reaches you. It is just possible that I may not come back to the West. I shall be for a time at your uncle Calvin's, and then my husband's friends think that they must have me. I should like to see you for a day or two, but if you do not care to see me, say so. If you let me come because you think you must, I shall find it out from your face in an hour. I should like to be something to you, or do something for you; but if I cannot, I would rather not come.

I like that letter.

I have written to her to come, and in such a way that I think she will understand me to mean what I say. I have not seen her since I was a child. I know that she was very much younger than my mother; that she spent her young ladyhood teaching at the South;—grandfather had enough with which to support her, but I have heard it said that she preferred to take care of herself;—that she finally married a poor minister, whose sermons people liked, but whose coat was shockingly shabby; that she left the comforts and elegances and friends of New England to go to the West and bury herself in an unheard-of little place with him (I think she must have loved him); that he afterwards settled in Lawrence; that there, after they had been married some childless years, this little Faith was born; and that there Uncle Forceythe died about three years ago; that is about all I know of her. I suppose her share of Grandfather Burleigh's little property supports her respectably. I understand that she has been living a sort of missionary life among her husband's people since his death, and that they think they shall never see her like again. It is they who keep her from coming home again, Uncle Calvin's wife told me once; they and one other thing,—her husband's grave.

I hope she will come to see me. I notice one strange thing about her letter. She does not use the ugly words "death" and "dying." I don't know exactly what she put in their places, but something that had a pleasant sound.

"To be happy because Roy is happy." I wonder if she really thinks it is possible.

I wonder what makes the words chase me about.

4

I am afraid that my brave resolutions are all breaking down.

The stillness of the May days is creeping into everything; the days in which the furlough was to come; in which the bitter Peace has come instead, and in which he would have been at home, never to go away from me any more.

The lazy winds are choking me. Their faint sweetness makes me sick. The moist, rich loam is ploughed in the garden; the grass, more golden than green, springs in the warm hollow by the front gate; the great maple, just reaching up to tap at the window, blazes and bows under its weight of scarlet blossoms. I cannot bear their perfume; it comes up in great breaths, when the window is opened. I wish that little cricket, just waked from his winter's nap, would not sit there on the sill and chirp at me. I hate the bluebirds flashing in and out of the carmine cloud that the maple makes, and singing, singing, everywhere.

It is easy to understand how Bianca heard "The nightingales sing through her head," how she could call them "Owl-like birds," who sang "for spite," who sang "for hate," who sang "for doom."

Most of all I hate the maple. I wish winter were back again to fold it away in white, with its bare, black fingers only to come tapping at the window. "Roy's maple" we used to call it. How much fun he had out of that old tree!

As far back as I can remember, we never considered spring to be officially introduced till we had a fight with the red blossoms. Roy used to pelt me well; but with that pretty chivalry of his, which was rare in such a little fellow, which developed afterwards into that rarer treatment of women, of which every one speaks who speaks of him, he would stop the play the instant it threatened roughness. I used to be glad, though, that I had strength and courage enough to make it some fun to him.

The maple is full of pictures of Roy. Roy, not yet over the dignity of his first boots, aiming for the cross-barred branch, coming to the ground with a terrible wrench on his ankle, straight up again before anybody could stop him, and sitting there on the ugly, swaying bough as white as a sheet, to wave his cap,—"There, I meant to do it, and I have!" Roy, chopping off the twigs for kindling-wood in his mud oven, and sending his hatchet right through the parlor window. Roy cutting leaves for me, and then pulling all my wreaths down over my nose every time I put them on! Roy making me jump half-way across the room with a sudden thump on my window, and, looking out, I would see him with his hat off and hair blown from his forehead, framed in by the scented blossoms, or the quivering green, or the flame of blood-red leaves. But there is not end to them if I begin.

I had planned, if he came this week, to strip the richest branches, and fill his room.

May 6.

The May-day stillness, the lazy winds, the sweetness in the air, are all gone. A miserable northeasterly storm has set in. The garden loam is a mass of mud; the golden grass is drenched; the poor little cricket is drowned in a mud-puddle; the bluebirds are huddled among the leaves, with their heads under their drabbled wings, and the maple blossoms, dull and shrunken, drip against the glass.

It begins to be evident that it will never do for me to live alone. Yet who is there in the wide world that I could bear to bring here—into Roy's place?

A little old-fashioned book, bound in green and gold, attracted my attention this morning while I was dusting the library. It proved to be my mother's copy of "Elia,"—one that father had given her, I saw by the fly-leaf, in their early engagement days. It is some time since I have read Charles Lamb; indeed, since the middle of February I have read nothing of any sort. Phoebe dries the Journal for me every night, and sometimes I glance at the Telegraphic Summary, and sometimes I don't.

"You used to be fond enough of books," Mrs. Bland says, looking puzzled,—"regular blue-stocking, Mr. Bland called you (no personal objection to you, of course, my dear, but he *doesn't* like literary women, which is a great comfort to me). Why don't you read and divert yourself now?"

But my brain, like the rest of me, seems to be crushed. I could not follow three pages of history with attention. Shakespeare, Wordsworth, Whittier, Mrs. Browning, are filled with Roy's marks,—and so down the shelf. Besides, poetry strikes as nothing else does, deep into the roots of things. One finds everywhere some strain at the fibres of one's heart. A mind must be healthily reconciled to actual life, before a poet—at least most poets—can help it. We must learn to bear and to work, before we can spare strength to dream.

To hymns and hymn-like poems, exception should be made. Some of them are like soft hands stealing into ours in the dark, and holding us fast without a spoken word. I do not know how many times Whittier's "Psalm," and that old cry of Cowper's, "God moves in a mysterious way," have quieted me,—just the sound of the words; when I was too wild to take in their meaning, and too wicked to believe them if I had.

As to novels, (by the way, Meta Tripp sent me over four yesterday afternoon, among which notice "Aurora Floyd" and "Uncle Silas,") the author of "Rutledge" expresses my feeling about them precisely. I do not remember her exact words, but they are not unlike these. "She had far outlived the passion of ordinary novels; and the few which struck the depths of her experience gave her more pain than pleasure."

However, I took up poor "Elia" this morning, and stumbled upon "Dream Children," to which, for pathos and symmetry, I have read few things superior in the language. Years ago, I almost knew it by heart, but it has slipped out of memory with many other things of late. Any book, if it be one of those which Lamb calls "books which *are* books," put before us at different periods of life, will unfold to us new meanings,—wheels within wheels, delicate springs of purpose to which, at the last reading, we were stone-blind; gems which perhaps the author ignorantly cut and polished.

A sentence in this "Dream Children," which at eighteen I passed by with a compassionate sort of wonder, only thinking that it gave me "the blues" to read it, and that I was glad Roy was alive, I have seized upon and learned all over again now. I write it down to the dull music of the rain.

"And how, when he died, though he had not been dead an hour, it seemed as if he had died a great while ago, such a distance there is betwixt life and death; and how I bore his death, as I thought, pretty well at first, but afterwards it haunted and haunted me; and though I did not cry or take it to heart as some do, and as I think he would have done if I had died, yet I missed him all day long, and knew not till then how much I had loved him. I missed his kindness and I missed his crossness, and wished him to be alive again to be quarrelling with him (for we quarrelled sometimes), rather than not have him again."

How still the house is! I can hear the coach rumbling away at the half-mile corner, coming up from the evening train. A little arrow of light has just cut the gray gloom of the West.

Ten o'clock.

The coach to which I sat listening rumbled up to the gate and stopped. Puzzled for the moment, and feeling as inhospitable as I knew how, I went down to the door. The driver was already on the steps, with a bundle in his arms that proved to be a rather minute child; and a lady, veiled, was just stepping from the carriage into the rain. Of course I came to my senses at that, and, calling to Phoebe that Mrs. Forceythe had come, sent her out an umbrella.

She surprised me by running lightly up the steps. I had imagined a somewhat advanced age and a sedate amount of infirmities, to be necessary concomitants of aunthood. She came in all sparkling with rain-drops, and, gently pushing aside the hand with which I was trying to pay her driver, said, laughing:—

"Here we are, bag and baggage, you see, 'big trunk, little trunk,' &c., &c. You did not expect me? Ah, my letter missed then. It is too bad to take you by storm in this way. Come, Faith! No, don't trouble about the trunks just now. Shall I go right in here?"

Her voice had a sparkle in it, like the drops on her veil, but it was low and very sweet. I took her in by the dining-room fire, and was turning to take off the little girl's things, when a soft hand stayed me, and I saw that she had drawn off the wet veil. A face somewhat pale looked down at me,—she is taller than I,—with large, compassionate eyes.

"I am too wet to kiss you, but I must have a look," she said, smiling. "That will do. You are like your mother, very like."

I don't know what possessed me, whether it was the sudden, sweet feeling of kinship with something alive, or whether it was her face or her voice, or all together, but I said:—

"I don't think you are too wet to be kissed," and threw my arms about her neck,—I am not of the kissing kind, either, and I had on my new bombazine, and she *was* very wet.

I thought she looked pleased.

Phoebe was sent to open the register in the blue room, and as soon as it was warm I went up with them, leading Faith by the hand. I am unused to children, and she kept stepping on my dress, and spinning around and tipping over, in the most astonishing manner. It strikingly reminded me of a top at the last gasp. Her mother observed that she was tired and sleepy. Phoebe was waiting around awkwardly up stairs, with fresh towels on her arm. Aunt Winifred turned and held out her hand.

"Well, Phoebe, I am glad to see you. This is Phoebe, I am sure? You have altered with everything else since I was here before. You keep bright and well, I hope, and take good care of Miss Mary?"

It was a simple enough thing, to be sure, her taking the trouble to notice the old servant with whom she had scarcely ever exchanged a half-dozen words; but I liked it. I liked the way, too, in which it was done. It reminded me of Roy's fine, well-bred manner towards his inferiors,—always cordial, yet always appropriate; I have heard that our mother had much the same.

I tried to make things look as pleasant as I could down stairs, while they were making ready for tea. The grate was raked up a little, a bright supper-cloth laid on the table, and the curtains drawn. Phoebe mixed a hasty cake of some sort, and brought out the heavier pieces of silver,—tea-pot, &c., which I do not use when I am alone, because it is so much trouble to take care of them, and because I like the little Wedgwood set that Roy had for his chocolate.

"How pleasant!" said Aunt Winifred, as she sat down with Faith in a high chair beside her. Phoebe had a great hunt up garret for that chair; it has been stowed away there since it and I parted company. "How pleasant everything is here! I believe in bright dining-rooms. There is an indescribable dinginess to most that I have seen, which tends to anything but thankfulness. Homesick, Faith? No; that's right. I don't think we shall be homesick at Cousin Mary's."

If she had not said that, the probabilities are that they would have been, for I have fallen quite out of the way of active housekeeping, and have almost forgotten how to entertain a friend. But I do not

24

want her good opinion wasted, and mean they shall have a good time if I can make it for them.

It was a little hard at first to see her opposite me at the table; it was Roy's place.

While she was sitting there in the light, with the dust and weariness of travel brushed away a little, I was able to make up my mind what this aunt of mine looks like.

She is young, then, to begin with, and I find it necessary to reiterate the fact, in order to get it into my stupid brain. The cape and spectacles, the little old woman's shawl and invalid's walk, for which I had prepared myself, persist in hovering before my bewildered eyes, ready to drop down on her at a moment's notice. Just thirty-five she is by her own showing; older than I, to be sure; but as we passed in front of the mirror together, once to-night, I could not see half that difference between us. The peace of her face and the pain of mine contrast sharply, and give me an old, worn look, beside her. After all, though, to one who had seen much of life, hers would be the true maturity perhaps,—the maturity of repose. A look in her eyes once or twice gave me the impression that she thinks me rather young, though she is far too wise and delicate to show it. I don't like to be treated like a girl. I mean to find out what she does think.

My eyes have been on her face the whole evening, and I believe it is the sweetest face—woman's face—that I have ever seen. Yet she is far from being a beautiful woman. It is difficult to say what makes the impression; scarcely any feature is accurate, yet the *tout ensemble* seems to have no fault. Her hair, which must have been bright bronze once, has grown gray—quite gray—before its time. I really do not know of what color her eyes are; blue, perhaps, most frequently, but they change with every word that she speaks; when quiet, they have a curious, far-away look, and a steady, lambent light shines through them. Her mouth is well cut and delicate, yet you do not so much notice that as its expression. It looks as if it held a happy secret, with which, however near one may come to her, one can never intermeddle. Yet there are lines about it and on her forehead, which are proof plain enough that she has not always floated on summer seas. She yet wears her widow's black, but relieves it pleasantly by white at the throat and wrists. Take her altogether, I like to look at her.

Faith is a round, rolling, rollicking little piece of mischief, with three years and a half of experience in this very happy world. She has black eyes and a pretty chin, funny little pink hands all covered with dimples, and a dimple in one cheek besides. She has tipped over two tumblers of water, scratched herself all over playing with the cat, and set her apron on fire already since she has been here. I stand in some awe of her; but, after I have become initiated, I think that we shall be very good friends.

"Of all names in the catalogue," I said to her mother, when she came down into the parlor after putting her to bed, "Faith seems to be about the *most* inappropriate for this solid-bodied, twinkling little bairn of yours, with her pretty red cheeks, and such an appetite for supper!"

"Yes," she said, laughing, "there is nothing *spirituelle* about Faith. But she means just that to me. I could not call her anything else. Her father gave her the name." Her face changed, but did not sadden; a quietness crept into it and into her voice, but that was all.

"I will tell you about it sometime,—perhaps," she added, rising and standing by the fire. "Faith looks like him." Her eyes assumed their distant look, "like the eyes of those who see the dead," and gazed away,—so far away, into the fire, that I felt that she would not be listening to anything that I might say, and therefore said nothing.

We spent the evening chatting cosily. After the fire had died down in the grate (I had Phoebe light a pine-knot there, because I noticed that Aunt Winifred fancied the blaze in the dining-room), we drew up our chairs into the corner by the register, and roasted away to our heart's content. A very bad habit, to sit over the register, and Aunt Winifred says she shall undertake to break me of it. We talked about everything under the sun,—uncles, aunts, cousins, Kansas and Connecticut, the surrenders and the assassination, books, pictures, music, and Faith,—O, and Phoebe and the cat. Aunt Winifred talks well, and does not gossip nor exhaust her resources; one feels always that she has material in reserve on any subject that is worth talking about.

For one thing I thank her with all my heart: she never spoke of Roy.

Upon reflection, I find that I have really passed a pleasant evening.

She knocked at my door just now, after I had written the last sentence, and had put away the book for the night. Thinking that it was Phoebe, I called, "Come in," and did not turn. She had come to the bureau where I stood unbraiding my hair, and touched my arm, before I saw who it was. She had on a crimson dressing-gown of warm flannel, and her hair hung down on her shoulders. Although so gray, her hair is massive yet, and coils finely when she is dressed.

"I beg your pardon," she said, "but I thought you would not be in bed, and I came in to say,—let me sit somewhere else at the breakfast-table, if you like. I saw that I had taken 'the vacant place.' Good night, my dear."

It was such a little thing! I wonder how many people would have noticed it or taken the trouble to speak of it. The quick perception, the unusual delicacy,—these too are like Roy.

I almost wish that she had stayed a little longer. I almost think that I could bear to have her speak to me about him.

Faith, in the next room, seems to have wakened from a frightened dream, and I can hear their voices through the wall. Her mother is soothing and singing to her in the broken words of some old lullaby with which Phoebe used to sing Roy and me to sleep, years and years ago. The unfamiliar, home-like sound is pleasant in the silent house. Phoebe, on her way to bed, is stopping on the garret-stairs to listen to it. Even the cat comes mewing up to the door, and purring as I have not heard the creature purr since the old Sunday-night singing, hushed so long ago.

5

I was awakened and nearly smothered this morning by a pillow thrown directly at my head.

Somewhat unaccustomed, in the respectable, old maid's life that I lead, to such a pleasant little method of salutation, I jerked myself upright, and stared. There stood Faith in her night-dress, laughing as if she would suffocate, and her mother in search of her was just knocking at the open door.

"She insisted on going to wake Cousin Mary, and wouldn't be washed till I let her; but I stipulated that she should kiss you softly on both your eyes."

"I did," said Faith, stoutly; "I kissed her eyes, both two of 'em, and her nose, and her mouth and her neck; then I pulled her hair, and then I spinched her; but I thought she'd have to be banged a little. *Wasn't* it a bang, though!"

It really did me good to begin the day with a hearty laugh. The days usually look so long and blank at the beginning, that I can hardly make up my mind to step out into them. Faith's pillow was the famous pebble in the pond, to which authors of original imagination invariably resort; I felt its little circles widening out all through the day. I wonder if Aunt Winifred thought of that. She thinks of many things.

For instance, afraid apparently that I should think I was afflicted with one of those professional visitors who hold that a chance relationship justifies them in imposing on one from the beginning to the end of the chapter, she managed to make me understand, this morning, that she was expecting to go back to Uncle Forceythe's brother on Saturday. I was surprised at myself to find that this proposition struck me with dismay. I insisted with all my heart on keeping her for a week at the least, and sent forth a fiat that her trunks should be unpacked.

We have had a quiet, homelike day. Faith found her way to the orchard, and installed herself there for the day, overhauling the muddy grass with her bare hands to find dandelions. She came in at dinner-time as brown as a little nut, with her hat hanging down her neck, her apron torn, and just about as dirty as I should suppose it possible for a clean child to succeed in making herself. Her mother, however, seemed to be quite used to it, and the expedition with which she made her presentable I regard as a stroke of genius.

While Faith was disposed of, and the house still, auntie and I took our knitting and spent a regular old woman's morning at the south window in the dining-room. In the afternoon Mrs. Bland came over, babies and all, and sent up her card to Mrs. Forceythe.

Supper-time came, and still there had not been a word of Roy. I began to wonder at, while I respected, this unusual silence.

While her mother was putting Faith to bed, I went into my room alone, for a few moments' quiet. An early dark had fallen, for it had clouded up just before sunset. The dull, gray sky and narrow horizon shut down and crowded in everything. A soldier from the village, who has just come home, was walking down the street with his wife and sister. The crickets were chirping in the meadows. The faint breath of the maple came up.

I sat down by the window, and hid my face in both my hands. I must have sat there some time, for I had quite forgotten that I had company to entertain, when the door softly opened and shut, and some one came and sat down on the couch beside me. I did not speak, for I could not, and, the first I knew, a gentle arm crept about me, and she had gathered me into her lap and laid my head on her shoulder, as she might have gathered Faith.

"There," she said, in her low, lulling voice, "now tell Auntie all about it."

I don't know what it was, whether the voice, or touch, or words, but it came so suddenly,—and nobody had held me for so long,— that everything seemed to break up and unlock in a minute, and I threw up my hands and cried. I don't know how long I cried.

She passed her hand softly to and fro across my hair, brushing it away from my temples, while they throbbed and burned; but she did not speak. By and by I sobbed out:—

"Auntie, Auntie, Auntie!" as Faith sobs out in the dark. It seemed to me that I must have help or die.

"Yes, dear. I understand. I know how hard it is. And you have been bearing it alone so long! I am going to help you, and you must tell me all you can."

The strong, decided words, "I am going to help you," gave me the first faint hope I have had, that I *could* be helped, and I could tell her—it was not sacrilege—the pent-up story of these weeks. All the time her hand went softly to and fro across my hair.

Presently, when I was weak and faint with the new comfort of my tears, "Aunt Winifred," I said, "I don't know what it means to be resigned; I don't know what it *means!*"

Still her hand passed softly to and fro across my hair.

"To have everything stop all at once! without giving me any time to learn to bear it. Why, you do not know,—it is just as if a great black gate had swung to and barred out the future, and barred out him, and left me all alone in any world that I can ever live in, forever and forever."

"My child," she said, with emphasis solemn and low upon the words,—"my child, I *do* know. I think you forget—my husband."

I had forgotten. How could I? We are most selfishly blinded by our own griefs. No other form than ours ever seems to walk with us in the furnace. Her few words made me feel, as I could not have felt if she had said more, that this woman who was going to help me had suffered too; had suffered perhaps more than I,—that, if I sat as a little child at her feet, she could teach me through the kinship of her pain.

"O my dear," she said, and held me close, "I have trodden every step of it before you,—every single step."

"But you never were so wicked about it! You never felt—why, I have been *afraid* I should hate God! You never were so wicked as that."

Low under her breath she answered "Yes,"—this sweet, saintly woman who had come to me in the dark as an angel might.

Then, turning suddenly, her voice trembled and broke:—

"Mary, Mary, do you think He *could* have lived those thirty-three years, and be cruel to you now? Think that over and over; only that. It may be the only thought you dare to have,—it was all I dared to have once,—but cling to it; *cling with both hands,* Mary, and keep it."

I only put both hands about her neck and clung there; but I hope—it seems, as if I clung a little to the thought besides; it was as new and sweet to me as if I had never heard of it in all my life; and it has not left me yet.

"And then, my dear," she said, when she had let me cry a little longer, "when you have once found out that Roy's God loves you more than Roy does, the rest comes more easily. It will not be as long to wait as it seems now. It isn't as if you never were going to see him again."

I looked up bewildered.

"What's the matter, dear?"

"Why, do you think I shall see him,—really see him?"

"Mary Cabot," she said abruptly, turning to look at me, "who has been talking to you about this thing?"

"Deacon Quirk," I answered faintly,—"Deacon Quirk and Dr. Bland."

She put her other arm around me with a quick movement, as if she would shield me from Deacon Quirk and Dr. Bland.

"Do I think you will see him again? You might as well ask me if I thought God made you and made Roy, and gave you to each other. See him! Why, of course you will see him as you saw him here."

"As I saw him here! Why, here I looked into his eyes, I saw him smile, I touched him. Why, Aunt Winifred, Roy is an angel!"

She patted my hand with a little, soft, comforting laugh.

"But he is not any the less Roy for that,—not any the less your own real Roy, who will love you and wait for you and be very glad to see you, as he used to love and wait and be glad when you came home from a journey on a cold winter night."

31

(handwritten in left margin: Quteojar / A different Christian God)

"And he met me at the door, and led me in where it was light and warm!" I sobbed.

"So he will meet you at the door in this other home, and lead you into the light and the warmth. And cannot that make the cold and dark a little shorter? Think a minute!"

"But there is God,—I thought we went to Heaven to worship Him, and—"

"Shall you worship more heartily or less, for having Roy again? Did Mary love the Master more or less, after Lazarus came back? Why, my child, where did you get your ideas of God? Don't you suppose He *knows* how you love Roy?"

I drank in the blessed words without doubt or argument. I was too thirsty to doubt or argue. Some other time I may ask her how she knows this beautiful thing, but not now. All I can do now is to take it into my heart and hold it there.

Roy my own again,—not only to look at standing up among the singers,—but close to me; somehow or other to be as near as—to be nearer than—he was here, *really* mine again! I shall never let this go.

After we had talked awhile, and when it came time to say good night, I told her a little about my conversation with Deacon Quirk, and what I said to him about the Lord's will. I did not know but that she would blame me.

"Some time," she said, turning her great, compassionate eyes on me,—I could feel them in the dark,—and smiling, "you will find out all at once, in a happy moment, that you can say those words with all your heart, and with all your soul, and with all your strength; it will come, even in this world, if you will only let it. But, until it does, you do right, quite right, not to scorch your altar with a false burnt-offering. God is not a God to be mocked. He would rather have only the old cry: 'I believe; help mine unbelief,' and wait till you can say the rest.

"It has often grated on my ears," she added, "to hear people speak those words unworthily. They seem to me the most solemn words that the Bible contains, or that Christian experience can utter. As far as my observation goes, the good people—for they are good people—who use them when they ought to know better are of two sorts. They are people in actual agony, bewildered, racked with rebellious doubts, unaccustomed to own even to themselves the secret seethings of sin; really persuaded that because it is a Christian duty to have no will but the Lord's, they are under obligations to affirm that they have no will but the Lord's. Or else they are people who know no more about this pain of bereavement than a child. An affliction has passed over them, put them into mourning, made them feel uncomfortable till the funeral was over, or ever caused them a shallow sort of grief, of which each week evaporates a little, till it is gone. These mourners air their trouble the longest, prate loudest about resignation, and have the most to say to you or me about our 'rebellious state of mind.' Poor things! One can hardly be vexed at them for pity. Think of being made so!"

"There is still another class of the cheerfully resigned," I suggested, "who are even more ready than these to tell you of your desperate wickedness—"

"People who have never had even the semblance of a trouble in all their lives," she interrupted. "Yes. I was going to speak of them. Of all miserable comforters, they are the most arrogant."

"As to real instant submission," she said presently, "there *is* some of it in the world. There are sweet, rare lives capable of great loves and great pains, which yet are kept so attuned to the life of Christ, that the cry in the Garden comes scarcely less honestly from their lips, than from his. Such, like the St. John, are but one among the Twelve. Such, it will do you and me good, dear, at least to remember."

"Such," I thought when I was left alone, "you new dear friend of mine, who have come with such a blessed coming into my lonely days,—such you must be now, whatever you were once."

If I should tell her that, how she would open her soft eyes!

33

¿6¿

As I was looking over the green book last night, Aunt Winifred came up behind me and softly laid a bunch of violets down between the leaves.

By an odd contrast, the contented, passionless things fell against those two verses that were copied from the German, and completely covered them from sight. I lifted the flowers, and held up the page for her to see.

As she read, her face altered strangely; her eyes dilated, her lip quivered, a flush shot over her cheeks and dyed her forehead up to the waves of her hair. I turned away quickly, feeling that I had committed a rudeness in watching her, and detecting in her, however involuntarily, some far, inner sympathy, or shadow of a long-past sympathy, with the desperate words.

"Mary," she said, laying down the book, "I believe Satan wrote that."

She laughed a little then, nervously, and paled back into her quiet, peaceful self.

"I mean that he inspired it. They are wicked words. You must not read them over. You will outgrow them sometime with a beautiful growth of trust and love. Let them alone till that time comes. See, I will blot them out of sight for you with colors as blue as heaven,— the *real* heaven, where God *will* be loved the most."

She shook apart the thick, sweet nosegay, and, taking a half-dozen of the little blossoms, pinned them, dripping with fragrant dew, upon the lines. There I shall let them stay, and, since she wishes it, I shall not lift them to see the reckless words till I can do it safely.

This afternoon Aunt Winifred has been telling me about herself. Somewhat more, or of a different kind, I should imagine, from what she has told most people. She seems to love me a little, not in a proper kind of way, because I happen to be her niece, but for my own sake. It surprises me to find how pleased I am that she should.

34

That Kansas life must have been very hard to her, in contrast as it was with the smooth elegance of her girlhood; she was very young, too, when she undertook it. I said something of the sort to her.

"They have been the hardest and the easiest, the saddest and the happiest, years of all my life," she answered.

I pondered the words in my heart, while I listened to her story. She gave me vivid pictures of the long, bright bridal journey, overshadowed with a very mundane weariness of jolting coaches and railway accidents before its close; of the little neglected hamlet which waited for them, twenty miles from a post-office and thirty from a school-house; of the parsonage, a log-hut among log-huts, distinguished and adorned by a little lath and plastering, glass windows, and a doorstep;—they drew in sight of it at the close of a tired day, with a red sunset lying low on the flats.

Uncle Forceythe wanted mission-work, and mission-work he found here with—I should say with a vengeance, if the expression were exactly suited to an elegantly constructed and reflective journal.

"My heart sank for a moment, I confess," she said, "but it never would do, you know, to let him suspect that, so I smiled away as well as I knew how, shook hands with one or two women in red calico who had been "slickin up inside," they said; went in by the fire,—it was really a pleasant fire,—and, as soon as they had left us alone, I climbed into John's lap, and, with both arms around his neck, told him that I knew we should be very happy. And I said—"

"Said what?"

She blushed a little, like a girl.

"I believe I said I should be happy in Patagonia,—with him. I made him laugh at last, and say that my face and words were like a beautiful prophecy. And, Mary, if they were, it was beautifully fulfilled. In the roughest times,—times of ragged clothes and empty flour-barrels, of weakness and sickness and quack doctors, of cold and discouragement, of prairie fires and guerillas,—from trouble to trouble, from year's end to year's end, we were happy together, we two. As long as we could have each other, and as long as we could be about our

Master's business, we felt as if we did not dare to ask for anything more, lest it should seem that we were ungrateful for such wealth of mercy."

It would take too long to write out here the half that she told me, though I wish I could, for it interested me more than any story that I have ever read.

After years of Christ-like toiling to help those rough old farmers and wicked bushwhackers to Heaven, the call to Lawrence came, and it seemed to Uncle Forceythe that he had better go. It was a pleasant, influential parish, and there, though not less hard at work, they found fewer rubs and more comforts; there Faith came, and there were their pleasant days, till the war.—I held my breath to hear her tell about Quantrell's raid. There, too, Uncle wasted through that death-in-life, consumption; there he "fell on sleep," she said, and there she buried him.

She gave me no further description of his death than those words, and she spoke them with her far-away, tearless eyes looking off through the window, and after she had spoken she was still for a time.

The heart knoweth its own bitterness; that grew distinct to me, as I sat, shut out by her silence. Yet there was nothing bitter about her face.

"Faith was six months old when he went," she said presently. "We had never named her: Baby was name enough at first for such a wee thing; then she was the only one, and had come so late, that it seemed to mean more to us than to most to have a baby all to ourselves, and we liked the sound of the word. When it became quite certain that John must go, we used to talk it over, and he said that he would like to name her, but what, he did not tell me.

"At last, one night, after he had lain for a while thinking with closed eyes, he bade me bring the child to him. The sun was setting, I remember, and the moon was rising. He had had a hard day; the life was all scorched out of the air. I moved the bed up by the window, that he might have the breath of the rising wind. Baby was wide awake, cooing softly to herself in the cradle, her bits of damp curls clinging to her head, and her pink feet in her hands. I took her up and brought her just as she was, and knelt down by the bed. The street was still. We could hear the frogs chanting a mile away. He lifted her little hands upon his own, and said—no matter about the words—but he told me that as he left the child, so he left the name, in my sacred charge,—that he had chosen it for me,—that, when he was out of sight, it might help me to have it often on my lips.

"So there in the sunset and the moonrise, we two alone together, he baptized her, and we gave our little girl to God."

When she had said this, she rose and went over to the window, and stood with her face from me. By and by, "It was the fourteenth," she said, as if musing to herself,—"the fourteenth of June."

I remembered now that Uncle Forceythe died on the fourteenth of June. It may have been that the words of that baptismal blessing were the last that they heard, either child or mother.

May 10.

It has been a pleasant day; the air shines like transparent gold; the wind sweeps like somebody's strong arms over the flowers, and gathers up a crowd of perfumes that wander up and down about one. The church bells have rung out like silver all day. Those bells—especially the Second Advent at the further end of the village—are positively ghastly when it rains.

Aunt Winifred was dressed bright and early for church. I, in morning dress and slippers, sighed and demurred.

"Auntie, *do* you expect to hear anything new?"

"Judging from your diagnosis of Dr. Bland,—no."

"To be edified, refreshed, strengthened, or instructed?"

"Perhaps not."

"Bored, then?"

"Not exactly."

"What do you expect?"

"There are the prayers and singing. Generally one can, if one tries, wring a little devotion from the worst of them. As to a minister, if he is good and commonplace, young and earnest and ignorant, and

I, whom he cannot help one step on the way to Heaven, consequently stay at home, Deacon Quirk, whom he might carry a mile or two, by and by stays at home also. If there is to be a 'building fitly joined together,' each stone must do its part of the upholding. I feel better to go half a day always. I never compel Faith to go, but I never have a chance, for she teases not to be left at home."

"I think it's splendid to go to church most the time," put in Faith, who was squatted on the carpet, counting sugared caraway seeds,— "all but the sermon. That isn't splendid. I don't like the gre-at big prayers 'n' things. I like caramary seeds, though; mother always gives 'em to me in meeting 'cause I'm a good girl. Don't you wish *you* were a good girl, Cousin Mary, so's you could have some? Besides, I've got on my best hat and my button-boots. Besides, there used to be a real funny little boy up in meeting at home, and he gave me a little tin dorg once over the top the pew. Only mother made me give it back. O, you ought to seen the man that preached down at Uncle Calvin's! I tell you he was a bully old minister,—*he banged the Bible like everything!*"

"There's a devotional spirit for you!" I said to her mother.

"Well," she answered, laughing, "it is better than that she should be left to play dolls and eat preserves, and be punished for disobedience. Sunday would invariably become a guilty sort of holiday at that rate. Now, caraways or 'bully old ministers' notwithstanding, she carries to bed with her a dim notion that this had been holy time and pleasant time. Besides, the associations of a church-going childhood, if I can manage them genially, will be a help to her when she is older. Come, Faith! go and pull off Cousin Mary's slippers, and bring down her boots, and then she'll have to go to church. No, I *didn't* say that you might tickle her feet!"

Feeling the least bit sorry that I had set the example of a stay-at-home Christian before the child, I went directly up stairs to make ready, and we started after all in good season.

Dr. Bland was in the pulpit. I observed that he looked—as indeed did the congregation bodily—with some curiosity into our slip, where it has been a rare occurrence of late to find me, and where the light, falling through the little stained glass oriel, touched Aunt Winifred's thoughtful smile. I wondered whether Dr. Bland thought it was wicked for people to smile in church. No, of course he has too much sense. I wonder what it is about Dr. Bland that always suggests such questions.

It has been very warm all day,—that aggravating, unseasonable heat, which is apt to come in spasms in the early part of May, and which, in thick spring alpaca and heavy sack, one finds intolerable. The thermometer stood at 75° on the church porch; every window was shut, and everybody's fan was fluttering. Now, with this sight before him, what should our observant minister do, but give out as his first hymn: "Thine earthly Sabbaths." "Thine earthly Sabbaths" would be a beautiful hymn, if it were not for those lines about the weather:—

"No midnight shade, *no clouded sun,*
But sacred, high, eternal noon"!

There was a great hot sunbeam striking directly on my black bonnet. My fan was broken. I gasped for air. The choir went over and over and *over* the words, spinning them into one of those indescribable tunes, in which everybody seems to be trying to get through first. I don't know what they called them,—they always remind me of a game of "Tag."

I looked at Aunt Winifred. She took it more coolly than I, but an amused little smile played over her face. She told me after church that she had repeatedly heard that hymn given out at noon of an intense July day. Her husband, she said, used to save it for the winter, or for cloudy afternoons. "Using means of grace," he called that.

However, Dr. Bland did better the second time, Aunt Winifred joined in the singing, and I enjoyed it, so I will not blame the poor man. I suppose he was so far lifted above this earth, that he would not have known whether he was preaching in Greenland's icy mountains, or on India's coral strand.

When he announced his text, "For our conversation is in Heav-

[handwritten margin note: religion is choking her?]

39

en," Aunt Winifred and I exchanged glances of content. We had been talking about heaven on the way to church; at least, till Faith, not finding herself entertained, interrupted us by some severe speculations as to whether Maltese kitties were mulattoes, and "why the bell-ringer didn't jump off the steeple some night, and see if he couldn't fly right up, the way Elijah did."

I listened to Dr. Bland as I have not listened for a long time. The subject was of all subjects nearest my heart. He is a scholarly man, in his way. He ought to know, I thought, more about it than Aunt Winifred. Perhaps he could help me.

His sermon, as nearly as I can recall it, was substantially this.

"The future life presented a vast theme to our speculation. Theories 'too numerous to mention,' had been held concerning it. Pagans had believed in a coming state of rewards and punishments. What natural theology had dimly foreshadowed, Revelation had brought in, like a full-orbed day, with healing on its wings." I am not positive about the metaphors.

"As it was fitting that we should at times turn our thoughts upon the threatenings of Scriptures, it was eminently suitable also that we should consider its promises.

"He proposed in this discourse to consider the promise of heaven, the reward offered by Christ to his good and faithful servants.

"In the first place: What is heaven?"

I am not quite clear in my mind what it was, though I tried my best to find out. As nearly as I can recollect, however,—

"Heaven is an eternal state.

"Heaven is a state of holiness.

"Heaven is a state of happiness."

Having heard these observations before, I will not enlarge as he did upon them, but leave that for the "vivid imagination" of the green book.

"In the second place: What will be the employments of heaven?

"We shall study the character of God.

"An infinite mind must of necessity be eternally an object of study to a finite mind. The finite mind must of necessity find in such study supreme delight. All lesser joys and interests will pale. He felt at moments, in reflecting on this theme, that that good brother who, on being asked if he expected to see the dead wife of his youth in heaven, replied, 'I expect to be so overwhelmed by the glory of the presence of God, that it may be thousands of years before I shall think of my wife,'—he felt that perhaps this brother was near the truth."

Poor Mrs. Bland looked exceedingly uncomfortable.

"We shall also glorify God."

He enlarged upon this division, but I have forgotten exactly how. There was something about adoration, and the harpers harping with their harps, and the sea of glass, and crying, Worthy the Lamb! and a great deal more that bewildered and disheartened me so that I could scarcely listen to it. I do not doubt that we shall glorify God primarily and happily, but can we not do it in some other way than by harping and praying?

"We shall moreover love each other with a universal and unselfish love."

"That we shall recognize our friends in heaven, he was inclined to think, after mature deliberation, was probable. But there would be no special selfish affections there. In this world we have enmities and favoritisms. In the world of bliss our hearts would glow with holy love alike to all other holy hearts."

I wonder if he really thought *that* would make "a world of bliss." Aunt Winifred slipped her hand into mine under her cloak. Ah, Dr. Bland, if you had known how that little soft touch was preaching against you!

"In the words of an eminent divine, who has long since entered into the joys of which he spoke: 'Thus, whenever the mind roves through the immense region of heaven, it will find, among all its innumerable millions, not an enemy, not a stranger, not an indifferent heart, not a reserved bosom. Disguise here, and even concealment, will be unknown. The soul will have no interests to conceal, *no thoughts to disguise.* A window will be opened in every breast, and show to every eye the rich and beautiful furniture within!'

"Thirdly: How shall we fit for heaven?"

He mentioned several ways, among which,—

"We should subdue our earthly affections to God.

"We must not love the creature as the Creator. My son, give *me* thy heart. When he removes our friends from the scenes of time (with a glance in my direction), we should resign ourselves to his will, remembering that the Lord gave and the Lord hath taken away in mercy; that He is all in all; that He will never leave us nor forsake us; that *He* can never change or die."

As if that made any difference with the fact, that his best treasures change or die!

"In conclusion,—

"We infer from our text that our hearts should not be set upon earthly happiness. (Enlarged.)

"That the subject of heaven should be often in our thoughts and on our lips." (Enlarged.)

Of course I have not done justice to the filling up of the sermon; to the illustrations, metaphors, proof-texts, learning, and eloquence,— for, though Dr. Bland cannot seem to think outside of the old grooves, a little eloquence really flashes through the tameness of his style sometimes, and when he was talking about the harpers, etc., some of his words were well chosen. "To be drowned in light," I have somewhere read, "may be very beautiful; it is still to be drowned." But I have given the skeleton of the discourse, and I have given the sum of the impressions that it left on me, an attentive hearer. It is fortunate that I did not hear it while I was alone; it would have made me desperate. Going hungry, hopeless, blinded, I came back empty, uncomforted, groping. I wanted something actual, something pleasant, about this place into which Roy has gone. He gave me glittering generalities, cold commonplace, vagueness, unreality, a God and a future at which I sat and shivered.

Dr. Bland is a good man. He had, I know, written that sermon with prayer. I only wish that he could be made to *see* how it glides over and sails splendidly away from wants like mine.

But thanks be to God who has provided a voice to answer me out of the deeps.

Auntie and I walked home without any remarks (we overheard Deacon Quirk observe to a neighbor: "That's what I call a good gospel sermon, now!"), sent Faith away to Phoebe, sat down in the parlor, and looked at each other.

"Well?" said I.

"I know it," said she.

Upon which we both began to laugh.

"But did he say the dreadful truth?"

"Not as I find it in my Bible."

"That it is probable, only *probable* that we shall recognize——"

"My child, do not be troubled about that. It is not probable, it is sure. If I could find no proof for it, I should none the less believe it, as long as I believe in God. He gave you Roy, and the capacity to love him. He has taught you to sanctify that love through love to Him. Would it be *like* Him to create such beautiful and unselfish loves,—most like the love of heaven of any type we know,—just for our threescore years and ten of earth? Would it be like Him to suffer two souls to grow together here, so that the separation of a day is pain, and then wrench them apart for all eternity? It would be what Madame de Gasparin calls, 'fearful irony on the part of God.'"

"But there are lost loves. There are lost souls."

"How often would I have gathered you, and ye would not! That is not his work. He would have saved both soul and love. They had their own way. We were speaking of His redeemed. The object of having this world at all, you know, is to fit us for another. Of what use will it have been, if on passing out of it we must throw by forever its gifts, its lessons, its memories? God links things together better than that. Be sure, as you are sure of Him, that we shall be *ourselves* in heaven. Would you be yourself not to recognize Roy?—consequently, not to love Roy, for to love and to be separated is misery, and heaven is joy."

"I understand. But you said you had other proof."

"So I have; plenty of it. If 'many shall come from the East and from the West, and shall sit down in the kingdom of God with Abraham, Isaac, and Jacob,' will they not be likely to know that they are with Abraham, Isaac, and Jacob? or will they think it is Shadrach, Meshech, and Abednego?

"What is meant by such expressions as 'risen *together,*' 'sitting *together* in heavenly places'? If they mean anything, they mean recognitions, friendships, enjoyments.

"Did not Peter and the others know Moses when they saw him?—know Elias when they saw him? Yet these men were dead hundreds of years before the favored fishermen were born.

"How was it with those 'saints which slept and arose' when Christ hung dead there in the dark? Were they not seen of many?"

"But that was a miracle."

"They were risen dead, such as you and I shall be some day. The miracle consisted in their rising then and there. Moreover, did not the beggar recognize Abraham? and—Well, one might go through the Bible finding it full of this promise in hints or assertions, in parables or visions. We are 'heirs of God,' 'joint heirs with Christ'; having suffered with Him, we shall be 'glorified *together.*' Christ himself has said many sure things: 'I will come and receive you, that where I am, there ye may be.' 'I will that they be with me where I am.' Using, too, the very type of Godhead to signify the eternal nearness and eternal love of just such as you and Roy, as John and me, he prays: 'Holy Father, keep them whom Thou hast given me, that *they may be one as we are.*'

"There is one place, though, where I find what I like better than all the rest; you remember that old cry wrung from the lips of the stricken king,—'I shall go to him; but he will not return to me.'"

"I never thought before how simple and direct it is; and that, too, in those old blinded days."

"The more I study the Bible," she said, "and I study not entirely in ignorance of the commentators and the mysteries, the more perplexed I am to imagine where the current ideas of our future come from. They certainly are not in this book of gracious promises. That heaven which we heard about to-day was Dr. Bland's, not God's. 'It's aye a wonderfu' thing to me,' as poor Lauderdale said, 'the way some preachers take it upon themselves to explain matters to the Almighty!' "

"But the harps and choirs, the throne, the white robes, are all in Revelation. Deacon Quirk would put his great brown finger on the verses, and hold you there triumphantly."

"Can't people tell picture from substance, a metaphor from its meaning? That book of Revelation is precisely what it professes to be,—a vision; a symbol. A symbol of something, to be sure, and rich with pleasant hopes, but still a symbol. Now, I really believe that a large proportion of Christian church-members, who have studied their Bible, attended Sabbath schools, listened to sermons all their lives, if you could fairly come at their most definite idea of the place where they expect to spend eternity, would own it to be the golden city, with pearl gates, and jewels in the wall. It never occurs to them, that, if one picture is literal, another must be. If we are to walk golden streets, how can we stand on a sea of glass? How can we 'sit on thrones'? How can untold millions of us 'lie in Abraham's bosom'?"

"But why have given us empty symbols? Why not a little fact?"

"They are not *empty* symbols. And why God did not give us actual descriptions of actual heavenly life, I don't trouble myself to wonder. He certainly had his reasons, and that is enough for me. I find from these symbols, and from his voice in my own heart, many beautiful things,—I will tell you some more of them at another time,—and, for the rest, I am content to wait. He loves me, and he loves mine. As long as we love Him, He will never separate Himself from us, or us from each other. That, at least, is *sure.*"

"If that is sure, the rest is of less importance;—yes. But Dr. Bland said an awful thing!"

"The quotation from a dead divine?"

"Yes. That there will be no separate interests, no thoughts to conceal."

"Poor good man! He has found out by this time that he should not have laid down nonsense like that, without qualification or demur, before a Bible-reading hearer. It was simply *his* opinion, not David's, or Paul's, or John's, or Isaiah's. He had a perfect right to put it in the form of a conjecture. Nobody would forbid his conjecturing that the inhabitants of heaven are all deaf and dumb, or wear green glasses, or shave their heads, if he chose, provided he stated that it was conjecture, not revelation."

"But where does the Bible say that we shall have power to conceal our thoughts?—and I would rather be annihilated than to spend eternity with heart laid bare,—the inner temple thrown open to be trampled on by every passing stranger!"

"The Bible specifies very little about the minor arrangements of eternity in any way. But I doubt if, under any circumstances, it would have occurred to inspired men to inform us that our thoughts shall continue to be our own. The fact is patent on the face of things. The dead minister's supposition would destroy individuality at one fell swoop. We should be like a man walking down a room lined with mirrors, who sees himself reflected in all sizes, colors, shades, at all angles and in all proportions, according to the capacity of the mirror, till he seems no longer to belong to himself, but to be cut up into ellipses and octagons and prisms. How soon would he grow frantic in such companionship, and beg for a corner where he might hide and hush himself in the dark?

"That we shall in a higher life be able to do what we cannot in this,—judge fairly of each other's *moral* worth,—is undoubtedly true. Whatever the Judgment Day may mean, that is the substance of it. But this promiscuous theory of refraction;—never!

"Besides, wherever the Bible touches the subject, it premises our individuality as a matter of course. What would be the use of talking, if everybody knew the thoughts of everybody else?"

"You don't suppose that people talk in heaven?"

Qsilence

"I don't suppose anything else. Are we to spend ages of joy, a company of mutes together? Why not talk?"

"I supposed we should sing,—but—"

"Why not talk as well as sing? Does not song involve the faculty of speech?—unless you would like to make canaries of us."

"Ye-es. Why, yes."

"There are the visitors at the beautiful Mount of Transfiguration again. Did not they *talk* with each other and with Christ? Did not John *talk* with the angel who 'shewed him those things'?"

"And you mean to say—"

"I mean to say that if there is such a thing as common sense, you will talk with Roy as you talked with him here,—only not as you talked with him here, because there will be no troubles nor sins, no anxieties nor cares, to talk about; no ugly shades of cross words or little quarrels to be made up; no fearful looking-for of separation."

I laid my head upon her shoulder, and could hardly speak for the comfort that she gave me.

"Yes, I believe we shall talk and laugh and joke and play—"

"Laugh and joke in heaven?"

"Why not?"

"But it seems so—so—why, so wicked and irreverent and all that, you know."

Just then Faith, who, mounted out on the kitchen table, was preaching at Phoebe in comical mimicry of Dr. Bland's choicest intonations, laughed out like the splash of a little wave.

The sound came in at the open door, and we stopped to listen till it had rippled away.

"There!" said her mother, "put that child, this very minute, with all her little sins forgiven, into one of our dear Lord's many mansions, and do you suppose that she would be any the less holy or less reverent for a laugh like that? Is he going to check all the sparkle and blossom of life when he takes us to himself? I don't believe any such thing.

"There were both sense and Christianity in what somebody wrote on the death of a humorous poet:—

'Does nobody laugh there, where he has gone,—
   This man of the smile and the jest?'

—provided there was any hope that the poor fellow *had* gone to heaven; if not, it was bad philosophy and worse religion.

"Did not David dance before the Lord with all his might? A Bible which is full of happy battle-cries:'Rejoice in the Lord! make a joyful noise unto him! Give thanks unto the Lord, for his mercy endureth!'—a Bible which exhausts its splendid wealth of rhetoric to make us understand that the coming life is a life of *joy,* no more threatens to make nuns than mutes of us. I expect that you will hear some of Roy's very old jokes, see the sparkle in his eye, listen to his laughing voice, lighten up the happy days as gleefully as you may choose; and that—"

Faith appeared upon the scene just then, with the interesting information that she had bitten her tongue; so we talked no more.

How pleasant—how pleasant this is! I never supposed before that God would let any one laugh in heaven.

I wonder if Roy has seen the President. Aunt Winifred says she does not doubt it. She thinks that all the soldiers must have crowded up to meet him, and "O," she says, "what a sight to see!"

₹7₹

May 12th.

Aunt Winifred has said something about going, but I cannot yet bear to hear of such a thing. She is to stay a while longer.

16th.

We have been over to-night to the grave.

She proposed to go by herself, thinking, I saw, with the delicacy with which she always thinks, that I would rather not be there with another. Nor should I, nor could I, with any other than this woman. It is strange. I wished to go there with her. I had a vague, unreasoning feeling that she would take away some of the bitterness of it, as she has taken the bitterness of much else.

It is looking very pleasant there now. The turf has grown fine and smooth. The low arbor-vitæ hedge and knots of Norway spruce, that father planted long ago for mother, drop cool, green shadows that stir with the wind. My English ivy has crept about and about the cross. Roy used to say that he should fancy a cross to mark the spot where he might lie; I think he would like this pure, unveined marble. May-flowers cover the grave now, and steal out among the clover-leaves with a flush like sunrise. By and by there will be roses, and, in August, August's own white lilies.

We went silently over, and sat silently down on the grass, the field-path stretching away to the little church behind us, and beyond, in front, the slope, the flats, the river, the hills cut in purple distance melting far into the east. The air was thick with perfume. Golden bees hung giddily over the blush in the grass. In the low branches that swept the grave a little bird had built her nest.

Aunt Winifred did not speak to me for a time, nor watch my face. Presently she laid her hand upon my lap, and I put mine into it.

"It is very pleasant here," she said then, in her very pleasant voice.

"I meant that it should be," I answered, trying not to let her see my lips quiver. "At least it must not look neglected. I don't suppose it makes any difference to *him*."

"I do not feel sure of that."

"What do you mean?"

"I do not feel sure that anything he has left makes no 'difference' to him."

"But I don't understand. He is in heaven. He would be too happy to care for anything that is going on in this woful world."

"Perhaps that is so," she said, smiling a sweet contradiction to her words, "but I don't believe it."

"What do you believe?"

49

"Many things that I have to say to you, but you cannot bear them now."

"I have sometimes wondered, for I cannot help it," I said, "whether he is shut off from all knowledge of me for all these years till I can go to him. It will be a great while. It seems hard. Roy would want to know something, if it were only a little, about me."

"I believe that he wants to know, and that he knows, Mary; though, since the belief must rest on analogy and conjecture, you need not accept it as demonstrated mathematics," she answered, with another smile.

"Roy never forgot me here!" I said, not meaning to sob.

"That is just it. He was not constituted so that he, remaining himself, Roy, could forget you. If he goes out into this other life forgetting, he becomes another than himself. That is a far more unnatural way of creeping out of the difficulty than to assume that he loves and remembers. Why not assume that? In fact, why assume anything else? Neither reason, nor the Bible, nor common sense, forbids it. Instead of starting with it as an hypothesis to be proved if we can, I lay it down as one of those probabilities for which Butler would say, 'the presumption amounts nearly to certainty'; and if any one can disprove it, I will hear what he has to say. There!" she broke off, laughing softly, "that is a sufficient dose of metaphysics for such a simple thing. It seems to me to lie just here: Roy loved you. Our Father, for some tender, hidden reason, took him out of your sight for a while. Though changed much, he can have forgotten nothing. Being *only out of sight,* you remember, not lost, nor asleep, nor annihilated, he goes on loving. To love must mean to think of, to care for, to hope for, to pray for, not less out of a body than in it."

"But that must mean—why, that must mean—"

"That he is near you. I do not doubt it."

The sunshine quivered in among the ivy-leaves, and I turned to watch it, thinking.

"I do not doubt," she went on, speaking low,—"I cannot doubt that our absent dead are very present with us. He said, 'I am with you always,' knowing the need we have of him, even to the end of the world. He must understand the need we have of them. I cannot doubt it."

I watched her as she sat with her absent eyes turned eastward, and her peculiar look—I have never seen it on another face—as of one who holds a happy secret; and while I watched I wondered.

"There is a reason for it," she said, rousing as if from a pleasant dream,—"a good sensible reason, too, it strikes me, independent of Scriptural or other proof."

"What is that?"

"That God keeps us briskly at work in this world."

I did not understand.

"Altogether too briskly, considering that it is a preparative world, to intend to put us from it into an idle one. What more natural than that we shall spend our best energies as we spent them here,—in comforting, teaching, helping, saving people whose very souls we love better than our own? In fact, it would be very unnatural if we did not."

"But I thought that God took care of us, and angels, like Gabriel and the rest, if I ever thought anything about it, which I am inclined to doubt."

"'God works by the use of means,' as the preachers say. Why not use Roy as well as Gabriel? What archangel could understand and reach the peculiarities of your nature as he could? or, even if understanding, could so love and bear with you? What is to be done? Will they send Roy to the planet Jupiter to take care of somebody's else sister?"

I laughed in spite of myself; nor did the laugh seem to jar upon the sacred stillness of the place. Her words were drawing away the bitterness, as the sun was blotting the dull, dead greens of the ivy into its glow of golden color.

"But the Bible, Aunt Winifred."

"The Bible does *not* say a great deal on this point," she said, "but it does not contradict me. In fact, it helps me; and, moreover, it would uphold me in black and white if it weren't for one little obstacle."

"And that?"

"That frowning 'original Greek,' which Gail Hamilton denounces with her righteous indignation. No sooner do I find a pretty verse that is exactly what I want, than up hops a commentator, and says, this isn't according to text, and means something entirely different; and Barnes says this, and Stuart believes that, and Olshausen has demonstrated the other, and very ignorant it is in you, too, not to know it! Here the other day I ferreted out a sentence in Revelation that seemed to prove beyond question that angels and redeemed men were the same; where the angel says to John, you know, 'Am I not of thy brethren the prophets?' I thought that I had discovered a delightful thing which all the Fathers of the church had overlooked, and went in great glee to your Uncle Calvin, to be told that something was the matter,—a noun left out, or some other unanswerable and unreasonable horror, I don't know what; and that it didn't mean that he was of thy brethren the prophets at all!

"You see, if it could be proved that the Christian dead become angels, we could have all that we need, direct from God, about—to use the beautiful old phrase—the communion of saints. From Genesis to Revelation the Bible is filled with angels who are at work on earth. They hold sweet converse with Abraham in his tent. They are intrusted to save the soul of Lot. An angel hears the wail of Hagar. The beautiful feet of an angel bring the good tidings to maiden Mary. An angel's noiseless step guides Peter through the barred and bolted gate. Angels rolled the stone from the buried Christ, and angels sat there in the solemn morning,—O Mary! if we could have seen them!

"Then there is that one question, direct, comprehensive,—we should not need anything else,—'Are they not all ministering spirits, sent forth to minister to the heirs of salvation?'

"But you see it never seems to have entered those commentators' heads that all these beautiful things refer to any but a superior race of beings, like those from whose ranks Lucifer fell."

"How stupid in them!"

"I take comfort in thinking so; but, to be serious, even admitting that these passages refer to a superior race, must there not be some similarity in the laws which govern existence in the heavenly world? Since these gracious deeds are performed by what we are accustomed to call 'spiritual beings,' why may they not as well be done by people from this world as from anywhere else? Besides, there is another point, and a reasonable one, to be made. The word angel in the original* means, strictly, *a messenger*. It applies to any servant of God, animate or inanimate. An east wind is as much an angel as Michael. Again, the generic terms, 'spirits,' 'gods,' 'sons of God,' are used interchangeably for saints and for angels. So, you see, I fancy that I find a way for you and Roy and me and all of us, straight into the shining ministry. Mary, Mary, wouldn't you like to go this very afternoon?"

She lay back in the grass, with her face upturned to the sky, and drew a long breath, wearily. I do not think she meant me to hear it. I did not answer her, for it came over me with such a hopeless thrill, how good it would be to be taken to Roy, there by his beautiful grave, with the ivy and the May-flowers and the sunlight and the clover-leaves round about; and that it could not be, and how long it was to wait,—it came over me so that I could not speak.

"There!" she said, suddenly rousing, "what a thoughtless, wicked thing it was to say! And I meant to give you only the good cheer of a cheery friend. No, I do not care to go this afternoon, nor any afternoon, till my Father is ready for me. Wherever he has most for me to do, there I wish,—yes, I think I *wish* to stay. He knows best."

After a pause, I asked again, "Why did He not tell us more about this thing,—about their presence with us? You see if I could *know* it!"

"The mystery of the Bible lies not so much in what it says, as in what it does not say," she replied. "But I suppose that we have been told all that we can comprehend in this world. Knowledge on one point might involve knowledge on another, like the links of a chain, till it stretched far beyond our capacity. At any rate, it is not for me

* αγγελος

to break the silence. That is God's affair. I can only accept the fact. Nevertheless, as Dr. Chalmers says: 'It were well for us all could we carefully draw the line between the secret things which belong to God and the things which are revealed and belong to us and to our children.' Some one else,—Whately, I think,—I remember to have noticed as speaking about these very subjects to this effect,—that precisely because we know so little of them, it is the more important that we 'should endeavor so to dwell on them as to make the most of what little knowledge we have.' "

"Aunt Winifred, you are such a comfort!"

"It needs our best faith," she said, "to bear this reticence of God. I cannot help thinking sometimes of a thing Lauderdale said,—I am always quoting him,—from 'Son of the Soil,' you remember: 'It's an awfu' marvel, beyond my reach, when a word of communication would make a' the difference, why it's no permitted, if it were but to keep a heart from breaking now and then.' Think of poor Eugénie de Guèrin, trying to continue her little journal 'To Maurice in Heaven,' till the awful, answerless stillness shut up the book and laid aside the pen.

"But then," she continued, "there is this to remember,—I may have borrowed the idea, or it may be my own,—that if we could speak to them, or they to us, there would be no death, for there would be no separation. The last, the surest, in some cases the only test of loyalty to God, would thus be taken away. Roman Catholic nature is human nature, when it comes upon its knees before a saint. Many lives—all such lives as yours and mine—would become—"

"Would become what?"

"One long defiance to the First Commandment."

I cannot become used to such words from such quiet lips. Yet they give me a curious sense of the trustworthiness of her peace. "Founded upon a rock," it seems to be. She has done what it takes a lifetime for some of us to do; what some of us go into eternity, leaving undone; what I am afraid I shall never do,—sounded her own nature. She knows the worst of herself, and faces it as fairly, I believe, as anybody can do in this world. As for the best of herself, she trusts that to Christ, and he knows it, and we. I hope she, in her sweet humbleness, will know it some day.

"I suppose, nevertheless," she said, "that Roy knows what you are doing and feeling as well as, perhaps better than, he knew it three months ago. So he can help you without harming you."

I asked her, turning suddenly, how that could be, and yet heaven be heaven,—how he could see me suffer what I had suffered, could see me sometimes when I supposed none but God had seen me,—and sing on and be happy.

"You are not the first, Mary, and you will not be the last, to ask that question. I cannot answer it, and I never heard of any who could. I feel sure only of this,—that he would suffer far less to see you than to know nothing about you; and that God's power of inventing happiness is not to be blocked by an obstacle like this. Perhaps Roy sees the end from the beginning, and can bear the sight of pain for the peace that he watches coming to meet you. I do not know,—that does not perplex me now; it only makes me anxious for one thing."

"What is that?"

"That you and I shall not do anything to make them sorry."

"To make them sorry?"

"Roy would care. Roy would be disappointed to see you make life a hopeless thing for his sake, or to see you doubt his Saviour."

"Do you think *that?*"

"Some sort of mourning over sin enters that happy life. God himself 'was grieved' forty years long over his wandering people. Among the angels there has been 'silence,' whatever that mysterious pause may mean, just as there is joy over one sinner that repenteth; another of my proof-texts, that, to show that they are allowed to keep us in sight."

"Then you think, you really think, that Roy remembers and loves and takes care of me; that he has been listening, perhaps, and is— why, you don't think he may be *here?*"

"Yes, I do. Here, close beside you all this time, trying to speak to

have a purpose

you through the blessed sunshine and the flowers, trying to help you, and sure to love you,—right here, dear. I do not believe God means to send him away from you, either."

My heart was too full to answer her. Seeing how it was, she slipped away, and, strolling out of sight with her face to the eastern hills, left me alone.

And yet I did not seem alone. The low branches swept with a little soft sigh across the grave; the May-flowers wrapped me in with fragrance thick as incense; the tiny sparrow turned her soft eyes at me over the edge of the nest, and chirped contentedly; the "blessed sunshine" talked with me as it touched the edges of the ivy-leaves to fire.

I cannot write it even here, how these things stole into my heart and hushed me. If I had seen him standing by the stainless cross, it would not have frightened or surprised me. There—not dead or gone, but *there*—it helps me, and makes me strong!

"Mamie! little Mamie!"

O Roy, I will try to bear it all, if you will only stay!

⟨ 8 ⟩

May 20.

The nearer the time has come for Aunt Winifred to go, the more it has seemed impossible to part with her. I have run away from the thought like a craven, till she made me face it this morning, by saying decidedly that she should go on the first of the week.

I dropped my sewing; the work-basket tipped over, and all my spools rolled away under the chairs. I had a little time to think while I was picking them up.

"There is the rest of my visit at Norwich to be made, you know," she said, "and while I am there I shall form some definite plans for the summer; I have hardly decided what, yet. I had better leave here by the seven o'clock train, if such an early start will not incommode you."

I wound up the last spool, and turned away to the window. There was a confused, dreary sky of scurrying clouds, and a cold wind was bruising the apple-buds. I hate a cold wind in May. It made me choke a little, thinking how I should sit and listen to it after she was gone,—of the old, blank, comfortless days that must come and go,—of what she had brought, and what she would take away. I was a bit faint, I think, for a minute. I had not really thought the prospect through, before.

"Mary," she said, "what's the matter? Come here."

I went over, and she drew me into her lap, and I put my arms about her neck.

"I can *not* bear it," said I, "and that is the matter."

She smiled, but her smile faded when she looked at me.

And then I told her, sobbing how it was; that I could not go into my future alone,—I could not do it! that she did not know how weak I was,—and reckless,—and wicked; that she did not know what she had been to me. I begged her not to leave me. I begged her to stay and help me bear my life.

"My dear! you are as bad as Faith when I put her to bed alone."

"But," I said, "when Faith cries, you go to her, you know."

"Are you quite in earnest, Mary?" she asked, after a pause. "You don't know very much about me, after all, and there is the child. It is always an experiment, bringing two families into lifelong relations under one roof. If I could think it best, you might repent your bargain."

"*I* am not 'a family,'" I said, feebly trying to laugh. "Aunt Winifred, if you and Faith only *will* make this your home, I can never thank you, never. I shall be entertaining my good angels, and that is the whole of it."

"I have had some thought of not going back," she said at last, in a low, constrained voice, as if she were touching something that gave

57

moving to Faith? (handwritten)
"save" Faith (handwritten)
revive Mary's Faith (handwritten)

her great pain, "for Faith's sake. I should like to educate her in New England, if— I had intended if we stayed to rent or buy a little home of our own somewhere, but I had been putting off a decision. We are most weak and most selfish sometimes when we think ourselves strongest and noblest, Mary. I love my husband's people. I think they love me. I was almost happy with them. It seemed as if I were carrying on his work for him. That was so pleasant!"

She put me down out of her arms and walked across the room.

"I will think the matter over," she said, by and by, in her natural tones, "and let you know to-night."

She went away up stairs then, and I did not see her again until to-night. I sent Faith up with her dinner and tea, judging that she would rather see the child than me. I observed, when the dishes came down, that she had touched nothing but a cup of coffee.

I began to understand, as I sat alone in the parlor through the afternoon, how much I had asked of her. In my selfish distress at losing her, I had not thought of that. Faces that her husband loved, meadows and hills and sunsets that he has watched, the home where his last step sounded and his last word was spoken, the grave where she has laid him,—this last more than all,—call after her, and cling to her with yearning closeness. To leave them, is to leave the last faint shadow of her beautiful past. It hurts, but she is too brave to cry out.

Tea was over, and Faith in bed, but still she did not come down. I was sitting by the window, watching a little crescent moon climb over the hills, and wondering whether I had better go up, when she came in and stood behind me, and said, attempting to laugh:—

"Very impolite in me to run off so, wasn't it? Cowardly, too, I think. Well, Mary?"

"Well, Auntie?"

"Have you not repented your proposition yet?"

"You would excel as an inquisitor, Mrs. Forceythe!"

"Then it shall be as you say; as long as you want us you shall have us,—Faith and me."

I turned to thank her, but could not when I saw her face. It was

Faith vs 1st (handwritten, left margin)

58

very pale; there was something inexpressibly sad about her mouth, and her eyelids drooped heavily, like one weary from a great struggle.

Feeling for the moment guilty and ashamed before her, as if I had done her wrong, "It is going to be very hard for you," I said.

"Never mind about that," she answered, quickly. "We will not talk about that. I knew, though I did not *wish* to know, that it was best for Faith. Your hands about my neck have settled it. Where the work is, there the laborer must be. It is quite plain now. I have been talking it over with them all the afternoon; it seems to be what they want."

"With *them?*" I started at the words; who had been in her lonely chamber? Ah, it is simply real to her. Who, indeed, but her Saviour and her husband?

She did not seem inclined to talk, and stole away from me presently, and out of doors; she was wrapped in her blanket shawl, and had thrown a shimmering white hood over her gray hair. I wondered where she could be going, and sat still at the window watching her. She opened and shut the gate softly; and, turning her face towards the churchyard, walked up the street and out of my sight.

She feels nearer to him in the resting-place of the dead. Her heart cries after the grave by which she will never sit and weep again; on which she will never plant the roses any more.

As I sat watching and thinking this, the faint light struck her slight figure and little shimmering hood again, and she walked down the street and in with steady step.

When she came up and stood beside me, smiling, with the light knitted thing thrown back on her shoulders, her face seemed to rise from it as from a snowy cloud; and for her look,—I wish Raphael could have had it for one of his rapt madonnas.

"Now, Mary," she said, with the sparkle back again in her voice, "I am ready to be entertaining, and promise not to play the hermit again very soon. Shall I sit here on the sofa with you? Yes, my dear, I am happy, quite happy."

So then we took this new promise of home that has come to make

[handwritten marginal note: relationship in faith / talking to angels]

my life, if not joyful, something less than desolate, and analyzed it in its practical bearings. What a pity that all pretty dreams have to be analyzed! I had some notion about throwing our little incomes into a joint family fund, but she put a veto to that; I suppose because mine is the larger. She prefers to take board for herself and Faith; but, if I know myself, she shall never be suffered to have the feeling of a boarder, and I will make her so much at home in my house that she shall not remember that it is not her own.

Her visit to Norwich she has decided to put off until the autumn, so that I shall have her to myself undisturbed all summer.

I have been looking at Roy's picture a long time, and wondering how he would like the new plan. I said something of the sort to her.

"Why put any 'would' in that sentence?" she said, smiling. "It belongs in the present tense."

"Then I am sure he likes it," I answered,—"he likes it," and I said the words over till I was ready to cry for rest in their sweet sound.

22d.

It is Roy's birthday. But I have not spoken of it. We used to make a great deal of these little festivals,—but it is of no use to write about that.

I am afraid I have been bearing it very badly all day. She noticed my face, but said nothing till to-night. Mrs. Bland was down stairs, and I had come away alone up here in the dark. I heard her asking for me, but would not go down. By and by Aunt Winifred knocked, and I let her in.

"Mrs. Bland cannot understand why you don't see her, Mary," she said, gently. "You know you have not thanked her for those English violets that she sent the other day. I only thought I would remind you; she might feel a little pained."

"I can't to-night,—not to-night, Aunt Winifred. You must excuse me to her somehow. I don't want to go down."

"Is it that you don't 'want to,' or *is* it that you can't?" she said, in that gentle, motherly way of hers, at which I can never take offence.

"Mary, I wonder if Roy would not a little rather that you would go down?"

It might have been Roy himself who spoke.

I went down.

$$\{9\}$$

Aunt Winifred went to the office this morning, and met Dr. Bland, who walked home with her. He always likes to talk with her.

A woman who knows something about fate, free-will, and fore-knowledge absolute, who is not ignorant of politics, and talks intelligently of Agassiz's latest fossil, who can understand a German quotation, and has heard of Strauss and Neander, who can dash her sprightliness ably against his old dry bones of metaphysics and theology, yet never speak an accent above that essentially womanly voice of hers, is, I imagine, a phenomenon in his social experience.

I was sitting at the window when they came up and stopped at the gate. Dr. Bland lifted his hat to me in his grave way, talking the while; somewhat eagerly, too, I could see. Aunt Winifred answered him with a peculiar smile and a few low words that I could not hear.

"But, my dear madam," he said, "the glory of God, you see, the glory of God is the primary consideration."

"But the glory of God *involves* these lesser glories, as a sidereal system, though a splendid whole, exists by the multiplied differing of one star from another star. Ah, Dr. Bland, you make a grand abstraction out of it, but it makes me cold,"—she shivered, half playfully, half involuntarily,—"it makes me cold. I am very much alive and human; and Christ was human God."

She came in smiling a little sadly, and stood by me, watching the minister walk over the hill.

"How much does that man love his wife and children?" she asked abruptly.

"A good deal. Why?"

"I am afraid that he will lose one of them then, before many more years of his life are past."

"What! he hasn't been telling you that they are consumptive or anything of the sort?"

"O dear me, no," with a merry laugh which died quickly away: "I was only thinking,—there is trouble in store for him; some intense pain,—if he is capable of intense pain,—which shall shake his cold, smooth theorizing to the foundation. He speaks a foreign tongue when he talks of bereavement, of death, of the future life. No argument could convince him of that, though, which is the worst of it."

"He must think you shockingly heterodox."

"I don't doubt it. We had a little talk this morning, and he regarded me with an expression of mingled consternation and perplexity that was curious. He is a very good man. He is not a stupid man. I only wish that he would stop preaching and teaching things that he knows nothing about.

"He is only drifting with the tide, though," she added, "in his views of this matter. In our recoil from the materialism of the Romish Church, we have, it seems to me, nearly stranded ourselves on the opposite shore. Just as, in a rebound from the spirit which would put our Saviour on a level with Buddha or Mahomet, we have been in danger of forgetting 'to begin as the Bible begins,' with his humanity. It is the grandeur of inspiration, that it knows how to *balance* truth."

It had been in my mind for several days to ask Aunt Winifred something, and, feeling in the mood, I made her take off her things and devote herself to me. My question concerned what we call the "intermediate state."

"I have been expecting that," she said; "what about it?"

"What *is* it?"

"Life and activity."

"We do not go to sleep, of course."

"I believe that notion is about exploded, though clear thinkers like Whately have appeared to advocate it. Where it originated, I do not know, unless from the frequent comparisons in the Scriptures of death with sleep, which refer solely, I am convinced, to the condition of body, and which are voted down by an overwhelming majority of decided statements relative to the consciousness, happiness, and tangibility of the life into which we immediately pass."

"It is intermediate, in some sense, I suppose."

"It waits between two other conditions,—yes; I think the drift of what we are taught about it leads to that conclusion. I expect to become at once sinless, but to have a broader Christian character many years hence; to be happy at once, but to be happier by and by; to find in myself wonderful new tastes and capacities, which are to be immeasurably ennobled and enlarged after the Resurrection, whatever that may mean."

"What does it mean?"

"I know no more than you, but you shall hear what I think, presently. I was going to say that this seems to be plain enough in the Bible. The angels took Lazarus at once to Abraham. Dives seems to have found no interval between death and consciousness of suffering."

"They always tell you that that is only a parable."

"But it must mean *something*. No story in the Bible has been pulled to pieces and twisted about as that has been. We are in danger of pulling and twisting all sense out of it. Then Judas, having hanged his wretched self, went to his own place. Besides, there was Christ's promise to the thief."

I told her that I had heard Dr. Bland say that we could not place much dependence on that passage, because "Paradise" did not necessarily mean heaven.

"But it meant living, thinking, enjoying; for 'To-day thou shalt *be with me.*' Paul's beautiful perplexed revery, however, would be enough if it stood alone; for he did not know whether he would rather stay in this world, or depart and be with Christ, which is far better. *With Christ,* you see; and His three mysterious days, which typify our intermediate state, were over then, and he had ascended to his Father. Would it be 'far better' either to leave this actual tangible life throbbing with hopes and passions, to leave its busy, Christ-like working, its quiet joys, its very sorrows which are near and human, for a nap of several ages, or even for a vague, lazy, half-alive, disembodied existence?"

"Disembodied? I supposed, of course, that it was disembodied."

"I do not think so. And that brings us to the Resurrection. All the *tendency* of Revelation is to show that an embodied state is superior to a disembodied one. Yet certainly we who love God are promised that death will lead us into a condition which shall have the advantage of this: for the good apostle to die 'was gain.' I don't believe, for instance, that Adam and Eve have been wandering about in a misty condition all these thousands of years. I suspect that we have some sort of body immediately after passing out of this, but that there is to come a mysterious change, equivalent, perhaps, to a re-embodiment, when our capacities for action will be greatly improved, and that in some manner this new form will be connected with this 'garment by the soul laid by.'"

"Deacon Quirk expects to rise in his own entire, original body, after it has lain in the First Church cemetery a proper number of years, under a black slate headstone, adorned by a willow, and such a 'cherubim' as that poor boy shot,—by the way, if I've laughed at that story once, I have fifty times."

"Perhaps Deacon Quirk would admire a work of art that I found stowed away on the top of your Uncle Calvin's bookcases. It was an old woodcut—nobody knows how old—of an interesting skeleton rising from his grave, and, in a sprightly and modest manner, drawing on his skin, while Gabriel, with apoplectic cheeks, feet uppermost in the air, was blowing a good-sized tin trumpet in his ear!

"No; some of the popular notions of resurrection are simple physiological impossibilities, from causes 'too tedious to specify.' Imagine, for instance, the resurrection of two Hottentots, one of whom has happened to make a dinner of the other some fine day. A little complication there! Or picture the touching scene, when that devoted husband, King Mausolas, whose widow had him burned and ate the ashes, should feel moved to institute a search for his body! It is no wonder that the infidel argument has the best of it, when we attempt to enforce a natural impossibility. It is worth while to remember that Paul expressly stated that we shall *not* rise in our entire earthly bodies. The simile which he used is the seed sown, dying in, and mingling with, the ground. How many of its original particles are found in the full-grown corn?"

"Yet you believe that *something* belonging to this body is preserved for the completion of another?"

"Certainly. I accept God's statement about it, which is as plain as words can make a statement. I do not know, and I do not care to know, how it is to be effected. God will not be at a loss for a way, any more than he is at a loss for a way to make his fields blossom every spring. For aught we know, some invisible compound of an annihilated body may hover, by a divine decree, around the site of death till it is wanted,—sufficient to preserve identity as strictly as a body can ever be said to preserve it; and stranger things have happened. You remember the old Mohammedan belief in the one little bone which is imperishable. Prof. Bush's idea of our triune existence is suggestive, for a notion. He believed, you know, that it takes a material body, a spiritual body, and a soul, to make a man. The spiritual body is enclosed within the material, the soul within the spiritual. Death is simply the slipping off of the outer body, as a husk slips off from its kernel. The deathless frame stands ready then for the soul's untrammelled occupation. But it is a waste of time to speculate over such useless fancies, while so many remain that will vitally affect our happiness."

It is singular; but I never gave a serious thought—and I have done some thinking about other matters—to my heavenly body, till that moment, while I sat listening to her. In fact, till Roy went, the Future was a miserable, mysterious blank, to be drawn on and on in eternal and joyless monotony, and to which, at times, annihilation seemed preferable. I remember, when I was a child, asking father once, if I were so good that I *had* to go to heaven, whether, after a hundred years, God would not let me "die out." More or less of the disposition of that same desperate little sinner I suspect has always clung to me. So I asked Aunt Winifred, in some perplexity, what she supposed our bodies would be like.

"It must be nearly all 'suppose,' " she said, "for we are nowhere definitely told. But this is certain. They will be as real as these."

"But these you can see, you can touch."

"What would be the use of having a body that you can't see and touch? A body is a *body,* not a spirit. Why should you not, having seen Roy's old smile and heard his own voice, clasp his hand again, and feel his kiss on your happy lips?

"It is really amusing," she continued, "to sum up the notions that good people—excellent people—even thinking people—have of the heavenly body. Vague visions of floating about in the clouds, of balancing—with a white robe on, perhaps—in stiff rows about a throne, like the angels in the old pictures, converging to an apex, or ranged in semi-circles like so many marbles. Murillo has one charming exception. I always take a secret delight in that little cherub of his, kicking the clouds, in the right-hand upper corner of the Immaculate Conception; he seems to be having a good time of it, in genuine baby-fashion. The truth is, that the ordinary idea, if sifted accurately, reduces our eternal personality to—*gas.*

"Isaac Taylor holds, that, as far as the abstract idea of spirit is concerned, it may just as reasonably be granite as ether.

"Mrs. Charles says a pretty thing about this. She thinks these 'super-spiritualized angels' very 'unsatisfactory' beings, and that 'the heart returns with loving obstinacy to the young men in long white garments' who sat waiting in the sepulchre.

"Here again I cling to my conjecture about the word 'angel'; for then we should learn emphatically something about our future selves.

"'As the angels in heaven,' or 'equal unto the angels,' we are told in another place,—that may mean simply what it says. At least, if we are to resemble them in the particular respect of which the words were spoken,—and that one of the most important which could well be selected,—it is not unreasonable to infer that we shall resemble them in others.'In the Resurrection,' by the way, means, in that connection and in many others, simply future state of existence, without any reference to the time at which the great bodily change is to come.

"'But this is a digression,' as the novelists say. I was going to say, that it bewilders me to conjecture where students of the Bible have discovered the usual foggy nonsense about the corporeity of heaven.

"If there is anything laid down in plain statement, devoid of metaphor or parable, simple and unequivocal, it is the definite contradiction of all that. Paul, in his preface to that sublime apostrophe to death, repeats and reiterates it, lest we should make a mistake in his meaning.

"'There are celestial *bodies.*' 'It is raised a spiritual *body.*' 'There is a spiritual *body.*' 'It *is* raised in incorruption.' 'It *is* raised in glory.' 'It *is* raised in power.' Moses, too, when he came to the transfigured mount in glory, had as real a *body* as when he went into the lonely mount to die."

"But they will be different from these?"

"The glory of the terrestrial is one, the glory of the celestial another. Take away sin and sickness and misery, and that of itself would make difference enough."

"You do not suppose that we shall look as we look now?"

"I certainly do. At least, I think it more than possible that the 'human form divine,' or something like it, is to be retained. Not only from the fact that risen Elijah bore it; and Moses, who, if he had not passed through his resurrection, does not seem to have looked different from the other,—I have to use those two poor prophets on all occasions, but, as we are told of them neither by parable nor picture, they are important,—and that angels never appeared in any

why is it necessary to believe we have a body?

67

other, but because, in sinless Eden, God chose it for Adam and Eve. What came in unmarred beauty direct from His hand cannot be unworthy of His other paradise 'beyond the stars.' It would chime in pleasantly, too, with the idea of Redemption, that our very bodies, free from all the distortion of guilt, shall return to something akin to the pure ideal in which He moulded them. Then there is another reason, and stronger."

"What is that?"

"The human form has been borne and dignified forever by Christ. And, further than that, He ascended to His Father in it, and lives there in it as human God to-day."

I had never thought of that, and said so.

"Yes, with the very feet which trod the dusty road to Emmaus; the very wounded hands which Thomas touched, believing; the very lips which ate of the broiled fish and honey-comb; the very voice which murmured 'Mary?' in the garden, and which told her that He ascended unto His Father and her Father, to His God and her God, He 'was parted from them,' and was 'received up into heaven.' His death and resurrection stand forever the great prototype of ours. Otherwise, what is the meaning of such statements as these: 'When He shall appear, we shall be *like Him*'; 'The first man (Adam) is of the earth; the second man is the Lord. As we have borne the image of the earthly, *we shall also bear the image of the heavenly*'? And what of this, when we are told that our 'vile bodies,' being changed, shall be fashioned *'like unto His glorious body'*?"

I asked her if she inferred from that, that we should have just such bodies as the freedom from pain and sin would make of these.

"Flesh and blood cannot inherit the kingdom," she said. "There is no escaping that, even if I had the smallest desire to escape it, which I have not. Whatever is essentially earthly and temporary in the arrangements of this world will be out of place and unnecessary there. Earthly and temporary, flesh and blood certainly are."

"Christ said 'A spirit hath not flesh and bones, as ye see me have.'"

"A *spirit* hath not; and who ever said that it did? His body had something that appeared like them, certainly. That passage, by the way, has led some ingenious writer on the Chemistry of Heaven to infer that our bodies there will be like these, minus *blood!* I don't propose to spend my time over such investigations. Summing up the meaning of the story of those last days before the Ascension, and granting the shade of mystery which hangs over them, I gather this,—that the spiritual body is real, is tangible, is visible, is human, but that 'we shall be changed.' Some indefinable but thorough change had come over Him. He could withdraw Himself from the recognition of Mary, and from the disciples, whose 'eyes were holden,' as it pleased Him. He came and went through barred and bolted doors. He appeared suddenly in a certain place, without sound of footstep or flutter of garment to announce His approach. He vanished, and was not, like a cloud. New and wonderful powers had been given to Him, of which, probably, His little bewildered group of friends saw but a few illustrations."

"And He was yet *man?*"

"He was Jesus of Nazareth until the sorrowful drama of human life that He had taken upon Himself was thoroughly finished, from manger to sepulchre, and from sepulchre to the right hand of His Father."

"I like to wonder," she said, presently, "what we are going to look like and be like. *Ourselves,* in the first place. 'It is I Myself,' Christ said. Then to be perfectly well, never a sense of pain or weakness,—imagine how much solid comfort, if one had no other, in being forever rid of all the ills that flesh is heir to! Beautiful, too, I suppose we shall be, every one. Have you never had that come over you, with a thrill of compassionate thankfulness, when you have seen a poor girl shrinking, as only girls can shrink, under the life-long affliction of a marred face or form? The loss or presence of beauty is not as slight a deprivation or blessing as the moralists would make it out. Your grandmother, who was the most beautiful woman I ever saw, the belle of the county all her young days, and the model for artists' fancy sketching even in her old ones, as modest as a violet and as honest as the sunshine, used to have the prettiest little way when we girls were in our teens, and she thought that we must be lectured a bit on youthful vanity, of adding, in her quiet voice, smoothing down her black silk apron as she spoke, 'But still it is a thing to be thankful for, my dear, to have a *comely countenance.*'

"But to return to the track and our future bodies. We shall find them vastly convenient, undoubtedly, with powers of which there is no dreaming. Perhaps they will be so one with the soul that to will will be to do,—hindrance out of the question. I, for instance, sitting here by you, and thinking that I should like to be in Kansas, would be there. There is an interesting bit of a hint in Daniel about Gabriel, who, 'being caused to fly swiftly, touched him about the time of the evening oblation.'"

"But do you not make a very material kind of heaven out of such suppositions?"

"It depends upon what you mean by 'material.' The term does not, to my thinking, imply degradation, except so far as it is associated with sin. Dr. Chalmers has the right of it, when he talks about *'spiritual materialism.'* He says in his sermon on the New Heavens and Earth,—which, by the way, you should read, and from which I wish a few more of our preachers would learn something,—that we 'forget that on the birth of materialism, when it stood out in the freshness of those glories which the great Architect of Nature had impressed upon it, that then the "morning stars sang together, and all the sons of god shouted for joy."' I do not believe in a *gross* heaven, but I believe in a *reasonable* one."

4th.

We have been devoting ourselves to feminine vanities all day out in the orchard. Aunt Winifred has been making her summer bonnet, and I some linen collars. I saw, though she said nothing, that she thought the *crêpe* a little gloomy, and I am going to wear these in the mornings to please her.

She has an accumulation of work on hand, and in the afternoon I offered to tuck a little dress for Faith,—the prettiest pink *barège* affair pale as a blush rose, and about as delicate. Faith, who had been making mud-pies in the swamp, and was spattered with black peat from curls to stockings, looked on approvingly, and wanted it to wear on a flag-root expedition to-morrow. It seemed to do me good to do something for somebody after all this lonely and—I suspect— selfish idleness.

6th.

I read a little of Dr. Chalmers to-day, and went laughing to Aunt Winifred with the first sentence.

"There is a limit to the revelations of the Bible about futurity, and it were a mental or spiritual trespass to go beyond it."

"Ah! but," she said, "look a little farther down."

And I read, "But while we attempt not to be 'wise above that which is written,' we should attempt, and that most studiously, to be wise *up to* that which is written." - not above the text but w/ the text

8th.

It occurred to me to-day, that it was a noticeable fact, that, among all the visits of angels to this world of which we are told, no one seems to have discovered in any the presence of a dead friend. If redeemed men are subject to the same laws as they, why did such a thing never happen? I asked Aunt Winifred, and she said that the question reminded her of St. Augustine's lonely cry thirty years after the death of Monica: "Ah, the dead do not come back; for, had it been possible, there has not been a night when I should not have seen my mother!" There seemed to be two reasons, she said, why there should be no exceptions to the law of silence imposed between us and those who have left us; one of which was, that we should be overpowered with familiar curiosity about them, which nobody seems to have dared to express in the presence of angels, and the secrets of their life God has decreed that it is unlawful to utter.

"But Lazarus, and Jairus's little daughter, and the dead raised at the Crucifixion,—what of them?" I asked.

"I cannot help conjecturing that they were suffered to forget their glimpse of spiritual life," she said. "Since their resurrection was a miracle, there might be a miracle throughout. At least, their lips must have been sealed, for not a word of their testimony has been saved. When Lazarus dined with Simon, after he had come back to life,— and of that feast we have a minute account in, I believe, every Gospel,—nobody seems to have asked, or he to have answered, any questions about it.

"The other reason is a sorrowfully sufficient one. It is that *every* lost darling has not gone to heaven. Of all the mercies that our Father has given, this blessed uncertainty, this long unbroken silence, may be the dearest. Bitterly hard for you and me, but what are thousands like you and me weighed against one who stands beside a hopeless grave? Think a minute what mourners there have been, and *whom* they have mourned! Ponder one such solitary instance as that of Vittoria Colonna, wondering, through her widowed years, if she could ever be 'good enough' to join wicked Pescara in another world! This poor earth holds—God only knows how many, God make them very few!—Vittorias. Ah, Mary, what right have *we* to complain?"

9th.

To-night Aunt Winifred had callers,—Mrs. Quirk and (O Homer aristocracy!) the butcher's wife,—and it fell to my lot to put Faith to bed.

The little maiden seriously demurred. Cousin Mary was very good,—O yes, she was good enough,—but her mamma was a great deal gooder; and why couldn't little peoples sit up till nine o'clock as well as big peoples, she should like to know!

Finally, she came to the gracious conclusion that perhaps I'd *do*, made me carry her all the way up stairs, and dropped, like a little lump of lead, half asleep, on my shoulder, before two buttons were unfastened.

Feeling under some sort of theological obligation to hear her say her prayers, I pulled her curls a little till she awoke, and went through with "Now I lay me down to sleep, I pway ve Lord," triumphantly. I supposed that was the end, but it seems that she has been also taught the Lord's Prayer, which she gave me promptly to understand.

"O, see here! That isn't all. I can say Our Father, and you've got to help me a lot!"

This very soon became a self-evident proposition; but by our united efforts we managed, after tribulations manifold, to arrive successfully at "For ever 'n' ever 'n' ever 'n' *A*-men."

"Dear me," she said, jumping up with a yawn, "I think that's a *dreadful long-tailed prayer*,—don't you, Cousin Mary?"

"Now I must kiss mamma good night," she announced, when she was tucked up at last.

"But mamma kissed you good night before you came up."

"O, so she did. Yes, I 'member. Well, it's papa I've got to kiss. I knew there was somebody."

I looked at her in perplexity.

"Why, there!" she said, "in the upper drawer,—my pretty little pap in a purple frame. Don't you know?"

I went to the bureau-drawer, and found in a case of velvet a small ivory painting of her father. This I brought, wondering, and the child took it reverently and kissed the pictured lips.

"Faith," I said, as I laid it softly back, "do you always do this?"

"Do what? Kiss papa good night? O yes, I've done that ever since I was a little girl, you know. I guess I've always kissed him pretty much. When I'm a naughty girl he feels *real* sorry. He's gone to heaven. I like him. O yes, and then, when I'm through kissing, mamma kisses him too."

[handwritten margin note: What is faith teaching here? Faith can be ruling?]

73

$\{10\}$

I was in her room this afternoon while she was dressing. I like to watch her brush her beautiful gray hair; it quite alters her face to have it down; it seems to shrine her in like a cloud, and the outlines of her cheeks round out, and she grows young.

"I used to be proud of my hair when I was a girl," she said with a slight blush, as she saw me looking at her; "it was all I had to be vain of, and I made the most of it. Ah well! I was dark-haired three years ago.

"O you regular old woman!" she added, smiling at herself in the mirror, as she twisted the silver coils flashing through her fingers. "Well, when I am in heaven, I shall have my pretty brown hair again."

It seemed odd enough to hear that; then the next minute it did not seem odd at all, but the most natural thing in the world.

June 14.

She said nothing to me about the anniversary, and, though it has been in my thoughts all the time, I said nothing to her. I thought that she would shut herself up for the day, and was rather surprised that she was about as usual, busily at work, chatting with me, and playing with Faith. Just after tea, she went away alone for a time, and came back a little quiet, but that was all. I was for some reason impressed with the feeling that she kept the day in memory, not so much as the day of her mourning, as of his release.

Longing to do something for her, yet not knowing what to do, I went in to the garden while she was away, and, finding some carnations, that shone like stars in the dying light, I gathered them all, and took them to her room, and, filling my tiny porphyry vase, left them on the bracket, under the photograph of Uncle Forceythe that hangs by the window.

When she found them, she called me, and kissed me.

"Thank you, dear," she said, "and thank God too, Mary, for me. That
he should have been happy,—happy and out of pain, for three long
beautiful years! O, think of that!"

When I was in her room with the flowers, I passed the table on
which her little Bible lay open. A mark of rich ribbon—a black ribbon—fell across the pages; it bore in silver text these words:—

"Thou shalt have no other gods before me."

20th.

"I thank thee, my God, the river of Lethe may indeed flow through
the Elysian Fields,—it does not water the Christian's Paradise."

Aunt Winifred was saying that over to herself in a dreamy undertone this morning, and I happened to hear her.

"Just a quotation, dear," she said, smiling, in answer to my look of
inquiry, "I couldn't originate so pretty a thing. *Isn't* it pretty?"

"Very; but I am not sure that I understand it."

"You thought that forgetfulness would be necessary to happiness?"

"Why,—yes; as far as I had ever thought about it; that is, after our
last ties with this world are broken. It does not seem to me that I
could be happy to remember all that I have suffered and all that I
have sinned here."

"But the last of all the sins will be as if it had never been. Christ
takes care of that. No shadow of a sense of guilt can dog you, or affect your relations to Him or your other friends. The last pain borne,
the last tear, the last sigh, the last lonely hour, the last unsatisfied ream,
forever gone by; why should not the dead past bury its dead?"

"Then why remember it?"

"'Save but to swell the sense of being blest.' Besides, forgetfulness
of the disagreeable things of this life implies forgetfulness of the pleasant ones. They are all tangled together."

"To be sure. I don't know that I should like that."

"Of course you wouldn't. Imagine yourself in a state of being
where you and Roy had lost your past; all that you had borne and
enjoyed, and hoped and feared, together; the pretty little memories

of your babyhood, and first 'half-days' at school, when he used to trudge along beside you,—little fellow! how many times I have watched him!—holding you tight by the apron-sleeve or hat-string, or bits of fat fingers, lest you should run away or fall. Then old Academy pranks, out of which you used to help each other; his little chivalry and elder-brotherly advice; the mischief in his eyes; some of the 'Sunday-night talks'; the first novel that you read and dreamed over together; the college stories; the chats over the corn-popper by firelight; the earliest, earnest looking-on into life together, its temptations conquered, its lessons learned, its disappointments faced together,—always you two,—would you like to, are you *likely* to, forget all this?

"Roy might as well be not Roy, but a strange angel, if you should. Heaven will be not less heaven, but more, for this pleasant remembering. So many other and greater and happier memories will fill up the time then, that after years these things may—probably will—seem smaller than it seems to us now they can ever be; but they will, I think, be always dear; just as we look back to our baby-selves with a pitying sort of fondness, and though the little creatures are of small enough use to us now, yet we like to keep good friends with them for old times' sake.

"I have no doubt that you and I shall sit down some summer afternoon in heaven and talk over what we have been saying to-day, and laugh perhaps at all the poor little dreams we have been dreaming of what has not entered into the heart of man. You see it is certain to be so much *better* than anything that I can think of; which is the comfort of it. And Roy—"

"Yes; some more about Roy, please."

"Supposing he were to come right into the room now,—and I slipped out,—and you had him all to yourself again— Now, dear, don't cry, but wait a minute!" Her caressing hand fell on my hair. "I did not mean to hurt you, but to say that your first talk with him, after you stand face to face, may be like that.

"Remembering this life is going to help us amazingly, I fancy, to appreciate the next," she added, by way of period. "Christ seems to have thought so, when he called to the minds of those happy people what, in that unconscious ministering of lowly faith which may never reap its sheaf in the field where the seed was sown, they had not had the comfort of finding out before,—'I was sick and in prison, and ye visited me.' And to come again to Abraham in the parable, did he not say, 'Son, *remember* that thou in thy lifetime hadst good things and Lazarus evil'?"

"I wonder what it is going to look like," I said, as soon as I could put poor Dives out of my mind.

"Heaven? Eye hath not seen, but I have my fancies. I think I want some mountains, and very many trees."

"Mountains and trees!"

"Yes; mountains as we see them at sunset and sunrise, or when the maples are on fire and there are clouds enough to make great purple shadows chase each other into lakes of light, over the tops and down the sides,—the *ideal* of mountains which we catch in rare glimpses, as we catch the ideal of everything. Trees as they look when the wind cooes through them on a June afternoon; elms or lindens or pines as cool as frost, and yellow sunshine trickling through on moss. Trees in a forest so thick that it shuts out the world, and you walk like one in a sanctuary. Trees pierced by stars, and trees in a bath of summer moons to which the thrill of 'Love's young dream' shall cling forever— But there is no end to one's fancies. Some water, too, I would like."

"There shall be no more sea."

"Perhaps not; though, as the sea is the great type of separation and of destruction, that may be only figurative. But I'm not particular about the sea, if I can have rivers and little brooks, and fountains of just the right sort; the fountains of this world don't please me generally. I want a little brook to sit and sing to Faith by. O, I forgot! she will be a large girl probably, won't she?"

"Never too large to like to hear your mother sing, will you, Faith?"

"O no," said Faith, who bobbed in and out again like a canary just then,—"not unless I'm *dreadful* big, with long dresses and a water-fall, you know. I s'pose, maybe, I'd have to have little girls myself to sing to, then. I hope they'll behave better'n Mary Ann does. She's lost her other arm, and all her sawdust is just running out. Besides, Kitty thought she was a mouse, and ran down cellar with her, and she's all shooken up, somehow. She don't look very pretty."

"Flowers, too," her mother went on, after the interruption. "*Not* all amaranth and asphodel, but a variety and color and beauty unimagined; glorified lilies of the valley, heavenly tea-rose buds, and spiritual harebells among them. O, how your poor mother used to say,—you know flowers were her poetry,—coming in weak and worn from her garden in the early part of her sickness, hands and lap and basket full: 'Winifred, if I only supposed I *could* have some flowers in heaven I shouldn't be half so afraid to go!' I had not thought as much about these things then as I have now, or I should have known better how to answer her. I should like, if I had my choice, to have day-lilies and carnations fresh under my windows all the time."

"Under your windows?"

"Yes. I hope to have a home of my own."

"Not a house?"

"Something not unlike it. In the Father's house are many mansions. Sometimes I fancy that those words have a literal meaning which the simple men who heard them may have understood better than we, and that Christ is truly 'preparing' my home for me. He must be there, too, you see,—I mean John."

I believe that gave me some thoughts that I ought not to have, and so I made no reply.

"If we have trees and mountains and flowers and books," she went on, smiling, "I don't see why not have houses as well. Indeed they seem to me as supposable as anything can be which is guess-work at the best; for what a homeless, desolate sort of sensation it gives one to think of people wandering over the 'sweet fields beyond the flood' without a local habitation and a name. What could be done with the millions who, from the time of Adam, have been gathering there, unless they lived under the conditions of organized society? Organized society involves homes, not unlike the homes of this world.

"What other arrangement could be as pleasant, or could be pleasant at all? Robertson's definition of a church exactly fits. 'More united in each other, because more united in God.' A happy home is the happiest thing in the world. I do not see why it should not be in any world. I do not believe that all the little tendernesses of family ties are thrown by and lost with this life. In fact, Mary, I cannot think that anything which has in it the elements of permanency is to be lost, but sin. Eternity cannot be—it cannot be the great blank ocean which most of us have somehow or other been brought up to feel that it is, which shall swallow up, in a pitiless, glorified way, all the little brooks of our delight. So I expect to have my beautiful home, and my husband, and Faith, as I had them here; with many differences and great ones, but *mine* just the same. Unless Faith goes into a home of her own,—the little creature! I suppose she can't always be a baby.

"Do you remember what a pretty little wistful way Charles Lamb has of wondering about all this?

"'Shall I enjoy friendships there, wanting the smiling indications which point me to them here,—the "sweet assurance of a look"? Sun, and sky, and breeze, and solitary walks, and summer holidays, and the greenness of fields, and the delicious juices of meats and fish, and society, . . . and candle-light and fireside conversations, and innocent vanities, and jests, and *irony itself,*—do these things go out with life?'"

"Now, Aunt Winifred!" I said, sitting up straight, "what am I to do with these beautiful heresies? If Deacon Quirk *should* hear!"

"I do not see where the heresy lies. As I hold fast by the Bible, I cannot be in much danger."

"But you don't glean your conjectures from the Bible."

"I conjecture nothing that the Bible contradicts. I do not believe as truth indisputable anything that the Bible does not give me. But I reason from analogy about this, as we all do about other matters.

Why should we not have pretty things in heaven? If this 'bright and beautiful economy' of skies and rivers, of grass and sunshine, of hills and valleys, is not too good for such a place as this world, will there be any less variety of the bright and beautiful in the next? There is no reason for supposing that the voice of God will speak to us in thunder-claps, or that it will not take to itself the thousand gentle, suggestive tongues of a nature built on the ruins of this, an unmarred system of beneficence.

"There is a pretty argument in the fact that just such sunrises, such opening of buds, such fragrant dropping of fruit, such bells in the brooks, such dreams at twilight, and such hush of stars, were fit for Adam and Eve, made holy man and woman. How do we know that the abstract idea of a heaven needs imply anything very much unlike Eden? There is some reason as well as poetry in the conception of a 'Paradise Regained.' A 'new earth wherein dwelleth righteousness.'"

"But how far is it safe to trust to this kind of argument?"

"Bishop Butler will answer you better than I. Let me see,—Isaac Taylor says something about that."

She went to the bookcase for his "Physical Theory of Another Life," and, finding her place, showed me this passage:—

"If this often repeated argument from analogy is to be termed, as to the conclusions it involves, a conjecture merely, we ought then to abandon altogether every kind of abstract reasoning; nor will it be easy afterwards to make good any principle of natural theology. In truth, the very basis of reasoning is shaken by a scepticism so sweeping as this."

And in another place:—

"None need fear the consequences of such endeavors who have well learned the prime principle of sound philosophy, namely, not to allow the most plausible and pleasing conjectures to unsettle our convictions of truth . . . resting upon positive evidence. If there be any who frown upon all such attempts . . . they would do well to consider, that although individually, and from the constitution of their

minds, they may find it very easy to abstain from every path of ex-
cursive meditation, it is not so with others who almost irresistibly
are borne forward to the vast field of universal contemplation,—a
field from which the human mind is not to be barred, and which is
better taken possession of by those who reverently bow to the authority of Christianity, than left open to impiety."

"Very good," I said, laying down the book. "But about those trees
and houses, and the rest of your 'pretty things'? Are they to be like
these?"

"I don't suppose that the houses will be made of oak and pine and
nailed together, for instance. But I hope for heavenly types of nature and art. *Something that will be to us then what these are now.* That is
the amount of it. They may be as 'spiritual' as you please; they will
answer all the purpose to us. As we are not spiritual beings yet, however, I am under the necessity of calling them by their earthly names.
You remember Plato's old theory, that the ideal of everything exists
eternally in the mind of God. If that is so,—and I do not see how it
can be otherwise,—then whatever of God is expressed to us in this
world by flower, or blade of grass, or human face, why should not
that be expressed forever in heaven by something corresponding to
flower, or grass, or human face? I do not mean that the heavenly
creation will be less real than these, but more so. Their 'spirituality'
is of such a sort that our gardens and forests and homes are but shadows of them.

"You don't know how I amuse myself at night thinking this all over
before I go to sleep; wondering what one thing will be like, and
another thing; planning what I should like; thinking that John has
seen it all, and wondering if he is laughing at me because I know so
little about it! I tell you, Mary, there's a 'deal o' comfort in 't,' as Phoebe
says about her cup of tea."

July 5.

Aunt Winifred has been hunting up a Sunday school class for herself
and one for me; which is a venture that I never was persuaded into

undertaking before. She herself is fast becoming acquainted with the poorer people of the town.

I find that she is a thoroughly busy Christian, with a certain "week-day holiness" that is strong and refreshing, like a west wind. Church-going, and conversations on heaven, by no means exhaust her vitality.

She told me a pretty thing about her class; it happened the first Sabbath that she took it. Her scholars are young girls of from fourteen to eighteen years of age, children of church-members, most of them. She seemed to have taken their hearts by storm. *She* says, "They treated me very prettily, and made me love them at once."

Clo Bentley is in the class; Clo is a pretty, soft-eyed little creature, with a shrinking mouth, and an absorbing passion for music, which she has always been too poor to gratify. I suspect that her teacher will make a pet of her. She says that in the course of her lesson, or, in her words,—

"While we were all talking together, somebody pulled my sleeve, and there was Clo in the corner, with her great brown eyes fixed on me. 'See here!' she said in a whisper, 'I can't be good! I would be good if I could *only* just have a piano!' 'Well, Clo,' I said, 'if you will be a good girl, and go to heaven, I think you will have a piano there, and play just as much as you care to.'

"You ought to have seen the look the child gave me! Delight and fear and incredulous bewilderment tumbled over each other, as if I had proposed taking her into a forbidden fairy-land.

"'Why, Mrs. Forceythe! Why, they won't let anybody have a piano up there! not in *heaven?*'

"I laid down the question-book, and asked what kind of place she supposed that heaven was going to be.

"'O,' she said, with a dreary sigh, 'I never think about it when I can help it. I suppose we *shall all just stand there!*'

"'And you?' I asked of the next, a bright girl with snapping eyes.

"'Do you want me to talk good, or tell the truth?' she answered me. Having been given to understand that she was not expected to

does not think of heaven

'talk good' in my class, she said, with an approving, decided nod: 'Well, then! I don't think it's going to be *anything nice* anyway. No, I don't! I told my last teacher so, and she looked just as shocked, and said I never should go there as long as I felt so. That made me mad, and I told her I didn't see but I should be as well off in one place as another, except for the fire.'

"A silent girl in the corner began at this point to look interested. 'I always supposed,' said she, 'that you just floated round in heaven—you know—all together—something like ju-jube paste!'

"Whereupon I shut the question-book entirely, and took the talking to myself for a while.

"'But I *never* thought it was anything like that,' interrupted little Clo, presently, her cheeks flushed with excitement. 'Why, I should like to go, if it is like that! I never supposed people talked, unless it was about converting people, and saying your prayers, and all that.'

"Now, weren't those ideas* alluring and comforting for young girls in the blossom of warm human life? They were trying with all their little hearts to 'be good,' too, some of then, and had all of them been to church and Sunday school all their lives. Never, never, if Jesus Christ had been Teacher and Preacher to them, would He have pictured their blessed endless years with Him in such bleak colors. They are not the hues of His Bible."

₹11₹

July 16.

We took a trip to-day to East Homer for butter. Neither angels nor principalities could convince Phoebe that any butter but "Stephen David's" might, could, would, or should be used in this family. So to Mr. Stephen David's, a journey of four miles, I meekly betake myself at stated periods in the domestic year, burdened with directions about

---

* Facts

firkins and half-firkins, pounds and half-pounds, salt and no salt, churning and "working-over"; some of which I remember and some of which I forget, and to all of which Phoebe considers me sublimely incapable of attending.

The afternoon was perfect, and we took things leisurely, letting the reins swing from the hook,—an arrangement to which Mr. Tripp's old gray was entirely agreeable,—and, leaning back against the buggy-cushions, wound along among the strong, sweet pine-smells, lazily talking or lazily silent, as the spirit moved, and as only two people who thoroughly understand and like each other can talk or be silent.

We rode home by Deacon Quirk's, and, as we jogged by, there broke upon our view a blooming vision of the Deacon himself, at work in his potato-field with his son and heir, who, by the way, has the reputation of being the most awkward fellow in the township.

The amiable church-officer, having caught sight of us, left his work, and coming up to the fence "in rustic modesty unscared," guiltless of coat or vest, his calico shirt-sleeves rolled up to his huge brown elbows, and his dusty straw hat flapping in the wind, rapped on the rails with his hoe-handle as a sign for us to stop.

"Are we in a hurry?" I asked, under my breath.

"O no," said Aunt Winifred. "He has somewhat to say unto me, I see by his eyes. I have been expecting it. Let us hear him out. Good afternoon, Deacon Quirk."

"Good afternoon, ma'am. Pleasant day?"

She assented to the statement, novel as it was.

"A very pleasant day," repeated the Deacon, looking for the first time in his life, to my knowledge, a little undecided as to what he should say next. "Remarkable fine day for riding. In a hurry?"

"Well, not especially. Did you want anything of me?"

"You're a church-member, aren't you, ma'am?" asked the Deacon, abruptly.

"I am."

"Orthodox?"

"O yes," with a smile. "You had a reason for asking?"

"Yes, ma'am; I had, as you might say, a reason for asking."

The Deacon laid his hoe on the top of the fence, and his arms across it, and pushed his hat on the back of his head in a becoming and argumentative manner.

"I hope you don't consider that I'm taking liberties if I have a little religious conversation with you, Mrs. Forceythe."

"It is no offence to me if you are," replied Mrs. Forceythe, with a twinkle in her eye; but both twinkle and words glanced off from the Deacon.

"My wife was telling me last night," he began, with an ominous cough, "that her niece, Clotildy Bentley—Moses Bentley's daughter, you know, and one of your sentimental girls that reads poetry, and is easy enough led away by vain delusions and false doctrine— was under your charge at Sunday school. Now Clotildy is intimate with my wife,—who is her aunt on her mother's side, and always tries to do her duty by her,—and she told Mrs. Quirk what you'd been a saying to those young minds on the Sabbath."

He stopped, and observed her impressively, as if he expected to see the guilty blushes of arraigned heresy covering her amused, attentive face.

"I hope you will pardon me, ma'am, for repeating it, but Clotildy said that you told her she should have a pianna in heaven. A *pianna,* ma'am!"

"I certainly did," she said quietly.

"You did? Well, now, I didn't believe it, nor I wouldn't believe it, till I'd asked you! I thought it warn't more than fair that I should ask you, before repeating it, you know. It's none of my business, Mrs. Forceythe, any more than that I take a general interest in the spiritooal welfare of the youth of our Sabbath school; but I am very much surprised! I am *very* much surprised!"

"I am surprised that you should be, Deacon Quirk. Do you believe that God would take a poor little disappointed girl like Clo, who has been all her life here forbidden the enjoyment of a perfectly innocent taste, and keep her in His happy heaven eternal years, without finding means to gratify it? I don't."

"I tell Clotildy I don't see what she wants of a pianna-forte," observed "Clotildy's" uncle, sententiously. "She can go to singin' school, and she's been in the choir ever since I have, which is six years come Christmas. Besides, I don't think it's our place to speckylate on the mysteries of the heavenly spere. My wife told her that she mustn't believe any such things as that, which were very irreverent, and contrary to the Scriptures, and Clo went home crying. She said: 'It was so pretty to think about.' It is very easy to impress these delusions of fancy on the young."

"Pray, Deacon Quirk," said Aunt Winifred, leaning earnestly forward in the carriage, "will you tell me what there is 'irreverent' or 'unscriptural' in the idea that there will be instrumental music in heaven?"

"Well," replied the Deacon after some consideration, "come to think of it, there will be harps, I suppose. Harpers harping with their harps on the sea of glass. But I don't believe there will be any piannas. It's a dreadfully material way to talk about that glorious world, to my thinking."

"If you could show me wherein a harp is less 'material' than a piano, perhaps I should agree with you."

Deacon Quirk looked rather nonplussed for a minute.

"What *do* you suppose people will do in heaven?" she asked again.

"Glorify God," said the Deacon, promptly recovering himself,— "glorify God, and sing Worthy the Lamb! We shall be clothed in white robes with palms in our hands, and bow before the Great White Throne. We shall be engaged in such employments as befit sinless creatures in a spiritooal state of existence."

"Now, Deacon Quirk," replied Aunt Winifred, looking him over from head to foot,—old straw hat, calico shirt, blue overalls, and cowhide boots, coarse, work-worn hands, and "narrow forehead braided tight,"—"just imagine yourself, will you? taken out of this life this minute, as you stand here in your potato-field (the Deacon changed his position with evident uneasiness), and put into another life,—not anybody else, but yourself, just as you left this spot,—and do you honestly think that you should be happy to go and put on a white dress and stand still in a choir with a green branch in one hand and a singing-book in the other, and sing and pray and never do anything but sing and pray, this year, next year, and every year forever?"

"We-ell," he replied, surprised into a momentary flash of carnal candor, "I can't say that I shouldn't wonder for a minute, maybe, *how Abinadab would ever get those potatoes hoed without me.*—Abinadab! go back to your work!"

The graceful Abinadab had sauntered up during the conversation, and was listening, hoe in hand and mouth open. He slunk away when his father spoke, but came up again presently on tiptoe when Aunt Winifred was talking. There was an interested, intelligent look about his square and pitifully embarrassed face, which attracted my notice.

"But then," proceeded the Deacon, re-enforced by the sudden recollection of his duties as a father and a church-member, "that couldn't be a permanent state of feeling, you know. I expect to be transformed by the renewing of my mind to appreciate the glories of the New Jerusalem, descending out of heaven from God. That's what I expect, marm. Now I heerd that you told Mrs. Bland, or that Mary told her, or that she heerd it someway, that you said you supposed there were trees and flowers and houses and such in heaven. I told my wife I thought your deceased husband was a Congregational minister, and I didn't believe you ever said it; but that's the rumor."

Without deeming it necessary to refer to her "deceased husband," Aunt Winifred replied that "rumor" was quite right.

"Well!" said the Deacon, with severe significance, "*I* believe in a spiritooal heaven."

I looked him over again,—hat, hoe, shirt, and all; scanned his obstinate old face with its stupid, good eyes and animal mouth. Then I glanced at Aunt Winifred as she leaned forward in the afternoon light; the white, finely cut woman, with her serene smile and rapt, saintly eyes,—every inch of her, body and soul, refined not only by birth and training, but by the long nearness of her heart to Christ.

"Of the earth, earthy. Of the heavens, heavenly." The two faces sharpened themselves into two types. Which, indeed, was the better able to comprehend a "spiritooal heaven"?

"It is distinctly stated in the Bible, by which I suppose we shall both agree," said Aunt Winifred, gently, "that there shall be a *new earth,* as well as new heavens. It is noticeable, also, that the descriptions of heaven, although a series of metaphors, are yet singularly earthlike and tangible ones. Are flowers and skies and trees less 'spiritual' than white dresses and little palm-branches? In fact, where are you going to get your little branches without trees? What could well be more suggestive of material modes of living, and material industry, than a city marked into streets and alleys, paved solidly with gold, walled in and barred with gates whose jewels are named and counted, and whose very length and breadth are measured with a celestial survey-or's chain?"

"But I think we'd ought to stick to what the Bible says," answered the Deacon, stolidly. "If it says golden cities and doesn't say flowers, it means cities and doesn't mean flowers. I dare say you're a good woman, Mrs. Forceythe, if you do hold such oncommon doctrine, and I don't doubt you mean well enough, but I don't think that we ought to trouble ourselves about these mysteries of a future state. *I'm* willing to trust them to God!"

The evasion of a fair argument by this self-sufficient spasm of piety was more than I could calmly stand, and I indulged in a subdued explosion.—Auntie says it sounded like Fourth of July crackers touched off under a wet barrel.

"Deacon Quirk! do you mean to imply that Mrs. Forceythe does not trust it to God? The truth is, that the existence of such a world as heaven is a fact from which you shrink. You know you do! She has twenty thoughts about it where you have one; yet you set up a claim to superior spirituality!"

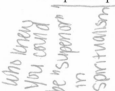
Who knew you could be "superior" in spiritualism

"Mary, Mary, you are a little excited, I fear. God is a spirit, and they that worship him must worship him in spirit and in truth!'"

The relevancy of this last, I confess myself incapable of perceiving, but the good man seemed to be convinced that he had made a point, and we rode off leaving him under that blissful delusion.

"If he *weren't* a good man!" I sighed. "But he is, and I must respect him for it."

"Of course you must; nor is he to blame that he is narrow and rough. I should scarcely have argued as seriously as I did with him, but that, as I fancy him to be a representative of a class, I wanted to try an experiment. Isn't he amusing, though? He is precisely one of Mr. Stopford Brooke's men 'who can understand nothing which is original.'"

"Are there, or are there not, more of such men in our church than in others?"

"Not more proportionately to numbers. But I would not have them thinned out. The better we do Christ's work, the more of uneducated, neglected, or debased mind will be drawn to try and serve Him with us. He sought out the lame, the halt, the blind, the stupid, the crotchety, the rough, as well as the equable, the intelligent, the refined. Untrained Christians in any sect will always have their eccentricities and their littlenesses, at which the silken judgment of high places, where the Carpenter's Son would be a strange guest, will sneer. That never troubles me. It only raises the question in my mind whether cultivated Christians generally are sufficiently *cultivators,* scattering their golden gifts on wayside ground."

"Now take Deacon Quirk," I suggested, when we had ridden along a little way under the low, green arches of the elms, "and put him into heaven as you proposed, just as he is, and what *is* he going to do with himself? He can dig potatoes and sell them without cheating, and give generously of their proceeds to foreign missions; but take away his potatoes, and what would become of him? I don't know a human being more incapacitated to live in such a heaven as he believes in."

89

"Very true, and a good, common-sense argument against such a heaven. I don't profess to surmise what will be found for him to do, beyond this,—that it will be some very palpable work that he can understand. How do we know that he would not be appointed guardian of his poor son here, to whom I suspect he has not been all that father might be in this life, and that he would not have his body as well as his soul to look after, his farm as well as his prayers? to him might be committed the charge of the dews and the rains and the hundred unseen influences that are at work on this very potato-field."

"But when his son has gone in his turn, and we have all gone, and there are no more potato-fields? An Eternity remains."

"You don't know that there wouldn't be any potato-fields; there may be some kind of agricultural employments even then. To whomsoever a talent is given, it will be given him wherewith to use it. Besides, by that time the good Deacon will be immensely changed. I suppose that the simple transition of death, which rids him of sin and of grossness, will not only wonderfully refine him, but will have its effect upon his intellect."

"If a talent is given, use will be found for it? Tell me some more about that."

"I fancy many things about it; but of course can feel sure of only the foundation principle. This life is a great school-house. The wise Teacher trains in us such gifts as, if we graduate honorably, will be of most service in the perfect manhood and womanhood that come after. He sees, as we do not, that a power is sometimes best trained by repression. 'We do not always lose an advantage when we dispense with it,' Goethe says. But the suffocated lives, like little Clo's there, make my heart ache sometimes. I take comfort in thinking how they will bud and blossom up in the air, by and by. There are a great many of them. We tread them underfoot in our careless stepping now and then, and do not see that they have not the elasticity to rise from our touch. 'Heaven may be a place for those who failed on earth,' the Country Parson says."

"Then there will be air enough for all?"

"For all; for those who have had a little bloom in this world, as well. I suppose the artist will paint his pictures, the poet sing his happy songs, the orator and author will not find their talents hidden in the eternal darkness of a grave; the sculptor will use his beautiful gift in the moulding of some heavenly Cararra; 'as well the singer as the player on instruments shall be here.' Christ said a thing that has grown on me with new meanings lately:—'He that *loseth his life for my sake shall find it.*' *It,* you see,—not another man's life, not a strange compound of powers and pleasures, but his own familiar aspirations. So we shall best 'glorify God,' not less there than here, by doing it in the peculiar way that He himself marked out for us. But—ah, Mary, you see it is only the life 'lost' for His sake that shall be so beautifully found. A great man never goes to heaven because he is great. He must go, as the meanest of his fellow-sinners go, with face towards Calvary, and every golden treasure used for love of Him who showed him how."

"What would the old pagans—and modern ones, too, for that matter—say to that? Wasn't it Tacitus who announced it as his belief, that immortality was granted as a special gift to a few superior minds? For the people who persisted in making up the rest of the world, poor things! as it could be of little consequence what became of them, they might die as the brute dieth."

"It seems an unbearable thing to me sometimes," she went on, "the wreck of a gifted soul. A man who can be, if he chooses, as much better and happier than the rest of us as the ocean reflects more sky than a mill-pond, must also be, if he chooses, more wicked and more miserable. It takes longer to reach sea-shells than river pebbles. I am compelled to think, also, that intellectual rank must in heaven bear some proportion to goodness. There are last and there are first that shall have changed places. As the tree falleth, there shall it lie, and with that amount of holiness of which a man leaves this life the possessor, he must start in another. I have seen great thinkers, 'foremost men' in science, in theology, in the arts, who, I solemnly believe, will turn aside in heaven,—and will turn humbly and heartily,—to let certain day-laborers and paupers whom I have known go up before them as kings and priests unto God."

"I believe that. But I was going to ask,—for poor creatures like your respected niece, who hasn't a talent, nor even a single absorbing taste, for one thing above another thing,—what shall she do?"

"Whatever she liketh best; something very useful, my dear, don't be afraid, and very pleasant. Something, too, for which this life has fitted you; though you may not understand how that can be, better than did poor Heine on his 'matrazzen-gruft,' reading all the books that treated his disease. 'But what good this reading is to do me I don't know,' he said, 'except that it will qualify me to give lectures in heaven on the ignorance of doctors on earth about diseases of the spinal marrow.'"

"I don't know how many times I have thought of—I believe it was the poet Gray, who said that his idea of heaven was to lie on the sofa and read novels. That touches the lazy part of us, though."

"Yes, they will be the active, outgoing, generous elements of our nature that will be brought into use then, rather than the self-centred and dreamy ones. Though I suppose that we shall read in heaven,—being influenced to be better and nobler by good and noble teachers of the pen, not less there than here."

"O think of it! To have books, and music,—and pictures?"

"All that Art, 'the handmaid of the Lord,' can do for us, I have no doubt will be done. Eternity will never become monotonous. Variety without end, charms unnumbered within charms, will be devised by Infinite ingenuity to minister to our delight. Perhaps,—this is just my fancying,—perhaps there will be whole planets turned into galleries of art, over which we may wander at will; or into orchestral halls where the highest possibilities of music will be realized to singer and to hearer. Do you know, I have sometimes had a flitting notion that music would be the language of heaven? It certainly differs in some indescribable manner from the other arts. We have most of us felt it in our different ways. It always seems to me like the cry of a

The outcome of Faith

great, sad life dragged to use in this world against its will. Pictures and statues and poems fit themselves to their work more contentedly. Symphony and song struggle in fetters. That sense of conflict is not good for me. It is quite as likely to harm as to help. Then perhaps the mysteries of sidereal systems will be spread out like a child's map before us. Perhaps we shall take journeys to Jupiter and to Saturn and to the glittering haze of nebulæ, and to the site of ruined worlds whose 'extinct light is yet travelling through space.' Occupation for explorers there, you see!"

"You make me say with little Clo, 'O, why, I want to go!' every time I hear you talk. But there is one thing,—you spoke of families living together."

"Yes."

"And you spoke of—your husband. But the Bible—"

"Says there shall be no marrying nor giving in marriage. I know that. Nor will there be such marrying or giving in marriage as there is in a world like this. Christ expressly goes on to state, that we shall be *as* the angels in heaven. How do we know what heavenly unions of heart with heart exist among the angels? It leaves me margin enough to live and be happy with John forever, and it holds many possibilities for the settlement of all perplexing questions brought about by the relations of this world. It is of no use to talk much about them. But it is on that very verse that I found my unshaken belief that they will be smoothed out in some natural and happy way, with which each one shall be content."

"But O, there is a great gulf fixed; and on one side one, and on the other another, and they loved each other."

Her face paled,—it always pales, I notice, at the mention of this mystery,—but her eyes never lost by a shade their steadfast trust.

"Mary, don't question me about *that*. That belongs to the unutterable things. God will take care of it. I *think* I could leave it to him even if he brought it for me myself to face. I feel sure that he will make it all come out right. Perhaps He will be so dear to us, that we could not love any one who hated him. In some way the void *must* be filled, for he shall wipe away tears. But it seems to me that the only thought in which there can be any *rest,* and in that there *can,* is this: that Christ, who loves us even as his Father loves him, can be happy in spite of the existence of a hell. If it is possible to him, surely he can make it possible to us."

"Two things that He has taught us," she said after a silence, "give me beautiful assurance that none of these dreams with which I help myself can be beyond his intention to fulfil. One is, that eye hath not seen it, nor ear heard it, nor the heart conceived it,—this lavishness of reward which he is keeping for us. Another is, that 'I shall be *satisfied* when I awake.'"

"With his likeness."

"With his likeness. And about that I have other things to say."

But Old Gray stopped at the gate and Phoebe was watching for her butter, and it was no time to say them then.

❧ *12* ❧

July 22.

Aunt Winifred has connected herself with our church. I think it was rather hard for her, breaking the last tie that bound her to her husband's people; but she had a feeling, that, if her work is to be done and her days ended here, she had better take up all such little threads of influence to make herself one with us.

25th.

To-day what should Deacon Quirk do but make a solemn call on Mrs. Forceythe, for the purpose of asking—and this with a hint that he wished he had asked before she became a member of the Homer First Congregational Church—whether there were truth in the rumors, now rife about town, that she was a Swedenborgian!

Aunt Winifred broke out laughing, and laughed merrily. The Deacon frowned.

"I used to fancy that I believed in Swedenborg," she said, as soon as she could sober down a little.

The Deacon pricked up his ears, with visions of excommunications and councils reflected on every feature.

"Until I read his books," she finished.

"Oh!" said the Deacon. He waited for more, but she seemed to consider the conversation at an end.

"So then you—if I understand—are *not* a Swedenborgian, ma'am?"

"If I were, I certainly should have had no inducement to join myself to your church," she replied, with gentle dignity. "I believe, with all my heart, in the same Bible and the same creed that you believe in, Deacon Quirk."

"And you *live* your creed, which all such genial Christians do not find it necessary to do," I thought, as the Deacon in some perplexity took his departure, and she returned with a smile to her sewing.

I suppose the call came about in this way. We had the sewing-circle here last week, and just before the lamps were lighted, and when people had dropped their work to group and talk in the corners, Meta Tripp came up with one or two other girls to Aunt Winifred, and begged "to hear some of those queer things people said she believed about heaven." Auntie is never obtrusive with her views on this or any other matter, but, being thus urged, she answered a few questions that they put to her, to the extreme scandal of one or two old ladies, and the secret delight of the rest.

"Well," said little Mrs. Bland, squeezing and kissing her youngest, who was at that moment employed in sticking very long darning-needles into his mother's water-fall, "I hope there'll be a great many babies there. I should be perfectly happy if I always could have babies to play with!"

The look that Aunt Winifred shot over at me was worth seeing.

She merely replied, however, that she supposed all our "highest aspirations,"—with an indescribable accent to which Mrs. Bland was safely deaf,—if good ones, would be realized; and added, laughing, that Swedenborg said that the babies in heaven—who outnumber the grown people—will be given into the charge of those women especially fond of them.

"Swedenborg is suggestive, even if you can't accept what seem to the uninitiated to be his natural impossibilities," she said, after we had discussed Deacon Quirk awhile. "He says a pretty thing, too, occasionally. Did I ever read you about the houses?"

She had not, and I wished to hear, so she found the book on Heaven and Hell, and read:—

"As often as I have spoken with the angels mouth to mouth, so often I have been with them in their habitations: their habitations are altogether like the habitations on earth which are called houses, but more beautiful; in them are parlors, rooms, and chambers in great numbers; there are also courts, and round about are gardens, shrubberies, and fields. Palaces of heaven have been seen, which were so magnificent that they could not be described; above, they glittered as if they were of pure gold, and below, as if they were of precious stones; one palace was more splendid than another; within, it was the same: the rooms were ornamented with such decorations as neither words nor sciences are sufficient to describe. On the side which looked to the south there were paradises, where all things in like manner glittered, and in some places the leaves were as of silver, and the fruits as of gold; and the flowers on their beds presented by colors as it were rainbows; at the boundaries again were palaces, in which the view terminated."

Aunt Winifred says that our hymns, taken all together, contain the worst and the best pictures of heaven that we have in any branch of literature.

"It seems to me incredible," she says, "that the Christian Church should have allowed that beautiful 'Jerusalem' in its hymnology so long, with the ghastly couplet,—

'Where congregations ne'er break up,
  And Sabbaths have no end.'

The dullest preachers are sure to give it out, and that when there are the greatest number of restless children wondering when it will be time to go home. It is only within ten years that modern hymn-books have altered it, returning in part to the original.

"I do not think we have chosen the best parts of that hymn for our 'service of song.' You never read the whole of it? You don't know how pretty it is! It is a relief from the customary palms and choirs. One's whole heart is glad of the outlet of its sweet refrain,—

'Would God that I were there!'

before one has half read it. You are quite ready to believe that

'There is no hunger, heat, nor cold,
  But *pleasure every way.*'

Listen to this:—

'Thy houses are of ivory,
  Thy windows crystal clear,
Thy tiles are made of beaten gold;
  O God, that I were there!

'We that are here in banishment
  Continually do moan.

* * * * * * *

'Our sweet is mixed with bitter gall,
  Our pleasure is but pain,
Our joys scarce last the looking on,
  Our sorrows still remain.

'But there they live in such delight,
  Such pleasure and such play,
As that to them a thousand years
  Doth seem as yesterday.'

And this:—

'Thy gardens and thy gallant walks
   Continually are green;
There grow such sweet and pleasant flowers
   As nowhere else are seen.

'There cinnamon, there sugar grows,
   There nard and balm abound,
What tongue can tell, or heart conceive
   The joys that there are found?

'Quite through the streets, with silver sound,
   The flood of life doth flow,
Upon whose banks, on every side,
   The wood of life doth grow.'

I tell you we may learn something from that grand old Catholic singer. He is far nearer to the Bible than the innovators on his MSS. Do
you not notice how like his images are to the inspired ones, and yet
how pleasant and natural is the effect of the entire poem?

"There is nobody like Bonar, though, to sing about heaven. There
is one of his, 'We shall meet and rest,'—do you know it?"

I shook my head, and knelt down beside her and watched her
face,—it was quite unconscious of me, the musing face,—while she
repeated dreamily:—

"Where the faded flower shall freshen,—
   Freshen nevermore to fade;
Where the shaded sky shall brighten,—
   Brighten nevermore to shade;
Where the sun-blaze never scorches;
   Where the star-beams cease to chill;
Where no tempest stirs the echoes
   Of the wood, or wave, or hill; . . .
Where no shadow shall bewilder;
   Where life's vain parade is o'er;
Where the sleep of sin is broken,

And the dreamer dreams no more;
Where the bond is never severed,—
  Partings, claspings, sob and moan,
Midnight waking, twilight weeping,
  Heavy noontide,—all are done;
Where the child has found its mother;
  Where the mother finds the child;
Where dear families are gathered,
  That were scattered on the wild; . . .
Where the hidden wound is healed;
  Where the blighted life reblooms;
Where the smitten heart the freshness
  Of its buoyant youth resumes; . . .
Where we find the joy of loving,
  As we never loved before,—
Loving on, unchilled, unhindered,
  Loving once, forevermore." . . .

30th.

Aunt Winifred was weeding her day-lilies this morning, when the gate creaked timidly, and then swung noisily, and in walked Abina-dab Quirk, with a bouquet of China pinks in the button-hole of his green-gray linen coat. He had taken evident pains to smarten himself up a little, for his hair was combed into two horizontal *dabs* over his ears, and the green-gray coat and blue-checked shirt-sleeves were quite clean; but he certainly is the most uncouth specimen of six feet five that it has ever been my privilege to behold. I feel sorry for him, though. I heard Meta Tripp laughing at him in Sunday school the other day,—"Quadrangular Quirk," she called him, a little too loud, and the poor fellow heard her. He half turned, blushing fiercely; then slunk down in his corner with as pitiable a look as is often seen upon a man's face.

He came up to Auntie awkwardly,—a part of the scene I saw from the window, and the rest she told me,—head hanging, and the tiny bouquet held out.

"Clo sent these to you," he stammered out,—"my cousin Clo. I was coming 'long, and she thought, you know,—she'd get me, you see, to—to—that is, to—bring them. She sent her—that is—let me see. She sent her respect—ful—respectful—no, her love; that was it. She sent her love 'long with 'em."

Mrs. Forceythe dropped her weeds, and held out her white, shapely hands, wet with the heavy dew, to take the flowers.

"O, thank you! Clo knows my fancy for pinks. How kind in you to bring them! Won't you sit down a few moments? I was just going to rest a little. Do you like flowers?"

Abinadab eyed the white hands, as his huge fingers just touched them, with a sort of awe; and, sighing, sat down on the very edge of the garden bench beside her. After a singular variety of efforts to take the most uncomfortable position of which he was capable, he succeeded to his satisfaction, and, growing then somewhat more at his ease, answered her question.

"Flowers are sech *gassy* things. They just blow out and that's the end of 'em. *I* like machine-shops best."

"Ah! well, that is a very useful liking. Do you ever invent machinery yourself?"

"Sometimes," said Abinadab, with a bashful smile. "There's a little improvement of mine for carpet-sweepers up before the patent-office now. Don't know whether they'll run it through. Some of the chaps I saw in Boston told me they thought they would do 't in time; it takes an awful sight of time. I'm alwers fussing over something of the kind; alwers did, since I was a baby; had my little wind-mills and carts and things; used to sell 'em to the other young uns. Father don't like it. He wants me to stick to the farm. I don't like farming. I feel like a fish out of water.—Mrs. Forceythe, marm!"

He turned on her with an abrupt change of tone, so funny that she could with difficulty retain her gravity.

"I heard you saying a sight of queer things the other day about heaven. Clo, she's been telling me a sight more. Now, *I* never believed in heaven!"

"Why?"

"Because I don't believe," said the poor fellow, with sullen decision, "that a benevolent God ever would ha' made sech a derned awkward chap as I am!"

Aunt Winifred replied by stepping into the house, and bringing out a fine photograph of one of the best of the St. Georges,—a rapt, yet very manly face, in which the saint and the hero are wonderfully blended.

"I suppose," she said, putting it into his hands, "that if you should go to heaven, you would be as much fairer than that picture as that picture is fairer than you are now."

"No! Why, would I, though? Jim-miny! Why, it would be worth going for, wouldn't it?"

The words were no less reverently spoken than the vague rhapsodies of his father; for the sullenness left his face, and his eyes—which are pleasant, and not unmanly, when one fairly sees them—sparkled softly, like a child's.

"Make it all up there, maybe?" musing,—"the girls laughing at you all your life, and all? That would be the bigger heft of the two then, wouldn't it? for they say there ain't any end to things up there. Why, so it might be fair in Him after all; more'n fair, perhaps. See here, Mrs. Forceythe, I'm not a church-member, you know, and father, he's dreadful troubled about me; prays over me like a span of ministers, the old gentleman does, every Sunday night. Now, I don't want to go to the other place anymore than the next man, and I've had my times, too, of thinking I'd keep steady and say my prayers reg'lar,—it makes a chap feel on a sight better terms with himself,—but I don't see how *I'm* going to wear white frocks and stand up in a choir,—never could sing no more'n a frog with a cold in his head,—it tires me more now, honest, to think of it, than it does to do a week's mowing. Look at me! Do you s'pose I'm fit for it? Father, he's always talking about the thrones, and the wings, and the praises, and the palms, and having new names in your foreheads, (shouldn't object to that, though, by any means), till he drives me into the toolhouse, or off on a spree. I tell him if God hain't got a place where chaps like me can do something He's fitted 'em to do in this world, there's no use thinking about it anyhow."

So Auntie took the honest fellow into her most earnest thought for half an hour, and argued, and suggested, and reproved, and helped him, as only she could do; and at the end of it seemed to have worked into his mind some distinct and not unwelcome ideas of what a Christ-like life must mean to him, and of the coming heaven which is so much more real to her than any life outside of it.

"And then," she told him, "I imagine that your fancy for machinery will be employed in some way. Perhaps you will do a great deal more successful inventing there than you ever will here."

"You don't say so!" said radiant Abinadab.

"God will give you something to do, certainly, and something that you will like."

"I might turn it to some religious purpose, you know!" said Abinadab, looking bright. "Perhaps I could help 'em build a church, or hist some of their pearl gates, or something like!"

Upon that he said that it was time to be at home and see to the oxen, and shambled awkwardly away.

Clo told us this afternoon that he begged the errand and the flowers from her. She says: "'Bin thinks there never was anybody like you, Mrs. Forceythe, and 'Bin isn't the only one, either." At which Mrs. Forceythe smiles absently, thinking—I wonder of what.

Monday night.

I saw as funny and as pretty a bit of a drama this afternoon as I have seen for a long time.

Faith had been rolling out in the hot hay ever since three o'clock, with one of the little Blands, and when the shadows grew long they came in with flushed cheeks and tumbled hair, to rest and cool upon the door-steps. I was sitting in the parlor, sewing energetically on some sun-bonnets for some of Aunt Winifred's people down town,— I found the heat to be more bearable if I kept busy,—and could see, unseen, all the little *tableaux* into which the two children grouped themselves; a new one every instant; in the shadow now,—now in a quiver of golden glow; the wind tossing their hair about, and their chatter chiming down the hall like bells.

"O what a funny little sunset there's going to be behind the maple-tree," said the blond-haired Bland, in a pause.

"Funny enough," observed Faith, with her superior smile, "but it's going to be a great deal funnier up in heaven, I tell you, Molly Bland."

"Funny in heaven? Why, Faith!" Molly drew herself up with a religious air, and looked the image of her father.

"Yes, to be sure. I'm going to have some little pink blocks made out of it when I go; pink and yellow and green and purple and—O, so many blocks! I'm going to have a little red cloud to sail round in, like that one up over the house, too, I shouldn't wonder."

Molly opened her eyes.

"O, I don't believe it!"

"*You* don't know much!" said Miss Faith, superbly. "I shouldn't s'pose you would believe it. P'r'aps I'll have some strawberries too, and some ginger-snaps,—I'm not going to have any old bread and butter up there,—O, and some little gold apples, and a lot of playthings; nicer playthings—why, nicer than they have in the shops in Boston, Molly Bland! God's keeping 'em up there a purpose."

"Dear me!" said incredulous Molly, "I should just like to know who told you that much. My mother never told it at me. Did your mother tell it at you?"

"O, she told me some of it, and the rest I thought out myself."

"Let's go and play One Old Cat," said Molly, with an uncomfortable jump; "I wish I hadn't got to go to heaven!"

"Why, Molly Bland! why, I think heaven's splendid! I've got my papa up there, you know. 'Here's my little girl!' That's what he's going to say. Mamma, she'll be there, too, and we're all going to live in the prettiest house. I have dreadful hurries to go this afternoon sometimes when Phoebe's cross and won't give me sugar. They don't let you in, though, 'nless you're a good girl."

"Who gets it all up?" asked puzzled Molly.

"Jesus Christ will give me all these beautiful fings," said Faith, evidently repeating her mother's words,—the only catechism that she has been taught.

"And what will he do when he sees you?" asked her mother, coming down the stairs and stepping up behind her.

"Take me up in His arms and kiss me."

"And what will Faith say?"

"Fank—you!" said the child, softly.

In another minute she was absorbed, body and soul, in the mysteries of One Old Cat.

"But I don't think she will feel much like being naughty for half an hour to come," her mother said; "hear how pleasantly her words drop! Such a talk quiets her, like a hand laid on her head. Mary, sometimes I think it is His very hand, as much as when He touched those other little children. I wish Faith to feel at home with Him and His home. Little thing! I really do not think that she is conscious of any fear of dying; I do not think it means anything to her but Christ, and her father, and pink blocks, and a nice time, and never disobeying me, or being cross. Many a time she wakes me up in the morning talking away to herself, and when I turn and look at her, she says: 'O mamma, won't we go to heaven to-day, you fink? *When* will we go, mamma?'"

"If there had been any pink blocks and ginger-snaps for me when I was at her age, I should not have prayed every night to 'die out.' I think the horrors of death that children live through, unguessed and unrelieved, are awful. Faith may thank you all her life that she has escaped them."

"I should feel answerable to God for the child's soul, if I had not prevented that. I always wanted to know what sort of mother that poor little thing had, who asked, if she were *very* good up in heaven, whether they wouldn't let her go down to hell Saturday afternoons, and play a little while!"

"I know. But think of it,—blocks and ginger-snaps!"

"I treat Faith just as the Bible treats us, by dealing in *pictures* of truth that she can understand. I can make Clo and Abinadab Quirk comprehend that their pianos and machinery may not be made of literal rosewood and steel, but will be some synonyme of the thing, which will answer just such wants of their changed natures as rosewood and steel must answer now. There will be machinery and pianos in the same sense in which there will be pearl gates and harps. Whatever enjoyment any or all of them represent now, something will represent then.

"But Faith, if I told her that her heavenly ginger-snaps would not be made of molasses and flour, would have a cry, for fear that she was not going to have any ginger-snaps at all; so, until she is older, I give her unqualified ginger-snaps. The principal joy of a child's life consists in eating. Faith begins, as soon as the light wanes, to dream of that gum-drop which she is to have at bedtime. I don't suppose she can outgrow that at once by passing out of her little round body. She must begin where she left off,—nothing but a baby, though it will be as holy and happy a baby as Christ can make it. When she says: 'Mamma, I shall be hungery and want my dinner, up there,' I never hesitate to tell her that she shall have her dinner. She would never, in her secret heart, though she might not have the honesty to say so, expect to be otherwise than miserable in a dinnerless eternity."

"You are not afraid of misleading the child's fancy?"

"Not so long as I can keep the two ideas—that Christ is her best friend, and that heaven is not meant for naughty girls—pre-eminent in her mind. And I sincerely believe that He would give her the very pink blocks which she anticipates, no less than He would give back a poet his lost dreams, or you your brother. He has been a child; perhaps, incidentally to the unsolved mysteries of atonement, for this very reason,—that He may know how to 'prepare their places' for them, whose angels do always behold His Father. Ah, you may be sure that, if of such is the happy Kingdom, He will not scorn to stoop and fit it to their little needs.

"There was that poor little fellow whose guinea-pig died,—do you remember?"

105

"Only half; what was it?"

"'O mamma,'" he sobbed out, behind his handkerchief,'don't great big elephants have souls?'

"'No, my son.'

"'Nor camels, mamma?'

"'No.'

"'Nor bears, nor alligators, nor chickens?'

"'O no, dear.'

"'O mamma, mamma! Don't little CLEAN—*white*—*guinea-pigs* have souls?'

"I never should have had the heart to say no to that; especially as we have no positive proof to the contrary.

"Then that scrap of a boy who lost his little red balloon the morning he bought it, and, broken-hearted, wanted to know whether it had gone to heaven. Don't I suppose if he had been taken there himself that very minute, that he would have found a little balloon in waiting for him? How can I help it?"

"It has a pretty sound. If people would not think it so material and shocking—"

"Let people read Martin Luther's letter to his little boy. There is the testimony of a pillar in good and regular standing! I don't think you need to be afraid of my balloon, after that."

I remembered that there was a letter of his on heaven, but, not recalling it distinctly, I hunted for it to-night, and read it over. I shall copy it, the better to retain it in mind.

"Grace and peace in Christ, my dear little son. I see with pleasure that thou learnest well, and prayed diligently. Do so, my son, and continue. When I come home I will bring thee a pretty fairing.

"I know a pretty, merry garden wherein are many children. They have little golden coats, and they gather beautiful apples under the trees, and pears, cherries, plums, and wheat-plums;—they sing, and jump, and are merry. They have beautiful little horses, too, with gold bits and silver saddles. And I asked the man to whom the garden belongs, whose children they were. And he said: 'They are the children that love to pray and to learn, and are good.' Then said I: 'Dear man, I have a son, too; his name is Johnny Luther. May he not also come into this garden and eat these beautiful apples and pears, and ride these fine horses?' Then the man said: 'If he loves to pray and to learn, and is good, he shall come into this garden, and Lippus and Jost too; and when they all come together, they shall have fifes and trumpets, lutes and all sorts of music, and they shall dance, and shoot with little cross-bows.'

"And he showed me a fine meadow there in the garden, made for dancing. There hung nothing but golden fifes, trumpets, and fine silver cross-bows. But it was early, and the children had not yet eaten; therefore I could not wait the dance, and I said to the man: 'Ah, dear sir! I will immediately go and write all this to my little son Johnny, and tell him to pray diligently, and to learn well, and to be good, so that he also may come to this garden. But he has an Aunt Lehne, he must bring her with him.' Then the man said: 'It shall be so; go, and write him so.'

"Therefore, my dear little son Johnny, learn and pray away! and tell Lippus and Jost, too that they must learn and pray. And then you shall come to the garden together. Herewith I commend thee to Almighty God. And greet Aunt Lehne, and give her a kiss for my sake.

"Thy dear Father,

"Martinus Luther.

"Anno 1530."

❧ *13* ❧

August 3.

The summer is sliding quietly away,—my desolate summer which I dreaded; with the dreams gone from its wild flowers, the crown from its sunsets, the thrill from its winds and its singing.

But I have found out a thing. One can live without dreams and crowns and thrills.

I have not lost them. They lie under the ivied cross with Roy for a little while. They will come back to me with him. "Nothing is lost," she teaches me. And until they come back, I see—for she shows me—fields groaning under their white harvest, with laborers very few. Ruth followed the sturdy reapers, gleaning a little. I, perhaps, can do as much. The ways in which I must work seem so small and insignificant, so pitifully trivial sometimes, that I do not even like to write them down here. In fact, they are so small that, six months ago, I did not see them at all. Only to be pleasant to old Phoebe, and charitable to Meta Tripp, and faithful to my *not* very interesting little scholars, and a bit watchful of worn-out Mrs. Bland, and— But dear me, I won't. They *are* so little!

But one's self becomes of less importance, which seems to be the point.

It seems very strange to me sometimes, looking back to those desperate winter days, what a change has come over my thoughts of Roy. Not that he is any less—O, never any less to me. But it is almost as if she had raised him from the grave. Why seek ye the living among the dead? Her soft, compassionate eyes shine with the question every hour. And every hour he is helping me,—ah, Roy, we understand one another now.

How he must love Aunt Winifred! How pleasant the days will be when we can talk her over, and thank her together!

"To be happy because Roy is happy." I remember how those first words of hers struck me. It does not seem to me impossible, now.

Aunt Winifred and I laugh at each other for talking so much about heaven. I see that the green book is filled with my questions and her answers. The fact is, not that we do not talk as much about mundane affairs as other people, but that this one thing interests us more.

If, instead, it had been flounces, or babies, or German philosophy, the green book would have filled itself just as unconsciously with flounces, or babies, or German philosophy. This interest in heaven is of course no sign of especial piety in me, nor could people with young, warm, uncrushed hopes throbbing through their days be expected to feel the same. It is only the old principle of, where the treasure is—the heart.

"How spiritual-minded Mary has grown!" Mrs. Bland observes, regarding me respectfully. I try in vain to laugh her out of the conviction. If Roy had not gone before, I should think no more, probably, about the coming life, than does the minister's wife herself.

But now—I cannot help it—that is the reality, this the dream; that the substance, this the shadow.

The other day Aunt Winifred and I had a talk which has been of more value to me than all the rest.

Faith was in bed; it was a cold, rainy evening; we were secure from callers; we lighted a few kindlers in the parlor-grate; she rolled up the easy-chair, and I took my cricket at her feet.

"Paul at the feet of Gamaliel! This is what I call comfort. Now, Auntie, let us go to heaven awhile."

"Very well. What do you want there now?"

I paused a moment, sobered by a thought that has been growing steadily upon me of late.

"Something more, Aunt Winifred. All these other things are beautiful and dear; but I believe I want—God.

"You have not said much about Him. The Bible says a great deal about Him. You have given me the filling-up of heaven in all its pleasant promise, but—I don't know—there seems to be an outline wanting."

She drew my hand up into hers, smiling.

"I have not done my painting by artistic methods, I know; but it was not exactly accidental.

"Tell me, honestly,—is God more to you or less, a more distinct Being or a more vague one, than He was six months ago? Is He, or is He not, dearer to you now than then?"

I thought about it a minute, and then turned my face up to her.

"Mary, what a light in your eyes! How is it?"

It came over me slowly, but it came with such a passion of gratitude and unworthiness, that I scarcely knew how to tell her—that He never has been to me, in all my life, what he is now at the end of these six months. He was once an abstract Grandeur which I struggled more in fear than love to please. He has become a living Presence, dear and real.

> "No dead fact stranded on the shore
>   Of the oblivious years;
> But warm, sweet, tender, even yet
>   A present help." . . .

He was an inexorable Mystery who took Roy from me to lose him in the glare of a more inexorable heaven. He is a Father who knew better than we that we should be parted for a while; but He only means it to be a little while. He is keeping him for me to find in the flush of some summer morning, on which I shall open my eyes no less naturally than I open them on June sunrises now. I always have that fancy of going in the morning.

She understood what I could not tell her, and said, "I thought it would be so."

"You, His interpreter, have done it," I answered her. "His heaven shows what He is,—don't you see?—like a friend's letter. I could no more go back to my old groping relations to Him, than I could make of you the dim and somewhat apocryphal Western Auntie that you were before I saw you."

"Which was precisely why I have dealt with this subject as I have," she said. "You had all your life been directed to an indefinite heaven, where the glory of God was to crowd out all individuality and all human joy from His most individual and human creatures, till the 'Glory of God' had become nothing but a name and a dread to you. So I let those three words slide by, and tried to bring you to them, as Christ brought the Twelve to believe in him, 'for the works' sake.'

"Yet, my child; clinging human loves, stifled longings, cries for rest, forgotten hopes, shall have their answer. Whatever the bewilderment of beauties folded away for us in heavenly nature and art, they shall

strive with each other to make us glad. These things have their pleasant place. But, through eternity, there will be always something beyond and dearer than the dearest of them. God himself will be first,—
naturally and of necessity, without strain of struggle, *first*."

When I sat here last winter with my dead in my house, those words
would have roused in me an agony of wild questionings. I should
have beaten about them and beaten against them, and cried in my
honest heart that they were false. I *knew* that I loved Roy more than
I loved such a Being as God seemed to me then to be. Now, they
strike me as simply and pleasantly true. The more I love Roy, the more
I love Him. He loves us both.

"You see it could not be otherwise," she went on, speaking low.
"Where would you be, or I, or they who seem to us so much dearer
and better than ourselves, if it were not for Jesus Christ? What can
heaven be to us, but a song of the love that is the same to us yesterday, to-day, and forever,—that, in the mystery of an intensity which
we shall perhaps never understand, could choose death and be glad
in the choosing, and, what is more than that, could live *life* for us for
three-and-thirty years?

"I cannot strain my faith—or rather my common sense—to the
rhapsodies with which many people fill heaven. But it seems to me
like this: A friend goes away from us, and it may be seas or worlds
that lie between us, and we love him. He leaves behind him his little
keepsakes; a lock of hair to curl about our fingers; a picture that has
caught the trick of his eyes or smile; a book, a flower, a letter. What
we do with the curling hair, what we say to the picture, what we dream
over the flower and the letter, nobody knows but ourselves. People
have risked life for such mementoes. Yet who loves the senseless gift
more than the giver,—the curl more than the young forehead on
which it fell,—the letter more than the hand which traced it?

"So it seems to me that we shall learn to see in God the centre of
all possibilities of joy. The greatest of these lesser delights is but the
greater measure of His friendship. They will not mean less of pleasure, but more of Him. They will not "pale," as Dr. Bland would say.

Human dearness will wax, not wane, in heaven; but human friends will be loved for love of Him."

"I see; that helps me; like a torch in a dark room. But there will be shadows in the corners. Do you suppose that we shall ever *fully* feel it in the body?"

"In the body, probably not. We see through a glass so darkly that the temptation to idolatry is always our greatest. Golden images did not die with Paganism. At times I fancy that, somewhere between this world and another, a revelation will come upon us like a flash, of what *sin* really is,—such a revelation, lighting up the lurid background of our past in such colors, that the consciousness of what Christ has done for us will be for a time as much as heart can bear. After that, the mystery will be, not how to love Him most, but that we ever *could* have loved any creature or thing as much."

"We serve God quite as much by active work as by special prayer, here," I said after some thought; "how will it be there?"

"We must be busily at work certainly; but I think there must naturally be more communion with Him then. Now, this phrase "communion with God" has been worn, and not always well worn.

"Prayer means to us, in this life, more often penitent confession than happy interchange of thought with Him. It is associated, too, with aching limbs and sleepy eyes, and nights when the lamp goes out. Obstacles, moral and physical, stand in the way of our knowing exactly what it may mean in the ideal of it.

"My best conception of it lies in the *friendship* of the man Christ Jesus. I suppose he will bear with him, eternally, the humanity which he took up with him from the Judean hills. I imagine that we shall see him in visible form like ourselves, among us, yet not of us; that he, himself, is 'Gott mit ihnen'; that we shall talk with him as a man talketh with his friend. Perhaps, bowed and hushed at his dear feet, we shall hear from his own lips the story of Nazareth, of Bethany, of Golgotha, of the chilly mountains where he used to pray all night long for us; of the desert places where he hungered; of his cry for help—think, Mary—*His!*—when there was not one in all the world to hear it, and there was silence in heaven, while angels strengthened him and man forsook him. Perhaps his voice—the very voice which has sounded whispering through our troubled life—"Could ye not watch one hour?"—shall unfold its perplexed meanings; shall make its rough places plain; shall show us step by step the merciful way by which he led us to that hour; shall point out to us, joy by joy, the surprises that he has been planning for us, just as the old father in the story planned to surprise his wayward boy come home.

"And such a 'communion,'—which is not too much, nor yet enough, to dare to expect of a God who was the 'friend' of Abraham, who 'walked' with Enoch, who did not call fishermen his servants,—*such* will be that 'presence of God,' that 'adoration,' on which we have looked from afar off with despairing eyes that wept, they were so dazzled, and turned themselves away as from the thing they greatly feared."

I think we neither of us cared to talk for a while after this. Something made me forget even that I was going to see Roy in heaven. "Three-and-thirty years. Three-and-thirty years." The words rang themselves over.

"It is on the humanity of Christ," she said after some musing, "that all my other reasons for hoping for such a heaven as I hope for, rest for foundation. He knows exactly what we are, for he has been one of us; exactly what we hope and fear and crave, for he has hoped and feared and craved, not the less humanly, but only more intensely.

" *'If it were not so,'*—do you take in the thoughtful tenderness of that? A mother, stilling her frightened child in the dark, might speak just so,—*'if it were not so, I would have told you.'* That brooding love makes room for all that we can want. He has sounded every deep of a troubled and tempted life. Who so sure as he to understand how to prepare a place where troubled and tempted lives may grow serene? Further than this; since he stands as our great Type, no less in death and after than before it, he answers for us many of these lesser questions on the event of which so much of our happiness depends.

"Shall we lose our personality in a vague ocean of ether,—you one puff of gas, I another?—

"He, with his own wounded body, rose and ate and walked and talked.

"Is all memory of this life to be swept away?—

"He, arisen, has forgotten nothing. He waits to meet his disciples at the old, familiar places; as naturally as if he had never been parted from them, he falls in with the current of their thoughts.

"Has any one troubled us with fears that in the glorified crowds of heaven we may miss a face dearer than all the world to us?—

"He made himself known to his friends; Mary, and the two at Emmaus, and the bewildered group praying and perplexed in their bolted room.

"Do we weary ourselves with speculations whether human loves can outlive the shock of death?—

"Mary knew how He loved her, when, turning, she heard him call her by her name. They knew, whose hearts 'burned within them while he talked with them by the way, and when he tarried with them, the day being far spent.'"

"And for the rest?"

"For the rest, about which He was silent, we can trust him, and if, trusting, we please ourselves with fancies, he would be the last to think it blame to us. There is one promise which grows upon me the more I study it, 'He that spared not his own Son, how shall he not also *with him freely give us all things?*' Sometimes I wonder if that does not infold a beautiful *double entendre,* a hint of much that you and I have conjectured,—as one throws down a hint of a surprise to a child.

"Then there is that pledge to those who seek first His kingdom: *'All these things shall be added unto you.'* 'These things,' were food and clothing, were varieties of material delight, and the words were spoken to men who lived hungry, beggared, and died the death of outcasts. If this passage could be taken literally, it would be very significant in its bearing on the future life; for Christ must keep his promise to the letter, in one world or another. It may be wrenching the verse, not as a verse, but from the grain of the argument, to insist on the literal interpretation,—though I am not sure."

₹*14*₹

August 15.

I asked the other day, wondering whether all ministers were like Dr. Bland, what Uncle Forceythe used to believe about heaven.

"Very much what I do," she said. "These questions were brought home to him, early in life, by the death of a very dear sister; he had thought much about them. I think one of the things that so much attached his people to him was the way he had of weaving their future life in with this, till it grew naturally and pleasantly into their frequent thought. O yes, your uncle supplied me with half of my proof-texts."

Aunt Winifred has not looked quite well of late, I fancy; though it may be only fancy. She has not spoken of it, except one day when I told her that she looked pale. It was the heat, she said.

20th.

Little Clo came over to-night. I believe she thinks Aunt Winifred the best friend she has in the world. Auntie has become much attached to all her scholars, and has a rare power of winning her way into their confidence. They come to her with all their little interests,—everything, from saving their souls to trimming a bonnet. Clo, however, is the favorite, as I predicted.

She looked a bit blue to-night, as girls will look; in fact, her face always has a tinge of sadness about it. Aunt Winifred, understanding at a glance that the child was not in a mood to talk before a third, led her away into the garden, and they were gone a long time. When it grew dark, I saw them coming up the path, Clo's hand locked in her teacher's, and her face, which was wet, upturned like a child's. They strolled to the gate, lingered a little to talk, and then Clo said good night without coming in.

Auntie sat for a while after she had gone, thinking her over, I could see.

"Poor thing!" she said at last, half to herself, half to me,—"poor little foolish thing! This is where the dreadful individuality of a human soul irks me. There comes a point, beyond which you *can't* help people."

"What has happened to Clo?"

"Nothing, lately. It has been happening for two years. Two miserable years are an eternity, at Clo's age. It is the old story,—a summer boarder; a little flirting; a little dreaming; a little pain; then autumn, and the nuts dropping on the leaves, and he was gone,—and knew not what he did,—and the child waked up. There was the future; to bake and sweep, to go to sewing-circles, and sing in the choir, and bear the moonlight nights,—and she loved him. She has lived through two years of it, and she loves him now. Reason will not reach such a passion in a girl like Clo. I did not tell her that she would put it away with other girlish things, and laugh at herself some happy day, as women have laughed at their young fancies before her; partly because that would be a certain way of repelling her confidence,—she does not believe it, and my believing could not make her; partly because I am not quite sure about it myself. Clo has a good deal of the woman about her, her introspective life is intense. She may cherish this sweet misery as she does her musical tastes, till it has struck deep root. There is nothing in the excellent Mrs. Bentley's household, nor in Homer anywhere, to draw the girl out from herself in time to prevent the dream from becoming a reality."

"Poor little thing! What did you say to her?"

"You ought to have heard what she said to me! I wish I were at liberty to tell you the whole story. What troubles her most is that it is not going to help the matter any to die. 'O Mrs. Forceythe,' she says, in a tone that is enough to give the heart-ache, even to such an old woman as Mrs. Forceythe, 'O Mrs. Forceythe, what is going to become of me up there? He never loved me, you see, and he never, never will, and he will have some beautiful, good wife of his own, and I won't have *any*body! For I can't love anybody else,— I've tried; I tried just as hard as I could to love my cousin 'Bin; he's real good, and—I'm—afraid 'Bin likes me, though I guess he likes his carpet-sweepers better. O, sometimes I think, and think, till it seems as if I could not bear it! I don't see how God can *make* me happy. I wish I could be buried up and go to sleep, and never have any heaven!'"

"And you told her—?"

"That she should have him there. That is, if not himself, some-thing,—somebody who would so much more than fill his place, that she would never have a lonely or unloved minute. Her eyes bright-ened, and shaded, and pondered, doubting. She 'didn't see how it could ever be.' I told her not to try and see how, but to leave it to Christ. He knew all about this little trouble of hers, and he would make it right.

"'Will he?' she questioned, sighing; 'but there are so many of us! There's 'Bin, and a plenty more, and I don't see how it's going to be smoothed out. Everything is in a jumble, Mrs. Forceythe, don't you see? for some people *can't* like and keep liking so many times.' Some-thing came into my mind about the rough places that shall be made plain, and the crooked things straight. I tried to explain to her, and at last I kissed away her tears, and sent her home, if not exactly com-forted, a little less miserable, I think, than when she came. Ah, well,— I wonder myself sometimes about these 'crooked things'; but, though I wonder, I never doubt."

She finished her sentence somewhat hurriedly, and half started from her chair, raising both hands with a quick, involuntary motion that attracted my notice. The lights came in just then, and, unless I am much mistaken, her face showed paler than usual; but when I asked her if she felt faint, she said, "O no, I believe I am a little tired, and will go to bed."

September 1.

I am glad that the summer is over. This heat has certainly worn on Aunt Winifred, with that kind of wear which slides people into conformed invalidism. I suppose she would bear it in her saintly way, as she bears everything, but it would be a bitter cup for her. I know she was always pale, but this is a paleness which—

Night.

A dreadful thing has happened!

I was in the middle of my sentence, when I heard a commotion in the street, and a child's voice shouting incoherently something about the doctor, and *"mother's killed! O, mother's killed! mother's burnt to death!"* I was at the window in time to see a blond-haired girl running wildly past the house, and to see that it was Molly Bland.

At the same moment I saw Aunt Winifred snatching her hat from its nail in the entry. She beckoned to me to follow, and we were half-way over to the parsonage before I had a distinct thought of what I was about.

We came upon a horrible scene. Dr. Bland was trying to do everything alone; there was not a woman in the house to help him, for they have never been able to keep a servant, and none of the neighbors had had time to be there before us. The poor husband was growing faint, I think. Aunt Winifred saw by a look that he could not bear much more, sent him after Molly for the doctor, and took everything meantime into her own charge.

I shall not write down a word of it. It was a sight that, once seen, will never leave me as long as I live. My nerves are thoroughly shaken by it, and it must be put out of thought as far as possible.

It seems that the little boy—the baby—crept into the kitchen by himself, and began to throw the contents of the match-box on the stove, "to make a bonfire," the poor little fellow said. In five minutes his apron was ablaze. His mother was on the spot at his first cry, and smothered the little apron, and saved the child, but her dress was muslin, and everybody was too far off to hear her at first,—and by the time her husband came in from the garden it was too late.

She is living yet. Her husband, pacing the room back and forth, and crouching on his knees by the hour, is praying God to let her die before the morning.

Morning.

There is no chance of life, the doctor says. But he has been able to find something that has lessened her sufferings. She lies partially unconscious.

Wednesday night.

Aunt Winifred and I were over at the parsonage to-night, when she roused a little from her stupor and recognized us. She spoke to her husband, and kissed me good by, and asked for the children. They were playing softly in the next room; we sent for them, and they came in,—the four unconscious, motherless little things,—with the sunlight in their hair.

The bitterness of death came into her marred face at sight of them, and she raised her hands to Auntie—to the only other mother there—with a sudden helpless cry:"I could bear it, I could bear it, if it weren't for *them*. Without any mother all their lives,—such little things,—and to go away where I can't do a single *thing* for them!"

Aunt Winifred stooped down and spoke low, but decidedly.

"You *will* do for them. God knows all about it. He will not send you away from them. You shall be just as much their mother, every day of their lives, as you have been here. Perhaps there is something to do for them which you never could have done here. He sees. He loves them. He loves you."

If I could paint, I might paint the look that struck through and through that woman's dying face; but words cannot touch it. If I were Aunt Winifred, I should bless God on my knees to-night for having shown me how to give such ease to a soul in death.

Thursday morning.

God is merciful. Mrs. Bland died at five o'clock.

10th.

How such a voice from the heavens shocks one out of the repose of calm sorrows and of calm joys. This has come and gone so suddenly that I cannot adjust it to any quiet and trustful thinking yet.

The whole parish mourns excitedly; for, though they worked their minister's wife hard, they loved her well. I cannot talk it over with the rest. It jars. Horror should never be dissected. Besides, my heart is too full of those four little children with the sunlight in their hair and the unconsciousness in their eyes.

15th.

Mrs. Quirk came over to-day in great perplexity. She had just come from the minister's.

"I don't know what we're a goin' to do with him!" she exclaimed in a gush of impatient, uncomprehending sympathy; "you can't let a man take on that way much longer. He'll sorry himself sick, and then we shall either lose him or have to pay his bills to Europe! Why, he jest stops in the house, and walks his study up and down, day and night; or else he jest sets and sets and don't notice nobody but the children. Now I've jest ben over makin' him some chicken-pie,— and he made believe to eat it, 'cause I'd ben at the trouble, I suppose, but how much do you suppose he swallowed? Jest three mouthfuls! Thinks says I, I won't spend my time over chicken-pie for the afflicted agin, and on ironing-day, too! When I knocked at the study door, he said, 'Come in, and stopped his walkin' and turned as quick.

" 'O,' says he, 'good morning. I thought it was Mrs. Forceythe.'

"I told him no, I wasn't Mrs. Forceythe, but I'd come to comfort him in his sorrer all the same. But that's the only thing I have agin our minister. He won't *be* comforted. Mary Ann Jacobs, who's ben there kind of looking after the children and things for him, you know, sence the funeral—she says he's asked three or four times for you,

Mrs. Forceythe. There's ben plenty of his people in to see him, but you haven't ben nigh him, Mary Ann says."

"I stayed away because I thought the presence of friends at this time would be an intrusion," Auntie said; "but if he would like to see me, that alters the case. I will go, certainly."

"I don't know," suggested Mrs. Quirk, looking over the tops of her spectacles,—"I s'pose it's proper enough, but you bein' a widow, you know, and his wife—"

Aunt Winifred's eyes shot fire. She stood up and turned upon Mrs. Quirk with a look the like of which I presume that worthy lady had never seen before, and is not likely to see soon again (it gave the beautiful scorn of a Zenobia to her fair, slight face), moved her lips slightly, but said nothing, put on her bonnet, and went straight to Dr. Bland's.

The minister, they told her, was in his study. She knocked lightly at the door, and was bidden in a lifeless voice to enter.

Shades and blinds were drawn, and the glare of the sun quite shut out. Dr. Bland sat by his study-table, with his face upon his hands. A Bible lay open before him. It had been lately used; the leaves were wet.

He raised his head dejectedly, but smiled when he saw who it was. He had been thinking about her, he said, and was glad that she had come.

I do not know all that passed between them, but I gather, from such hints as Auntie in her unconsciousness throws out, that she had things to say which touched some comfortless places in the man's heart. No Greek and Hebrew "original," no polished dogma, no link in his stereotyped logic, not one of his eloquent sermons on the future state, came to his relief.

These were meant for happy days. They rang cold as steel upon the warm needs of an afflicted man. Brought face to face, and sharply, with the blank heaven of his belief, he stood up from before his dead, and groped about it, and cried out against it in the bitterness of his soul.

"I had no chance to prepare myself to bow to the will of God," he said, his reserved ministerial manner in curious contrast with the caged way in which he was pacing the room,—"I had no chance. I am taken by surprise, as by a thief in the night. I had a great deal to say to her, and there was no time. She could tell me what to do with my poor little children. I wanted to tell her other things. I wanted to tell her— Perhaps we all of us have our regrets when the Lord removes our friends; we may have done or left undone many things; we might have made them happier. My mind does not rest with assurance in its conceptions of the heavenly state. If I never can tell her—"

He stopped abruptly, and paced into the darkest shadows of the shadowed room, his face turned away.

"You said once some pleasant things about heaven?" he said at last, half appealingly, stopping in front of her, hesitating; like a man and like a minister, hardly ready to come with all the learning of his schools and commentators and sit at the feet of a woman.

She talked with him for a time in her unobtrusive way, deferring, when she honestly could, to his clerical judgment, and careful not to wound him by any word; but frankly and clearly, as she always talks.

When she rose to go he thanked her quietly.

"This is a somewhat novel train of thought to me," he said; "I hope it may not prove an unscriptural one. I have been reading the book of Revelation to-day with these questions especially in mind. We are never too old to learn. Some passages may be capable of other interpretations than I have formerly given them. No matter what I *wish,* you see, I must be guided by the Word of my God."

Auntie says that she never respected the man so much as she did when, hearing those words, she looked up into his haggard face, convulsed with its human pain and longing.

"I hope you do not think that *I* am not guided by the Word of God," she answered. "I mean to be."

"I know you mean to be," he said cordially. "I do not say that you are not. I may come to see that you are, and that you are right. It will be a peaceful day for me if I can ever quite agree with your methods of reasoning. But I must think these things over. I thank you once more for coming. Your sympathy is grateful to me."

Just as she closed the door he called her back.

"See," he said, with a saddened smile. "At least I shall never preach *this* again. It seems to me that life is always undoing for us something that we have just laboriously done."

He held up before her a mass of old blue manuscript, and threw it, as he spoke, upon the embers left in his grate. It smoked and blazed up and burned out.

It was that sermon on heaven of which there is an abstract in this journal.

20th.

Aunt Winifred hired Mr. Tripp's gray this afternoon, and drove to East Homer on some unexplained errand. She did not invite me to go with her, and Faith, though she teased impressively, was left at home. Her mother was gone till late,—so late that I had begun to be anxious about her, and heard through the dark the first sound of the buggy wheels, with great relief. She looked very tired when I met her at the gate. She had not been able, she said, to accomplish her errand at East Homer, and from there had gone to Worcester by railroad, leaving Old Gray at the East Homer Eagle till her return. She told me nothing more, and I asked no questions.

೭ *15* ೨

Sunday.

Faith has behaved like a witch all day. She knocked down three crickets and six hymn-books in church this morning, and this afternoon horrified the assembled and devout congregation by turning round in the middle of the long prayer, and, in a loud and distinct voice, asking Mrs. Quirk for "'nother those pepp'mints such as you gave me one Sunday a good many years ago, you 'member." After church, her mother tried a few Bible questions to keep her still.

"Faith, who was Christ's father?"

"Jerusalem!" said Faith, promptly.

"Where did his parents take Jesus when they fled from Herod?"

"O, to Europe. Of course I knew that! Everybody goes to Europe."

To-night, when her mother had put her to bed, she came down laughing.

"Faith does seem to have a hard time with the Lord's Prayer. To-night, being very sleepy and in a hurry to finish, she proceeded with great solemnity:—'Our Father who art in heaven, hallowed be thy name; six days shalt thou labor and do all thy work, and— Oh!'

"I was just thinking how amused her father must be."

Auntie says many such things. I cannot explain how pleasantly they strike me, nor how they help me.

29th.

Dr. Bland gave us a good sermon yesterday. There is an indescribable change in all his sermons. There is a change, too, in the man, and that something more than the haggardness of grief. I not only respect him and am sorry for him, but I feel more ready to be taught by him than ever before. A certain indefinable *humanness* softens his eyes and tones, and seems to be creeping into everything that he says. Yet, on the other hand, his people say that they have never heard him speak such pleasant, helpful things concerning his and their relations to God. I met him the other night, coming away from his wife's grave, and was struck by the expression of his face. I wondered if he were not slowly finding the "peaceful day," of which he told Aunt Winifred.

She, by the way, has taken another of her mysterious trips to Worcester.

30th.

We were wondering to-day where it will be,—I mean heaven.

"It is impossible to do more than wonder," Auntie said, "though we are explicitly told that there will be new heavens *and* a new earth, which seems, if anything can be taken literally in the Bible, to point to this world as the future home of at least some of us."

"Not for all of us, of course?"

"I don't feel sure. I know that somebody spent his valuable time in estimating that all the people who have lived and died upon the earth would cover it, alive or buried, twice over; but I know that somebody else claims with equal solemnity to have discovered that they could all be buried in the State of Pennsylvania! But it would be of little consequence if we could not all find room here, since there must be other provision for us."

"Why?"

"Certainly there is 'a place' in which we are promised that we shall be 'with Christ,' this world being yet the great theatre of human life and battle-ground of Satan; no place, certainly, in which to confine a happy soul without prospect of release. The Spiritualistic notion of 'circles' of dead friends revolving over us is to me intolerable. I want my husband with me when I need him, but I hope he has a place to be happy in, which is out of this woful world.

"The old astronomical idea, stars around a sun, and systems around a centre, and that centre the Throne of God, is not an unreasonable one. Isaac Taylor, among his various conjectures, inclines, I fancy, to suppose that the sun of each system is the heaven of that system. Though the glory of God may be more directly and impressively exhibited in one place than in another, we may live in different planets, and some of us, after its destruction and renovation, on this same dear old, happy and miserable, loved and maltreated earth. I hope I shall be one of them. I should like to come back and build me a beautiful home in Kansas,—I mean in what was Kansas,—among the happy people and the familiar, transfigured spots where John and I worked for God so long together. That—with my dear Lord to see and speak with every day—would be 'Heaven our Home.'"

"There will be no *days,* then?"

"There will be succession of time. There may not be alternations of twenty-four hours dark or light, but 'I use with thee an earthly language,' as the wife said in that beautiful little 'Awakening,' of Therrmin's. Do you remember it? Do read it over, if you haven't read it lately.

"As to our coming back here, there is an echo to Peter's assertion, in the idea of a world under a curse, destroyed and regenerated,— the atonement of Christ reaching, with something more than poetic force, the very sands of the earth which he trod with bleeding feet to make himself its Saviour. That makes me feel—don't you see?— what a taint there is in sin. If dumb dust is to have such awful cleansing, what must be needed for you and me?

"How many pleasant talks we have had about these things, Mary! Well, it cannot be long, at the longest, before we know, even as we are known."

I looked at her smiling white face,—it is always very white now,— and something struck slowly through me, like a chill.

October 16, midnight.

There is no such thing as sleep at present. Writing is better than thinking.

Aunt Winifred went again to Worcester to-day. She said that she had to buy trimming for Faith's sack.

She went alone, as usual, and Faith and I kept each other company through the afternoon,—she on the floor with Mary Ann, I in the easy-chair with Macaulay. As the light began to fall level on the floor, I threw the book aside,—being at the end of a volume,—and, Mary Ann having exhausted her attractions, I surrendered unconditionally to the little maiden.

She took me up garret, and down cellar, on top of the wood-pile, and into the apple-trees; I fathomed the mysteries of Old Man's Castle and Still Palm; I was her grandmother, I was her baby, I was a rabbit, I was a chestnut horse, I was a watch-dog, I was a mild-tempered giant, I was a bear "warranted not to eat little girls," I was a roaring hippopotamus and a canary bird, I was Jeff Davis and I was Moses in the bulrushes, and of what I was, the time faileth me to tell.

It comes over me with a curious, mingled sense of the ludicrous

and the horrible, that I should have spent the afternoon like a baby
and almost as happily, laughing out with the child, past and future
forgotten, the tremendous risks of "I spy" absorbing all my present;
while what was happening was happening, and what was to come
was coming. Not an echo in the air, not a prophecy in the sunshine,
not a note of warning in the song of the robins that watched me
from the apple-boughs!

As the long, golden afternoon slid away, we came out by the front
gate to watch for the child's mother. I was tired, and, lying back on
the grass, gave Faith some pink and purple larkspurs, that she might
amuse herself in making a chain of them. The picture that she made
sitting there on the short, dying grass—the light which broke all
about her and over her at the first, creeping slowly down and away
to the west, her little fingers linking the rich, bright flowers tube into
tube, the dimple on her cheek and the love in her eyes—has photo-
graphed itself into my thinking.

How her voice rang out, when the wheels sounded at last, and the
carriage, somewhat slowly driven, stopped!

"Mamma, mamma! see what I've got for you, mamma!"

Auntie tried to step from the carriage, and called me: "Mary, can
you help me a little? I am—tired."

I went to her, and she leaned heavily on my arm, and we came up
the path.

"Such a pretty little chain, all for you, mamma," began Faith, and
stopped, struck by her mother's look.

"It has been a long ride, and I am in pain. I believe I will lie right
down on the parlor sofa. Mary, would you be kind enough to give
Faith her supper and put her to bed?"

Faith's lip grieved.

"Cousin Mary isn't *you,* mamma. I want to be kissed. You haven't
kissed me."

Her mother hesitated for a moment; then kissed her once, twice;
put both arms about her neck; and turned her face to the wall without a word.

"Mamma is tired, dear," I said; "come away."

She was lying quite still when I had done what was to be done for the child, and had come back. The room was nearly dark. I sat down on my cricket by her sofa.

"Shall Phoebe light the lamp?"

"Not just yet."

"Can't you drink a cup of tea if I bring it?"

"Not just yet."

"Did you find the sack-trimming?" I ventured, after a pause.

"I believe so,—yes."

She drew a little package from her pocket, held it a moment, then let it roll to the floor forgotten. When I picked it up, the soft, tissue-paper wrapper was wet and hot with tears.

"Mary?"

"Yes."

"I never thought of the little trimming till the last minute. I had another errand."

I waited.

"I thought at first I would not tell you just yet. But I suppose the time has come; it will be no more easy to put it off. I have been to Worcester all these times to see a doctor."

I bent my head in the dark, and listened for the rest.

"He has his reputation; they said he could help me if anybody could. He thought at first he could. But to-day—Mary, see here."

She walked feebly towards the window, where a faint, gray light struggled in, and opened the bosom of her dress . . .

There was silence between us for a long while after that; she went back to the sofa, and I took her hand and bowed my face over it, and so we sat.

The leave rustled out of doors. Faith, up stairs, was singing herself to sleep with a droning sound.

"He talked of risking an operation," she said, at length, "but de-cided to-day that it was quite useless. I suppose I must give up and be sick now; I am feeling the reaction from having kept up so long. He thinks I shall not suffer a very great deal. He thinks he can relieve me, and that it may be soon over."

"There is no chance?"

"No chance."

I took both of her hands, and cried out, I believe, as I did that first night when she spoke to me of Roy,—"Auntie, Auntie, Auntie!" and tried to think what I was doing, but only cried out the more.

"Why, Mary!" she said,—"why, Mary!" and again, as before, she passed her soft hand to and fro across my hair, till by and by I began to think, as I had thought before, that I could bear anything which God who loved us all—who *surely* loved us all—should send.

So then, after I had grown still, she began to tell me about it in her quiet voice, and the leaves rustled, and Faith had sung herself to sleep, and I listened wondering. For there was no pain in the quiet voice,—no pain, nor tone of fear. Indeed, it seemed to me that I detected, through its subdued sadness, a secret, suppressed buoyancy of satisfaction, with which something struggled.

"And you?" I asked, turning quickly upon her.

"I should thank God with all my heart, Mary, if it were not for Faith and you. But it *is* for Faith and you. That's all."

When I had locked the front door, and was creeping up here to my room, my foot crushed something, and a faint, wounded perfume came up. It was the little pink and purple chain.

﹛*16*﹜

October 17.

"The Lord God a'mighty help us! but His ways are past finding out. What with one thing and another thing, that child without a mother, and you with the crape not yet rusty for Mr. Roy'l, it doos seem to me as if His manner of treating folks beats all! But I tell you this, Miss Mary, my dear; you jest say your prayers reg'lar and *stick to Him,* and He'll pull you through, sure!"

This was what Phoebe said when I told her.

November 8.

To-night, for the first time, Auntie fairly gave up trying to put Faith to bed. She had insisted on it until now, crawling up by the banisters like a wounded thing. This time she tottered and sank upon the second step. She cried out, feebly: "I am afraid I must give it up to Cousin Mary. Faith!"—the child clung with both hands to her,— "Faith, Faith! Mother's little girl!"

It was the last dear care of motherhood yielded; the last link snapped. It seemed to be the very bitterness of parting.

I turned away, that they might bear it together, they two alone.

19th.

Yet I think that took away the sting.

The days are slipping away now very quietly, and—to her I am sure, and to me for her sake—very happily.

She suffers less than I had feared, and she lies upon the bed and smiles, and Faith comes in and plays about, and the cheery morning sunshine falls on everything, and when her strong hours come, we have long talks together, hand clasped in hand.

Such pleasant talks! We are quite brave to speak of anything, since we know that what is to be is best just so, and since we fear no parting. I tell her that Faith and I will soon learn to shut our eyes and think we see her, and try to make it *almost* the same, for she will never be very far away, will she? And then she shakes her head smiling, for it pleases her, and she kisses me softly. Then we dream of how it will all be, and how we shall love and try to please each other quite as much as now.

"It will be like going around a corner, don't you see?" she says. "You will know that I am there all the while, though hidden, and that if you call me I shall hear." Then we talk of Faith, and of how I shall comfort her; that I shall teach her this, and guard her from that, and how I shall talk with her about heaven and her mother. Sometimes Faith comes up and wants to know what we are saying, and lays poor Mary Ann, sawdust and all, upon the pillow, and wants "her toof-ache kissed away." So Auntie kisses away the dolly's "toof-ache"; and kisses the dolly's little mother, sometimes with a quiver on her lips, but more often with a smile in her eyes, and Faith runs back to play, and her laugh ripples out, and her mother listens—listens—

Sometimes, too, we talk of some of the people for whom she cares; of her husband's friends; of her scholars, or Dr. Bland, or Clo, or poor 'Bin Quirk, or of somebody down town whom she was planning to help this winter. Little Clo comes in as often as she is strong enough to see her, and sends over untold jellies and blanc-manges, which Faith and I have to eat. "But don't let the child know that," Auntie says.

But more often we talk of the life which she is so soon to begin; of her husband and Roy; of what she will try to say to Christ; how much dearer He has grown to her since she has lain here in pain at His bidding, and how He helps her, at morning and at eventide and in the night-watches.

We talk of the trees and the mountains and the lilies in the garden, on which the glory of the light that is not the light of the sun may shine; of the "little brooks" by which she longs to sit and sing to Faith; of the treasures of art which she may fancy to have about her; of the home in which her husband may be making ready for her coming, and wonder what he has there, and if he knows how near the time is now.

But I notice lately that she more often and more quickly wearies of these things; that she comes back, and comes back again to some loving thought—as loving as a child's—of Jesus Christ. He seems to be—as she once said she tried that He should be to Faith—her "*best* friend."

Sometimes, too, we wonder what it means to pass out of the body, and what one will be first conscious of.

"I used to have a very human, and by no means slight, dread of the physical pain of death," she said to-day; "but, for some reason or other, that is slowly leaving me. I imagine that the suffering of any fatal sickness is worse than the immediate process of dissolution. Then there is so much beyond it to occupy one's thoughts. One thing I have thought much about; it is that, whatever may be our first experience after leaving the body, it is not likely to be a *revolutionary* one. It is more in analogy with God's dealings that a quiet process, a gentle accustoming, should open our eyes on the light that would blind if it came in a flash. Perhaps we shall not see Him,—perhaps we could not bear it to see Him at once. It may be that the faces of familiar human friends will be the first to greet us; it may be that the touch of the human hand dearer than any but His own shall lead us, as we are able, behind the veil, till we are a little used to the glory and the wonder, and lead us so to Him.

"Be that as it may, and be heaven where it may, I am not afraid. With all my guessing and my studying and my dreaming over these things, I am only a child in the dark. 'Nevertheless, I am not afraid of the dark. God bless Mr. Robertson for saying that! I'm going to bless him when I see him. How pleasant it will be to see him, and some other friends whose faces I never saw in this world. David, for instance, or Paul, or Cowper, or President Lincoln, or Mrs. Browning. The only trouble is that *I* am nobody to them! However, I fancy that they will let me shake hands with them.

"No, I am quite willing to trust all these things to God.

'And what if much be still unknown?
    Thy Lord shall teach thee that,
When thou shalt stand before His throne,
    Or sit as Mary sat.'

I may find them very different from what I have supposed. I know that I shall find them infinitely *more* satisfying than I have supposed. As Schiller said of his philosophy, 'Perhaps I may be ashamed of my raw design, at sight of the true original. This may happen; I expect it; but then, it will be a more majestic, a more delightful surprise.'

"I believe nothing that God denies. I cannot overrate the beauty of his promise. So it surely can have done no harm for me to take the comfort of my fancying till I am there; and what a comfort it has been to me, God only knows. I could scarcely have borne some things without it.

"You are never afraid that anything proving a little different from what you expect might—"

"Might disappoint me? No; I have settled that in my heart with God. I do not *think* I shall be disappointed. The truth is, he has obviously not *opened* the gates which bar heaven from our sight, but he has as obviously not *shut* them; they stand ajar, with the Bible and reason in the way, to keep them from closing; surely we should look in as far as we can, and surely, if we look with reverence, our eyes will be holden, that we may not cheat ourselves with mirages. And, as the little Swedish girl said, the first time she saw the stars: 'O father, if the *wrong side* of heaven is so beautiful, what must the *right side* be?'"

January.

I write little now, for I am living too much. The days are stealing away and lessening one by one, and still Faith plays about the room, though very softly now, and still the cheery sunshine shimmers in, and still we talk with clasping hands, less often and more pleasantly. Morning and noon and evening come and go; the snow drifts down and the rain falls softly; clouds form and break and hurry past the windows; shadows melt and lights are shattered, and little rainbows are prisoned by the icicles that hang from the eaves.

I sit and watch them, and watch the sick-lamp flicker in the night, and watch the blue morning crawl over the hills; and the old words are stealing down my thought: *That is the substance, this the shadow; that the reality, this the dream.*

I watch her face upon the pillow; the happy secret on its lips; the smile within its eyes. It is nearly a year now since God sent the face to me. What it has done for me He knows; what the next year and all the years are to be without it, He knows, too.

It is slipping away,—slipping. And I—must—lose it.

Perhaps I should not have said what I said to-night; but being weak from watching, and seeing how glad she was to go, seeing how all the peace was for her, all the pain for us, I cried, "O Auntie, Auntie, why can't we go too? Why *can't* Faith and I go with you?"

But she answered me only, "Mary, He knows."

We will be brave again to-morrow. A little more sunshine in the room! A little more of Faith and the dolly!

The Sabbath.

She asked for the child at bedtime to-night, and I laid her down in her night-dress on her mother's arm. She kissed her, and said her prayers, and talked a bit about Mary Ann, and to-morrow, and her snow man. I sat over by the window in the dusk, and watched a little creamy cloud that was folding in the moon. Presently their voices grew low, and at last Faith's stopped altogether. Then I heard in fragments this:—

"Sleepy, dear? But you won't have many more talks with mamma. Keep awake just a minute, Faith, and hear—can you hear? Mamma will never, *never* forget her little girl; she won't go away very far; she will always love you. Will you remember as long as you live? She will always see you, though you can't see her, perhaps. Hush, my darling, *don't* cry! Isn't God naughty? No, God is good; God is always good. He won't take mamma a great way off. One more kiss? There! now you may go to sleep. One more! Come, Cousin Mary."

June 6.

It is a long time since I have written here. I did not want to open the book till I was sure that I could open it quietly, and could speak as she would like to have me speak, of what remains to be written.

But a very few words will tell it all.

It happened so naturally and so happily, she was so glad when the time came, and she made me so glad for her sake, that I cannot grieve. I say it from my honest heart, I cannot grieve. In the place out of which she has gone, she has left me peace. I think of something that Miss Procter said about the opening of that golden gate,

"round which the kneeling spirits wait.
The halo seems to linger round those kneeling closest to the door:
The joy that lightened from that place shines still upon the watch-
er's face."

I think more often of some things that she herself said in the very last of those pleasant talks, when, turning a leaf in her little Bible, she pointed out to me the words:—

"It is expedient for you that I go away; for, if I go not away, the Comforter will not come."

It was one spring-like night,—the twenty-ninth of March.

She had been in less pain, and had chatted and laughed more with us than for many a day. She begged that Faith might stay till dark, and might bring her Noah's ark and play down upon the foot of the bed where she could see her. I sat in the rocking-chair with my face to the window. We did not light the lamps.

The night came on slowly. Showery clouds flitted by, but there was a blaze of golden color behind them. It broke through and scattered them; it burned them and melted them; it shot great pink and pur-ple jets up to the zenith; it fell and lay in amber mist upon the hills. A soft wind swept by, and darted now and then into the glow, and shifted it about, color away from color, and back again.

"See, Faith!" she said softly; "put down the little camel a minute, and look!" and added after, but neither to the child nor to me, it seemed: "At eventide there shall be light." Phoebe knocked presently, and I went out to see what was wanted, and planned a little for Auntie's breakfast, and came back.

Faith, with her little ark, was still playing quietly upon the bed. I sat down again in my rocking-chair with my face to the window. Now and then the child's voice broke the silence, asking Where should she put the elephant, and was there room there for the yellow bird? and now and then her mother answered her, and so presently the skies had faded, and so the night came on.

I was thinking that it was Faith's bedtime, and that I had better light the lamp, when a few distinct, hurried words from the bed attracted my attention.

"Faith, I think you had better kiss mamma now, and get down."

There was a change in the voice. I was there in a moment, and lifted the child from the pillow, where she had crept. But she said, "Wait a minute, Mary; wait a minute,"—for Faith clung to her, with one hand upon her cheek, softly patting it.

I went over and stood by the window.

It was her mother herself who gently put the little fingers away at last.

"Mother's own little girl! Good night, my darling, my darling."

So I took the child away to Phoebe, and came back, and shut the door.

"I thought you might have some message for Roy," she said.

"Now?"

"Now, I think."

We had often talked of this, and she had promised to remember it, whatever it might be. So I told her— But I will not write what I told her.

I saw that she was playing weakly with her wedding-ring, which hung very loosely below its little worn guard.

"Take the little guard," she said, "and keep it for Faith; but bury the other with me: he put it on; nobody else must take it—"

The sentence dropped, unfinished.

I crept up on the bed beside her, for she seemed to wish it. I asked if I should light the lamp, but she shook her head. The room seemed light, she said, quite light. She wondered then if Faith were asleep, and if she would waken early in the morning.

After that I kissed her, and then we said nothing more, only presently she asked me to hold her hand.

It was quite dark when she turned her face at last towards the window.

"John" she said,—"why, John!"

❋

They came in, with heads uncovered and voices hushed, to see her, in the days while she was lying down stairs among the flowers.

Once when I thought that she was alone, I went in,—it was at twilight,—and turned, startled by a figure that was crouched sobbing on the floor.

"O, I want to go too, *I want* to go too!" it cried.

"She's ben there all day long," said Phoebe, wiping her eyes, "and she won't go home for a mouthful of victuals, poor creetur! but she jest sets there and cries and cries, an' there's no stoppin' of her!"

It was little Clo.

At another time, I was there with fresh flowers, when the door opened, creaking a little, and 'Bin Quirk came in on tiptoe, trying in vain to still the noise of his new boots. His eyes were red and wet, and he held out to me timidly a single white carnation.

"Could you put it somewhere, where it wouldn't do any harm? I walked way over to Worcester and back to get it. If you could jest hide it under the others out of sight, seems to me it would do me a sight of good to feel it was there, you know."

I motioned him to lay it himself between her fingers.

"O, I darsn't. I'm not fit, *I'm* not. She'd rether have you."

But I told him that I knew she would be as pleased that he should give it to her himself as she was when he gave her the China pinks on that distant summer day. So the great awkward fellow bent down, as simply as a child, as tenderly as a woman, and left the flower in its place.

"*She* liked 'em," he faltered; "maybe, if what she used to say is all so, she'll like 'em now. She liked 'em better than she did machines. I've just got my carpet-sweeper through; I was thinking how pleased she'd be; I wanted to tell her. If I should go to the good place,—if ever I do go, it will be just her doin's,—I'll tell her then, maybe, I—"

He forgot that anybody was there, and, sobbing, hid his face in his great hands.

So we are waiting for the morning when the gates shall open,— Faith and I. I, from my stiller watches, am not saddened by the music of her life. I feel sure that her mother wishes it to be a cheery life. I feel sure that she is showing me, who will have no motherhood by which to show myself, how to help her little girl.

And Roy,—ah, well, and Roy,—he knows. Our hour is not yet come. If the Master will that we should be about His Father's business, what is that to us?

Beyond the Gates

To my brother,
Stuart,
who passed beyond, August 29, 1883

It should be said, that, at the time of the departure
of him to whose memory this little book is consecrated,
the work was already in press; and that these pages owe
more to his criticism than can be acknowledged here.

—E.S.P.

Gloucester, Mass., September 1883

₹ *1* ₹

I had been ill for several weeks with what they called brain fever. The events which I am about to relate happened on the fifteenth day of my illness.

Before beginning to tell my story, it may not be out of place to say a few words about myself, in order to clarify to the imagination of the reader points which would otherwise involve numerous explanatory digressions, more than commonly misplaced in a tale dealing with the materials of this.

I am a woman forty years of age. My father was a clergyman; he had been many years dead. I was living, at the time I refer to, in my mother's house in a factory town in Massachusetts. The town need not be more particularly mentioned, nor genuine family names given, for obvious reasons. I was the oldest of four children; one of my sisters was married, one was at home with us, and there was a boy at college.

I was an unmarried, but not an unhappy woman. I had reached a very busy, and sometimes I hoped a not altogether valueless, middle age. I had used life and loved it. Beyond the idle impulse of a weary moment, which signifies no more than the reflex action of a mental muscle, and which I had been in the habit of rating accordingly, I had never wished to die. I was well, vigorous, and active. I was not of a dependent or a despondent temperament.

I am not writing an autobiography, and these things, not of importance in themselves, require only the briefest allusion. They will serve to explain the general cast of my life, which in turn may define the features of my story.

There are two kinds of solitary: he who is drawn by the inward, and he who chooses the outward life. To this latter class I had belonged. Circumstances, which it is not necessary to detail here, had thrust me into the one as a means of self-preservation from the other, while I was yet quite young.

I had been occupied more largely with the experiences of other people than with my own. I had been in the habit of being depended upon. It had been my great good fortune to be able to spend a part of my time among the sick, the miserable, and the poor. It had been, perhaps, my better chance to be obliged to balance the emotional perils of such occupations by those of a different character. My business was that of a school-teacher, but I had traveled somewhat; I had served as a nurse during the latter years of the war; in the Sanitary Commission; upon the Freedmen's Bureau; as an officer in a Woman's Prison, and had done a little work for the State Bureau of Labor among the factory operatives of our own town. I had therefore, it will be seen, been spared the deterioration of a monotonous existence. At the time I was taken ill I was managing a private school, rather large for the corps of assistants which I could command, and had overworked. I had been at home, thus employed, with my mother who needed me, for two years.

It may not be unsuitable, before proceeding with my narrative, to say that I had been a believer in the truths of the Christian religion; not, however, a devotee. I had not the ecstatic temperament, and was not known among my friends for any higher order of piety than that which is implied in trying to do one's duty for Christ's sake, and saying little about it for Him,—less than I wish I had sometimes. It was natural to me to speak in other ways than by words; that does not prove that it was best. I had read a little, like all thinking people with any intellectual margin to their lives, of the religious controversies of the day, and had not been without my share of pressure from the fashionable reluctance to believe. Possibly this had affected a temperament not too much inclined towards the supernatural, but it had never conquered my faith, which I think had grown to be dearer to me because I had not kept it without a fight for it. It certainly had become, for this reason, of greater practical value. It certainly had become, for this and every reason, the most valuable thing I had, or hoped to have. I believed in God and immortality, and in the history of Jesus Christ. I respected and practiced prayer, but chiefly decided what I ought to do next minute. I loved life and lived it. I neither feared death nor thought much about it.

When I had been ill a fortnight, it occurred to me that I was very sick, but not that I could possibly die. I suffered a good deal at first; after that much less. There was great misery for lack of sleep, and intolerable restlessness. The worst, however, was the continuity of care. Those who have borne heavy responsibilities for any length of time will understand me. The incessant burden pressed on: now a pupil had fallen into some disgraceful escapade; now the investments of my mother's, of which I had the charge, had failed on the dividends; then I had no remittance for the boy at college; then my sister, in a heart-breaking emergency, confided to me a peril against which I could not lift a finger; the Governor held me responsible for the typhoid among the prisoners; I added eternal columns of statistics for the Charity Boards, and found forever a mistake in each report; a dying soldier called to me in piercing tones for a cup of water; the black girl to whom I read the Gospel of John, drowned her baby; I ran six looms in the mill for the mother of six children till her seventh should be born; I staked the salvation of my soul upon answering the argument of Strauss to the satisfaction of an unbelieving friend, and lost my wager; I heard my classes in Logic, and was unable to repeat anything but the "Walrus and the Carpenter," for the "Barbara Celarent." Suddenly, one day, in the thick of this brain-battle, I slipped upon a pause, in which I distinctly heard a low voice say,

"But Thine eternal thoughts move on,
Thine undisturbed affairs."

It was my mother's voice. I perceived then that she sat at my bedside in the red easy-chair, repeating hymns, poor soul! in the hope of calming me.

I put out my hand and patted her arm, but it did not occur to me to speak till I saw that there were masses of pansies and some mignonette upon the table, and I asked who sent them, and she told me the school-girls had kept them fresh there every day since I was taken ill. I felt some pleasure that they should take the trouble to select the flowers I preferred. Then I asked her where the jelly came from, and the grapes, and about other trifles that I saw, such as accumulate in any sick-room. Then she gave me the names of different friends and neighbors who had been so good as to remember me. Chiefly I was touched by the sight of a straggly magenta geranium which I noticed growing in a pot by the window, and which a poor woman from the mills had brought the day before. I asked my mother if there were any letters, and she said, many, but that I must not hear them read; she spoke of some from the prison. The door-bell often rang softly, and I asked why it was muffled, and who called. Alice had come in, and said something in an undertone to mother about the Grand Army and resolutions and sympathy; and she used the names of different people I had almost forgotten, and this confused me. They stopped talking, and I became at once very ill again.

The next point which I recall is turning to see that the doctor was in the room. I was in great suffering, and he gave me a few spoonfuls of something which he said would secure sleep. I desired to ask him what it was, as I objected to narcotics, and preferred to bear whatever was before me with the eyes of my mind open, but as soon as I tried to speak I forgot what I wished to say.

I do not know how long it was before the truth approached me, but it was towards evening of the day, the fifteenth, as I say, of my illness, that I said aloud:

"Mother, Tom is in the room. Why has Tom come home?"

Tom was my little brother at college. He came towards the bed as I spoke. He had his hat in his hand, and he put it up before his eyes.

"Mother!" I repeated louder than before. *"Why have you sent for Tom?"*

But Mother did not answer me. She leaned over me. I saw her looking down. She had the look that she had when my father died; though I was so young when that happened, I had never forgotten my mother's look; and I had never seen it since, from that day until this hour.

"Mother! am I so sick as *that*? Mother!"

"Oh, my dear!" cried Mother. "Oh my dear, my dear!" . . .

So after that I understood. I was greatly startled that they should feel me to be dangerously ill; but I was not alarmed.

"It is nonsense," I said, after I had thought about it a little while. "Dr. Shadow was always a croaker. I have no idea of dying! I have nursed too many sicker people than I am. I don't *intend* to die! I am able to sit up now, if I want to. Let me try."

"I'll hold you," said Tom, softly enough. This pleased me. He lifted all the pillows, and held me straight out upon his mighty arms. Tom was a great athlete—took the prizes at the gymnasium. No weaker man could have supported me for fifteen minutes in the strained position by which he found that he could give me comfort and so gratify my whim. Tom held me a long time; I think it must have been an hour; but I began to suffer again, and could not judge of time. I wondered how that big boy got such infinite tenderness into those iron muscles. I felt a great respect for human flesh and bone and blood, and for the power and preciousness of the living human body. It seemed much more real to me, then, than the spirit. It seemed an absurdity that any one should suppose that I was in danger of being done with life. I said:—

"I'm going to live, Tom! Tell Mother I have no idea of dying. I prefer to live."

Tom nodded; he did not speak; I felt a hot dash of tears on my face, which surprised me; I had not seen Tom cry since he lost the foot-ball match when he was eleven years old.

They gave me something more out of the spoon, again, I think, at that moment, and I felt better. I said to Tom:—

"You see!" and bade them send Mother to lie down, and asked Alice to make her beef-tea, and to be sure and make it as we did in the army. I do not remember saying anything more after this. I certainly did not suffer any more. I felt quiet and assured. Nothing farther troubled me. The room became so still that I thought they must all have gone away, and left me with the nurse, and that she, finding me so well, had herself fallen asleep. This rested me—to feel that I was no longer causing them pain—more than anything could have done; and I began to think the best thing I could do would be to take a nap myself.

With this conviction quietly in mind I turned over, with my face towards the wall, to go to sleep. I grew calmer, and yet more calm, as I lay there. There was a cross of Swiss carving on the wall, hanging over a picture of my father. Leonardo's Christ—the one from the drawing for the Last Supper, that we all know—hung above both these. Owing to my position, I could not see the other pictures in the room, which was large, and filled with little things, the gifts of those who had been kind to me in a life of many busy years. Only these three objects—the cross, the Christ, and my father—came within range of my eyes as the power of sleep advanced. The room was darkened, as it had been since I became so ill, so that I was not sure whether it were night or day. The clock was striking. I think it struck two; and I perceived the odor of the mignonette. I think it was the last thing I noticed before going to sleep, and I remembered, as I did so, the theories which gave to the sense of smell greater significance than any of the rest; and remembered to have read that it was either the last or the first to give way in the dying. (I could not recall, in my confused condition, which.) I thought of this with pleased and idle interest; but did not associate the thought with the alarm felt by any friends about my condition.

I could have slept but a short time when I woke, feeling much easier. The cross, the Christ, and the picture of my father looked at me calmly from the wall on which the sick-lamp cast a steady, soft light. Then I remembered that it was night, of course, and felt chagrined that I could have been confused on this point.

The room seemed close to me, and I turned over to ask for more air.

As I did so, I saw some one sitting in the cushioned window-seat by the open window—the eastern window. No one had occupied this seat, on account of the draught and chill, since my illness. As I looked steadily, I saw that the person who sat there was my father.

His face was turned away, but his figure and the contour of his noble head were not to be mistaken. Although I was a mere girl when he died, I felt no hesitation about this. I knew at once, and beyond all doubt, that it was he. I experienced pleasure, but little, if any, surprise.

As I lay there looking at him, he turned and regarded me. His deep eyes glowed with a soft, calm light; but yet, I know not why, they expressed more love than I had ever seen in them before. He used to love us nervously and passionately. He had now the look of one whose whole nature is saturated with rest, and to whom the fitfulness, distrust, or distress of intense feeling acting upon a super-sensitive organization, were impossible. As he looked towards me, he smiled. He had one of the sweetest smiles that ever illuminated a mortal face.

"Why, Father!" I said aloud. He nodded encouragingly, but did not speak.

"Father?" I repeated, "Father, is this *you?*" He laughed a little, softly, putting up one hand and tossing his hair off from his forehead—an old way of his.

"What are you here for?" I asked again. "Did Mother send for *you,* too?"

When I had said this, I felt confused and troubled; for though I did not remember that he was dead—I mean I did not put the thought in any such form to myself, or use that word or any of its synonyms— yet I remembered that he had been absent from our family circle for a good while, and that if Mother had sent for him because I had a brain fever, it would have been for some reason not according to her habit.

"It is strange," I said. "It isn't like her. I don't understand the thing at all."

Now, as I continued to look at the corner of the room where my father was sitting, I saw that he had risen from the cushioned window-seat, and taken a step or two towards me. He stopped, however, and stood quite still, and looked at me most lovingly and longingly; and *then* it was that he held out his arms to me.

"Oh," cried I, "I wish I could come! But you don't know how sick I am. I have not walked a step for over two weeks."

He did not speak even yet, but still held out his arms with that look of unutterably restful love. I felt the elemental tie between parent and child draw me. It seemed to me as if I had reached the foundation of all human feeling; as if I had gone down—how shall I say it?— below the depths of all other love. I had always known I loved him, but not like that. I was greatly moved.

"But you don't understand me," I repeated with some agitation. "I *can't* walk." I thought it very strange that he did not, in consideration of my feebleness, come to me.

Then for the first time he spoke.

"Come," he said gently. His voice sounded quite natural; I only noticed that he spoke under his breath, as if not to awake the nurse, or any person who was in the room.

At this, I moved, and sat up on the edge of my bed; although I did so easily enough, I lost courage at that point. It seemed impossible to go farther. I felt a little chilly, and remembered, too, that I was not dressed. A warm white woolen wrapper of my own, and my slippers, were within reach, by the head of the bed; Alice wore them when she watched with me. I put these things on, and then paused, expecting to be overcome with exhaustion after the effort. I believe, rather, I felt a little stronger. As I put the clothes on, I noticed the magenta geranium across the room. These, I think, were the only things which attracted my attention.

"Come here to me," repeated Father; he spoke more decidedly, this time with a touch of authority. I remembered hearing him speak just so when Tom was learning to walk; he began by saying, "Come, sonny boy!" but when the baby played the coward, he said, "My son, come here!"

As if I had been a baby, I obeyed. I put my feet to the floor, and found that I stood strongly. I experienced a slight giddiness for a moment, but when this passed, my head felt clearer than before. I walked steadily out into the middle of the room. Each step was firmer than the other. As I advanced, he came to meet me. My heart throbbed. I thought I should have fallen, not from weakness, but from joy.

"Don't be afraid," he said encouragingly; "that is right. You are doing finely. Only a few steps more. There!"

It was done. I had crossed the distance which separated us, and my dear Father, after all those years, took me, as he used to do, into his arms . . .

He was the first to speak, and he said:-

"You poor little girl!—But it is over now."

"Yes, it is over now," I answered. I thought he referred to the difficult walk across the room, and to my long illness, now so happily at an end. He smiled and patted me on the cheek, but made no other answer.

"I must tell Mother that you are here," I said presently. I had not looked behind me or about me. Since the first sight of my father sitting in the window, I had not observed any other person, and could not have told who was in the room.

"Not yet," my father said. "We may not speak to her at present. I think we had better go."

I lifted my face to say, "Go where?" but my lips did not form the question. It was just as it used to be when he came from the study and held out his hand, and said "Come," and I went anywhere with him, neither asking, nor caring, so long as it was with him; and then he used to play or walk with me, and I forgot the whole world besides. I put my hand in his without a question, and we moved towards the door.

"I suppose *you* had better go this way," he said, with a slight hesitation, as we passed out and across the hall.

"Any way you like best," I said joyfully. He smiled, and still keeping my hand, led me down the stairs. As we went down, I heard the little Swiss clock, above in my room, strike the half hour after two.

I noticed everything in the hall as we descended; it was as if my vision, as well as the muscles of motion, grew stronger with each moment. I saw the stair-carpeting with its faded Brussels pattern, once rich, and remembered counting the red roses on it the night I went up with the fever on me; reeling and half delirious, wondering how I could possibly afford to be sick. I saw the hat-tree with Tom's coat, and Alice's blue Shetland shawl across the old hair-cloth sofa. As we opened the door, I saw the muffled bell. I stood for a moment upon the threshold of my old home, not afraid but perplexed.

My father seemed to understand my thoughts perfectly, though I had not spoken, and he paused for my reluctant mood. I thought of all the years I has spent there. I thought of my childhood and girlhood; of the tempestuous periods of life which that quiet roof had hidden; of the calms upon which it had brooded. I thought of sorrows that I had forgotten, and those which I had prayed in vain to forget. I thought of temptations and of mistakes and of sins, from which I had fled back asking these four walls to shelter me. I thought of the comfort and blessedness that I had never failed to find in the old house. I shrank from leaving it. It seemed like leaving my body.

When the door had been opened, the night air rushed in. I could see the stars, and knew, rather than felt, that it was cold. As we stood waiting, an icicle dropped from the eaves, and fell, breaking into a dozen diamond flashes at our feet. Beyond, it was dark.

"It seems to me a great exposure," I said reluctantly, "to be taken out into a winter night,—at such an hour, too! I have been so very sick."

"Are you cold?" asked my father gently. After some thought I said:—

"No, sir."

For I was not cold. For the first time I wondered why.

"Are you tired?"

No, I was not tired.

"Are you afraid?"

"A little, I think, sir."

"Would you like to go back, Molly, and rest awhile?"

"If you please, Papa."

The old baby-word came instinctively in answer to the baby-name. He led me like a child, and like a child I submitted. It was like him to be so thoughtful of my weakness. My dear father was always one of those rare men who think of little things largely, and so bring, especially into the lives of women, the daily comfort which makes the infinite preciousness of life.

We went into the parlor and sat down. It was warm there and pleasant. The furnace was well on, and embers still in the grate. The lamps were not lighted, yet the room was not dark. I enjoyed being down there again after all those weeks up-stairs, and was happy in looking at the familiar things, the afghan on the sofa, and the magazines on the table, uncut because of my illness; Mother's work-basket, and Alice's music folded away.

"It was always a dear old room," said Father, seating himself in his own chair, which we had kept for twenty years in its old place. He put his head back, and gazed peacefully about.

When I felt rested, and better, I asked him if we should start now.

"Just as you please," he said quietly. "There is no hurry. We are never hurried."

"If we have anything to do," I said, "I had rather do it now I think."

"Very well," said Father "that is like you." He rose and held out his hand again. I took it once more, and once more we went out to the threshold of our old home. This time I felt more confidence, but when the night air swept in, I could not help shrinking a little in spite of myself, and showing the agitation which overtook me.

"Father!" I cried, "Father! *where* are we going?"

My father turned at this, and looked at me solemnly. His face seemed to shine and glow. He looked from what I felt was a great height. He said:—

"Are you really afraid, Mary, to go *any*where with me?"

"No, no!" I protested in a passion of regret and trust, "my dear father! I would go anywhere in earth or Heaven with you!"

"Then come," he said softly.

I clasped both hands, interlocking them though his arm, and we shut the door and went down the steps together and out into the winter dawn.

2

It was neither dark nor day; and as we stepped into the village streets the confused light trembled about us delicately. The stars were still shining. Snow was on the ground; and I think it had freshly fallen in the night, for I noticed that the way before us lay quite white and untrodden. I looked back over my shoulders as my father closed the gate, which he did without noise. I meant to take a gaze at the old house, from which, with a thrill at the heart, I began to feel that I was parting under strange and solemn conditions. But when I glanced up the path which we had taken, my attention was directed altogether from the house, and from the slight sadness of the thought I had about it.

The circumstances which arrested me was this. Neither my father's foot nor mine had left any prints upon the walk. From the front door to the street, the fine fair snow lay unbroken; it stirred, and rose in restless flakes like winged creatures under the gentle wind, flew a little way, and fell again, covering the surface of the long white path with a foam so light, it seemed as if thought itself could not have passed upon it without impression. I can hardly say why I did not call my father's attention to this fact.

As we walked down the road the dawn began to deepen. The stars paled slowly. The intense blue-black and purple of the night sky gave way to the warm grays that precede sunrise in our climate. I saw that the gold and the rose were coming. It promised to be a mild morning, warmer than for several days. The deadly chill was out of the air. The snow yielded on the outlines of the drifts, and relaxed as one looked at it, as snow does before melting, and the icicles had an air of expectation, as if they hastened to surrender to the annunciation of a warm and impatient winter's day.

"It's going to thaw," I said aloud.

"It seems so to you," replied my father, vaguely.

"But at least it is very pleasant," I insisted.

"I'm glad you find it so," he said; "I should have been disappointed if it had struck you as cold, or—gloomy—in any way."

It was still so early that all the village was asleep. The blinds and curtains of the houses were drawn and the doors yet locked. None of our neighbors were astir, nor were there any signs of traffic yet in the little shops. The great factory-bell, which woke the operatives at half-past four, had rung, but this was the only evidence as yet of human life or motion. It did not occur to me, till afterwards, to wonder at the inconsistency between the hour struck by my own Swiss clock and the factory time.

I was more interested in another matter which just then presented itself to me.

The village, as I say, was still asleep. Once I heard the distant hoofs of a horse sent clattering after the doctor, and ridden by a messenger from a house in mortal need.

Up to this, we two had seemed to be the only watchers in all the world.

Now, as I turned to see if I could discover whose horse it was and so who was in emergency, I observed suddenly that the sidewalk was full of people. I say full of people; I mean that there was a group behind us; a few, also, before us; some, too, were crossing the street. They conversed together standing at the corners, or walked in twos, as father and I were doing; or strolled, some of them alone. Some of them seemed to have immediate business and to be in haste; others sauntered as he who has no occupation. Some talked and gesticulated earnestly, or laughed loudly. Others went with a thoughtful manner, speaking not at all.

As I watched them I began to recognize here and there, a man, or a woman;—there were more men than women among them, and there were no children.

A few of these people, I soon saw, were old neighbors of ours; some I had known when I was a child, and had forgotten till this moment. Several of them bowed to us as we passed along. One man stopped and waited for us, and spoke to Father, who shook hands with him; intimating, however, pleasantly enough, that he was in haste, and must be excused for passing on.

"Yes, yes, I see," said the man with a glance at me. I then distinctly saw this person's face, and knew him beyond a doubt, for an old neighbor, a certain Mr. Snarl, a miserly, sanctimonious man—I never liked him.

"Father!" I stopped short. "Father, that man is dead. He has been dead for twenty years!"

Now, at this, I began to tremble; yet not from fear, I think; from amazement, rather, and the great confusion which I felt.

"And there"—I pointed to a pale young man who had been thrown from his carriage (it was said because he was in no condition to drive)—"there is Bobby Bend. He died last winter."

"Well," said Father quietly, "and what then?"

"And over there—why, certainly that is Mrs. Mersey!"

I had known Mrs. Mersey for a lovely woman. She died of a fever contracted in the care of a poor, neglected creature. I saw her at this moment across and far down the street, coming from a house where there was trouble. She came with a swift, elastic motion, unlike that of any of the others who were about us; the difference was marked, and yet one which I should have found it at that time impossible to describe. Perhaps I might have said that she hovered above rather than touched the earth; but this would not have defined the distinction. As I looked after her she disappeared; in what direction I could not tell.

"So they *are* dead people," I said, with a sort of triumph; almost as if I had dared my father to deny it. He smiled.

"Father, I begin to be perplexed. I have heard of these hallucinations, of course, and read the authenticated stories, but I never supposed I could be a subject of such illusions. It must be because I have been so sick."

"Partly because you have been so sick—yes," said Father drawing down the corners of his mouth, in that way he had when he was amused. I went on to tell him that it seemed natural to see him, but that I was surprised to meet those others who had left us, and that I did not find it altogether agreeable.

"Are you afraid?" he asked me, as he had before. No, I could not say that I was afraid.

"Then hasten on," he said in a different tone, "our business is not with them, at present. See! we have already left them behind."

And, indeed, when I glanced back, I saw that we had. We, too, were now traveling alone together, and at a much faster speed, towards the outskirts of the town. We were moving eastward. Before us the splendid day was coming up. The sky was unfolding, shade above shade, paler at the edge, and glowing at the heart, like the petals of a great rose.

The snow was melting on the moors towards which we bent our steps; the water stood here and there in pools, and glistened. A little winter bird—some chickadee or wood-pecker—was bathing in one of these pools; his tiny brown body glowed in the brightness, flashing to and fro. He chirped and twittered and seemed bursting with joy. As we approached the moors, the stalks of the sumachs, the mulberries, the golden-rod, and asters, all the wayside weeds and the brown things that we never know and never love till winter, rose beautiful from the snow; the icicles melted and dripped from them; the dead-gold-colored leaves of the low oaks rustled; at a distance we heard the sweet sough from a grove of pines; behind us the morning bells of the village broke into bubbles of cheerful sound. As we walked on together I felt myself become stronger at every step; my heart grew light.

"It is a good world," I cried, "it is a good world!"

"So it is," said my father heartily, "and yet—my dear daughter"— He hesitated; so long that I looked into his face earnestly, and then I saw that a strange gravity had settled upon it. It was not like any look that I had ever seen there before.

"I have better things to show you," he said gently.

"I do not understand you, sir."

"We have only begun our journey, Mary; and—if you do not understand—but I thought you would have done so by this time— I wonder if she *is* going to be frightened after all!"

We were now well out upon the moors, alone together, on the side of the hill. The town looked far behind us and insignificant. The earth dwindled and the sky grew, as we looked from one to the other. It seemed to me that I had never before noticed how small a portion of our range of vision is filled by the surface of earth, and what occupies it; and how immense the proportion of the heavens. As we stood there, it seemed to overwhelm us.

"Rise," said my father in a voice of solemn authority, "rise quickly!"

I struggled at his words, for he seemed to slip from me, and I feared to lose him. I struggled and struck out into the air; I felt a wild excitement, like one plunged into a deep sea, and desperately swimming, as animals do, and a few men, from blind instinct, having never learned. My father spoke encouragingly, and with tenderness. He never once let go my hand. I felt myself, beyond all doubt, soaring— slowly and weakly—but surely ascending above the solid ground.

"See! there is nothing to fear," he said from time to time. I did not answer. My heart beat fast. I exerted all my strength and took a stronger stroke. I felt that I gained upon myself. I closed my eyes, looking neither above nor below.

Suddenly, as gently as the opening of a water lily, and yet as swiftly as the cleaving of the lightning, there came to me a thought which made my brain whirl, and I cried aloud:

"Father, *am I* DEAD?" My hands slipped—I grew dizzy—wavered—and fluttered. I was sure that I should fall. At that instant I was caught with the iron of tenderness and held, like a very young child, in my father's arms. He said nothing, only patted me on the cheek, as we ascended, he seeing, and I blind; he strength, and I weakness; he who knew all, and I who knew nothing, silently with the rising sun athwart the rose-lit air.

I was awed, more than there are words to say; but I felt no more fear than I used to do when he carried me on his shoulder up the garden walk, after it grew dark, when I was tired out with play.

¿3¿

I use the words "ascension" and "arising" in the superficial sense of earthly imagery. Of course, carefully speaking, there can be no up or down to the motion of beings detached from a revolving globe, and set adrift in space. I thought of this in the first moment, with the keenness which distinguishes between knowledge and experience. I knew when our journey came to an end, by the gradual cessation of our rapid motion; but at first I did not incline to investigate beyond this fact. Whether I was only tired, or giddy, or whether a little of what we used to call faintness overcame me, I can hardly say. If this were so, it was rather a spiritual than a physical disability; it was a faintness of the soul. Now I found this more energetic than the bodily sensations I had known. I scarcely sought to wrestle against it, but lay quite still, where we had come to a halt.

I wish to say here, that if you ask me where this was, I must answer that I do not know. I must say distinctly that, though after the act of dying I departed from the surface of the earth, and reached the confines of a different locality, I cannot yet instruct another *where* this place may be.

My impression that it was not a vast distance (measured, I mean, by an astronomical scale) from our globe, is a strong one, which, however, I cannot satisfactorily defend. There seemed to be flowers about me; I wondered what they were, but lay with my face hidden in my arm, not caring yet to look about. I thought of that old-fashioned allegory called "The Distant Hills," where the good girl, when she died, sank upon a bed of violets; but the bad girl slipped upon rolling stones beneath a tottering ruin. This trifling memory occupied me for some moments; yet it had so great significance to me, that I recall it, even now, with pungent gratitude.

"I shall remember what I have read." This was my first thought in the new state to which I had come. Minna was the name of the girl in the allegory. The illustrations were very poor, but had that uncanny fascination which haunts allegorical pictures—often the more powerful because of their rudeness.

As I lay there, still not caring, or even not daring to look up, the fact that I was crushing flowers beneath me became more apparent; a delicate perfume arose and surrounded me; it was like and yet unlike any that I had ever known; its familiarity entranced, its novelty allured me. Suddenly I perceived what it was—

"Mignonette!"

I laughed at my own dullness in detecting it, and could not help wondering whether it were accident of design that had given me for my first experience in the new life, the gratification of a little personal taste like this. For a few moments I yielded to the pure and exquisite perfume, which stole into my whole nature, or it seemed to me so then. Afterwards I learned how little I knew of my "whole nature" at that time.

Presently I took courage, and lifted my head. I hardly know what I expected to see. Visions of the Golden City in the Apocalypse had flitted before me. I thought of the River of Death in the "Pilgrim's Progress," of the last scene in the "Voyage of Life," of Theremin's "Awakening," of several famous books and pictures which I have read or seen, describing what we call Heaven. These works of the human imagination—stored away perhaps in the frontal lobes of the brain, as scientists used to tell us—had influenced my anticipations more than I could have believed possible till that moment.

I was indeed in a beautiful place; but it did not look, in any respect, as I had expected. No; I think not in any respect. Many things which happened to me later, I can describe more vividly than I can this first impression. In one way it was a complex, in another, a marvelously simple one. Chiefly, I think I had a consciousness of safety—infinite safety. All my soul drew a long breath—"Nothing more can happen to me!" Yet, at the same time, I felt that I was at the outset of all experience. It was as if my heart cried aloud, "Where shall I begin?"

I looked about and abroad. My father stood at a little distance from me, conversing with some friends. I did not know them. They had great brightness and beauty of appearance. So, also, had he. He had altered perceptibly since he met me in the lower world, and seemed to glow and become absorbent of light from some source yet unseen. This struck me forcibly in all the people whom I saw—there were many of them, going to and fro busily—that they were receptive and reflecting beings. They differed greatly in the degree in which they gave this impression; but all gave it. Some were quite pale, though pure in color; others glowed and shone. Yet when I say color, I use an earthly word, which does not express my meaning. It was more the atmosphere of penumbra, in which each moved, that I refer to, perhaps, than the tint of their bodies. They had bodies, very like such as I was used to. I saw that I myself was not, or so it appeared, greatly changed. I had form and dress, and I moved at will, and experienced sensations of pleasure and, above all, of magnificent health. For a while I was absorbed, without investigating details, in the mere sense of physical ease and power. I did not wish to speak, or to be spoken to, nor even to stir and exercise my splendid strength. It was more than enough to feel it, after all those weeks of pain. I lay back again upon the mignonette; as I did so, I noticed that the flowers where my form had pressed them were not bruised; they had sprung erect again; they had not wilted, nor even hung their heads as if they were hurt—I lay back upon, and deep within, the mignonette, and, drowned in the delicate odor, gazed about me.

Yes; I was truly in a wonderful place. It was in the country (as we should say below), though I saw signs of large centres of life, outlines of distant architecture far away. There were hills, and vast distances, and vistas of hill tints in the atmosphere. There were forests of great depth. There was an expanse of shining water. There were fields of fine extent and color, undulating like green seas. The sun was high—if it were the sun. At least there was great brilliance about me. Flowers must have been abundant, for the air was live with perfumes.

When I have said this, I seem to have said little or nothing. Certain it is that these first impressions came to me in broad masses, like the sweep of a large brush or blender upon canvas. Of details I received few, for a long time. I was overcome with a sense of Nature—freedom—health—beauty, as if—how shall I say it?—as if for the first time I understood what generic terms meant; as if I had entered into the secret of all abstract glory; as if what we had known as philosophical or as poetical phrases were now become attainable facts, each possessing that individual existence in which dreamers upon earth dare to believe, and of which no doubter can be taught.

I am afraid I do not express this with anything like the simplicity with which I felt it; and to describe it with anything resembling the power would be impossible.

I felt my smallness and ignorance in view of the wonders which lay before me. "I shall have time enough to study them," I thought, but the thought itself thrilled me throughout, and proved far more of an excitant than a sedative. I rose slowly, and stood trembling among the mignonette. I shielded my eyes with my hand, not from any glare or dazzle or strain, but only from the presence and the pressure of beauty, and so stood looking off. As I did so, certain words came to mind with the haunting voice of a broken quotation:

"Neither have entered into the heart of man"—

"The things which God hath prepared"—

It was a relief to me to see my father coming towards me at that moment, for I had, perhaps, undergone as much keen emotion as one well bears, compressed into a short space of time. He met me smiling.

"And how is it, Mary?"

"My first Bible verse has just occurred to me, Father—the first religious thought I've had in Heaven yet!" I tried to speak lightly, feeling too deeply for endurance. I repeated the words to him, for he asked me what they were which had come to me.

"That is a pleasant experience," he said quietly. "It differs with us all. I have seen people enter in a transport of haste to see the Lord Himself—noticing nothing, forgetting everything. I have seen others come in a transport of terror—so afraid they were of Him."

"And I had scarcely thought about seeing Him till now!" I felt ashamed of this. But my father comforted me by a look.

"Each comes to his own by his own," he said. "The nature is never forced. He expects nothing of us but to be natural."

This seemed to me a deep saying; and the more I thought of it the deeper it seemed. I said so as we walked, separate still from the others, through the beautiful weather. The change from a New England winter to the climate in which I found myself was, in itself, not the least of the great effects and delights which I experienced that first day.

If nothing were expected of us but to be natural, it was the more necessary that it should be natural to be right.

I felt the full force of this conviction as it had never been possible to feel it in the other state of being, where I was under restraint. The meaning of *liberty* broke upon me like a sunburst. Freedom was in and of itself the highest law. Had I thought that death was to mean release from personal obedience? Lo, death itself was but the elevation of moral claims, from lower to higher. I perceived how all demands of the larger upon the lesser self must be increased in the condition to which I had arrived. I felt overpowered for the moment with the intensity of these claims. It seemed to me that I had never really known before, what obligation meant. Conduct was now the least of difficulties. For impulse, which lay behind conduct, for all force which wrought out fact in me, I had become accountable.

"As nearly as I can make it out, Father," I said, "henceforth I shall be responsible for my nature."

"Something like that; not altogether."

"The force of circumstance and heredity,"—I began, using the old earthly *patois.* "Of course I'm not to be called to account for what I start with here, any more than I was for what I started with there. That would be neither science nor philosophy."

"We are neither unscientific nor unphilosophical, you will find," said my father, patiently.

"I am very dull, sir. Be patient with me. What I am trying to say, I believe, is that I shall feel the deepest mortification if I do not find it natural to do right. This feeling is so keen, that to be wrong must be the most unnatural thing in the world. There is certainly a great difference from what it used to be; I cannot explain it. Already I am ashamed of the smallness of my thoughts when I first looked about in this place. Already I cannot understand why I did not spring like a fountain to the Highest, to the Best. But then, Father, I never was a devotee, you know."

When I had uttered these words I felt a recoil from myself, and sense of discord. I was making excuses for myself. That used to be a fault of the past life. One did not do it here. It was as if I had committed some grave social indecorum. I felt myself blushing. My father noticed my embarrassment, and called my attention to a brook by which we were walking, beginning to talk of its peculiar translucence and rhythm, and other little novelties, thus kindly diverting me from my distress, and teaching me how we were spared everything we could be in heaven, even in trifles like this. I was not so

much as permitted to bear the edge of my regret, without the velvet of tenderness interposing to blunt the smart. It used to be thought
among us below that one must be allowed to suffer from error, to
learn. It seemed to be found here, that one learned by being saved
from suffering. I wondered how it would be in the case of a really
grave wrong which I might be so miserable as to commit; and if I
should ever be so unfortunate as to discover by personal experience.

This train of thought went on while I was examining the brook.
It had brilliant colors in the shallows, where certain strange agates
formed pebbles of great beauty. There were also shells. A brook with
shells enchanted me. I gathered some of them; they had opaline tints,
and some were transparent as spun glass; they glittered in the hand,
and did not dull when out of the water, like the shells we were used
to. The shadows of strange trees hung across the tiny brown current,
and unfamiliar birds flashed like tossed jewels overhead, through the
branches and against the wonderful color of the sky. The birds were
singing. One among them had a marvelous note. I listened to it for
some time before I discovered that this bird was singing a Te Deum.
How I knew that it was a Te Deum I cannot say. The others were
more like earthly birds, except for the thrilling sweetness of their
notes—and I could not see this one, for she seemed to be hidden
from sight upon her nest. I observed that the bird upon the nest sang
here as well as that upon the bough; and that I understood her: *"Te
Deum laudamus—laudamus"* as distinctly as if I had been listening to
a human voice.

When I had comprehended this, and stood entranced to listen, I
began to catch the same melody in the murmur of the water, and
perceived, to my astonishment, that the two, the brook and the bird,
carried parts of the harmony of a solemn and majestic mass. Apparently these were but portions of the whole, but all which it was
permitted me to hear. My father explained to me that it was not every
natural beauty which had the power to join in such surpassing chorals; these were selected, for reasons which he did not attempt to
specify. I surmised that they were some of the simplest of the won-

ders of this mythical world, which were entrusted to new-comers, as being first within the range of their capacities. I was enraptured with what I heard. The light throbbed about me. The sweet harmony rang on. I bathed my face in the musical water—it was as if I absorbed the sound at the pores of my skin. Dimly I received a hint of the possible existence of a sense or senses of which I had never heard.

What wonders were to come! What knowledge, what marvel, what stimulation and satisfaction! And I had but just begun! I was overwhelmed with this thought, and looked about; I knew not which way to turn; I had not what to say. Where was the first step? What was the next delight? The fire of discovery kindled in my veins. Let us hasten, that we may investigate Heaven!

"Shall we go on?" asked Father, regarding me earnestly.

"Yes, yes!" I cried, "let us go on. Let us see more—learn all. What a world have I come to! Let us begin at the beginning, and go to the end of it! Come quickly!"

I caught his hand, and we started on my eager mood. I felt almost a superabundance of vitality, and sprang along; there was everlasting health within my bounding arteries; there was eternal vigor in my firm muscle and sinews. How shall I express, to one who has never experienced it, the consciousness of life that can never die?

I could have leaped, flown, or danced like a child. I knew not how to walk sedately, like others whom I saw about us, who looked at me smiling, as older people look at the young on earth. "I, too, have felt thus—and thus." I wanted to exercise the power of my arms and limbs. I longed to test the triumphant poise of my nerve. My brain grew clearer and clearer, while for the gladness in my heart there is not any earthly word. As I bounded on, I looked more curiously at the construction of the body in which I found myself. It was, and yet it was not, like that which I had worn on earth. I seemed to have slipped out of one garment into another. Perhaps it was nearer the truth to say that it was like casting off an outer for an inner dress. There were nervous and arterial and other systems, it seemed, to which I had been accustomed. I cannot explain wherein they differed, as they surely did, and did enormously, from their representatives below. If I say that I felt as if I had got into the *soul of a body,* shall I be understood? It was as if I had been encased, one body within the other, to use a small earthly comparison, like the ivory figures which curious Chinese carvers cut within temple windows. I was constantly surprised at this. I do not know what I had expected, but assuredly nothing like the fact. Vague visions of gaseous or meteoric angelic forms have their place in the imaginations of most of us below; we picture our future selves as a kind of nebulosity. When I felt the spiritual flesh, when I used the strange muscle, when I heard the new heart-beat of my heavenly identity, I remembered certain words, with a sting of mortification that I had known them all my life, and paid so cool a heed to them: "There is a terrestrial body, and there is a celestial body." The glory of the terrestrial was one. Behold, the glory of the celestial was another. St. Paul had set this tremendous assertion revolving in the sky of the human mind, like a star which we had not brought into our astronomy.

It was not a hint or a hope that he gave; it was the affirmation of a man who presumed to know. In common with most of his readers, I had received his statement with a poor incredulity or cold disregard. Nothing in the whole range of what we used to call the Bible, had been more explicit than those words; neither metaphor, nor allegory, nor parable befogged them; they were as clear cut as the dictum of Descartes. I recalled them with confusion, as I bounded over the elastic and wondrously-tinted grass.

Never before, at least, had I known what the color of green should be; resembling, while differing from that called by the name on earth—a development of a color, a blossom from a bud, a marvel from a commonplace. Thus the sweet and common clothing which God had given to our familiar earth, transfigured, wrapped again the hills and fields of Heaven. And oh, what else? what next? I turned to my father to ask him in which direction we were going; at this moment an arrest of the whole current of feeling checked me like a great dam.

Up to this point I had gone dizzily on; I had experienced the thousand diversions of a traveler in a foreign land; and, like such a traveler, I had become oblivious of that which I had left. The terrible incapacity of the human mind to retain more than one class of strong impressions at once, was temporarily increased by the strain of this, the greatest of all human experiences. The new had expelled the old. In an intense revulsion of feeling, too strong for expression, I turned my back on the beautiful landscape. All Heaven was before me, but dear, daily love was behind.

"Father," I said, choking, "I never forgot them before in all my life. Take me home! Let me go at once. I am not fit to be alive if Heaven itself can lead me to neglect my mother."

4

In my distress I turned and would have fled, which way I knew not. I was swept up like a weed on a surge of self-reproach and longing. What was eternal life if she had found out that I was dead? What were the splendors of Paradise, if she missed me? It was made evident to me that my father was gratified at the turn my impulses had taken, but he intimated that it might not be possible to follow them, and that this was a matter which must be investigated before acting. This surprised me, and I inquired of him eagerly—yet, I think not passionately, not angrily, as I should once have done at the thwarting of such a wish as that—what he meant by the doubt he raised.

"It is not always permitted," he said gravely. "We cannot return when we would. We go upon these errands when it is Willed. I will go and learn what the Will may be for you touching this matter. Stay here and wait for me."

Before I could speak, he had departed swiftly, with the great and glad motion of those who go upon sure business in this happy place; as if he himself, at least, obeyed unseen directions, and obeyed them with his whole being. To me, so lately from a lower life, and still so choked with its errors, this loving obedience of the soul to a great central Force which I felt on every hand, but comprehended not, as yet, affected me like the discovery of a truth in science. It was as if I had found a new law of gravitation, to be mastered only by infinite attention. I fell to thinking more quietly after my father had left me alone. There came a subsidence to my tempestuous impulse, which astonished myself. I felt myself drawn and shaped, even like a wave by the tide, by something mightier far than my own wish. But there was this about the state of feeling into which I had come: that which controlled me was not only greater, it was dearer than my desire. Already a calmness conquered my storm. Already my heart awaited, without outburst or out-thrust, the expression of that other desire which should decide my fate in this most precious matter. All the old rebellion was gone, even as the protest of a woman goes on earth before the progress of a mighty love. I no longer argued and explained. I did not require or insist. Was it possible that I did not even doubt? The mysterious, celestial law of gravitation grappled me. I could no more presume to understand it than I could withstand it.

I had not been what is called a submissive person. All my life, obedience had torn me in twain. Below, it had cost me all I had to give, to cultivate what believers called trust in God.

I had indeed tried, in a desperate and faulty fashion, but I had often been bitterly ashamed at the best result which I could achieve, feeling that I scarcely deserved to count myself among His children, or to call myself by the Name which represented the absolute obedience of the strongest nature that human history had known. Always, under all, I had doubted whether I accepted God's will because I wanted to, so much as because I had to. This fear had given me much pain, but being of an active temperament, far, perhaps too far, removed from mysticism, I had gone on to the next fight, or the next duty, without settling my difficulties; and so like others of my sort, battled along through life, as best or as worst I might. I had always hurried more than I had grown. To be sure, I was not altogether to blame for this, since circumstances had driven me fast, and I had yielded to them not always for my own sake; but clearly, it may be as much of a misfortune to be too busy, as to be idle; and one whose subtlest effects are latest perceived. I could now understand it to be reasonable, that if I had taken more time on earth to cultivate myself for the conditions of Heaven, I might have had a different experience at the outset of this life, in which one was never in a hurry.

My father returned from his somewhat protracted absence, while I was thinking of these things thus quietly. My calmer mood went out to meet his face, from which I saw at once what was the result of his errand, and so a gentle process prepared me for my disappointment when he said that it was not Willed that I should go to her at this immediate time. He advised me to rest awhile before taking the journey, and to seek this rest at once. No reasons were given for this command; yet strangely, I felt it to be the most reasonable thing in the world.

No; blessedly no! I did not argue, or protest, I did not dash out my wild wish, I did not ask or answer anything—how wonderful!

Had I needed proof any longer that I was dead and in Heaven, this marvelous adjustment of my will to that other would in itself have told me what and where I was.

I cannot say that this process took place without effort. I found a certain magnificent effort in it, like that involved in the free use of my muscles; but it took place without pain. I did indeed ask,—

"Will it be long?"

"Not long."

"That is kind in Him!" I remember saying, as we moved away. For now, I found that I thought first rather of what He gave than of what He denied. It seemed to me that I had acquired a new instinct. My being was larger by the acquisition of a fresh power. I felt a little as I used to do below, when I had conquered a new language.

I had met, and by his loving mercy I had mastered, my first trial in the eternal life. This was to be remembered. It was like the shifting of a plate upon a camera.

More wearied than I had thought by the effort, I was glad to sink down beneath the trees in a nook my father showed me, and yield to the drowsiness that stole upon me after the great excitement of the day. It was not yet dark, but I was indeed tired. A singular subsidence, not like our twilight, but still reminding one of it, had fallen upon the vivid color of the air. No one was passing; the spot was secluded; my father bade me farewell for the present, saying that he should return again; and I was left alone.

The grass was softer than eider of the lower world; and lighter than snow-flakes, the leaves that fell from low-hanging boughs about me. Distantly, I heard moving water; and more near, sleepy birds. More distant yet, I caught, and lost, and caught again, fragments of orchestral music. I felt infinite security. I had the blessedness of weariness that knew it could not miss of sleep. Dreams stole upon me with motion and touch so exquisite that I thought: "Sleep itself is a new joy; what we had below was only a hint of the real thing," as I sank into deep and deeper rest.

Do not think that I forgot my love and longing to be elsewhere. I think the wish to see her and to comfort her grew clearer every moment. But stronger still, like a comrade marching beside it, I felt the pacing of that great desire which had become dearer than my own.

⸨ 5 ⸩

When I waked, I was still alone. There seemed to have been showers, for the leaves and grass about me were wet; yet I felt no chill or dampness, or any kind of injury from this fact. Rather I had a certain refreshment, as if my sleeping senses had drunk of the peace and power of the dew that flashed far and near about me. The intense excitement under which I had labored since coming to this place was calmed. All the fevers of feeling were laid. I could not have said whether there had been what below we called night, or how the passage of time had marked itself; I only knew that I had experienced the recuperation of night, and that I sprang to the next duty or delight of existence with the vigor of recurring day.

As I rose from the grass, I noticed a four-leaved clover, and remembering the pretty little superstition we used to have about it, I plucked it, and held it to my face, and so learned that the rain-drop in this new land had perfume; an exquisite scent; as if into the essence of brown earth and spicy roots, and aromatic green things, such as summer rain distills with us from out a fresh-washed world, there were mingled an inconceivable odor drawn out of the heart of the sky. Metaphysicians used to tell us that no man ever imagined a new perfume, even in his dreams. I could see that they were right, for anything like the perfume of clover after a rain in Heaven, had never entered into my sense or soul before. I saved the clover "for good luck," as I used to do.

Overhead there was a marvel. There seemed to have been clouds—their passing and breaking, and flitting—and now, behold the heavens themselves, bared of all their storm-drapery, had drawn across their dazzling forms a veil of glory. From what, for want of better knowledge, I still called East to West, and North to South, one supernal prism swept. The whole canopy of the sky was a rainbow.

It is impossible to describe this sight in any earthly tongue, to any dwellers of the earth. I stood beneath it, as a drop stands beneath the ocean. For a time I could only feel the surge of beauty—mere beauty—roll above me. Then, I think, as the dew had fallen from the leaf, so I sunk upon my knees. I prayed because it was natural to pray, and felt God in my soul as the prism feels the primary color, while I thanked Him that I was immortally alive. It had never been like this before, to pray; nay, prayer itself was now one of the discoveries of Heaven. It throbbed through me like the beat of a new heart. It seemed to me that He must be very near me. Almost it was, as if He and I were alone together in the Universe. For the first time, the passionate wish to be taken into His very visible presence,—that intense desire which I had heard of, as overpowering so many of the newly dead,—began to take possession of me. But I put it aside, since it was not permitted, and a consciousness of my unfitness came to me, that made the wish itself seem a kind of mistake. I think this feeling was not unlike what we called below a sense of sin. I did not give it that name at that time. It had come to me so naturally and gradually, that there was no strain or pain about it. Yet when I had it, I could no longer conceive of being without it. It seemed to me that I was a stronger and wiser woman for it. A certain gentleness and humility different from what I had been used to, in my life of activity, wherein so many depended on me, and on the decided faculties of my nature, accompanied the growing sense of personal unworthiness with which I entered on the blessedness of everlasting life.

I watched the rainbow of the sky till it had begun to fade—an event in itself an exquisite wonder, for each tint of the prism flashed out and ran in lightning across the heavens before falling to its place in the primary color, till at last the whole spectacle was resolved into the three elements, the red, the yellow, and the blue; which themselves moved on and away, like a conqueror dismissing a pageant.

When this gorgeous scene had ended, I was surprised to find that though dead and in Heaven, I was hungry. I gathered fruits which grew near, of strange form and flavor, but delicious to the taste past anything I had ever eaten, and I drank of the brook where the shells were, feeling greatly invigorated thereby. I was beginning to wonder where my father was, when I saw him coming towards me. He greeted me with his old good-morning kiss, laying his hand upon my head in a benediction that filled my soul.

As we moved on together, I asked him if he remembered how we used to say below:

"What a heavenly day!"

Many people seemed to be passing on the road which we had chosen, but as we walked on they grew fewer.

"There are those who wish to speak with you," he said with a slight hesitation, "but all things can wait here; we learn to wait ourselves. You are to go to your mother now."

"And not with you?" I asked, having a certain fear of the mystery of my undertaking. He shook his head with a look more nearly like disappointment than anything I had seen upon his face in this new life; explaining to me, however, with cheerful acquiescence, that it was not Willed that he should join me on my journey.

"Tell her that I come shortly," he added, "and that I come alone. She will understand. And have no fear; you have much to learn, but it will come syllable by syllable."

Now swiftly, at the instant while he spoke with me, I found myself alone and in a mountainous region, from which a great outlook was before me. I saw the kingdoms of heaven and the glory of them, spread out before me like a map. A mist of the colors of amethyst and emerald interfused, enwrapped the outlines of the landscape. All details grew blurred and beautiful like a dream at which one snatches vainly in the morning. Off, and beyond, the infinite ether throbbed. Yonder, like a speck upon a sunbeam, swam the tiny globe which we called earth. Stars and suns flashed and faded, revolving and waiting in their places. Surely it was growing dark, for they sprang out like mighty light-houses upon the grayness of the void.

The splendors of the Southern cross streamed far into the strange light, neither of night nor day, not of twilight or dawn, which surrounded me.

Colored suns, of which astronomers had indeed taught us, poured undreamed-of light upon unknown planets. I passed worlds whose luminaries gave them scarlet, green, and purple days. "These too," I thought, "I shall one day visit." I flashed through currents of awful color, and measures of awful night. I felt more than I perceived, and wondered more than I feared. It was some moments before I realized, by these few astronomical details, that I was adrift, alone upon the mystery and mightiness of Space.

Of this strange and solitary journey, I can speak so imperfectly, that it were better almost to leave it out of my narrative. Yet, when I remember how I have sometimes heard those still upon earth conceive, with the great fear and ignorance inseparable from earth-trained imagination, of such transits of the soul from point to point in ether, I should be glad to express at least the incomplete impressions which I received from this experience.

The strongest of these, and the sweetest, was the sense of safety— and still the sense of safety; unassailable, everlasting; blessed beyond the thought of an insecure life to compass. To be dead was to be dead to danger, dead to fear. To be dead was to be alive to a sense of assured good chance that nothing in the universe could shake.

So I felt no dread, believe me, though much awe and amazement, as I took my first journey from Heaven to earth. I have elsewhere said that the distance, by astronomical calculation, was in itself perhaps not enormous. I had an impression that I was crossing a great sphere or penumbra, belonging to the earth itself, and having a certain relation to it, like the soul to the body of a man.

Was Heaven located within or upon this world-soul? The question occurred to me, but up to this time, I am still unable to answer it. The transit itself was swift and subtle as a thought. Indeed, it seemed to me that thought itself might have been my vehicle of conveyance; or perhaps I should say, feeling. My love and longing took me up like pollen taken by the wind. As I approached the spot where my dear ones dwelt and sorrowed for me, desire and speed both increased by a might momentum.

Now I did not find this journey as difficult as that other, when I had departed, a freshly-freed soul, from earth to Heaven. I learned that I was not subject to other natural laws. A celestial gravitation controlled the celestial body, as that of the earth had compelled the other. I was upborne in space by this new and mysterious influence. Yet there was not dispute between it and the other law, the eternal law of love, which drew me down. Between soul and body, in the heavenly existence, there could be no more conflict than between light and an ether wave.

I do not say that I performed this journey without effort or intelligence. The little knowledge I ever had was taxed in view of the grandeurs and the mysteries around me. Shall I be believed if I say that I recalled all the astronomy and geography that my life as a teacher had left still somewhat freshly imprinted on the memory? that the facts of physics recurred to me, even in that inroad of feeling? and that I guided myself to the Massachusetts town as I would have found it upon a globe at school? Already I learned that no acquisition of one life is lost in the next. Already I thanked God for everything I knew, only wishing, with the passion of ignorance newly revealed to itself by the dawn of wisdom, that my poor human acquirements had ever truly deserved the high name of study, or stored my thought with its eternal results.

⸲ 6 ⸳

As I approached the scene of my former life, I met many people. I had struck a realm of spirits who at first perplexed me. They did not look happy, and seemed possessed by great unrest. I observed that, though they fluttered and moved impatiently, none rose far above the surface of the earth. Most of them were employed in one way or another upon it. Some bought and sold; some eat and drank; others occupied themselves in coarse pleasures, from which one could but turn away the eyes. There were those who were busied in more refined ways:—students with eyes fastened to dusty volumes; virtuosos who hung about a picture, a statue, a tapestry, that had enslaved them; one musical creature I saw, who ought to have been of exquisite organization, judging from his hands—he played perpetually upon an instrument that he could not tune; women, I saw too, who robed and disrobed without a glint of pleasure in their faded faces.

There were ruder souls than any of these—but one sought for them in the dens of the earth; their dead hands still were red with stains of blood, and in their dead hearts reigned the remnants of hideous passions.

Of all these appearances, which I still found it natural to call phenomena as I should once have done, it will be remembered that I received the temporary and imperfect impression of a person passing swiftly through a crowd, so that I do not wish my account to be accepted for anything more trustworthy than it is.

While I was wondering greatly what it meant, some one joined and spoke to me familiarly, and turning, I saw it to be that old neighbor, Mrs. Mersey, to whom I have alluded, who, like myself, seemed to be bent upon an errand, and to be but a visitor upon the earth. She was a most lovely spirit, as she had always been, and I grasped her hand cordially while we swept on rapidly together to our journey's end.

"Do tell me," I whispered, as soon as I could draw her near enough, "who all these people are, and what it means. I fear to guess. And yet indeed they seem like the dead who cannot get away."

"Alas," she sighed, "you have said it. They loved nothing, they lived for nothing, they believed in nothing, they cultivated themselves for nothing but the earth. They simply lack the spiritual momentum to get away from it. It is as much the working of a natural law as the progress of a fever. Many of my duties have been among such as these. I know them well. They need time and tact in treatment, and oh, the greatest patience! At first it discouraged me, but I am learning the enthusiasm of my work."

"These, then," I said, "were those I saw in that first hour, when my father led me out of the house, and through the street. I saw you among them, Mrs. Mersey, but I knew even then that you were not of them. But surely they do not stay forever prisoners of the earth? Surely such a blot on the face of spiritual life cannot but fade away? I am a new-comer. I am still quite ignorant, you see. But I do not understand, any more than I did before, how that could be."

"They have their choice," she answered vaguely. But when I saw the high solemnity of her aspect, I feared to press my questions. I could not, however, or I did not forbear saying:—

"At least *you* must have already persuaded many to sever themselves from such a condition as this?"

"Already some, I hope," she replied evasively, as she moved away. She always had remarkably fine manners, of which death had by no means deprived her. I admired her graciousness and dignity as she passed from my side to that of one we met, who, in a dejected voice, called her by her name, and intimated that he wished to speak with her. He was a pale and restless youth, and I thought, but was not sure, for we separated so quickly, that it was the little fellow I spoke of, Bobby Bend. I looked back, after I had advanced some distance on my way, and saw the two together, conversing earnestly. While I was still watching them, it seemed to me, though I cannot be positive upon this point, that they had changed their course, and were quietly ascending, she leading, he following, above the dismal sphere in which she found the lad, and that his heavy, awkward, downward motions became freer, struggling upward, as I gazed.

I had now come to the location of my old home, and, as I passed through the familiar village streets, I saw that night was coming on. I met many whom I knew, both of those called dead and living. The former recognized me, but the latter saw me not. No one detained me, however, for I felt in haste which I could not conceal.

With high-beating heart, I approached the dear old house. No one was astir. As I turned the handle of the door, a soft, sickening touch crawled around my wrist; recoiling, I found that I was entwisted in a piece of crape that the wind hand blown against me.

I went in softly; but I might have spared myself the pains. No one heard me, though the heavy door creaked, I thought, as emphatically as it always had—loudest when we were out latest, and longest when we shut it quickest. I went into the parlor and stood, for a moment, uncertain what to do.

Alice was there, and my married sister Jane, with her husband and little boy. They sat about the fire, conversing sadly. Alice's pretty eyes were disfigured with crying. They spoke constantly of me. Alice was relating to Jane and her family the particulars of my illness. I was touched to hear her call me "patient and sweet;"—none the less because she had often told me I was the most impatient member of the family.

No one had observed my entrance. Of course I was prepared for this, but I cannot tell why I should have felt it, as I certainly did. A low bamboo chair, cushioned with green *crétonne,* stood by the table. I had a fancy for this chair, and, pleased that they had left it unoccupied, advanced and took it, in the old way. It was with something almost like a shock, that I found myself unnoticed in the very centre of their group.

While I sat there, Jane moved to fix the fire, and, in returning, made as if she would take the bamboo chair.

"Oh, don't!" said Alice, sobbing freshly. Jane's own tear sprang, and she turned away.

"It seems to me," said my brother-in-law, looking about with the patient grimace of a business man compelled to waste time at a funeral, "that there has a cold draught come into this room from somewhere. Nobody has left the front door open, I hope? I'll go and see."

He went, glad of the excuse to stir about, poor fellow, and I presume he took a comfortable smoke outside.

The little boy started after his father, but was bidden back, and crawled up into the chair where I was sitting. I took the child upon my lap, and let him stay. No one removed him, he grew so quiet, and he was soon asleep in my arms. This pleased me; but I could not be contented long, so I kissed the boy and put him down. He cried bitterly, and ran to his mother for comfort.

While they were occupied with him, I stole away. I thought I knew where Mother would be, and was ashamed of myself at the reluctance I certainly had to enter my own room, under these exciting circumstances.

Conquering this timidity, as unwomanly and unworthy, I went up and opened the familiar door. I had begun to learn that neither sound nor sight followed my motions now, so that I was not surprised at attracting no attention from the lonely occupant of the room. I closed the door—from long habit I still made an effort to turn the latch softly—and resolutely examined what I saw.

My mother was there, as I had expected. The room was cold—there was no fire,—and she had on her heavy blanket shawl. The gas was lighted, and one of my red candles, but both burned dimly. The poor woman's magenta geranium had frozen. My mother sat in the red easy-chair, which, being a huge, old-fashioned thing, surrounded and shielded her from the draught. My clothes, and medicines, and all the little signs of sickness had been removed. The room was swept, and orderly. Above the bed, the pictures and the carved cross looked down.

Below them, calm as sleep, and cold as frost, and terrible as silence, lay that which had been I.

She did not shrink. She was sitting close beside it. She gazed at it with the tenderness which death itself could not affright. Mother was not crying. She did not look as if she had shed tears for a long time. But her wanness and the drawn lines about her mouth were hard to see. Her aged hands trembled as she cut the locks of hair from the neck of the dead. She was growing to be an old woman. And I—her first-born—I had been her staff of life, and on me she had thought to lean in her widowed age. She seemed to me to have grown feeble fast in the time since I had left her.

All my soul rushed to my lips, and I cried out—it seemed that either the dead or the living must hear that cry—

"Mother! Oh, my dear *mother*!"

But deaf as life, she sat before me. She had just cut off the lock of hair she wanted; as I spoke, the curling ends of it twined around her fingers; I tried to snatch it away, thinking thus to arrest her attention.

The lock of hair trembled, turned, and clung the closer to the living hand. She pressed it to her lips with the passion of desolation.

"But, Mother," I cried once more, "I am *here*." I flung my arms about her and kissed her again and again. I called and entreated her by every dear name that household love had taught us. I besought her to turn, to see, to hear, to believe, to be comforted. I told her how blest was I, how bountiful was death.

"I am alive," I said. "I am alive! I see you, I touch you, hear you, love you, hold you!" I tried argument and severity; I tried tenderness and ridicule.

She turned at this: it seemed to me that she regarded me. She stretched her arms out; her aged hands groped to and fro as if she felt for something and found it not; she shook her head, her dim eyes gazed blankly into mine. She sighed patiently, and rose as if to leave the room, but hesitated,—covered the face of the dead body—caressed it once or twice as if it had been a living infant—and then, taking up her Bible, which had been upon the chair beside her, dropped upon her knees, and holding the book against her sunken cheek, abandoned herself to silent prayer.

This was more than I could bear just then, and, thinking to collect myself by a few moments' solitude, I left her. But as I stood in the dark hall, uncertain and unquiet, I noticed a long, narrow line of light at my feet, and, following it confusedly, found that it came from the crack in the closed, but unlatched door of another well-remembered room. I pushed the door open hurriedly and closed it behind me.

My brother sat in this room alone. His fire was blazing cheerfully and, flashing, revealed the deer's-head from the Adirondacks, the stuffed rose-curlew from Florida, the gull's wing from Cape Ann, the gun and rifle and bamboo fish-pole, the class photographs over the mantel, the feminine features on porcelain in velvet frames, all the little trappings with which I was familiar. Tom had been trying to study, but his Homer lay pushed away, with crumpled leaves, upon the table. Buried in his lexicon—one strong elbow intervening—down, like a hero thrown, the boy's face had gone.

"Tom," I said quietly—I always spoke quietly to Tom, who had a constitutional fear of what he called "emotions"—"Tom, you'd better be studying your Greek. I'd much rather see you. Come, I'll help you."

He did not move, poor fellow, and as I came nearer, I saw, to my heart-break, that our Tom was crying. Sobs shook his huge frame, and down between the iron fingers, toughened by base-ball matches, tears had streamed upon the pages of the Odyssey.

"Tom, Tom, old fellow, *don't!*" I cried, and, hungry as love, I took the boy. I got upon the arm of the smoking chair, as I used to, and so had my hands about his neck, and my cheek upon his curly hair, and would have soothed him. Indeed, he did grow calm, and calmer, as if he yielded to my touch; and presently he lifted his wet face, and looked about the room, half ashamed, half defiant, as if to ask who saw that.

"Come, Tom," I tried again. "It really isn't so bad as you think. And there is Mother catching cold in that room. Go and get her away from the body. It is no place for her. She'll get sick. Nobody can manage her as well as you."

As if he heard me, he arose. As if he knew me, he looked for the flashing of an instant into my eyes.

"I don't see how a girl of her sense can be *dead,*" said the boy aloud. He stretched his arms once above his head, and out into the bright, empty room, and I heard him groan in a way that wrung my heart. I went impulsively to him, and as his arms closed, they closed about me strongly. He stood for a moment quite still. I could feel the nervous strain subsiding all over his big soul and body.

"Hush," I whispered. "I'm no more dead than you are."

If he heard, what he felt, God knows. I speak of a mystery. No optical illusion, no tactual hallucination could hold the boy who took all the medals at the gymnasium. The hearty, healthy fellow could receive no abnormal sign from the love and longing of the dead. Only spirit unto spirit could attempt that strange out-reaching. Spirit unto spirit, was it done? Still, I relate a mystery, and what shall I say? His professor in the class-room of metaphysics would teach him next week that grief owns the law of the rhythm of motion; and that at the oscillation of the pendulum the excitement of anguish shall subside into apathy which mourners alike tread as a disloyalty to the dead, and court as a nervous relief to the living.

Be this as it may, the boy grew suddenly calm, and even cheerful, and followed me at once. I led him directly to his mother, and left them for a time alone together.

After this my own calm, because my own confidence, increased. My dreary sense of helplessness before the suffering of those I loved, gave place to the consciousness of power to reach them. I detected this power in myself in an undeveloped form, and realized that it might require exercise and culture, like all other powers, if I would make valuable use of it. I could already regard the cultivation of the faculty which would enable love to defy death, and spirit to conquer matter, as likely to be one of the occupations of a full life.

I went out into the fresh air for a time to think these thoughts through by myself, undisturbed by the sight of grief that I could not remove; and strolled up and down the village streets in the frosty night.

When I returned to the house they had all separated for the night, sadly seeking sleep in view of the events of the morrow, when, as I had already inferred, the funeral would take place.

I spent the night among them, chiefly with my mother and Tom, passing unnoticed from room to room, and comforting them in such ways as I found possible. The boy had locked his door, but after a few trials I found myself able to pass the medium of this resisting matter, and to enter and depart according to my will. Tom finished his lesson in the Odyssey, and I sat by and helped him when I could. This I found possible in simple ways, which I may explain farther at another time. We had often studied together, and his mind the more readily, therefore, responded to the influence of my own. He was soon well asleep, and I was free to give all my attention to my poor mother. Of those long and solemn hours, what shall I say? I thought she would never, never rest. I held her in these arms the live-long night. With these hands I caressed and calmed her. With these lips I kissed her.

With this breath I warmed her cold brow and fingers. With all my soul and body I willed that I would comfort her, and I believe, thank God, I did. At dawn she slept peacefully; she slept late, and rose refreshed. I remained closely by her throughout the day.

They did their best, let me say, to provide me with a Christian funeral, partly in accordance with some wishes I had expressed in writing, partly from the impulse of their own good sense. Not a curtain was drawn to darken the house of death. The blessed winter sunshine flowed in like the current of a broad stream, through low, wide windows. No ghastly "funeral flowers" filled the room; there was only a cluster of red pinks upon the coffin, and the air was sweet but not heavy with the carnation perfume that they knew I loved. My dead body and face they had covered with a deep red pall, just shaded off the black, as dark as darkness could be, and yet be redness. Not a bell was tolled. Not a tear—at least, I mean, by those nearest me—not a tear was shed. As the body was carried from the house, the voices of unseen singers lifted the German funeral chant:—

"Go forth! go on, with solemn song,
Short is the way; the rest is long!"

At the grave they sang:—

"Softly now the light of day,"

since my mother had asked for one of the old hymns; and besides the usual Scriptural Burial Service, a friend, who was dear to me, read Mrs. Browning's "Sleep."

It was all as I would have had it, and I looked on peacefully. If I could have spoken I would have said: "You have buried me cheerfully, as Christians ought, as a Christian ought to be."

I was greatly touched, I must admit, at the grief of some of the poor, plain people who followed my body on its final journey to the village church-yard. The woman who sent the magenta geranium refused to be comforted, and there were one or two young girls whom I had been so fortunate as to assist in difficulties, who, I think, did truly mourn. Some of my boys from the Grand Army were there, too,—some, I mean, whom it had been my privilege to care for in the hospitals in the old war days. They came in uniform, and held their caps before their eyes. It did please me to see them there.

When the brief service at the grave was over, I would have gone home with my mother, feeling that she needed me more than ever; but as I turned to do so, I was approached by a spirit whose presence I had not observed. It proved to be my father. He detained me, explaining that I should remain where I was, feeling no fear, but making no protest, till the Will governing my next movement might be made known to me. So I bade my mother good-by, and Tom, as well as I could in the surprise and confusion, and watched them all as they went away. She, as she walked, seemed to those about her to be leaning only upon her son. But I beheld my father tenderly hastening close beside her, while he supported her with the arm which had never failed her yet, in all their loving lives. Therefore I could let her go, without distress.

The funeral procession departed slowly; the grave was filled; one of the mill-girls came back and threw in some arbor vitæ and a flower or two,—the sexton hurried her, and both went away. It grew dusk, dark. I and my body were left alone together.

Of that solemn watch, it is not for me to chatter to any other soul. Memories over-swept me, which only we two could share. Hopes possessed me which it were not possible to explain to another organization. Regret, resolve, awe, and joy, every high human emotion excepting fear, battled about us. While I knelt there in the windless night, I heard chanting from a long distance, but yet distinct to the dead, that is to the living ear. As I listened, the sound deepened, approaching, and a group of singing spirits swept by in the starlit air, poised like birds, or thoughts, above me:

"It is sown a natural—it is raised a spiritual body."

"Death! where is thy sting?—Grave!—thy victory?"

"Believing in Me, though he were dead, yet shall he live."

I tried my voice, and joined, for I could no longer help it, in the thrilling chorus. It was the first time since I died, that I had felt myself invited or inclined to share the occupations of others, in the life I had entered. Kneeling there, in the happy night, by my own grave, I lifted all my soul and sense into the immortal words, now for the first time comprehensible to me:

"*I believe, I believe in the resurrection of the dead.*"

It was not long thereafter that I received the summons to return. I should have been glad to go home once more, but was able to check my own preference without wilful protest, or an aching heart. The conviction that all was well with my darlings and myself, for life and for death, had now become an intense yet simple thing, like consciousness itself.

I went as, and where I was bidden, joyfully.

₹7₹

Upon reëntering the wonderful place which I had begun to call Heaven, and to which I still give that name, though not, I must say, with perfect assurance that the word is properly applied to that phase of the life of which I am the yet most ignorant recorder, I found myself more weary than I had been at any time since my change came. I was looking about, uncertain where to go, feeling, for the first time, rather homeless in this new country, when I was approached by a stranger, who inquired of me what I sought:

"Rest," I said promptly.

"A familiar quest," observed the stranger, smiling.

"You are right, sir. It is a thing I have been seeking for forty years."

"And never found?"

"Never found."

"I will assist you," he said gently, "that is, if you wish it. What will you have first?"

"Sleep, I think, first, then food. I have been through exciting scenes.

I have a touch—a faint one—of what below we called exhaustion. Yet now I am conscious in advance of the rest which is sure to come. Already I feel it, like the ebbing of the wave that goes to form the flow of the next. How blessed to know that one *can't* be ill!"

"How do you know that?" asked my companion.

"On the whole, I don't know that I do," I answered, with embarrassment, "I suppose it is a remnant of one's old religious teaching: 'The inhabitant shall not say I am sick.' Surely there were such words."

"And you trusted them?" asked the stranger.

"The Bible was a hard book to accept," I said quickly, "I would not have you overestimate my faith. I tried to believe that it was God's message. I think I *did* believe it. But the reason was clear to me. I could not get past that if I wished to."

"What, then, was the reason," inquired my friend, solemnly, "why you trusted the message called the Word of God, as received by the believing among His children on earth?"

"Surely," I urged, "there is but one reason. I refer to the history of our Lord. I do not know whether all in this place are Christians; but I was one.—Sir! I anticipate your question. I was a most imperfect, useless one—to my sorrow and my shame I say it—but, so far as I went, I was an honest one."

"Did you love Him?—Him whom you called Lord?" asked the stranger, with an air of reserve. I replied that I thought I could truly say that He was dear to me.

I began to be deeply moved by this conversation. I stole a look at the stranger, whom I had at first scarcely noticed, except as one among many passing souls. He was a man of surpassing majesty of mien, and for loveliness of feature I had seen no mortal to vie with him. "This," I thought, "must be one of the beings we called angels." Astonishing brightness rayed from him at every motion, and his noble face was like the sun itself. He moved beside me like any other spirit, and condescended to me so familiarly, yet with so unapproachable a dignity, that my heart went out to him as breath upon the air. It did not occur to me to ask him who he was, or wither he led me.

It was enough that he led, and I followed without question or reply. We walked and talked for a long time together.

He renewed the conversation by asking me whether I had really staked my immortal existence upon the promise of that obscure, uneducated Jew, twenty centuries in his grave,—that plain man who lived a fanatic's life, and died a felon's death, and whose teachings had given rise to such bigotry and error upon the earth. I answered that I had never been what is commonly called a devout person, not having a spiritual temperament, but that I had not held our Master responsible for the mistakes of either his friends or his foes, and that the greatest regret I had brought with me into Heaven was that I had been so unworthy to bear His blessed name. He next inquired of me, if I truly believed that I owed my entrance upon my present life to the interposition of Him of whom we spoke.

"Sir," I said, "you touch upon sacred nerves. I should find it hard to tell you how utterly I believe that immortality is the gift of Jesus Christ to the human soul."

"I believed this on earth," I added, "I believe it in Heaven. I do not *know* it yet, however. I am a new-comer; I am still very ignorant. No one has instructed me. I hope to learn 'syllable by syllable.' I am impatient to be taught; yet I am patient to be ignorant till I am found worthy to learn. It may be, that you, sir, who evidently are of a higher order of life than ours, are sent to enlighten me?"

My companion smiled, neither dissenting from, nor assenting to my question, and only asked me in reply, if I had yet spoken with the Lord. I said that I had not even seen Him; nay, that I had not even asked to see Him. My friend inquired why this was, and I told him frankly that it was partly because I was so occupied at first—nay, most of the time until I was called below.

"I had not much room to think. I was taken from event to event, like a traveler. This matter that you speak of seemed out of place in every way at that time."

Then I went on to say that my remissness was owing partly to a little real self-distrust, because I feared I was not the kind of believer to whom He would feel quickly drawn; that I felt afraid to propose such a preposterous thing as being brought into His presence; that I supposed, when He saw fit to reveal Himself to me, I should be summoned in some orderly way, suitable to this celestial community; that, in fact, though I had cherished this most sweet and solemn desire, I had not mentioned it before, not even to my own father who conducted me to this place.

"I have not spoken of it," I said, "to any body but to you."

The stranger's face wore a remarkable expression when I said this; as if I had deeply gratified him; and there glittered from his entire form and features such brightness as well-nigh dazzled me. It was as if, where a lesser being would have spoken, or stirred, he shone. I felt as if I conversed with him by radiance, and that living light had become a vocabulary between us. I have elsewhere spoken of the quality of reflecting light as marked among the ordinary inhabitants of this new life; but in this case I was aware of a distinction, due, I thought, to the superior order of existence to which my friend belonged. He did not, like the others, reflect; he radiated glory. More and more, as we had converse together, this impressed, until it awed me. We remained together for a long time. People who met us, greeted the angel with marked reverence, and turned upon me glances of sympathetic delight; but no one interrupted us. We continued our walk into a more retired place, by the shore of a sea, and there we had deep communion.

My friend had inquired if I were still faint, and if I preferred to turn aside for food and rest; but when he asked me the question I was amazed to find that I no longer had the need of either. Such delight had I in his presence, such invigoration in his sympathy, that glorious recuperation had set in upon my earth-caused weariness. Such power had the soul upon the celestial body! Food for the first was force to the other.

It seemed to me that I had never known refreshment of either before; and that Heaven itself could contain no nutriment that would satisfy me after this upon which I fed in that high hour.

It is not possible for me to repeat the solemn words of that interview. We spoke of grave and sacred themes. He gave me great counsel and fine sympathy. He gave me affectionate rebuke and unfathomable resolve. We talked of those inner experiences which, on earth, the soul protects, like struggling flame, between itself and the sheltering hand of God. We spoke much of the Master, and of my poor hope that I might be permitted after I had been a long time in Heaven, to become worthy to see Him, though at the vast distance of my unworthiness. Of that unworthiness too, we spoke most earnestly; while we did so, the sense of it grew within me like a new soul; yet so divinely did my friend extend his tenderness to me, that I was strengthened far more than weakened by these finer perceptions of my unfitness, which he himself had aroused in me. The counsel that he gave me, Eternity could not divert out of my memory, and the comfort which I had from him I treasure to this hour. "Here," I thought, "here, at last, I find reproof as gentle as sympathy, and sympathy as invigorating as reproof. Now, for the first time in all my life, I find myself truly understood. What could I not become if I possessed the friendship of such a being! How shall I develop myself so as to obtain it? How can I endure to be deprived of it? Is this too, like friendship on earth, a snatch, a compromise, a heart-ache, a mirror in which one looks only long enough to know that it is dashed away? Have I begun that old pain again, *here*?"

For I knew, as I sat in that solemn hour with my face to the sea and my soul with him, while sweeter than any song of all the waves of Heaven or earth to sea-lovers sounded his voice who did commune with me,—verily I knew, for then and forever, that earth had been a void to me because I had him not, and that Heaven could be no Heaven to me without him.

All which I had known of human love; all that I had missed; the dreams from which I had been startled; the hopes that had evaded me; the patience which comes from knowing that one may not even try not to be misunderstood; the struggle to keep a solitary heart sweet; the anticipation of desolate age which casts its shadow backward upon the dial of middle life; the paralysis of feeling which creeps on with its disuse; the distrust of one's own atrophied faculties of loving; the sluggish wonder if one is ceasing to be lovable; the growing difficulty of explaining oneself even when it is necessary, because no one being more than any other cares for the explanation; the things which a lonely life converts into silence that cannot be broken, swept upon me like rapids, as, turning to look into his dazzling face, I said: "This—*all* this he understands."

But when, thus turning, I would have told him so, for there seemed to be no poor pride in Heaven, forbidding soul to tell the truth to soul,—when I turned, my friend had risen, and was departing from me, as swiftly and mysteriously as he came. I did not cry out to him to stay, for I felt ashamed; nor did I tell him how he had bereft me, for that seemed a childish folly. I think I only stood and looked at him.

"If there is any way of being worthy of your friendship," I said below my breath, "I will have it, if I toil for half Eternity to get it."

Now, though these words were scarcely articulate, I think he heard them, and turning, with a smile which will haunt my dreams and stir my deeds as long as I shall live, he laid his hand upon my head, and blessed me—but what he said I shall tell no man—and so departed from me, and I was left upon the shore alone, fallen, I think, in a kind of sleep or swoon.

When I awoke, I was greatly calmed and strengthened, but disinclined, at first, to move. I had the reaction from what I knew was the intensest experience of my life, and it took time to adjust my feelings to my thoughts.

A young girl came up while I sat there upon the sands, and employed herself in gathering certain marvelous weeds that the sea had tossed up. These weeds fed upon the air, as they had upon the water, remaining fresh upon the girl's garments, which she decorated with them. She did not address me, but strolled up and down silently. Presently, feeling moved by the assurance of congeniality that one detects so much more quickly in Heaven than on earth, I said to the young girl:—

"Can you tell me the name of the angel—you must have met him—who has but just left me, and with whom I have been conversing?"

"Do you then truly not know?" she asked, shading her eyes with her hand, and looking off in the direction my friend had taken; then back again, with a fine, compassionate surprise at me.

"Indeed I know not."

"That was the Master who spoke with you."

"What did you *say*?"

"That was our Lord Himself."

₹ 8 ₹

After the experience related in the last chapter, I remained for some time in solitude. Speech seemed incoherence, and effort impossible. I needed a pause to adapt myself to my awe and my happiness; upon neither of which will it be necessary for me to dwell. Yet I think I may be understood if I say that from this hour I found that what we call Heaven had truly begun for me. Now indeed for the first time I may say that I believed without wonder in the life everlasting; since now, for the first time, I had a reason sufficient for the continuance of existence. A force like the cohesion of atoms held me to eternal hope. Brighter than the dawn of friendship upon a heart bereft, more solemn than the sunrise of love itself upon a life that had thought itself unloved, stole on the power of the Presence to which I had been admitted in so surprising, and yet, after all, how natural a way! Henceforth the knowledge that this experience might be renewed for me at any turn of thought or act, would illuminate joy itself, so that "it should have no need of the sun to lighten it." I recalled these words, as one recalls a familiar quotation repeated for the first time on some foreign locality of which it is descriptive. Now I knew what he meant, who wrote: "The Lamb is the Light thereof."

When I came to myself, I observed the young girl who had before addressed me still strolling on the shore. She beckoned, and I
went to her, with a new meekness in my heart. What will He have
me to do? If, by the lips of this young thing, He choose to instruct
me, let me glory in the humility with which I will be a learner!

All things seemed to be so exquisitely ordered for us in this new
life, all flowed so naturally, like one sound-wave into another, with
ease so apparent, yet under law so superb, that already I was certain
Heaven contained no accidents, and no trivialities; as it did no shocks
or revolutions.

"If you like," said the young girl, "we will cross the sea."

"But how?" I asked, for I saw no boat.

"Can you not, then, walk upon the water yet?" she answered.
"Many of us do, as He did once below. But we no longer call such
things miracles. They are natural powers. Yet it is an art to use them.
One has to learn it, as we did swimming, or such things, in the old
times."

"I have only been here a short time," I said, half amused at the little celestial "airs" my young friend wore so sweetly. "I know but little yet. Can you teach me how to walk on water?"

"It would take so much time," said the young girl, "that I think
we should not wait for that. We go on to the next duty, now. You
had better learn, I think, from somebody wiser than I. I will take you
over another way."

A great and beautiful shell, not unlike a nautilus, was floating near
us, on the incoming tide, and my companion motioned to me to step
into this. I obeyed her, laughing, but without any hesitation. "Neither shall there be any more death," I thought as I glanced over the
rose-tinted edges of the frail thing into the water, deeper than any I
had ever seen, but unclouded, so that I looked to the bottom of the
sea. The girl herself stepped out upon the waves with a practiced air,
and lightly drawing the great shell with one hand, bore me after her,
as one bears a sledge upon ice. As we came into mid-water we began to meet others, some walking, as she did, some rowing or drift-

ing like myself. Upon the opposite shore uprose the outlines of a more thickly settled community than any I had yet seen.

Watching this with interest that deepened as we approached the shore, I selfishly or uncourteously forgot to converse with my companion, who did not disturb my silence until we landed. As she gave me her hand, she said in a quick, direct tone:

"Well, Miss Mary, I see that you do not know me, after all."

I felt, as I had already done once or twice before, a certain social embarrassment (which in itself instructed me, as perpetuating one of the minor emotions of life below that I had hardly expected to renew) before my lovely guide, as I shook my head, struggling with the phantasmal memories evoked by her words. No, I did not know her.

"I am Marie Sauvée. I *hope* you remember."

She said these words in French. The change of language served instantly to recall the long train of impressions stored away, who knew how or where, about the name and memory of this girl.

"Marie Sauvée! *You*—HERE!" I exclaimed in her own tongue.

At the name, now, the whole story, like the bright side of a dark-lantern, flashed. It was a tale of sorrow and shame, as sad, perhaps, as any that it had been my lot to meet. So far as I had ever known, the little French girl, thrown in my way while I was serving in barracks at Washington, had baffled every effort I had made to win her affection or her confidence, and had gone out of my life as the thistle-down flies on the wind. She had cost me many of those precious drops of the soul's blood which all such endeavor drains; and in the laboratory of memory I had labelled them, "Worse than Wasted," and sadly wondered if I should do the same again for such another need, at just such hopeless expenditure, and had reminded myself that it was not good spiritual economy, and said that I would never repeat the experience, and known all the while that I should.

Now here, a spirit saved, shining as the air of Heaven, "without spot or any such thing"—here, wiser in heavenly lore than I, longer with Him than I, nearer to Him than I, dearer to Him, perhaps, than I—*here* was Marie Sauvée.

"I do not know how to apologize," I said, struggling with my emotion, "for the way in which I spoke to you just now. Why should you not be here? Why, indeed? Why am I here? Why"—

"Dear Miss Mary," cried the girl, interrupting me passionately, "but for you it might never have been as it is. Or never for ages—I cannot say. I might have been a ghost, bound yet to the hated ghost of the old life. It was your doing, at the first—down there—all those years ago. Miss Mary, you were the first person I ever loved. You didn't know it. I had no idea of telling you. But I did, I loved you. After you went away, I loved you; ever since then, I loved you. I said, I will be fit to love her before I die. And then I said, I will go where she is going, for I shall never get at her anywhere else. And when I entered this place—for I had no friend or relative here that I knew, to meet me—I was more frightened than it is possible for any one like you to understand, and wondered what place there could be for one like me in all this country, and how I could ever get accustomed to their ways, and whether I should shock and grieve them—you *can't* understand *that;* I dreaded it so, I was afraid I should swear after I got to Heaven; I was afraid I might say some evil word, and shame them all, and shame myself more than I could ever get over. I knew I wasn't educated for any such society. I knew there wasn't anything in me that would be at home here, but just"—

"But just what, Marie?" I asked, with a humility deeper than I could have expressed.

"But just my love for you, Miss Mary. That was all. I had nothing to come to Heaven on, but loving you and meaning to be a better girl because I loved you. That was truly all."

"That is impossible!" I said quickly. "Your love for me never brought you here of itself alone. You are mistaken about this. It is neither Christianity nor philosophy."

"There is no mistake," persisted the girl, with gentle obstinacy, smiling delightedly at my dogmatism, "I came here because I loved you. Do you not see? In loving you, I loved—for the first time in my life I loved—goodness. I really did. And when I got to this place,

I found out that goodness was the same as God. And I had been getting the love of God into my heart, all that time, in that strange way, and never knew how it was with me, until—Oh, Miss Mary, who do you think it was, Who, that met me within an hour after I died?"

"It was our Master," she added in an awe-struck, yet rapturous whisper, that thrilled me through. "It was He Himself. He was the first, for I had nobody, as I told you, belonging to me in this holy place, to care for a wretch like me.—*He* was the first to meet *me*! And it was He who taught me everything I had to learn. It was He who made me feel acquainted and at home. It was He who took me on from love of you, to love of Him, as you put one foot after another in learning to walk after you have had a terrible sickness. And it was *He* who never reminded me—never once reminded me—of the sinful creature I had been. Never, by one word or look, from that hour to this day, has He let me feel ashamed in Heaven. That is what *He* is!" cried the girl, turning upon me, in a little sudden, sharp way she used to have; her face and form were so transfigured before me, as she spoke, that it seemed as if she quivered with excess of light, and were about to break away and diffuse herself upon the radiant air, like song, or happy speech, or melting color.

"Die for Him!" she said after a passionate silence. "If I could die everlastingly and everlastingly and everlastingly, to give Him any pleasure, or to save Him any pain— But then, that's nothing," she added, "I love Him. That is all that means.—And I've only got to live everlastingly instead. That is the way He has treated me—*me*!"

9

The shore upon which we had landed was thickly populated, as I have said. Through a sweep of surpassingly beautiful suburbs, we approached the streets of a town. It is hard to say why I should have been surprised at finding in this place the signs of human traffic, philanthropy, art, and study—what otherwise I expected, who can say? My impressions, as Marie Sauvée led me through the city, had the confusion of sudden pleasure. The width and shining cleanliness of the streets, the beauty and glittering material of the houses, the frequent presence of libraries, museums, public gardens, signs of attention to the wants of animals, and places of shelter for travelers such as I had never seen in the most advanced and benevolent of cities below,—these were the points that struck me most forcibly.

The next thing, which in a different mood might have been the first that impressed me was the remarkable expression of the faces that I met or passed. No thoughtful person can have failed to observe, in any throng, the preponderant look of unrest and dissatisfaction in the human eye. Nothing, to a fine vision, so emphasizes the isolation of being, as the faces of people in a crowd. In this new community to which I had been brought, that old effect was replaced by a delightful change. I perceived, indeed, great intentness of purpose here, as in all thickly-settled regions; the countenances that passed me indicated close conservation of social force and economy of intellectual energy; these were people trained by attrition with many influences, and balanced with the conflict of various interests. But these were men and women, busy without hurry, efficacious without waste; they had ambition without unscrupulousness, power without tyranny, success without vanity, care without anxiety, effort without exhaustion,—hope, fear, toil, uncertainty it seemed, elation it was sure—but a repose that it was impossible to call by any other name than divine, controlled their movements, which were like the pendulum of a golden clock whose works are out of sight. I watched these people with delight. Great numbers of them seemed to be students, thronging what we should call below colleges, seminaries, or schools of art, or music, or science. The proportion of persons pursuing some form of intellectual acquisition struck me as large. My little guide, to whom I mentioned this, assented to the fact, pointing out to me a certain institution we had passed, at which she herself was, she said, something like a primary scholar, and from which she had been given a holiday to meet me as she did, and conduct me through the journey that had been appointed for me on that day. I inquired of her what her studies might be like; but she told me that she was hardly wise enough as yet to explain to me what I could learn for myself when I had been longer in this place, and when my leisure came for investigating its attractions at my own will.

"I am uncommonly ignorant, you know," said Marie Sauvée humbly, "I have everything to learn. There is book knowledge and thought knowledge and soul knowledge, and I have not any of these. I was as much of what you used to call a heathen, as any Fiji-Islander you gave your missionaries to. I have so much to learn, that I am not sent yet upon other business such as I should like."

Upon my asking Marie Sauvée what business this might be, she hesitated. "I have become ambitious in Heaven," she answered slowly. "I shall never be content till I am fit to be sent to the worst woman that can be found—no matter which side of death—I don't care in what world—I want to be sent to one that nobody else will touch; I think I might know how to save her. It is a tremendous ambition!" she repeated. "Preposterous for the greatest angel there is here! and yet I—*I* mean to do it."

I was led on in this way by Marie Sauvée, through and out of the city into the western suburbs; we had approached from the east, and had walked a long distance. There did not occur to me, I think, till we had made the circuit of the beautiful town, one thing, which, when I did observe it, struck me as, on the whole, the most impressive that I had noticed. "I have not seen," I said, stopping suddenly, "I have not seen a poor person in all this city."

"Nor an aged one, have you?" asked Marie Sauvée, smiling.

"Now that I think of it,—no. Nor a sick one. Not a beggar. Not a cripple. Not a mourner. Not—and yet what have we here? This building, by which you are leading me, bears a device above the door, the last I should ever have expected to find *here.*"

It was an imposing building, of a certain translucent material that had the massiveness of marble, with the delicacy of thin agate illuminated from within. The rear of this building gave upon the open country, with a background of hills, and the vision of the sea which I had crossed. People strolled about the grounds, which had more than the magnificence of Oriental gardens. Music came from the building, and the saunterers, whom I saw, seemed nevertheless not to be idlers, but persons busily employed in various ways—I should have said, under the close direction of others who guided them. The inscription above the door of this building was a word, in a tongue unknown to me, meaning "Hospital," as I was told.

"They are the sick at heart," said Marie Sauvée, in answer to my look of perplexity, "who are healed there. And they are the sick of soul; those who were most unready for the new life; they whose spiritual being was diseased through inaction, *they* are the invalids of Heaven. There they are put under treatment, and slowly cured. With some, it takes long. I was there myself when I first came, for a little; it will be a most interesting place for you to visit, by-and-by."

I inquired who were the physicians of this celestial sanitarium.

"They who unite the natural love of healing to the highest spiritual development."

"By no means, then, necessarily they who were skilled in the treatment of diseases on earth?" I asked, laughing.

"Such are oftener among the patients," said Marie Sauvée sadly. To me, so lately from the earth, and our low earthly way of finding amusement in facts of this nature, this girl's gravity was a rebuke. I thanked her for it, and we passed by the hospital—which I secretly made up my mind to investigate at another time—and so out into the wider country, more sparsely settled, but it seemed to me more beautiful than that we had left behind.

"There," I said, at length, "is to my taste the loveliest spot we have seen yet. That is the most homelike of all these homes."

We stopped before a small and quiet house built of curiously inlaid woods, that reminded me of Sorrento work as a great achievement may remind one of a first and faint suggestion. So exquisite was the carving and coloring, that on a larger scale the effect might have interfered with the solidity of the building, but so modest were the proportions of this charming house, that its dignity was only enhanced by its delicacy. It was shielded by trees, some familiar to me, others strange. There were flowers—not too many; birds; and I noticed a fine dog sunning himself upon the steps. The sweep of landscape from all the windows of this house must have been grand. The wind drove up from the sea. The light, which had a peculiar depth and color, reminding me of that which on earth flows from under the edge of a breaking storm-cloud at the hour preceding sunset, formed an aureola about the house. When my companion suggested my examining this place, since it so attracted me, I hesitated, but yielding to her wiser judgment, strolled across the little lawn, and stood, uncertain, at the threshold. The dog arose as I came up, and met me cordially, but no person seemed to be in sight.

"Enter," said Marie Sauvée in a tone of decision, "You are expected. Go where you will."

I turned to remonstrate with her, but the girl had disappeared. Finding myself thus thrown on my own resources, and having learned already the value of obedience to mysterious influences in this new life, I gathered courage, and went into the house. The dog followed me affectionately, rather than suspiciously.

For a few moments I stood in the hall or ante-room, alone and perplexed. Doors opened at right and left, and vistas of exquisitely-ordered rooms stretched out. I saw much of the familiar furniture of a modest home, and much that was unfamiliar mingled therewith. I desired to ask the names or purposes of certain useful articles, and the characters and creators of certain works of art. I was bewildered and delighted. I had something of the feeling of a rustic visitor taken for the first time to a palace or imposing town-house.

Was Heaven an aggregate of homes like this? Did everlasting life move on in the same dear ordered channel—the dearest that human experiment had ever found—the channel of family love? Had one, after death, the old blessedness without the old burden? The old sweetness without the old mistake? The familiar rest, and never the familiar fret? Was there always in the eternal world "somebody to come home to"? And was there always the knowledge that it could not be the wrong person? Was all *that* eliminated from celestial domestic life? Did Heaven solve the problem on which earth had done no more than speculate?

While I stood, gone well astray on thoughts like these, feeling still too great a delicacy about my uninvited presence in this house, I heard the steps of the host, or so I took them to be; they had the indefinable ring of the master's foot. I remained where I was, not without embarrassment, ready to apologize for my intrusion as soon as he should come within sight. He crossed the long room at the left, leisurely; I counted his quiet footsteps; he advanced, turned, saw me—I too, turned—and so, in this way, it came about that I stood face to face with my own father.

. . . I had found the eternal life full of the unexpected, but this was almost the sweetest thing that had happened to me yet.

Presently my father took me over the house and the grounds; with a boyish delight, explaining to me how many years he had been building and constructing and waiting with patience in his heavenly home for the first one of his own to join him. Now, he too, should have "somebody to come home to." As we dwelt upon the past and glanced at the future, our full hearts overflowed. He explained to me that my new life had but now, in the practical sense of the word, begun; since a human home was the centre of all growth and blessedness. When he had shown me to my own portion of the house, and bidden me welcome to it, he pointed out to me a certain room whose door stood always open, but whose threshold was never crossed. I hardly feel that I have the right, in this public way, to describe, in detail, the construction or adornment of this room. I need only say that Heaven itself seemed to have been ransacked to bring together the daintiest, the most delicate, the purest, thoughts and fancies that celestial skill or art could create. Years had gone to the creation of this spot; it was a growth of time, the occupation of that loneliness which must be even in the happy life, when death has temporarily separated two who had been one. I was quite prepared for his whispered words, when he said,—

"Your mother's room, my dear. It will be all ready for her at any time."

This union had been a *marriage*—not one of the imperfect ties that pass under the name, on earth. Afterwards, when I learned more of the social economy of the new life, I perceived more clearly the rarity and peculiar value of an experience which had in it the elements of what might be called (if I should be allowed the phrase) eternal permanency, and which involved, therefore, none of the disintegration and redistribution of relations consequent upon passing from temporary or mistaken choices to a fixed and perfect state of society.

Later, on that same evening, I was called eagerly from below. I was resting, and alone;—I had, so to speak, drawn my first breath in Heaven; once again, like a girl in my own room under my father's roof; my heart at anchor, and my peace at full tide. I ran as I used to run, years ago, when he called me, crying down,—

"I'm coming, Father," while I delayed a moment to freshen my dress, and to fasten it with some strange white flowers that climbed over my window, and peered, nodding like children, into the room.

When I reached the hall, or whatever might be the celestial name for the entrance room below, I did not immediately see my father, but I heard the sound of voices beyond, and perceived the presence of many people in the house. As I hesitated, wondering what might be the etiquette of these new conditions, and whether I should be expected to play the hostess at a reception of angels or saints, some one came up from behind me, I think, and held out his hand in silence.

"St. Johns!" I cried, "Jamie St. Johns! The last time I saw *you*"—

"The last time you saw me was in a field-hospital after the battle of Malvern Hills," said St. Johns. "I died in your arms, Miss Mary. Shot flew about you while you got me that last cup of water. I died hard. You sang the hymn I asked for—'Ye who tossed on beds of pain'—

and the shell struck the tent-pole twenty feet off, but you sang right on. I was afraid you would stop. I was almost gone. But you never faltered. You sang my soul out—do you remember? I've been watching all this while for you. I've been a pretty busy man since I got to this place, but I've always found time to run in and ask your father when he expected you.

"I meant to be the first all along; but I hear there's a girl got ahead of me. She's here, too, and some more women. But most of us are the boys, to-night, Miss Mary,—come to give you a sort of house-warming—just to say we've never forgotten! . . . and you see we want to say 'Welcome home at last' to *our* army woman—God bless her—as she blessed us!

"Come in, Miss Mary! Don't feel bashful. It's nobody but your own boys. Here we are. There's a thing I remember—you used to read it. *'For when ye fail'*—you know I never could quote straight—*'they shall receive you into everlasting habitations'*—Wasn't that it? Now here. See! Count us! *Not one missing,* do you see? You said you'd have us all here yet—all that died before you did. You used to tell us so. You prayed it, and you lived it, and you did it, and, by His everlasting mercy, here we are. Look us over. Count again. I couldn't make a speech on earth and I can't make one in Heaven—but the fellows put me up to it. *Come* in, Miss Mary! *Dear* Miss Mary—why, we want to shake hands with you, all around! We want to have some of the old songs, and— What! Crying, Miss Mary?—*You?* We never saw you cry in all our lives. Your lip used to tremble. You got pretty white; but you weren't that kind of woman. Oh, see here! *Crying in* HEAVEN?"—

${10}$

From this time, the events which I am trying to relate began to assume in fact a much more orderly course; yet in form I scarcely find them more easy to prevent. Narrative, as has been said of conversation, "is always but a selection," and in this case the peculiar difficulties of choosing from an immense mass of material that which can be most fitly compressed into the compass allowed me by these few pages, are so great, that I have again and again laid down my task in despair; only to be urged on by my conviction that it is more clearly my duty to speak what may carry comfort to the hearts of some, than to worry because my imperfect manner of expression may offend the heads of others. All I can presume to hope for this record of an experience is, that it may have a passing value to certain of my readers whose anticipations of what they call "the Hereafter" are so vague or so dubious as to be more of a pain than a pleasure to themselves.

From the time of my reception into my father's house, I lost the sense of homelessness which had more or less possessed me since my entrance upon the new life, and felt myself becoming again a member of an organized society, with definite duties as well as assured pleasures before me.

These duties I did not find astonishingly different in their essence, while they had changed greatly in form, from those which had occupied me upon earth. I found myself still involved in certain filial and domestic responsibilities, in intellectual acquisition, in the moral support of others, and in spiritual self-culture. I found myself a member of an active community in which not a drone nor an invalid could be counted, and I quickly became, like others who surrounded me, an exceedingly busy person. At first my occupations did not assume sharp professional distinctiveness, but had rather the character of such as would belong to one in training for a more cultivated condition. This seemed to be true of many of my fellow-citizens; that they were still in a state of education for superior usefulness or happiness. With others, as I have intimated, it was not so. My father's business, for instance, remained what it had always been—that of a religious teacher; and I met women and men as well, to whom, as in the case of my old neighbor, Mrs. Mersey, there had been set apart an especial fellowship with the spirits of the recently dead or still living, who had need of great guidance. I soon formed, by observation, at least, the acquaintance, too, of a wide variety of natures;—I met artisans and artists, poets and scientists, people of agricultural pursuits, mechanical inventors, musicians, physicians, students, tradesmen, aerial messengers to the earth, or to other planets, and a long list besides, that would puzzle more than it would enlighten, should I attempt to describe it. I mention these points, which I have no space to amplify, mainly to give reality to any allusions that I shall make to my relations in the heavenly city, and to let it be understood that I speak of a community as organized and as various as Paris or New York; which possessed all the advantages and none of the evils that we are accustomed to associate with massed population; that such a community existed without sorrow, without sickness, without death, without anxiety, and without sin; that the evidences of almost incredible harmony, growth, and happiness which I saw before me in that one locality, I had reason to believe extended to uncounted others in unknown regions, thronging with joys and activities the mysteries of space and time.

For reasons which will be made clear as I approach the end of my narrative, I cannot speak as fully of many high and marvelous matters in the eternal life, as I wish that I might have done. I am giving impressions which, I am keenly aware, have almost the imperfection of a broken dream. I can only crave from the reader, on trust, a patience which he may be more ready to grant me at a later time.

I now began, as I say, to assume regular duties and pleasures; among the keenest of the latter was the constant meeting of old friends and acquaintances. Much perplexity, great delight, and some disappointment awaited me in these *dénouements* of earthly story.

The people whom I had naturally expected to meet earliest were often longest delayed from crossing my path; in some cases, they were altogether missing. Again, I was startled by coming in contact with individuals that I had never associated, in my conceptions of the future, with a spiritual existence at all; in these cases I was sometimes humbled by discovering a type of spiritual character so far above my own, that my fancies in their behalf proved to be unwarrantable self-sufficiency. Social life in the heavenly world, I soon learned, was a series of subtle or acute surprises. It sometimes reminded me of a simile of George Eliot's, wherein she likened human existence to a game of chess in which each one of the pieces had intellect and passions, and the player might be beaten by his own pawns. The element of unexpectedness, which constitutes the first and yet the most unreliable charm of earthly society, had here acquired a permanent dignity. One of the most memorable things which I observed about heavenly relations was, that people did not, in the degree or way to which I was accustomed, tire of each other. Attractions, to begin with, were less lightly experienced; their hold was deeper; their consequences more lasting. I had not been under my new conditions long, before I learned that here genuine feeling was never suffered to fall a sacrifice to intellectual curiosity, or emotional caprice; that here one had at last the stimulus of social attrition without its perils. I learned, of course, much else, which it is more than difficult, and some things which it is impossible, to explain. I testify only of what I am permitted.

Among the intellectual labors that I earliest undertook was the command of the Universal Language, which I soon found necessary to my convenience. In a community like that I had entered, many nationalities were represented, and I observed that while each retained its own familiar earthly tongue, and one had the pleasant opportunity of acquiring as many others as one chose, yet a common vocabulary became a desideratum of which, indeed, no one was compelled to avail himself contrary to his taste, but in which many, like myself, found the greatest pleasure and profit. The command of this language occupied much well-directed time.

I should not omit to say that a portion of my duty and my privilege consisted in renewed visits to the dearly-loved whom I had left upon the earth. These visits were sometimes matters of will with me. Again, they were strictly occasions of permission, and again, I was denied the power to make them when I most deeply desired to do so. Herein I learned the difference between trial and trouble, and that while the last was stricken out of heavenly life, the first distinctly remained. It is pleasant to me to remember that I was allowed to be of more than a little comfort to those who mourned for me; that it was I who guided them from despair to endurance, and so through peace to cheerfulness, and the hearty renewal of daily human content. These visits were for a long time—excepting the rare occasions on which I met Him who had spoken to me upon the sea-shore—the deepest delight which was offered me.

Upon one point I foresee that I shall be questioned by those who have had the patience so far to follow my recital. What, it will be asked, was the political constitution of the community you describe? What place in celestial society has worldly caste?

When I say, strictly none at all, let me not be misunderstood. I observed the greatest varieties of rank in the celestial kingdom, which seemed to me rather a close Theocracy than a wild commune. There were powers above me, and powers below; there were natural and harmonious social selections; there were laws and their officers; there was obedience and its dignity; there was influence and its authority; there were gifts and their distinctions. I may say that I found far more reverence for differences of rank or influence that I was used to seeing, at least in my own corner of the earth. The main point was that the basis of the whole thing had undergone a tremendous change. Inheritance, wealth, intellect, genius, beauty, all the old passports to power, were replaced by one so simple yet so autocratic, that I hardly know how to give any idea at once of its dignity and its sweetness. I may call this personal holiness. Position, in the new life, I found depended upon spiritual claims. Distinction was the result of character. The nature nearest to the Divine Nature ruled the social forces. Spiritual culture was the ultimate test of individual importance.

I inquired one day for a certain writer of world-wide—I mean of earth-wide—celebrity, who, I had learned, was a temporary visitor in the city, and whom I wished to meet. I will not for sufficient reasons mention the name of this man, who had been called the ge-

nius of his century, below. I had anticipated that a great ovation would
be given him, in which I desired to join, and I was surprised that his
presence made little or no stir in our community. Upon investigating the facts, I learned that his public influence was, so far, but a slight
one, though it had gradually gained, and was likely to increase with
time. He had been a man whose splendid powers were dedicated to
the temporary and worldly aspects of Truth, whose private life was
selfish and cruel, who had written the most famous poem of his age,
but "by all his searching" had not found out God.

In the conditions of the eternal life, this genius had been obliged
to set itself to learning the alphabet of spiritual truth; he was still a
pupil, rather than a master among us, and I was told that he himself
ardently objected to receiving a deference which was not as yet his
due; having set the might of his great nature as strenuously now to
the spiritual, as once to the intellectual task; in which, I must say, I
was not without expectation that he would ultimately outvie us all.

On the same day when this distinguished man entered and left our
city (having quietly accomplished his errand), I heard the confusion
of some public excitement at a distance, and hastening to see what
it meant, I discovered that the object of it was a plain, I thought in
her earthly life she must have been a poor woman, obscure, perhaps,
and timid. The people pressed towards her, and received her into the
town by acclamation. They crowned her with amaranth and flung
lilies in her path. The authorities of the city officially met her; the
people of influence hastened to beseech her to do honor to their
homes by her modest presence; we crowded for a sight of her, we
begged for a word from her, we bewildered her with our tributes,
till she hid her blushing face and was swept out of our sight.

"But who is this," I asked and eager passer, "to whom such an
extraordinary reception is tendered? I have seen nothing like it since
I came here."

"Is it possible you do not know ⸺ ⸺?"

My informant gave a name which indeed was not unfamiliar to me;
it was that of a woman who had united to extreme beauty of private

character, and a high type of faith in invisible truths, life-long devotion to an unpopular philanthropy. She had never been called a "great" woman on earth. Her influence had not been large. Her cause had never been the fashion, while she herself was living. Society had never amused itself by adopting her, even to the extent of a parlor lecture. Her name, so far as it was familiar to the public at all, had been the synonym of a poor zealot, a plain fanatic, to be tolerated for her conscientiousness and—avoided for her earnestness. Since her death, the humane consecration which she represented had marched on like a conquering army over her grave. Earth, of which she was not worthy, had known her too late. Heaven was proud to do honor to the spiritual foresight and sustained self-denial, as royal as it was rare.

I remember, also, being deeply touched by a sight upon which I chanced, one morning, when I was strolling about the suburbs of the city, seeking the refreshment of solitude before the duties of the day began. For, while I was thus engaged, I met our Master, suddenly. He was busily occupied with others, and, beyond the deep recognition of His smile, I had no converse with Him. He was followed at a little distance, as He was apt to be, by a group of playing children; but He was in close communion with two whom I saw to be souls newly-arrived from the lower life. One of these was a man—I should say he had been a rough man, and had come out of a rude life— who conversed with Him eagerly but reverently, as they walked on towards the town. Upon the other side, our Lord held with His own hand the hand of a timid, trembling woman, who scarcely dared to raise her eyes from the ground; now and then she drew His garment's edge furtively to her lips, and let it fall again, with the slow motion of one who is in a dream of ecstasy. These two people, I judged, had no connection with each other beyond the fact that they were simultaneous new-comers to the new country, and had, perhaps, both borne with them either special need or merit, I could hardly decide which. I took occasion to ask a neighbor, an old resident of the city, and wise in its mysteries, what he supposed to be the explanation of the scene before us, and why these two were so distinguished by the favor of Him whose least glance made holiday in the soul of any one of us. It was then explained to me, that the man about whom I had inquired was the hero of a great calamity, with which the lower world was at present occupied. One of the most frightful railway accidents of this generation had been averted, and the lives of four hundred helpless passengers saved, by the sublime sacrifice of this locomotive engineer, who died (it will be remembered) a death of voluntary and unique torture to save his train. All that could be said of the tragedy was that it held the essence of self-sacrifice in a form seldom attained by man. At the moment I saw this noble fellow, he had so immediately come among us that the expression of physical agony had hardly yet died out of his face, and his eye still blazed with the fire of his tremendous deed.

"But who is the woman?" I asked.

"She was a delicate creature—sick—died of the fright and shock; the only passenger on the train who did not escape."

I inquired why she too was thus preferred; what glorious deed had she done, to make her so dear to the Divine Heart?

"She? Ah, she," said my informant, "was only one of the household saints. She had been notable among celestial observers for many years. You know the type I mean—shy, silent—never thinks of herself, scarcely knows she has a self—toils, drudges, endures, prays; expects nothing of her friends, and gives all; hopes for little, even from her Lord, but surrenders everything; full of religious ideals, not all of them theoretically wise, but practically noble; a woman ready to be cut to inch pieces for her faith in an invisible Love that has never apparently given her anything in particular. Oh, you know the kind of woman: has never had anything of her own, in all her life—not even her own room—and a whole family adore her without knowing it, and lean upon her like infants without seeing it. We have been watching for this woman's coming. We knew there would be an especial greeting for her. But nobody thought of her accompanying the engineer. Come! Shall we not follow, and see how they will be received? If I am not mistaken, it will be a great day in the city."

¿11¿

Among the inquiries that must be raised by my fragmentary recital, I am only too keenly aware of the difficulty of answering one
which I do not see my way altogether to ignore. I refer to that af-
fecting the domestic relations of the eternal world.

It will be readily seen that I might not be permitted to share much
of the results of my observation in this direction, with earthly curiosity, or even earthly anxiety. It is not without thought and prayer
for close guidance that I suffer myself to say, in as few words as possible, that I found the unions which go to form heavenly homes so
different from the marriage relations of earth, in their laws of selection and government, that I quickly understood the meaning of our
Lord's few revealed words as to that matter; while yet I do not find
myself at liberty to explain either the words or the facts. I think I
cannot be wrong in adding, that in a number of cases, so great as to
astonish me, the marriages of earth had no historic effect upon the
ties of Heaven. Laws of affiliation uniting soul to soul in a relation
infinitely closer than a bond, and more permanent than any which
the average human experience would lead to if it were socially a free
agent, controlled the attractions of this pure and happy life, in a
manner of which I can only say that it must remain a mystery to the
earthly imagination. I have intimated that in some cases the choices
of time were so blessed as to become the choices of Eternity. I may
say, that if I found it lawful to utter the impulse of my soul, I should
cry throughout the breadth of the earth a warning to the lightness,
or the haste, or the presumption, or the mistake that chose to love
for one world, when it might have loved for two.

For, let me say most solemnly, that the relations made between man
and woman on earth I found to be, in importance to the individual,
second to nothing in the range of human experience, save the adjustment of the soul to the personality of God Himself.

If I say that I found earthly marriage to have been a temporary expedient for preserving the form of the eternal fact; that freedom in this as in all other things became in Heaven the highest law; that the great sea of human misery, swelled by the passion of love on earth, shall evaporate to the last drop in the blaze of bliss to which no human counterpart can approach any nearer than a shadow to the sun,—I may be understood by those for whose sake alone it is worth while to allude to this mystery at all; for the rest it matters little.

Perhaps I should say, once for all, that every form of pure pleasure or happiness which had existed upon the earth had existed as a type of a greater. Our divinest hours below had been scarcely more than suggestions of their counterparts above. I do not expect to be understood. It must only be remembered that, in all instances, the celestial life develops the soul of a thing. When I speak of eating and drinking, for instance, I do not mean that we cooked and prepared our food as we do below. The elements of nutrition continued to exist for us as they had in the earth, the air, the water, though they were available without drudgery or anxiety. Yet I mean distinctly that the sense of taste remained, that it was gratified at need, that it was a finer one and gave a keener pleasure than its coarser prototype below. I mean that the *soul of a sense* is a more exquisite thing than what we may call the body of the sense, as developed to earthly consciousness.

So far from there being any diminution in the number or power of the senses in the spiritual life, I found not only an acuter intensity in those which we already possessed, but that the effect of our new conditions was to create others of whose character we had never dreamed. To be sure, wise men had forecast the possibility of this fact, differing among themselves even as to the accepted classification of what they had, as Scaliger who called speech the sixth sense, or our English contemporary who included heat and force in his list (also of six); or more imaginative men who had admitted the conceivability of inconceivable powers in an order of being beyond the human. Knowing a little of these speculations, I was not so much surprised at the facts as overwhelmed by their extent and variety. Yet if I try to explain them, I am met by an almost insurmountable obstacle.

It is well known that missionaries are often thwarted in their religious labors by the absence in savage tongues of any words corresponding to certain ideas such as that of purity or unselfishness. Philologists have told us of one African tribe in whose language exist six different words descriptive of murder; none whatever expressive of love. In another no such word as gratitude can be found. Perhaps no illustration can better serve to indicate the impediments which bar the way to my describing to beings who possess but five senses and their corresponding imaginative culture, the habits or enjoyments consequent upon the development of ten senses or fifteen. I am allowed to say as much as this: that the growth of these celestial powers was variable with individuals throughout the higher world, or so much of it as I became acquainted with. It will be readily seen what an illimitable scope for anticipation or achievement is given to daily life by such an evolution of the nature. It should be carefully remembered that this serves only as a single instance of the exuberance of what we call everlasting life.

Below, I remember that I used sometimes to doubt the possibility of one's being happy forever under any conditions, and had moods in which I used to question the value of endless existence. I wish most earnestly to say, that before I had been in Heaven days, Eternity did not seem long enough to make room for the growth of character, the growth of mind, the variety of enjoyment and employment, and the increase of usefulness that practically constituted immortality.

It could not have been long after my arrival at my father's house that he took me with him to the great music hall of our city. It was my first attendance at any one of the public festivals of these happy people, and one long to be treasured in thought. It was, in fact, nothing less than the occasion of a visit by Beethoven, and the performance of a new oratorio of his own, which he conducted in person. Long before the opening hour the streets of the city were thronged. People with holiday expressions poured in from the country. It was a gala-day with all the young folks especially, much as such matters go below. A beautiful thing which I noticed was the absence of all personal insistence in the crowd. The weakest, or the saddest, or the most timid, or those who, for any reason, had the more need of this great pleasure, were selected by their neighbors and urged on into the more desirable positions. The music hall, so-called, was situated upon a hill just outside the town, and consisted of an immense roof supported by rose-colored marble pillars. There were no walls to the building, so that there was the effect of being no limit to the audience, which extended past the line of luxuriously covered seats provided for them, upon the grass, and even into the streets leading to the city. So perfect were what we should call below the telephonic arrangement of the community, that those who remained in their own homes or pursued their usual avocations were not deprived of the music. My impressions are that every person in the city, who desired to put himself in communication with it, heard the oratorio; but I am not familiar with the system by which this was effected. It involved a high advance in the study of acoustics, and was one of the things which I noted to be studied at a wiser time.

Many distinguished persons known to you below, were present, some from our own neighborhood, and others guests of the city. It was delightful to observe the absence of all jealousy or narrow criticism among themselves, and also the reverence with which their superiority was regarded by the less gifted. Every good or great thing seemed to be so heartily shared with every being capable of sharing it, and all personal gifts to become material for such universal pride, that one experienced a kind of transport at the elevation of the public character.

I remembered how it used to be below, when I was present at some musical festival in the familiar hall where the bronze statue of Beethoven, behind the sea of sound, stood calmly. How he towered above our poor unfinished story! As we grouped there, sitting each isolated with his own thirst, brought to be slaked or excited by the flood of music; drinking down into our frivolity or our despair the outlet of that mighty life, it used to seem to me that I heard, far above the passion of the orchestra, his own high words,—his own music made articulate,—*"I go to meet Death with joy."*

When there came upon the people in that heavenly audience-room a stir, like the rustling of a dead leaf upon crusted snow; when the stir grew to a solemn murmur; when the murmur ran into a lofty cry; when I saw that the orchestra, the chorus, and the audience had risen like one breathless man, and knew that Beethoven stood before us, the light of day darkened for that instant before me. The prelude was well under way, I think, before I dared lift my eyes to his face.

The great tide swept me on. When upon earth had he created sound like this? Where upon earth had we heard its like? There he is, one listening nerve from head to foot, he who used to stand deaf in the middle of his own orchestra—desolate no more, denied no more forever, all the heavenly senses possible to Beethoven awake to the last delicate response; all the solemn faith in the invisible, in the holy, which he had made his own, triumphant now; all the powers of his mighty nature in action like a rising storm—there stands Beethoven immortally alive.

What knew we of music, I say, who heard its earthly prototype? It was but the tuning of the instruments before the eternal orchestra shall sound. Soul! swing yourself free upon this mighty current. Of what will Beethoven tell us whom he dashes on like drops?

As the pæan rises, I bow my life to understand. What would be with us whom God chose to make Beethoven everlastingly? What is the burden of this master's message, given now in Heaven, as once on earth? Do we hear aright? Do we read the score correctly?

"Holy—holy"—

A chorus of angel voices, trained since the time when morning stars sang together with the sons of God, take up the word:

"Holy, *holy,* HOLY is the Lord."

. . . .

When the oratorio has ended, and we glide out, each hushed as a hidden thought, to his own ways, I stay beneath a linden-tree to gather breath. A fine sound, faint as the music of a dream, strikes my ringing ears, and, looking up, I see that the leaf above my head is singing. Has it, too, been one of the great chorus yonder? Did he command the forces of nature, as he did the seraphs of Heaven, or the powers of earth?

The strain falls away slowly form the lips of the leaf:

"Holy, holy, holy,"—

It trembles, and is still.

₹12₹

That which it is permitted me to relate to you moves on swiftly before the thoughts, like the compression in the last act of a drama. The next scene which starts from the variousness of heavenly delight I find to be the Symphony of Color.

There was a time in the history of art, below, when this, and similar phrases, had acquired almost a slang significance, owing to the affectation of their use by the shallow. I was, therefore, the more surprised at meeting a fact so lofty behind the guise of the familiar words; and noted it as but one of many instances in which the earthly had deteriorated from the ideals of the celestial life.

It seemed that the development of color had reached a point never conceived of below, and that the treatment of it constituted an art by itself. By this I do not mean its treatment under the form of painting, decoration, dress, or any embodiment whatever. What we were called to witness was an exhibition of color, pure and simple.

This occasion, of which I especially speak, was controlled by great colorists, some of earthly, some of heavenly renown. Not all of them were artists in the accepted sense of designers; among them were one or two select creatures in whom the passion of color had been remarkable, but, so far as the lower world was concerned, for the great part inactive, for want of any scientific means of expression.

We have all known the *color natures,* and, if we have had a fine sympathy, have compassionated them as much as any upon earth, whether they were found among the disappointed disciples of Art itself, or hidden away in plain homes, where the paucity of existence held all the delicacy and the dream of life close prisoners.

Among the managers of this Symphony I should say that I observed, at a distance, the form of Raphael. I heard it rumored that Leonardo was present, but I did not see him. There was another celebrated artist engaged in the work, whose name I am not allowed to give. It was an unusual occasion, and had attracted attention at a distance. The Symphony did not take place in our own city, but in an adjacent town, to which our citizens, as well as those of other places, repaired in great numbers. We sat, I remember, in a luxurious coliseum, closely darkened. The building was circular in form; it was indeed a perfect globe, in whose centre, without touching anywhere the superficies, we were seated. Air without light entered freely, I know not how, and fanned our faces perpetually. Distant music appealed to the ear, without engaging it. Pleasures, which we could receive or dismiss at will, wandered by, and were assimilated by those extra senses which I have no means of describing. Whatever could be done to put soul and body in a state of ease so perfect as to admit of complete receptivity, and in a mood so high as to induce the loftiest interpretation of the purely æsthetic entertainment before us, was done in the amazing manner characteristic of this country. I do not know that I had ever felt so keenly as on this occasion the delight taken by God in providing happiness for the children of His discipline and love. We had suffered so much, some of us, below, that it did not seem natural, at first, to accept sheer pleasure as an end in and of itself. But I learned that this, like many other fables in Heaven, had no moral. Live! Be! Do! Be glad! Because He lives, ye live also. Grow! Gain! Achieve! Hope! *That* is to glorify Him and enjoy Him forever. Having fought—rest. Having trusted—know. Having endured—enjoy. Being safe—venture. Being pure—fear not to be sensitive. Being in harmony with the Soul of all delights—dare to indulge thine own soul to the brim therein. Having acquired holiness—thou hast no longer any broken law to fear. Dare to be happy. This was the spirit of daily life among us. "Nothing was required of us but to be natural," as I have said before. And it "was natural to be right," thank God, at last.

Being a new-comer, and still so unlearned, I could not understand the Color Symphony as many of the spectators did, while yet I enjoyed it intensely, as an untaught musical organization may enjoy the most complicated composition. I think it was one of the most stimulating sights I ever saw, and my ambition to master this new art flashed fire at once.

Slowly, as we sat silent, at the centre of that great white globe—it was built of porphyry, I think, or some similar substance—there began to breathe upon the surface pure light. This trembled and deepened, till we were enclosed in a sphere of white fire. This I perceived, to scholars in the science of color, signified distinct thought, as a grand chord does to the musician. Thus it was with the hundred effects which followed. White light quivered into pale blue. Blue struggled with violet. Gold and orange parted. Green and gray and crimson glided on. Rose—the living rose—blushed upon us, and faltered under—over—yonder, till we were shut into a world of it, palpitating. It was as if we had gone behind the soul of a woman's blush, or the meaning of a sunrise. Whoever has known the passion for that color will understand why some of the spectators were with difficulty restrained from flinging themselves down into it, as into a sea of rapture.

There were others more affected by the purple, and even by the scarlet; some, again, by the delicate tints in which was the color of the sun, and by colors which were hints rather than expressions. Marvelous modifications of rays set in. They had their laws, their chords, their harmonies, their scales; they carried their melodies and "execution;" they had themes and ornamentation. Each combination had its meaning. The trained eye received it, as the trained ear receives orchestra or oratory. The senses melted, but the intellect was astir. A perfect composition of color unto color was before us, ex-

quisite in detail, magnificent in mass. Now it seemed as if we ourselves, sitting there ensphered in color, flew around the globe with
the quivering rays. Now as if we sank into endless sleep with repos-
ing tints; now as if we drank of color; then as if we dreamed it; now
as if we felt it—clasped it; then as if we heard it. We were taken into
the heart of it; into the mystery of the June sky, and the grass-blade,
the blue-bell, the child's cheek, the cloud at sunset, the snow-drift
at twilight. The apple-blossom told us its secret, and the down on
the pigeon's neck, and the plume of the rose-curlew, and the rob-
in's-egg, and the hair of blonde women, and the scarlet passion-flower,
and the mist over everglades, and the power of a dark eye.

It may be remembered that I have alluded once to the rainbow
which I saw soon after reaching the new life, and that I raised a question at the time as to the number of rays exhibited in the celestial
prism. As I watched the Symphony, I became convinced that the variety of colors unquestionably far exceeded those with which we were
familiar on earth. The Indian occultists indeed had long urged that
they saw fourteen tints in the prism; this was the dream of the mystic,
who, by a tremendous system of education, claims to have subjected
the body to the soul, so that the ordinary laws of nature yield to his
control. Physicists had also taught us that the laws of optics involved
the necessity of other colors beyond those whose rays were admissi-
ble by our present vision; this was the assertion of that science which
is indebted more largely to the imagination than the worshiper of the
Fact has yet arisen from prone posture high enough to see.

Now, indeed, I had the truth before me. Colors which no artist's
palette, no poet's rapture knew, played upon optic nerves exquisitely trained to receive such effects, and were appropriated by other
senses empowered to share them in a manner which human language
supplies me with no verb or adjective to express.

As we journeyed home after the Symphony, I was surprised to find
how calming had been the effect of its intense excitement. Without
fever of pulse or revel fancy or wearied nerve, I looked about upon
the peaceful country. I felt ready for any duty. I was strong for all

deprivation. I longed to live more purely. I prayed to live more un-selfishly. I greatly wished to share the pleasure, with which I had been blessed, with some denied soul. I thought of uneducated people, and coarse people, who had yet to be trained to so many of the highest varieties of happiness. I thought of sick people, all their earthly lives invalids, recently dead, and now free to live. I wished that I had sought some of these out, and taken them with me to the Symphony.

It was a rare evening, even in the blessed land. I enjoyed the change of scene as I used to do in traveling, below. It was delightful to look abroad and see everywhere prosperity and peace. The children were shouting and tumbling in the fields. Young people strolled laughing by twos or in groups. The vigorous men and women busied them-selves or rested at the doors of cosy homes. The ineffable landscape of hill and water stretched on behind the human foreground. No-where a chill or a blot; nowhere a tear or a scowl, a deformity, a dis-ability, or an evil passion. There was no flaw in the picture. There was no error in the fact. I felt that I was among a perfectly happy people. I said, "I am in a holy world."

The next day was a Holy Day; we of the earth still called it the Sabbath, from long habit. I remember an especial excitement on that Holy Day following the Color Symphony, inasmuch as we assem-bled to be instructed by one whom, above all other men that had ever lived on earth, I should have taken most trouble to hear. This was no other than St. John the Apostle.

I remember that we held the service in the open air, in the fields beyond the city, for "there was no Temple therein." The Beloved Disciple stood above us, on the rising ground. It would be impossi-ble to forget, but it is well-nigh impossible to describe, the appear-ance of the preacher. I think he had the most sensitive face I ever saw in any man; yet his dignity was unapproachable. He had a ring-ing voice of remarkable sweetness, and great power of address. He seemed more divested of himself than any orator I had heard. He poured his personality out upon us, like one of the forces of nature, as largely, and as unconsciously.

He taught us much. He reasoned of mysteries over which we had pored helplessly all our lives below. He explained intricate points in the plan of human life. He touched upon the perplexities of religious faith. He cast a great light backward over the long, dim way by which we had crept to our present blessedness. He spoke to us of our deadliest doubts. He confirmed for us our patient belief. He made us ashamed of our distrust and our restlessness. He left us eager for faith. He gave vigor to our spiritual ideals. He spoke to us of the love of God, as the light speaks of the sun. He revealed to us how we had misunderstood Him. Our souls cried out within us, as we remembered our errors. We gathered ourselves like soldiers as we knew our possibilities. We swayed in his hands as the bough sways in the wind. Each man looked at his neighbor as one whose eyes ask: "Have I wronged thee? Let me atone." "Can I serve thee? Show me how." All our spiritual life arose like an athlete, to exercise itself; we sought hard tasks; we aspired for far prizes; we turned to our daily lives like new-created beings; so truly we had kept Holy Day. When the discourse was over, there followed an anthem sung by a choir or child-angels hovering in mid-air above the preacher, and beautiful exceedingly to the sight and to the ear. "God," they sang, "is Love—*is* Love—is LOVE." In the refrain we joined with our own awed voices.

The chant died away. All the air of all the worlds was still. The beloved Disciple raised his hand in solemn signal. A majestic Form glided to his side. To whom should the fisherman of Galilee turn with a look like *that*? Oh, grace of God! what a smile was there! The Master and Disciple stand together; they rise above us. See! He falls upon his knees before that Other. So we also, sinking to our own, hide our very faces from the sight.

Our Lord steps forth, and stands alone. To us in glory, as to them of old in sorrow, He is the God made manifest. We do not lift our bowed heads, but we feel that He has raised His piercéd hands above us, and that His own lips call down the Benediction of His Father upon our eternal lives.

¿13 ς

My father had been absent from home a great deal, taking journeys with whose object he did not acquaint me. I myself had not visited the earth for some time; I cannot say how long. I do not find it possible to divide heavenly time by an earthly calendar, and cannot even decide how much of an interval, by human estimates, had been indeed covered by my residence in the Happy Country, as described upon these pages.

My duties had called me in other directions, and I had been exceedingly busy. My father sometimes spoke of our dear hearts at home, and reported them as all well; but he was not communicative about them. I observed that he took more pains than usual, or I should say more pleasure than usual, in the little domestic cares of our heavenly home. Never had it been in more perfect condition. The garden and the grounds were looking exquisitely. All the trifling comforts or ornaments of the house were to his mind. We talked of them much, and wandered about in our leisure moments, altering or approving details. I did my best to make him happy, but my own heart told me how lonely he must be despite me. We talked less of her coming than we used to do. I felt that he had accepted the separation with the unquestioning spirit which one gains so deeply in Heaven; and that he was content, as one who trusted, still to wait.

One evening, I came home slowly and alone. My father had been away for some days. I had been passing several hours with some friends, who, with myself, had been greatly interested in an event of public importance. A messenger was needed to carry certain tidings to a great astronomer, known to us of old on earth, who was at that time busied in research in a distant planet. It was a desirable embassy, and many sought the opportunity for travel and culture which it gave. After some delay in the appointment, it was given to a person but just arrived from below: a woman not two days dead. This surprised me till I had inquired into the circumstances, when I learned that the new-comer had been on earth an extreme sufferer, bed-ridden for forty years. Much of this time she had been unable even to look out of doors. The airs of Heaven had been shut from her darkened chamber. For years she had not been able to sustain conversation with her own friends, except on rare occasions. Possessed of a fine mind, she had been unable to read, or even to bear the human voice in reading. Acute pain had tortured her days. Sleeplessness had made horror of her nights. She was poor. She was dependent. She was of a refined organization. She was of a high spirit, and of energetic temperament. Medical science, holding out no cure, assured her that she might live to old age. She lived. When she was seventy-six years old, death remembered her. This woman had sometimes been inquired of, touching her faith in that Mystery which we call God. I was told that she gave but one answer; beyond this, revealing no more of experience than the grave itself, to which, more than to any other simile, her life could be likened.

"Though He slay me," she said, "I will trust."

"But, do you never doubt?"

"I *will* trust."

To this rare spirit, set free at last and re-embodied, the commission of which I have spoken was delegated; no one in all the city grudged her its coveted advantages. A mighty shout rose in the public ways when the selection was made known. I should have thought she might become delirious with the sudden access of her freedom, but it was said that she received her fortune quietly, and, slipping out of sight, was away upon her errand before we saw her face.

The incident struck me as a most impressive one, and I was occupied with it, as I walked home thoughtfully. Indeed, I was so absorbed that I went with my eyes cast down, and scarcely noticed when I had reached our own home. I did not glance at the house, but continued my way up the winding walk between the trees, still drowned in my reverie.

It was a most peaceful evening. I felt about me the fine light at which I did not look; that evening glow was one of the new colors,—one of the heavenly colors that I find it impossible to depict. The dog came to meet me as usual; he seemed keenly excited, and would have hurried me into the house. I patted him absently as I strolled on.

Entering the house with a little of the sense of loss which, even in the Happy World, accompanies the absence of those we love, and wondering when my father would be once more with me, I was startled at hearing his voice—no, voices; there were two; they came from an upper chamber, and the silent house echoed gently with their subdued words.

I stood for a moment listening below; I felt the color flash out of my face; my heart stood still. I took a step or two forward—hesitated—advanced with something like fear. The dog pushed before me, and urged me to follow. After a moment's thought I did so, resolutely.

The doors stood open everywhere, and the evening air blew in with a strong and wholesome force. No one had heard me. Guided by the voices of the unseen speakers I hurried on, across the hall, through my own room, and into that sacred spot I have spoken of, wherein for so many solitary years my dear father had made ready for her coming who was the joy of his joy, in Heaven, as she had been on earth.

For that instant, I saw all the familiar details of the room in a blur of light. It was as if a sea of glory filled the place. Across it, out beyond the window, on the balcony which overlooked the hill-country and the sea, stood my father and my mother, hand in hand.

She did not hear me, even yet. They were talking quietly, and were absorbed. Uncertain what to do, I might even have turned and left them undisturbed, so sacred seemed that hour of theirs to me; so separate in all the range of experience in either world, or any life. But her heart warned her, and she stirred, and so saw me—my dear mother—come to us, at last.

Oh, what arms can gather like a mother's, whether in earth or Heaven? Whose else could be those brooding touches, those raining tears, those half-inarticulate maternal words? And for her, too, the bitterness is passed, the blessedness begun. Oh, my dear mother! My dear mother! I thank God I was the child appointed to give you welcome—thus . . .

"And how is it with Tom,—poor Tom!"

"He has grown such a fine fellow; you cannot think. I leaned upon him. He was the comfort of my old age."

"Poor Tom!"

"And promises to make such a man, dear! A good boy. No bad habits, yet. Your father is so pleased that he makes a scholar."

"Dear Tom! And Alice?"

"It was hard to leave Alice. But she is young. Life is before her. God is good."

"And you, my dearest, was it hard for you at the last? Was it a long sickness? Who took care of you? Mother! did you suffer *much?*"

"Dear, I never suffered any. I had a sudden stroke I think. I was sitting by the fire with the children. It was vacation and Tom was at home. They were all at home. I started to cross the room, and it grew dark. I did not know that I was dead till I found I was standing there upon the balcony, in your father's arms."

"I had to tell her what had happened. She wouldn't believe me at the first."

"Were you with her all the time below?"

"All the time; for days before the end."

"And you brought her here yourself, easily?"

"All the way, myself. She slept like a baby, and wakened—as she says."

14

But was it possible to feel desolate in Heaven? Life now filled to the horizon. Our business, our studies, and our pleasures occupied every moment. Every day new expedients of delight unfurled before us. Our conceptions of happiness increased faster than their realization. The imagination itself grew, as much as the aspiration. We saw height beyond height of joy, as we saw outline above outline of duty. How paltry looked our wildest earthly dream! How small our largest worldly deed! One would not have thought it possible that one could even want so much as one demanded here; or hope so far as one expected now.

What possibilities stretched on; each leading to a larger, like newly-discovered stars, one beyond another; as the pleasure or the achievement took its place, the capacity for the next increased. Satiety or its synonyms passed out of our language, except as a reminiscence of the past. See, what were the conditions of this eternal problem. Given: a pure heart, perfect health, unlimited opportunity for usefulness, infinite chance of culture, home, friendship, love; the elimination from practical life of anxiety and separation; and the intense spiritual stimulus of the presence of our dear Master, through whom we approached the mystery of God—how incredible to anything short of experience the sum of happiness!

I soon learned how large a part of our delight consisted in anticipation; since now we knew anticipation without alloy of fear. I thought much of the joys in store for me, which yet I was not perfected enough to attain. I looked onward to the perpetual meeting of old friends and acquaintances, both of the living and the dead; to the command of unknown languages, arts, and sciences, and knowledges manifold; to the grandeur of helping the weak, and revering the strong; to the privilege of guarding the erring or the tried, whether of earth or heaven, and of sharing all attainable wisdom with the less wise, and of even instructing those too ignorant to know that they were not wise, and of ministering to the dying, and of assisting in bringing together the separated. I looked forward to meeting select natures, the distinguished of earth or Heaven; to reading history backward by contact with its actors, and settling its knotty points by their evidential testimony. Was I not in a world where Loyola, and Jeanne d'Arc, or Luther, or Arthur, could be asked questions?

I would follow the experiments of great discoverers, since their advent to this place. What did Newton, and Columbus, and Darwin in the eternal life?

I would keep pace with the development of art. To what standard had Michaelangelo been raising the public taste all these years?

I would join the fragments of those private histories which had long been matter of public interest. Where, and whose now, was Vittoria Colonna?

I would have the *finales* of the old Sacred stories. What use had been made of the impetuosity of Peter? What was the private life of Saint John? With what was the fine intellect of Paul now occupied? What was the charm in the Magdalene? In what sacred fields did the sweet nature of Ruth go gleaning? Did David write the new anthems for the celestial chorals? What was the attitude of Moses towards the Persistence of Force? Where was Judas? And did the Betrayed plead for the betrayer?

I would study the sociology of this explanatory life. Where, if anywhere, were the Cave-men? In what world, and under what educators, were the immortal souls of Laps and Bushmen trained? What social position had the early Christian martyrs? What became of Caligula, whose nurse, we were told, smeared her breasts with blood, and so developed the world-hated tyrant from the outraged infant? Where was Buddha, "the Man who knew"? What affectionate relation subsisted between him and the Man who Loved?

I would bide my time patiently, but I, too, would become an experienced traveler through the spheres. Our Sun I would visit, and scarlet Mars, said by our astronomers below to be the planet most likely to contain inhabitants. The colored suns I would observe, and the nebulæ, and the mysteries of space, powerless now to chill one by its reputed temperature, said to be forever at zero. Where were the Alps of Heaven? The Niagara of celestial scenery? The tropics of the spiritual world? Ah, how I should pursue Eternity with questions!

What was the relation of mechanical power to celestial conditions? What use was made of Watts and Stevenson?

What occupied the ex-hod-carriers and cooks?

Where were all the songs of all the poets? In the eternal accumulation of knowledge, what proportion sifted through the strainers of spiritual criticism? What *were* the standards of spiritual criticism? What became of those creations of the human intellect which had acquired immortality? Were there instances where these figments of fancy had achieved an eternal existence lost by their own creators? Might not one of the possible mysteries of our new state of existence be the fact of a world peopled by the great creatures of our imaginations known to us below? And might not one of our pleasures consist in visiting such a world? Was it incredible that Helen, and Lancelot, and Sigfried, and Juliet, and Faust, and Dinah Morris, and the Lady of Shalott, and Don Quixote, and Colonel Newcome, and Sam Weller, and Uncle Tom, and Hester Prynne and Jean Valjean existed? could be approached by way of holiday, as one used to take up the drama or the fiction, on a leisure hour, down below?

Already, though so short a time had I been in the upper life, my imagination was overwhelmed with the sense of its possibilities. They seemed to overlap one another like the molecules of gold in a ring, without visible juncture of practical end. I was ready for the inconceivable itself. In how many worlds should I experience myself? How many lives should I live? Did eternal existence mean eternal variety of growth, suspension, renewal? Might youth and maturity succeed each other exquisitely? Might individual life reproduce itself from seed, to flower, to fruit, like a plant, through the cycles? Would childhood or age be a matter of personal choice? Would the affectional or the intellectual temperaments at will succeed each other? Might one try the domestic or the public career in different existences? Try the bliss of love in one age, the culture of solitude in another? Be oneself yet be all selves? Experience all glories, all discipline, all knowledge, all hope? Know the ecstasy of assured union with the one creature chosen out of time and Eternity to complement the soul? And yet forever pursue the unattainable with the rapture and the reverence of newly-awakened and still ungratified feeling?

Ah me! was it possible to feel desolate even in Heaven?

I think it may be, because I had been much occupied with thoughts like these; or it may be that, since my dear mother's coming, I had been, naturally, thrown more by myself in my desire to leave those two uninterrupted in their first reunion—but I must admit that I had lonely moments, when I realized that Heaven had yet failed to provide me with a home of my own, and that the most loving filial position could not satisfy the nature of a mature man or woman in any world. I must admit that I began to be again subject to retrospects and sadnesses which had been well brushed away from my heart since my advent to this place. I must admit that in experiencing the immortality of being, I found that I experienced no less the immortality of love.

Had I to meet that old conflict *here*? I never asked for everlasting life. Will He impose it, and not free me from *that*? God forgive me! Have I evil in my heart still? Can one sin in Heaven? Nay, be merciful, be merciful! I will be patient. I will have trust. But the old nerves are not dead. The old ache has survived the grave.

Why was this permitted, if without a cure? Why had death no power to call decay upon that for which eternal life seemed to have provided no health? It had seemed to me, so far as I could observe the heavenly society, that only the fortunate affections of preëxistence survived. The unhappy, as well as the imperfect, were outlived and replaced. Mysteries had presented themselves here, which I was not yet wise enough to clear up. I saw, however, that a great ideal was one thing which never died. The attempt to realize it often involved effects which seemed hardly less than miraculous.

But for myself, events had brought no solution of the problems of my past; and with the tenacity of a constant nature I was unable to see any for the future.

I mused one evening, alone with these long thoughts. I was strolling upon a wide, bright field. Behind me lay the city, glittering and glad. Beyond, I saw the little sea which I had crossed. The familiar outline of the hills uprose behind. All Heaven seemed heavenly. I heard distant merry voices and music. Listening closely, I found that the Wedding March that had stirred so many human heart-beats was perfectly performed somewhere across the water, and that the wind bore the sounds towards me. I then remembered to have heard it said that Mendelssohn was himself a guest of some distinguished person in an adjacent town, and that certain music of his was to be given for the entertainment of a group of people who had been deaf-mutes in the lower life.

As the immortal power of the old music filled the air, I stayed my steps to listen. The better to do this, I covered my eyes with my hands, and so stood blindfold and alone in the midst of the wide field.

The passion of earth and the purity of Heaven—the passion of Heaven and the deferred hope of earth—what loss and what possession were in the throbbing strains!

As never on earth, they called the glad to rapture. As never on earth, they stirred the sad to silence. Where, before, had soul or sense been called by such a clarion? What music was, we used to dream. What it is, we dare, at last, to know.

And yet—I would have been spared this if I could, I think, just now. Give me a moment's grace. I would draw breath, and so move on again, and turn me to my next duty quietly, since even Heaven denies me, after all.

I would—what would I? Where am I? Who spoke, or stirred? Who called me by a name unheard by me of any living lip for almost twenty years?

In a transport of something not unlike terror, I could not remove my hands from my eyes, but still stood, blinded and dumb, in the middle of the shining field. Beneath my clasped fingers, I caught the radiance of the edges of the blades of grass that the low breeze swept against my garment's hem; and strangely in that strange moment, there came for me, for the only articulate thought I could command, these two lines of an old hymn:

"Sweet fields beyond the selling flood
Stand dressed in living green."

"Take down your hands," a voice said quietly. "Do not start or fear. It is the most natural thing in the world that I should find you. Be calm. Take courage. Look at me."

Obeying, as the tide obeys the moon, I gathered heart, and so, lifting my eyes, I saw him whom I remembered standing close beside me. We two were alone in the wide, bright field. All Heaven seemed to have withdrawn to leave us to ourselves for this one moment.

I had known that I might have loved him, all my life. I had never loved any other man. I had not seen him for almost twenty years. As our eyes met, our souls challenged one another in silence, and in strength. I was the first to speak:

"Where is she?"

"Not with me."

"When did you die?"

"Years ago."

"I had lost all trace of you."

"It was better so, for all concerned."

"Is she—is she"—

"She is on earth, and of it; she has found comfort long since; another fills my place. I do not grieve to yield it. Come!"

"But I have thought—for all these years—it was not right—I put the thought away—I do not understand"—

"Oh, come! I, too, have waited twenty years."

"But is there no reason—no barrier—are you sure? God help me! You have turned Heaven into Hell for me, if this is not right."

"Did I ever ask you to give me one pitying thought that was not right?"

"Never, God knows. Never. You helped me to be right, to be noble. You were the noblest man I ever knew. I was a better woman for having known you, though we parted—as we did."

"Then do you trust me? Come!"

"I trust you as I do the angels of God."

"And I love you as His angels may. Come!"

"For how long—am I to come?"

"Are we not in Eternity? I claim you as I have loved you, without limit and without end. Soul of my immortal soul! Life of my eternal life!—Ah, come."

⁊*15*⸝

And yet so subtle is the connection in the eternal life between the soul's best moments and the Source of them, that I felt unready for my joy until it had His blessing whose Love was the sun of all love, and whose approval was sweeter than all happiness.

Now, it was a part of that beautiful order of Heaven, which we ceased to call accident, that while I had this wish upon my lips, we saw Him coming to us, where we still stood alone together in the open field.

We did not hasten to meet Him, but remained as we were until He reached our side; and then we sank upon our knees before Him, silently. God knows what gain we had for the life that we had lost below. The pure eyes of the Master sought us with a benignity from which we thanked the Infinite Mercy that our own had not need to droop ashamed. What weak, earthly comfort could have been worth the loss of a moment such as this? He blesses us. With His sacred hands He blesses us, and by His blessing lifts our human love into so divine a thing that this seems the only life in which it could have breathed.

By-and-by, when our Lord has left us, we join hands like children, and walk quietly through the dazzling air, across the field, and up the hill, and up the road, and home. I seek my mother, trembling, and clasp her, sinking on my knees, until I hide my face upon her lap. Her hands stray across my hair and cheek.

"What is the matter, Mary?—*dear* Mary!"

"Oh, Mother, I have Heaven in my heart at last!"

"Tell me all about it, my poor child. Hush! There, there! my dear!"

"*Your poor child?* . . . Mother! What *can* you mean?"—

What can she mean, indeed? I turn and gaze into her eyes. My face was hidden in her lap. Her hands stray across my hair and cheek.

"*What is the matter, Mary?—dear Mary!*"

"*Oh, Mother, I have Heaven in my heart at last!*"

"*Tell me all about it, my poor child. Hush! There, there! my dear!*"

"*Your poor child? Mother! What* CAN *this mean?*"

She broods and blesses me, she calms and gathers me. With a mighty cry, I fling myself against her heart, and sob my soul out, there.

"You are better, child," she says. "Be quiet. You will live."

Upon the edge of the sick-bed, sitting strained and weary, she leans to comfort me. The night-lamp burns dimly on the floor behind the door. The great red chair stands with my white woolen wrapper thrown across the arm. In the window the magenta geranium droops freezing. Mignonette is on the table, and its breath pervades the air. Upon the wall, the cross, the Christ, and the picture of my father look down.

The doctor is in the room; I hear him say that he shall change the medicine, and some one, I do not notice who, whispers that it is thirty hours since the stupor, from which I have aroused, began. Alice comes in, and Tom, I see, has taken Mother's place, and holds me—dear Tom!—and asks me if I suffer, and why I look so disappointed.

Without, in the frosty morning, the factory-bells are calling the poor girls to their work. The shutter is ajar, and through the crack I see the winter day dawn on the world.

The Gates Between

Write the things which thou hast seen,
and the things which are, and
the things which shall be hereafter.

—REVELATION

ξ 1 ξ

If the narrative which I am about to recount perplex the reader, it can hardly do so more than it has perplexed the narrator. Explanations, let me say at the start, I have none to offer. That which took place I relate. I have had no special education or experience as a writer; both my nature and my avocation have led me in other directions. I can claim nothing more in the construction of these pages than the qualities of a faithful reporter. Such, I have tried to be.

It was on the twenty-fifth of November of the year 187—, that I, Esmerald Thorne, fell upon the event whose history and consequences I am about to describe.

Autobiographies I do not like. I should have been positive at any time during my life of forty-nine years that no temptation could drag me over that precipice of presumption and illusion which awaits the man who confides himself to the world. As it is the unexpected which happens, so it is the unwelcome which we choose. I do not tell this story for my own gratification. I tell it to fulfill the heaviest responsibility of my life. However I may present myself upon these pages is the least of my concern; whether well or ill, that is of the smallest possible consequence. Touching the manner of my telling the story, I have heavy thoughts; for I know that upon the manner of the telling will depend effects too far beyond the scope of any one human personality for me to regard them indifferently. I wish I could. I have reason to believe myself the bearer of a message to many men. This belief is in itself enough, one would say, to deplete a man of paltry purpose. I wish to be considered only as the messenger, who comes and departs, and is thought of no more. The message remains, and should remain, the only material of interest.

Owing to some peculiarities in the situation, I am unable to delegate, and do not see my way to defer, a duty—for I believe it to be a duty—which I shall therefore proceed to perform with as little apology as possible. I must trust to the gravity of my motive to overcome every trifling consideration in the mind of my readers; as it has solemnly done in my own.

In order to give force to my narrative, it will be necessary for me to be more personal in some particulars than I could have chosen, and to revert to certain details of my early history belonging to that category which people of my profession or temperament are wont to dismiss as "emotional." I have had strange occasion to learn that this is a deep and delicate word, which can never be scientifically used, which cannot be so much as elementally understood, except by delicacy and by depth. These are precisely the qualities of which this is to be said,—he who most lacks them will be most unaware of the lack.

There is a further peculiarity about such unconsciousness; that it is not material for education. You can teach a man that he is not generous, or true, or able. You can never teach him that he is superficial, or that he is not fine.

I have been by profession a physician; the son of a chemist; the grandson of a surgeon; a man fairly illustrative of the subtler significance of these circumstances; born and bred, as the children of science are;—a physical fact in a world of physical facts; a man who rises, if ever, by miracle, to a higher set of facts; who thinks the thought of his father, who does the deed of his father's father, who contests the heredity of his mother, who shuts the pressure of his special education like a clasp about his nature, and locks it down with the iron experience of his calling.

It was given to me, as it is not given to all men of my kind, to know a woman strong enough—and sweet enough—to fit a key unto this lock.

Strong enough *or* sweet enough, I should rather have said. The two are truly the same. The old Hebrew riddle read well, that "out of strength shall come forth sweetness." There is the lioness behind the rarest honey.

Like others of my calling, I had seen the best and the worst and the most of women. The pathological view of that complex subject is the most unfortunate which a man can well have. The habit of classifying a woman as neuralgic, hysteric, dyspeptic, instead of un-selfish, intellectual, high-minded, is not a wholesome one for the classifier. Something of the abnormal condition of the *clientèle* ex-tends to the adviser. A physician who has a healthy and natural view of women has the making of a great man in him.

I was not a great man. I was only a successful doctor; more con-scious in those days of the latter fact, and less of the former, be it admitted, than I am now. A man's avocation may be at once his ruin and his exculpation. I do not know whether I was more self-confi-dent or even more willful than other men to whom is given the autocracy of our profession, and the dependence of women which accompanies it. I should not wish to have the appearance of saying an unmanly thing, if I add that this dependence had wearied me.

It is more likely to be true that I differed from most other men in this: that in all my life I have known but one woman whom I loved, or wished to make my wife. I was forty-five years old be-fore I saw her.

Who of us has not felt at the Play, the strong allegorical power in the coming of the first actress before the house? The hero may pose, the clown dance, the villain plot, the warrior, the king, the merchant, the page, fuddle the attention for the nonce: it is a dreary business; it is like parsing poetry; it is a grammatical duty; the Play could not, it seems, go on without these superfluities. We listen, weary, regret, find fault, and acquire an aversion, when lo! upon the monotonous, masculine scene, some slender creature, shining, all white gown and yellow hair and soft arms and sweet curves comes gliding—and, hush! with the Everwomanly, the Play begins.

I do not think this feeling is one peculiar to our sex alone; I have heard women express the same in the strongest terms.

So, I have sometimes thought it is with the coming of the Woman upon the stage of a man's life. If the scenes have shifted for a while too long, monopolized by the old dismal male actors whose trick and pose and accent he knows so well and understands too easily,— and if, then, half-through the drama, late and longed-for, tardily and splendidly, comes the Star, and if she be a fine creature, of a high fame, and worthy of it,—ah, then look you to her spectator. Rapt and rapturous she will hold him till the Play is done.

So she found me—held me—holds me. The best of it, thank God, is the last of it. So, I can say, she holds me to this hour, where and as we are.

It was on this wise. On my short summer vacation of that year from which I date my happiness, and which I used to call The Year of my Lady, as others say The Year of Our Lord, I tarried for a time in a mountain village, unfashionable and beautiful, where my city patients were not likely to hunt me down. Fifty-three of them had followed me to the seashore the year before, and I went back to town a harder-worked man than I left it. Even a doctor has a right to life, liberty, and the pursuit of a vacation, and that time I struck out for my rights. I cut adrift—denied my addresses even to my partner—and set forth upon a walking tour alone, among the hills. Upon one point my mind was made up: I would not see a sick woman for two weeks.

I arrived at this little town of which I speak upon a Saturday evening. I remember that it was an extraordinary evening. Thunder came up, and clouds of colors such as I found remarkable. I am not an adept in describing these things, but I remember that they moved me. I went out and followed the trout-brook, which was a graceful little stream, and watched the pageant in the skies above the tops of the forest. The trees on either side of the tiny current had the look of souls regarding each other across a barrier, so solemn were they. They stood with their gaze upon the heavens and their feet rooted to the earth, and seemed like sentient creatures who know why this was as it was.

I, walking with my eyes upon them, feet unguarded, and fancy following a cloud or rose-color that hung fashioned in the outline of a mighty wing above me, caught my foot in a gnarled old hickory root and fell heavily. When I tried to rise I found that I was considerably hurt.

I was a well, vigorous man, not accustomed to pain, which took a vigorous form with me; and I was mortified to find myself quite faint, too much so even to disturb myself over the situation, or to wonder who would be likely to institute a searching-party for me,—a stranger, but an hour since, registered at the hotel.

With that ease which I condemned so hotly in my patients I abandoned myself to the physical pang, got back somehow against the hickory, and closed my eyes; devoid even of curiosity as to the consequences of the accident; only "attentive to my sensations," as a great writer of my day put it. I had often quoted him to nervous people whom I considered as exaggerating their sufferings; I did not recall the quotation at that moment.

"Oh! you are hurt!" a low voice said.

I was a bit fastidious in voices at that time of my life. To say that this was the sweetest I had ever heard would not express what I mean. It was the *dearest* I had ever heard. From that first moment,—before I saw her face,—drowned as I was in that wave of mean physical agony, given over utterly to myself, I knew, and to myself I said: "It is the dearest voice in all this world."

A woman on the further side of the trout-brook stood uncertain, pitifully regarding me. She was not a girl,—quite a woman; ripe, and self-possessed in bearing. She had a beautiful head, and bright dark hair; her head was bare, and her straw mountain-hat hung across one arm by the strings. She had been bathing her face in the water, which was of a pink tint like the wing above it. As she stood there, she seemed to be shut in and guarded by, dripping with, that rose-color,—

to inhale it, to exhale it, to be a part of it, to be *it*. She looked like a blossom of the live and wonderful evening.

"You are seriously hurt," she repeated. "I must get to you. Have patience; I will find a way. I will help you."

The bridge was at some distance from us, and the little stream was brawling and strong.

"But it is not deep," she said. "Do not feel any concern. It will do me no harm." As she spoke, she swung herself lightly over into the brook, stepping from stone to stone, till these came to an abrupt end in the current. There, for an instant poised, but one could not say uncertain, she hung shining before me—for her dress was white, and it took and took and took the rose-color as if she were a white rose, blushing. She then plunged directly into the water, which was knee-deep at least, and waded straight across to me.

As she climbed the bank, her thick wet dress clinging to her love-ly limbs, and her hands outstretched as if in hurrying pity, I closed my eyes again before her. I thought, as I did so, how much exquisite pleasure was like perfect pain.

She climbed the bank and stooped from her tall height to look at me; knelt upon the moss, and touched me impersonally, like the spirit that she seemed.

"You are very wet!" I cried. "The water is cold. I know these mountain brooks. You will be chilled through. Pray get home and send me—somebody."

"Where are you hurt?" she answered, with a little authoritative wave of the hand, as if she waved my words away. She had firm, fine hands.

"I have injured the patella—I mean the knee-pan," I replied. She smiled indulgently. She did not take the trouble to tell me that my lesson in elementary anatomy was at all superfluous. But when I saw her smile I said:—

"That was unconscious cerebration."

"Why, of course," she answered, nodding pleasantly.

"Go home," I urged. "Go and get yourself out of these wet things.

No lady can bear it; it will injure you." She lifted her head,—I thought she carried it like a Greek,—and regarded me with her wide, grave eyes. I met hers firmly, and for a moment we considered each other.

"It is plain that you are a doctor," she said lightly, with a second smile. "I presume you never see a well woman; at least—believe you see one now. I shall mind this wetting no more than if I were a trout or a gray squirrel. I am perfectly able to give you whatever help you require. And by your leave, I shall not go home and get into a dry dress until I see you properly cared for. Now! Can you step? Or shall I get a wagon, and a farm-hand? I think we could back a horse down almost to this spot. But it would take time. So?—Will you try it? Gently. Slowly. Don't *let* me hurt you, or blunder. I see that you are in great pain. Don't be afraid to lean on me. I am quite strong. I am able. If you can crawl a few steps"—

Steps! I would have crawled a few miles. For she put her sweet arms about me as simply and nobly as if I had been a wounded child; and with such strength of the flesh and unconsciousness of the spirit as I had never beheld in any woman, she did indeed support me out of the forest in such wise that my poor pain of the body became a great and glorified fact, for the joy of soul that I had because of her.

It had begun to be easy, in my day, to make a mock at many dear and delicate beliefs; not those alone which pertain to the life eternal, but those belonging to the life below. The one followed from the other, perhaps. That which we have been accustomed to call love was an angel whose wings had been bruised by our unbelieving clutch. It was not the fashion to love greatly. One of the leading scientists of my time and of my profession had written: "There is nothing particularly holy about love." So far as I had given thought to the subject, I had, perhaps, agreed with him. It is easy for a physician to agree to anything which emphasizes the visible, and erases the invisible fact. If there were any one form of the universal delusion more than all others "gone out" in the days of which I speak, it was the dear, old-fashioned delirium called loving at first sight. I was never exactly a scoffer; but I had mocked at this fable as other men of my

sort mock,—a subject for prophylactics, like measles or scarlet fever; and when you said that, you had said the whole. Be it, then, recorded, be it admitted, without let or hindrance, that I, Esmerald
Thorne, physician and surgeon, forty-five years old, and of sane mind,
did love that one woman, and her only, and her always, from the
moment that my unworthy eyes first looked into her own, as she
knelt before me on the moss beside the mountain brook,—from that
moment to this hour.

2

Thus half in perfect poetry, part in simplest prose, opened the first
canto of that long song which has made music in me; which has made
music *of* me, since that happy night. Of the countless words which
we have exchanged together in times succeeding, these, the few of
our first meeting are carved upon my brain as salutations are carved
in stone above the doorways of mansions. He that has loved as I did,
may say why this should be so, if he can. I cannot. Time and storm
beat against these inscriptions, and give them other coloring,—the
tints of years and weather; but while the house lasts and the rock holds
the salutation lives. In most other matters, the force of recurring
experience weakens association. He who loves cherishes the first
words of the beloved as he cherishes her last.

The situation was simple enough: an injured man and a lovely
woman, guests of the same summer hotel; a slow recovery; a leisurely sweet acquaintance; the light that never was on hill or shore; and
so the charm was wrought. My accident held me a prisoner for six
weeks. But my love put me in chains in six minutes.

Her name was Helen; like her of old

"Who fired the topmost towers of Ilium."

I liked the stately name for her, for she was of full womanhood,—

thirty-three years old; the age at which the French connoisseur said that a charming woman charmed the most.

Upon the evening before we parted, I ventured—for we sat at the sheltered end of the piazza, away from the patterers and chatterers, a little by ourselves—to ask her a brave question. I had learned that one might ask her anything; she had originality; she was not of the feminine pattern; she had no paltriness nor pettiness in her thoughts; she looked *out,* as men do, upon a subject; not *down,* as women are wont. She was a woman with whom a man could converse. He need not adapt himself and conceal himself, and play the part of a gallant at real matters which were above gallantry. He could confide in her. Now it was new to me to consider that I could confide in any person. In my calling, one becomes such a receptacle of human confidence,—once soaks up other people's lives till one becomes a great sponge, absorptive and absorbing forever, as sponges should. Who notices when the useful thing gets too full? That is what it is there for. Pour on—scalding hot, or freezing cold, or pure or foul—pour away. If one day it refuses to absorb any more, and lies limp and valueless—why, the Doctor has broken down; or the Doctor is dead. Who ever thought anything could happen to the *Doctor?* One thing in the natural history of the sponge is apt to be overlooked. When the process of absorption reaches a certain point, let the true hand touch the wearied thing, and grasp it in the right way, and lo! back rushes the instinct of confidence, *out,* not in.

Something of this sort had happened to me. The novelty of real acquaintance with a woman who did not need me had an effect upon me which perhaps few outside of my profession can understand. This woman truly needed nothing of me. She had not so much as a toothache or a sore throat. If she had cares or troubles they were her own. She leaned upon me no more than the sunrise did upon the mountain. She was as radiant, as healthful, as vivid, and as calm; she surrounded me, she overflowed me like the color of the air. Nay, beyond this it was I who had need; it was she who ministered. It was I who suffered the whims and longings of weakness,—the thousand little cravings of the sick for the well. It was I who learned to know that I have never known the meaning of what is called "diversion." I learned to suspect that I had yet to learn the true place of sympathy in therapeutics. I learned, in short, some serious professional lessons which were the simplest human ones.

But the question that I spoke of was on this wise. It did not indeed wear the form, but she gave it the hospitality, of a question.

"I wish I knew," I said, "why you have not married. I wish you thought me worthy to know."

"The whole world might know," she answered, with her sweet straightforward look.

"And I, then, as the most unworthy part of it?" For my heart sank at the terms upon which I was admitted to the answer.

"I have never seen any man whom I wished to marry. I have no other reason."

"Nor I," I said, "a woman"—And there I paused. Yes, precisely there, where I had not meant to; for she gave me a large, grave look, upon which I could no more have intruded than I could have touched her.

This was in September. The year had made the longest circuit of my life before I gathered the courage to finish that sentence, broken by the weight of a delicate look; before I dared to say to her:—

"Nor I a woman—until now."

I hope I was what we call "above" the petty masculine instinct which values a woman who is hard to win chiefly for that circumstance. Perhaps I was not as I thought myself. But it seemed to me that the anguish of wooing in doubt overcame all paltry sense of pleasure in pursuit of my delight. My thoughts of her moved like slow travelers up the sides of a mountain of snow. That other feeling would have been a descent to me. So wholly did she rule my soul— how could I stoop to care the more for hers, because she was beyond my reach?

Be this as it may, beyond my reach for yet another year she did remain. Gently as she inclined toward me, to love she made no haste. The force of my feeling was so great at times, it seemed incredible that hers did not rush to meet me like part of the same incoming wave broken by a coast island and joining—seemingly two, but in reality one—upon the shoreward side. For the first time in my life, in that rising tide of my great love, I truly knew humility. My unworthiness of her was more present with me even than my longing for her. If I could have scourged my soul clear of all unfitness for her as our Saviour was said to have scourged the tradesmen out of the Temple, I should have counted myself blessed, even though I never won her; though I beat out my last hope of her with the very blows which I inflicted upon myself.

In the vibrations of my strong emotion it used to surprise me that my will was such a cripple against the sensibilities of that delicate creature. I was a man of as much will as was naturally good for me; and my training had made it abnormal like a prize-fighter's bicepital muscle. People of my profession need some counter-irritant, which they seldom get, to the habit of command. To be the ultimate control for a *clientèle* of a thousand people, to enforce the personal opinion in every matter from a broken constitution to a broken heart, deprives a man of the usual human challenges to an athletic will. In his case, if ever, motion follows least resistance. His will-power grows by a species of pommeling; not by the higher tactics of wrestling.

But I, who gave the fiat on which life or death hung poised as unhesitatingly as I controlled the fluctuations of an influenza; and I, to whom the pliability of the feminine will had long since become an accepted and somewhat elemental fact, like the nature of milk-toast; I, Dr. Thorne, who had the habit of success, who expected to make his point, who was accustomed to receive obedience, who fought death or hysteria, an opposing school or a tricky patient, with equal fidelity, as one who pursues the avocation of life,—I stood, conquered before this slender woman whose eyes, like the sword of flame, turned this way and that, guarding the barred gates of the only Eden I had ever chosen to enter.

In short, for the first time in my life I found myself a suppliant; and I found myself thus and there for the sake of a feeling.

It was not for science' sake, it was not for the sake of personal fame, or for the glory of an idea, or for the promulgation of a discovery. I had not been overcome upon the intellectual side of my nature. I had been conquered by an emotion. I had been beaten by a thing for which, all my life, I had been prescribing as confidently as I would for a sprain. Medical men will understand me and some others may, when I say that I experienced surprise to come face to face at last, and in this unanswerable personal way, with an invisible, intangible power of the soul and of the body, which could not be treated as "a symptom."

I loved her. That was enough, and beyond. I loved her. That was the beginning and end. I loved her. I found nothing in the Materia Medica that could cure the fact. I loved her. Science gave me no explanation of the phenomenon. I did not love her scientifically. I loved her terribly.

I was a man of middle-age, and had called myself a scientist and philosopher. I had thought, if ever, to love soberly and philosoph-ically. Instead of that, I loved as poets sing, as artists paint, as the statues look, as the great romances read, as ideals teach,—as the young love.

As the young do? Nay. What young creature ever loved like that?

> They know not love who sip it at the spring.
> Youth is a fragile child that plays at love,
> Tosses a shell, and trims a little sail,
> Mimics the passion of the gathered years,
> And is a loiterer on the shallow bank
> Of the great flood that we have waited for.

I do not think of any other thing which a man cannot do better at forty, than at twenty. Why, then, should he not the better love?

My lady had a stately soul; but she gave it sweet graciousness and little womanly appeals and curves, that were to my heart as the touch of her hand was to my pulse. I was so happy in her presence that I could not believe I had ever been sad; and I longed so for her in absence that I could scarcely believe I had become happy. She was to my thoughts as the light is to the crystal. She came into my life as the miracles came to the unbelieving. She moved through my days and through my dreams, as the rose-cloud moved upon the mountain sky. She floated between me and my sick. She hovered above me and my dying. She was a mist between me and my books. Once when I took the knife for a dangerous operation, the steel blade caught a sunbeam and flashed; and I looked at the flash—it seemed to contain a new world—and I thought: "She is my own. I am a happy man!" But I was sorry for my patient. I was not rough with him. And the operation succeeded.

What is to be said? I loved her. Love is like faith. He who has it understands before you speak. But to him who has it not, it cannot be explained.

A year from the time of my most blessed accident beside the trout-brook,—in one year and two months from that day, upon a warm and wonderful September afternoon, my lady and I were married, and I brought her from her mother's house to the mountain village where first we saw each other. There we spent the first week of our happiness. It was as near to Eden as we could find. The village was left almost to its own rare resources; the summer tourists were well-nigh gone; the peaceful roads gave no stare of intrusion to our joy. The hills looked down upon us and made us feel how high love was. The forest inclosed us, and made us understand that love was large. The holiness of beauty was the hostess of our delight. Oh, I had won her! She was my wife. She was my own. She loved me.

If I cherished her as my own soul, what could I give her back, who had given herself to me?

I said, "I will make you the happiest woman who was ever beloved by man upon this earth."

"But you *have*," she whispered, lifting her dear face. "It is worth being alive for, if it came to an end to-morrow."

"Love has no end," I cried. "Happiness *is* life. It cannot die. It has an immortal soul. If ever I make you sad, if I am untender to you,—may God strike me"—

"Hush," she cried, clinging to me, and closing my lips with a kiss for which I would have died; "Hush, love! hush!"

₹3₹

It ought to be said, at this point in my story, that I had never been what would be called an even-tempered man. Truth to tell, I was a spoiled boy. My mother was a saint, but she was a soft-hearted one. My father was a scholar. Like many another boy of decided individuality, I came up anyhow. Nobody managed me. At an early age my profession made it my duty to manage everybody else. I had a nervous temperament to start on; neither my training nor my occupation had poised it. I do not think I was malicious nor even ill-natured. As men go, I was perhaps a kind man. The thing which I am trying to say is, that I was an irritable one.

As I look back upon the whole subject I can see, from my present point of view, that this irritability had seldom struck me as a personal disadvantage. I do not think it usually makes that impression upon temperaments similarly vitiated. As nearly as I can remember, I thought of myself rather as the possessor of an eccentricity, than as the victim of a vice. My father was an overworked college professor,—a quick-tempered man; my mother,—so he told me with streaming tears, upon the day that he buried her,—my mother never spoke one irritated word to him in all her life: he had chafed and she had soothed, he had slashed and she had healed, from the beginning to the end of their days together. A boy imitates for so many years before he reflects, that the liberty to say what one felt like saying appeared to me a mere identification of sex long before it occurred to me that mine might not be the only sex endowed by nature with this form of expression. I regarded it as one regards a beard, or a waistcoat,—simple signs of the variation of species.

My mother—Heaven rest her sweet soul—did not, that I recall, obviously oppose me in this view. After the time of the first moustache she obeyed her son, as she had obeyed her husband.

As has been already said, the profession to which I fell heir failed to recommend to me a different personal attitude toward the will of others. My sick people were my pawns upon the chess-board of life. I played my game with humane intentions, not wholly, I believe, with selfish ones. But I suffered the military dangers of character, without the military apologies for them. He whose duty to God and men requires him to command all with whom he comes in contact should pray God, and not expect men, to have mercy on his soul.

It is possible, I do not deny, that I put this view of the case without what literary critics call "the light touch." I is quite possible that I emphasize it. Circumstances have made this natural; and if I need any excuse for it I must seek it in them. Whether literary or not, it is not human to cherish a light view of a heavy experience.

I loved my wife. This I think, I have sufficiently made plain. I loved her as I might have discovered a new world; and I tried to express this fact, as I should have learned a new, unworldly language. I could no more have spoken unkindly to her than I could vivisect a humming-bird. I obeyed her lightest look as if she had given me an anæsthetic. Her love intoxicated me. I seemed to be the first lover who had ever used this phrase. My heart originated it, with a sense of surprise at my own imaginative quality. I was chloroformed with joy. Oh, I loved her! I return to that. I find I can say nothing beyond it. I loved her as other people love,—patients, and uninstructed persons. I, Esmerald Thorne, President of the State Medical Society, and Foreign Correspondent of the National Evolutionary Association, forty-six years old, and a Darwinian,—I loved my wife like any common, ardent, unscientific fellow.

It is easy to toss words and a smile at it all, now. There have been times when either would have been impossible from very heartbreak. There, again, is another of the phrases to which experience has been my only vocabulary. My patients used to talk to me about their broken hearts. I took the temperature and wrote a prescription. I added that she would be better to-morrow; I would call again in a week. I assured her that I understood the case. I was as well fitted to diagnose the diseases of the Queen of some purple planet which the telescope has not yet given to astronomy.

I have said that I found it impossible to be irritable to my dear wife. I cannot tell the precise time when it became possible. When does the dawn become the day upon the summer sky? When does the high tide begin to turn beneath the August moon? Rather, I might say, when does the blue become the violet, within the prism? Did I love her the less, because the distance of the worshiper had dwindled to the lover's clasp?

I could have shot the scoffer who told me so. What then? What shall I call that difference with which the man's love differs when he has won the woman? Had the miracle gone out of it? God forbid.

It was no longer the marvel of the fire come down from heaven to smite the altar. It was the comfortable miracle of the daily manna. Had my goddess departed from her divinity, my queen from her throne, my star from her heaven? Rather, in becoming mine she had become myself, and if there were a loss, that loss was in my own nature. I should have risen by reason of hers. If I descended, it was by force of my own gravitation. Her wing was too light to carry me.

It is easier to philosophize about these things than it is to record them in cold fact. With shame and sorrow do I say it, but say it I must: My love went the way of the love of other men who feel (this was and remains the truth) far less than I. I, who had believed myself to love like no other before me, and none to come after me, and I, who had won the dearest woman in all the world—I stooped to suffer myself to grow used to my blessedness, like any low man who was incapable of winning or of wearing it.

It cannot be said, it shall not be said, that I loved my wife less than the day I married her. It must be written that I became accustomed to my happiness.

That ideal of myself, which my ideal of her created in me, and which no emergency of fate could have shaken, slipped in the old, fatal quicksand of use. Our ideal of ourselves is to our highest life like the heart to the pulsation. It is the divinest art of the love of woman for man that she clasps him to his vision of himself, as breath and being are held together.

Until the time mentioned at the beginning of my narrative, I had in no sense appreciated the state of the case, as it lay between my ideal and my fact. That I had been more or less impatient of speech in my own home for some time past, is probably true. The ungoverned lip is a terrible master; and I had been a slave too long. I was in the habit of finding fault with my patients. I was accustomed to be what we call "quick" with servants. Neither had, I thought, as a rule, seemed to care the less for me on this account. If I lost a patient or a coachman now and then, I could afford to. The item did not trouble me. I was inconsiderate at times with personal friends. They said, It is his way, and bore with me. People usually bore with me; they always had. I looked upon this as one of the rights of temperament, so far as I looked upon it at all. I do not think this indulgence had occurred to me as other than a tribute. It is common enough in dealing with men of my sort. (And, alas, there are enough of my sort; I must be looked upon rather as a type than a specimen.) Such indulgence is a movement of self-defense, or else of philosophy, upon the part of those who come in contact with us. To this view of the subject I had given no attention.

I had lived to be almost fifty years old, and no person had ever said to me: "Esmerald Thorne, you trust your attractive qualities too far. Power and charm do not give a man a permit to be disagreeable. Your temperament does not release you from the commonplace human duty of self-restraint. A gentleman has no more right to get uncontrollably angry than he has to get drunk. The patience with which others receive you is not a testimony to your strength; it is a concession to your weakness. You are living upon concessions like disease, or childhood, or age."

No one had said this—surely not my wife. I can recall an expression of bewilderment at times upon her beautiful face, which for the moment perplexed me. After I had gone out, I would remember that I had been nervous in my manner. I do not think I had ever spoken with actual roughness to her, until this day of which I write. That I had been sometimes cross enough, is undoubtedly the case.

On that November day I had been overworked. This was no novelty, and I offer it as no excuse. I had been up for two nights with a dangerous case. I had another in the suburbs, and a consultation out of town. There was a quarrel at the hospital, and a panic in Stock Street. I had seen sixty patients that day. I had been attacked in the "Therapeutic Quarterly" upon my famous theory of Antisepsis. Perhaps I may add the circumstance that my baby was teething.

This was, naturally, less important to me than to his mother, who thought the child was ill. I knew better, and it annoyed me that my knowledge did not remove her apprehension. In point of fact, he had cried at night for a week or two, more than he ought to have done. She could not understand why I denied him a Dover's powder. I needed sleep, and could not get it. We were both worn, and—I might fill my chapter to the brim with the little reasons for my great error. Let it suffice that they were small and that it was large.

We had been married three years, and our boy was a year old. He was a fine fellow. Helen lost her Greek look and took on the Madonna expression after he was born. Any woman who is fit to be a mother gains that expression with her first child. My wife was a very happy mother.

She was sitting in the library when I came in that evening. It was a warm, red library, with heavy curtains and an open fire—a deep room that absorbed color. I fancied the room, and it was my wife's pleasure to await me in it with the child each evening at the earliest hour when I might by any chance be expected home. She possessed to the full the terrible power of waiting which women have. Although three years married, she could not read, or write, or play when she was listening for my step. I do not mean that she told me this. I found it out. She never called my attention to such little feminine weaknesses. She was never over-fond. My wife had a noble reserve. I had never seen the hour when I felt that her tenderness was a treasure to be lightly had, or indifferently treated.

It should be said that the library opened from the parlors, and was at that time separated from them by a heavy portière of crimson stuff, the doors not being drawn. This drapery she was in the habit of folding apart at the hours of my probable return, and as I came through the long parlors my eyes had the first greeting of her, before my voice or arms. Upon this evening, as upon others, I entered by the parlor door, and came—more quickly than usual—toward the library. I was in a great hurry; one of the acute attacks of the chronic condition which besets the busy doctor. As I crossed the length of the thick carpet, the rooms shook beneath my tread; I burst into, rather than entered, the library,—not seeing her, I think, or not pausing to see her, in the accustomed manner. When I had come to her I found that the child was not with her, as usual. She was sitting alone by the library table under the drop-light, which held a shade of red lace. She had a gown of white wool trimmed with ermine; a costume which gave me pleasure, and which she wore upon cool evenings, not too often for me to weary of it. She regarded my taste in dress as delicately and as delightedly as she did every other wish or will of mine.

She had been trying to read; but the magazine lay closed upon her knee below her folded hands. Her face wore an anxious look as she turned the fine contours of her head toward me.

"Oh," she cried, "at last!"

She moved to reach me, swiftly, murmuring something which I did not hear, or to which I did not attend; and under the crimson curtains met me, warm and dear and white, putting up her sweet arms.

I kissed her carelessly—would to God that I could forget it! I kissed her as if it did not matter much, and said:—

"Helen, I must have my dinner this instant!"

"Why, surely," she said, retreating from me with a little shock of pained surprise. "It is all ready, Esmerald. I will ring."

She melted from my arms. Oh, if I had known, if I had known! She stirred and slipped and was gone from me, and I stood stupidly looking at her; her figure, against the tall, full book-cases, shone mistily, while she touched the old-fashioned bell-rope of gold cord.

"Really, I hadn't time to come home at all," I added testily. "I am driven to death. I've got to go again in ten minutes. But I supposed you would worry if I didn't show myself. It is a foolish waste of time. I don't know how I am ever going to get through. I wish I hadn't come."

⁓4⁓

She changed color—from fair to flush, from red to white again—and her hand upon the gold cord trembled. I remembered it afterward, though I was not conscious of noticing it at the time.

"You need not," she replied, in her low, controlled voice, "on my account. You need never come again."

"It is easier to come," I answered, irritably, "than to know that you sit here making yourself miserable because I don't."

"Have I ever fretted you about coming, Esmerald? I did not know it."

"It would be easier if you did fret!" I cried crossly. "I'd rather you'd *say* a thing than look it. Any man would."

Indeed, it would have been a paltry satisfaction to me just then if I could have found her to blame. Her blamelessness irritated my self-complacence as the light irritates defective eyes.

"I am due at the hospital in twenty-two minutes," I went on, excitedly. "Chirugeon is behaving like Apollyon. If I'm not there to handle him, nobody will. The whole staff are afraid of him—everybody but me. We shan't get the new ward built these two years if he carries the day to-night. I've got a consultation at the Decker's—the old lady is dying. It's no sort of use dragging a tired man out there; I can't do her any good; but they will have it. I'm at the beck and call of every whim. Isn't that dinner ready? I wish I had time to change my boots! They are wet through. My head aches horribly. Brake telegraphed me to get down to Stock Street before two o'clock to save what is left of that Santa Ma stock. I couldn't go. I had an enormous office—forty people. I've lost ten thousand dollars in this panic. I've got to see Brake on my way to Decker's. I lost a patient this morning—that little girl of the Harrowhart's. She was a poor little scrofulous thing. But they are terribly cut up about it. . . . Chowder? I wish you'd had a good clear soup. I don't feel as if I could touch chowder. I hope you have some roast beef, better than the last. You mustn't let Parsnip cheat you. Quail? There's no nourishment in a quail for a man in my state. The gas leaks. Can't you have it attended to? Hurry up the coffee. I must swallow it and go. I've got more than ten men could do."

"It is more than one woman can do"—she began gently, when I came to the end of this outbreak and my breath together.

"What did you say? Do speak louder!"

"I said it seems to be more than one woman can do, to rest you."

"Yes," I said carelessly, "it is. You can't do the first thing for me, except to do me the goodness to ring for a decent cup of coffee. I can't drink this."

"Esmerald"—

"Oh, what? I can't stop to talk. There, I've burned my tongue, now. If there's anything I can't stand, it is going to a consultation with a burned tongue."

"How tired you are, Esmerald! I was only going to say that I am sorry. I can't *let* you go without saying that."

"I can't see that it helps it any. I am so tired I don't want to be touched. Never mind my coat. I'll put it on myself. Tell Joe—no. I left the horse standing. I don't want Joe. I suppose Donna is uneasy by this time. She won't stand at night—she's *got to*. I'll get that whim out of her. Now, don't look that way. The horse is safe enough. Don't you suppose I know how to drive? You're always having opinions of your own against mine. There. I must be off."

"Where's the baby, Helen?" I turned, with my hand upon the latch of my heavy oaken door, and jerked the question out, as cross men do.

"The baby isn't just right, somehow, Esmerald. I hated to bother you, for you never think it is anything. I dare say he will be better, but I thought I wouldn't let him come out of the nursery. Jane is with him. I've been a *little* troubled about him. He has cried all the afternoon."

"He cries because you coddle him!" I exploded. "It is all nonsense, Helen. Nothing ails the child. I won't encourage this sort of thing. I'll see him when I come home. I can't possibly wait—I am driven to death—for every little whim"—

But at the door I stopped. If the baby had been a patient he would have seen no doctor that night. But the father in me got the better of me, and without a word further to my wife I ran up to the nursery.

She stayed below; she perceived (Helen was always quick), although I had not said so, that I did not wish her to follow me. I examined the child hastily. The little fellow stopped crying at the sight of me, and put up both arms to be taken. I said:—

"No, Boy. Papa can't stop now," and put him gently back into his crib. When I had reached the nursery door I remember that I returned and kissed him. I was very angry, but I could not be angry with my baby. With the touch of his little lips dewy and sweet, upon mine, I rushed down to my wife and tempestuously began again:—

"Helen, I must have an end to this nonsense. Nothing ails the baby; he is only a trifle feverish with a new tooth. It really is very unpleasant to me that you make such a fuss over him. If you had married a green-grocer it might have been pardonable. Pray remember that you have married a physician who understands his business, and do leave me to manage it. Take the child out of the nursery. Carry him down-stairs as usual for a few minutes. He will sleep better. There! I'm eight minutes behindhand already, all for this senseless anxiety of yours. It is a pity you can't trust me, like other men's wives! I wish I'd married a woman with a little wifely spirit!—or else not married at all."

I shut the door; I am afraid I slammed it. I cleared the steps at a bound, and ran fiercely out into the night air. The wind was rising, and the weather was growing sharp. It was frosty and noisy. Donna, my chestnut mare, stood pawing the pavement in high temper, and called to me as she heard my step. She had dragged at her weight a little; she was thoroughly displeased with the delay. It occurred to me that she felt as I had acted. It even occurred to me to go back and tell my wife that I was ashamed of myself.

I turned and looked in through the parlor windows. The shades were up, and the gas was low. Dimly beyond, the bright panel of the lighted library arose between the crimson curtains. She stood against it, midway between the two rooms. Her hands had dropped closed one into the other before her. Her face was toward the street. She seemed to be gazing at me, whom she could not see. Her white dress, which hung in thick folds, the pallor of her face and her delicate hands, gave her the look of a statue; its purity, and to my fancy at that moment its permanence. She seemed to be carved there, like something that must stay.

I turned to go back—yes, I would have gone. It is little enough for a man to say for himself under circumstances like these; but perhaps I may be allowed to say it, since to exculpate myself is the last of my motives. I had made a step or two up the flagging between the deep grass-plots that fronted the house, when the mare, disturbed beyond endurance at a movement of delay which she too well understood, gave a shrill whinny, and reared, pulling and dragging at her weight fiercely. She was a powerful creature, and the weight yielded, hitting at her heels. In an instant she had cramped the wheels, and I saw that the buggy would go over. To spring back, reach the bit, snatch the reins, leap over the wheel, and whirl away in the reeling carriage was the work of something less than a thought; it was the elemental instinct by which a man must manage his horse, come life or death.

Like most doctors, I was something of a horseman, and the ideal of being thwarted by any of Donna's whims had never occurred to me. I knew that the horse was pulling hard, but beyond that, I could not be said to have knowledge, much less fear; the mad conflict between the brute and the man possessed me to the exclusion of intelligence.

It was some moments before it struck me that my own horse was running away with me.

My first, perhaps I may say my only emotion at the discovery was one of overpowering rage.

I did not mean to strike her. No driver, even if an angry one, would have done that. But I had the whip in my hand, around which the reins were knotted for the struggle, and when the horse broke into a gallop the jerk gave her a flick. I was not in the habit of whipping her. She felt herself insulted. It was now her turn to be angry; and an angry runaway means a bad business. Donna put down her head, struck out viciously from behind, and kicked the dasher flat. From that moment I lost all control of her.

I thought:—

"She is headed down town. At this rate, in five minutes she will be in the thick of travel. I have so many minutes more."

For how long I cannot tell, I had beyond this no other intelligent idea. Then I thought:—

"I should not like to be the man who has got to tell Helen." This repeated itself dully: "I should not care to be the fellow who will be sent to tell Helen."

I had ceased to call to the mare; it only made matters worse; but there was great hubbub in the streets as we leaped on. There were several attempts to head her off, I think. One man caught at her bridle. This frightened her; she threw him off, and threw him down. I think she must have hurt him. We were now well down town. Window lights and carriage lights flared by deliriously. The wind, which was high, at speed like that seemed something demoniac. I remember how much it added to my sense of danger. I remember that my favorite phrase occurred to me:—

"I am driven to death."

Suddenly I saw approaching an open landau. The street was full of vehicles, some of which I was sure to run down; but none of them seemed to give me concern except this one carriage. It contained a lady and a little boy, patients of mine. I recognized them forty feet away. He was a pretty little fellow, and she was fond of me; sent for me for everything; trusted me beyond reason; could not live without her doctor—that kind of patient. She had been a great sufferer. It seemed infernal to me that it should be *they*.

I shouted to her coachman:—

"Henry! For God's sake—to the left! To the *left!*"

But Henry stared at me like one struck dead. I thought I heard him say:—

"Marm, it's the *doctor!*" and after that I heard no more.

As the crash came, I saw the woman's face. She had recognized me with her look of sweet trustfulness; it froze to mortal horror. She clasped the child. I saw his cap come off from his yellow curls, and one little hand tossed out as the landau went over.

The mare, now mad as any maniac, ran on.

Something had broken, but it mattered little what. I think we turned a corner. I think she struck a lamp-post or a tree. At all events, the buggy went over; and, scooped into the top, and dragged, and blinded, and stunned, I came to the ground.

As I went down, I uttered the two words of all that are human, most solemn; perhaps, one may add, most automatic. Believer or skeptic, saint or sinner, we find that mortal danger hurls them from us, as it wrests the soul from out our bodies.

I said, *"My God!"* precisely as I threw out my arms, to catch at whatever could hold me when I could no longer hold myself.

5

How long I had lain stunned upon the pavement I had no means of knowing; I thought not long. I was surprised, on coming to myself, to find that my injuries were not more severe.

My head felt uncomfortable, and I had a certain numbness or stiffness, as one does from the first trial of long-disused limbs. I had always limped a trifle since that accident beside the trout-brook; and, as I staggered to my feet, I thought:—

"This will play the mischief with that old injury. I shouldn't wonder if it came to crutches."

On the contrary, when I had walked some dozen steps I found that an interesting thing had happened. The shock had dispersed the limp.

It was with a perfectly even and natural gait, although, as I say, rather a weak one, that I trod the pavement to try what manner of man the runaway had left me. I said:—

"It is one of those cases of nervous rearrangement. The shock has acted like a battery upon the nerve-centres. Instead of a broken neck, I have a cured leg. I'm a lucky fellow."

Having already, however, considered myself a lucky fellow for the greater part of my life, this conclusion did not impress me with the force which it might some other men; and, laughing lightly, as lucky people do, at fortune, I turned to examine the condition of my horse and carriage.

Donna was not to be seen. She had broken the traces, the breeching, the shafts, everything, in short, she could, and cleared herself. I had been unconscious long enough to give her time to make herself invisible, and she had made the most of it; in what direction she had gone, it was impossible for me to tell. The buggy was a wreck. No one was in sight who seemed to have interest or anxiety in the matter. I wondered that I did not find myself the victim of a gaping crowd. But I reflected that the mishap had taken place in a quiet dwelling street, not traveled at that hour, and that my fate, therefore, had attracted no attention. I remembered, too, my patient, Mrs. Faith, and her boy, and that dolt of a Henry's helpless face—the whole thing came to mind, vividly. It occurred to me that the crowd might be at the scene of an accident so terrible that no loafer was left to regard my lesser misfortune. It was they who had been sacrificed. It was I who escaped.

My first thought was to go at once and learn the worst; but I found myself a little out of my way. I really did not recognize the street in which I stood. I had been for so many years accustomed to driving everywhere that, like other doctors, I hardly knew my way back to the great thoroughfare where I had collided with Mrs. Faith's carriage, no trace of the tragedy was to be found; or at least I could not find any. After looking in vain, for a while, I stopped a man, and asked him if there had not been a carriage accident there within half an hour. He lifted his eyes to me stupidly, and went on. I put the same question to some one else—a lazy fellow, who was leaning against an iron railing and staring at me. But he shook his head decidedly.

A young priest passed by, at this moment, saying an Ave with moving lips and unworldly eyes, and I made inquiries of him whether a lady and a child had just been injured in that vicinity by a runaway.

"Nay," he said, gazing at me with a luminous look. "Nay, I see nothing."

After an instant's hesitation the priest made the sign of the cross both upon himself and me; and then stretched his hands in blessing over me, and silently went his way. I thought this very kind in him; and I bowed, as we parted, saying aloud:—

"Thank you, Father," for my heart was touched, despite myself, at the manner of the young devotee.

It had surely been my intention, on failing to find any traces of the accident in the spot where I supposed that it had taken place, to go at once to the house of Mrs. Faith, and inquire for her welfare and the boy's. It was the least I could do, under the circumstances.

Apparently, however, I myself was more shaken than I had thought; for after my brief interview with the priest I speedily lost my way, and could not find my patient's street or number. I searched for it for some time confusedly; but the brain was clearly still affected by the concussion—so much so that it was not long before I forgot what I was searching for, and went my ways with a dim and idle purpose, such as must accompany much of the action of those in whom the relation between mind and body has become, for any cause, disarranged.

After an interval—how long I cannot tell—of this suspended intelligence, my brain grew more clear and natural, and I remembered that I was very late at the hospital, at the consultation, at Brake's, at every appointment of the evening; so late that my accustomed sense of haste now began to possess me to the exclusion of everything else. I remembered by wife, indeed, and wondered if I had better go back and tell her that I was not hurt. But it did not strike me as necessary. Donna, if she had not broken her neck somewhere, by this time, would run straight for the stable; she would not go home. The buggy was a wreck, and the police might clear it away. There was no reason to suppose that Helen would hear of the accident, that I could see, from any source. There would be no scare. I had better go about my business, and tell her when I got home. News like this would keep an hour or two, and everybody the better for the keeping.

Reasoning in this manner, if it can be said to be reasoning, I took my way to the hospital as fast as possible. I did not happen to find a cab; and I gave myself the unusual experience of hailing a horse-car. The car did not stop for my signal, and I flung myself aboard as best I might; for a man so recently shaken up, with creditable ease, I thought.

Trusting to this circumstance, when we reached the hospital I leaped from the car, which was going at full speed; it was not till I was well up the avenue that I recalled having forgotten to offer my fare, which the conductor had omitted to demand.

"My head is not straight yet," I said. The little incident annoyed me.

In the hospital I found, as I expected, a professional cyclone raging. The staff were all there, except myself, and so hotly engaged in discussion that my arrival was treated with indifference. This was undoubtedly good for me, but it was not, therefore, agreeable to me; and I entered at once with some emphasis upon the dispute in hand.

"You are entirely wrong," I began, turning upon my opponents. "This institution had seven hundred more applicants than it could accommodate last year. We are not chartered to turn away suffering. We exist to relieve it. It is our business to find the means to do so, as much as it is to find the true remedy for the individual case. It is"—

"It is an act of financial folly," interrupted my most systematic professional enemy, a certain Dr. Gazell. He had a bland voice which irritated me like sugar sauce put upon horse-radish. "It cannot be done without mortgaging ourselves up to our ears—or our eaves. I maintain that the hospital can better bear to turn off patients than to turn on debt."

"And I maintain," I cried, tempestuously, "that this hospital cannot bear to do either! If the gentlemen gathered here to-night—the members of this staff, representing as they do, the wealthiest and most influential *clientèles* in the city—if we cannot among us pledge from our patients the sum needed to put this thing through, I say it is a poor show for ourselves. I, for one, am ready to raise fifteen thousand dollars within three months. If the rest of you will do your share in proportion"—

"Dr. Thorne has always been a little too personal, in this matter," said Gazell, reddening; he did not look at me, for embarrassment, but addressed the chairman of the meeting with a vague air of being in earnest, if any one could be got to believe it.

"No doubt about that," said one of the staff in an undertone. "Thorne is"—I thought I caught the added words, "unreasonable fellow," but I would not give myself the appearance of having done so.

"But we can't afford to quarrel with him altogether," suggested Chirugeon, still in a tone not meant for me to overhear. And with this they went at it again, till the discussion reached such warmth, and the motion to leave the subject with the trustees such favor, that, in disgust, I seized my hat and strode out of the room.

Smarting, I rushed away from them, and angrily out-of-doors again. I was exceedingly angry; but this gave me no more, perhaps (though I thought, a little), than the usual discomfort.

From the hospital I hurried to the consultation; where I was now well over-due. I found the attendant physician about to leave; in fact, I met him on the stairs, up which I had run rapidly, as soon as my ring was answered in the familiar house. This man was followed by old Madam Decker's daughter, who was weeping.

"She died at six o'clock, Dr. Halt," Miss Decker sobbed, "at six precisely, for I noticed. We didn't expect it so soon."

"Nor I, either," said Halt, soothingly. "I did not anticipate"—

"Dead!" I cried. "Mrs. Decker dead? I did my best—I have met with an accident. I could not come till now. Did she ask for me?"

"She talked of Dr. Thorne," sobbed Miss Decker, "as long as she could talk of anything. She wondered if he knew, she said, how sick she was."

I hastened to explain, to protest, to sympathize, to say the idle words with which we waste ourselves and weary mourners, at such times; but the daughter paid little attention to me. She was evidently hurt at my delay; and, thinking it best to spare her my presence, I bowed my head in silence, and left the house.

Halt followed me, and we stood together for a moment outside, where his carriage and driver awaited him.

"Was she conscious to the end?" I asked.

"Yes," he murmured. "Yes, yes, yes. It is a pity. I'm sorry for that girl."

Nodding shortly in my direction, he sprang into his coupé, and drove away.

I had now begun to be very restless to get home. It seemed suddenly important to see Helen. I felt, I knew not why, uneasy and impatient, and turned my steps toward town.

"But I must stop at Brake's," I thought. This seemed imperative; so much so that I went out of my course a little, to reach his house, a pretty, suburban place. I remember passing under trees; and the depth of their shadow; it seemed like a bay of blackness into which the night flowed. I looked up through it at the sky; stars showed through the massed clouds which the wind whipped along like a flock of titanic celestial creatures. I had not looked up before, since the accident. The act gave me strange sensations, as if the sky had lowered, or I had risen; the sense of having lost the usual scale of measurement. This reminded me that I was still not altogether right.

"I have really hurt my head," I thought, "I ought to get home. I must hurry this business with Brake. I must get to Helen."

But Brake was not at home. As I went up the steps, his servant was ushering out some one, to whom I heard the man say that Mr. Brake had left word not to expect him to-night.

"Does he ever stay late at the office?" I asked, thinking that the panic might render this possible.

The man turned the expressionless countenance of a well-trained servant upon me; and repeated:—

"Mr. Brake is not at home. I know nothing further about Mr. Brake's movements."

This reply settled the matter in my own mind, and I made my way to Stock Street as fast as I might. I could not make it seem unnecessary to see Brake. But Helen— Helen— The sooner this wretched detention was over, the sooner to see her. I had begun to be as nervous as a woman; and, I might add, as unreasonable as a sick one. I had got myself under the domination of one of those fixed ideas with which I had so little patience in the sick. I could not see Helen till I had seen Brake: this was the delusion. I succumbed to it, and knew that I succumbed to it, and could not help it, and knew that I could not help it, and did the deed it bade me. As I hurried on my way, I thought:—

"There has been considerable concussion. But Helen will take care of me. It's a pity I spoke so to Helen."

Stock Street, when I reached it, had a strange look to me. I was not used to being there at such an hour; few of us are. The relative silence, the few passers, the long empty spaces on the great thoroughfare, told me that the hour was later than I thought. This added to my restlessness, and I sought to look at my watch, for the first time since the accident; it was gone. I glanced at the high clock at the head of the street; but the light was imperfect, and with the vertigo which I had I did not make out the hour. It might, indeed, be really late. This troubled me, and I hastened my steps till I broke into a run.

It occurred to me, indeed, that I might be arrested for the suspicions under which such a pace, at such an hour and on such a street, would place me. But as I knew most of the members of the force in that region more or less well, this did not trouble me. I ran on, undisturbed, passing a watchman or two, and came quickly to Brake's place. It was locked.

This distressed me. I think I had confidently expected to find him there. It did not seem to me possible to go home without seeing my broker. I stood, uncertain, rattling at the heavy door with imbecile impatience. This act brought the police to the spot in three minutes.

It was Inspector Drayton who came up, the well-known inspector, so long on duty in Stock Street; a man famed for his professional shrewdness and his gentlemanly manner.

"I wish," I said, "Mr. Inspector, that you would be good enough to let me in. I want to see Brake. I have reason to believe he is in his office. I must get in."

"It is very important," I added; for the inspector did not answer immediately, but looked at me searchingly.

"There was certainly some one meddling with this lock," he said, after a moment's hesitation, looking stealthily up and down and around the street.

"It was I," I replied, eagerly. "It was only I, Dr. Thorne. Come, Drayton, you know me. I want to see Brake. I must see Brake. It is a matter brought up by this panic—you know—the Santa Ma. He sent for me. I absolutely must see Brake. It is a matter of thousands to me. Let me in, Mr. Inspector."

"Come," for he still delayed and doubted, "let me in somehow. You fellows have a way. Communicate with his watchman—do the proper thing—anyhow—I don't care—only let me in."

"I will see," murmured the inspector, with a perplexed air; he had not his usual cordial manner with me, though he was still as polished as possible, and wore the best of kid gloves. I think the inspector touched one of their electric signals—I am not clear about this—but at any rate, a sleepy watchman came from within, holding a safety lantern before him, and gingerly opened the huge door an inch or two.

"Let me come in," said the inspector, decidedly. "It is I—Drayton. I have a reason. I wish to go to Mr. Brake's rooms, if you please."

The inspector slipped in like a ghost, and I followed him. Neither of us said anything further to the watchman; we went directly to Brake's place. He was not there.

"I will wait a few minutes," I said. "I think he will be here. I must see Brake."

The inspector glanced at me as one does at a fellow who is behaving a little out of the common course of human conduct; but he did not enter into conversation with me, seeing me averse to it. I sank down wearily upon Brake's biggest brown leather office chair, and put my head down upon his table. I was now thoroughly tired and confused. I wished with all my heart that I had gone straight home to Helen. The inspector and the watchman busied themselves in examining the building, for some purpose to which I paid no attention. They conversed in low tones. "I heard a noise at the door, sir, myself," the watchman said.

"Why don't you tell him it was I?" I called; but I did not left my head. I was too tired to trouble myself. I must have fallen into a kind of stupor.

I do not know how long I had remained in this position and condition, whether minutes or hours; but when at last I roused myself, and looked about, a singular thing had happened.

The inspector had gone. The watchman had gone. I was alone in the broker's office. And I was locked in.

6

So often and so idly it is out custom to say, I shall never forget! that the words scarcely cause a ripple of comment in the mind; whereas, in fact, they are among the most audacious which we ever take upon our lips. How know we what law of selection our memories will obey in that system of mental relations which we call "forever"?

I, who believe myself to have obtained some especial knowledge upon this point, not possessed by all my readers, and to be more free than many another to use such language, still retreat before the phrase, and content myself with saying, "I have never forgotten." Up to this time I have never been able to forget the smallest detail of that night whose history I am now to record. It seems to me impossible in any set of conditions that memory could blot that experience from my being; but of that, what know I? No more than I know of the politics of a meteor.

Upon discovering my predicament I was, of course, greatly disturbed. I tried the door, and tried again; I urged the latch violently; I exerted myself till the mere moral sense of my helplessness overcame my strength. I called to the watchman, whose distant steps I heard, or fancied that I heard, pacing the corridors. There was a Safe Deposit in the basement, and the great building was heavily guarded. I shouted for my liberty, I pleaded for it, I demanded it; but I did not get it. No one answered me. I ran to the barred windows and shook the iron casement as prisoners and madmen do. Nobody heard me. I bethought me of the private telegraph which stood by Brake's desk, mute and mysterious, like a thing that waited an order to speak. I could not help wondering, with something like superstition, what would be the next words which would pass the lips of the silent metal. It occurred to me, of course, to telegraph for relief; but I did not know how, and a kind of respect for the intelligence and power of the instrument deterred me from meddling with it to no visible end. Suddenly I remembered the elec-

tric signal which so often communicates with watchman or police in places of this kind. This, after some search, I found in a corner, over the desk of Brake's assistant, and this I touched. My effort brought no reply. I pressed the button again with more force
and more desperation; I might say, with more personality.

"Obey me!" I cried, setting my teeth, and addressing the electric
influence as a man addresses a menial.

Instantly a thrill passed from the wire to the hand. A distant sound
jarred upon the air. Steps shuffled somewhere beyond the massive
walls. I even thought that I heard voices, as of the watchman and
others in possible consultation. No one approached the broker's door.
I urged the signal again and again. I became quite frantic, for I had
now begun to think with dismay of the effect of all this upon my
wife. I railed upon that signal like a delirious patient at the order of
a physician. A commotion seemed to follow, in some distant part of
the building. But no one came within hearing of my voice; the noise
soon ceased, and my efforts at freedom with it.

It having now become evident that I must spend the night where
I was, I proceeded to make the best of it; and a very bad best it was.
I was exhausted, I was angry, and I was distressed.

The full force of the situation was beginning to fall upon me. The
inspector had put a not unnatural interpretation upon my condition;
he thought so little of a gentleman who had dined too freely; it was
a perfectly normal incident in his experience. He had mistaken the
character of the stupor caused by my accident, and left me in that
office for a drunken man. The fact that he was not accustomed to
view me in such a light in itself probably explained the originality
of his method. We were on pleasant terms. Drayton was a good fellow. Who knew better than he what would be the professional significance of the circumstance that Dr. Thorne was seen intoxicated down
town at midnight? The city would ring with it in twelve hours, and
it would not be for me, though I had been the most popular doctor
in town, to undo the deed of that slander, if once it so much as lifted its invisible hand against the proud and pure reputation in whose

shelter I lived and labored, and had been suffered to become what we call "eminent." It was possible, too, that the inspector had some human regard for my family in this matter, and reasoned that to spare them the knowledge of my supposed disgrace was the truest kindness wherewith it was in his power to serve me. He meant to leave me where I was and as I was to sleep it off till morning. He would return in good season and release me quietly, and nobody the wiser but the watchman; who could be feed. This was plainly the purpose and the programme.

But Helen—

I returned to the table near which I had been sitting, and took the office chair again, and tried, like a reasonable creature, to calm myself.

What would Helen think by this time? I looked about the office stupidly. At first the dreary scene presented few details to me; but after a time they took on the precision and permanence which trifles acquire in emergencies. The gas was not lighted, but I could see with considerable ease, owing to the overwrought brain condition. It occurred to me that I saw like a cat or a medium; I noted this, as indicative of a certain remedy; and then it further occurred to me that I might as well prescribe for myself, having nothing better to do; and plainly there was something wrong. I therefore put my hand in my pocket for my case. It was gone.

Now, a physician of my sort is as ill at ease without his case as he would be without his body; and this little circumstance added disproportionately to my discomfort. With some irritable exclamation on my lips I leaned back in the chair, and once more regarded my environment. It was a rather large room, dim now, and as solitary as a graveyard after twilight. Before me stood the table, an oblong table covered with brown felt. A blue blotter, of huge dimensions, was spread from end to end; it was a new blotter, not much blurred. Inkstand, pens, paper-weight, calendar, and other trifles of a strictly necessary nature stood upon the blotter. Letters on file, and brokers' memoranda neatly stabbed by the iron stiletto—I forget the name of the thing—for that purpose made and provided, attracted my sick attention. An advertisement from a Western mortgage firm had escaped the neat hand of the clerk who put the office in order for the night, and fell fluttering to my feet. It would be impossible to say how important this seemed to me. I picked it up conscientiously, and filed it, to the best of my remembrance, with an invitation to the Merchant's Banquet, and a subscription list in behalf of the blind man who sold tissue-paper roses at the head of the street.

In one corner of the room, as I have said, was the clerk's desk; the electric signal shone faintly above it; it had, to my eyes, a certain phosphorescent appearance. Opposite, the steam radiator stood like a skeleton. There was a grate in the room, with a Cumberland coal fire laid. On the wall hung a map of the State, and another setting forth the proportions of a great Western railroad. At the extreme end of the room stood chairs and settees provided for auctions. Between myself and these, the high, guarded public desk of the broker rose like a rampart.

In this sombre and severe place I now abandoned myself to my thoughts; and these gave me no mercy.

My wife was a reasonable woman; but she was a loving and sensitive one. I was accustomed to spare her all unnecessary uncertainty as to my movements—being more careful in this respect, perhaps, than most physicians would be; our profession covers a multitude of little domestic sins. I had not taken the ground that I was never to be expected till I came. A system of affectionate communication as to my whereabouts existed between us; it was one of the pleasant customs of our honeymoon which had lasted over. The telegraph and the messenger boy we had always with us; it was a little matter for a man to take the trouble to tell his wife why and where he was kept away all night. I do not remember that I had ever failed to do so. It was a bother sometimes, I admit, but the pleasure it gave her usually repaid me; such is the small, sweet coin of daily love.

As I sat there at the broker's desk, like a creature in a trap, all that long and wretched night, the image of my wife seemed to devour my brain and my reason.

The great clock on the neighboring church struck one with a heavy and a solemn intonation, of which I can only say that it was to me unlike anything I had ever heard before. It gave me a shudder to hear it, as if I listened to some supernatural thing. The first hour of the new day rang like a long cry. Some freak of association brought to my mind that angel in the Apocalypse who proclaimed with a mighty voice that Time should be no more. I caught myself thinking this preposterous thing: Suppose it were all over? Suppose we never saw each other again? Suppose my wife were to die? To-night? Suppose some accident befell her? If she tripped upstairs? If the child's crib took fire and she put it out, and herself received one of those deadly shocks from burns not in themselves mortal?

Suppose—she herself opening the door to let in the messenger expected from me—that some drunken fellow, or some tramp—

"This," I said aloud, "is the kind of thing *she* does when I am delayed. This is what it means to wait. Men don't do it often enough to know what it is. I wonder if we have any scale of measurement for what women suffer?"

What she, for instance, by that time was suffering, oh, who in the wide world else could guess or dream? There were such suffering cells in that exquisite nature! Who but me could understand?

I brought my clinched hand down upon the broker's blue blotting-paper, and laid my heavy head upon it.

Suppose somebody had got the news to her that the horse had been seen dashing free of the buggy, or had returned alone to the stable, panting and cut?

Suppose Helen thought that my unaccountable absence had something to do with that scene between us? Suppose she thought—or if she suspected—perhaps she imagined—

I hid my face within my shaking hands and groaned. A curse upon the cruel words that I had spoken to the tenderest of souls, to the dearest and the gentlest of women! A curse upon the lawless temper that had fired them! Accursed the hot lips that had uttered them, the unmanly heart that could have let them slip!

I thought of her face—I really had not thought of her face before, that wretched night. I had not strictly dared. Now I found that daring had nothing to do with it. I thought because I had to think. I dwelt upon her expression when I spoke to her—God forgive me!—as I did; her attitude, the way her hands fell, her silence, the quiver in her delicate mouth. I saw the dim parlor, the lighted room beyond her, the scarlet shade upon the gas; she standing midway, tall and mute, like a statue carved by one stroke of a sword.

My own words came back to me; and I was not apt to remember things I said to people. So many impressions passed in and out of my mind in the course of one busy day, that I became their victim rather than their master. But now my language to my wife that unhappy evening returned to my consciousness with incredible vividness and minuteness. It will be seen from the precision with which I have already recorded it, how inexorable this minuteness was.

It occurred to me that I might as well have struck her.

In this kind of moral pommeling which sensitive women feel—as they do—how could I have indulged! I, who knew what a sensitive woman is, what fearful and wonderful nervous systems these delicate creatures have to manage; I, with what I was pleased to term my high organization and special training—I, like any brutal hind, had berated my wife. I, who was punctilious to draw the silken portière for her, who could not let her pick up so much as her own lace handkerchief, nor allow her to fold a wrap of the weight of a curlew's feather about her own soft throat—I had belabored her with the bludgeons that bruise the life out of women's souls. I wondered, indeed, if I should have been a less amiable fellow if I had worn cowhide boots and kicked her.

My reproaches, my remorses, my distresses, it is now an idle tale to tell. That night passed like none before it, and none which have come after it. My mind moved with a piteous monotony over and over and about the aching thought: to see Helen—to see Helen—to be patient till morning, and tell Helen— Only to get through this horrible night, and hurry, rushing to the morning air, to the nearest cab dashing down the street, and making the mad haste of love and shame, to see my wife—to tell my wife—

As never in all our lives before, I should tell her how dear she was; how unworthy was I to love her; how I loved her just as much as if I were worthy, and could not help it though I tried—or (as we say) could not help it though I died! I should run up, ringing the bell, never waiting to find the latch-key—for I could wait for nothing. I should spring into the house, and find her up-stairs, in our own room; it would be so early; she would be only half-dressed, yet, pale and lovely, looking like a spirit, far across the rich colors of the room, her long hair loose about her. I should gather her to my heart before she saw me; my arms and lips should speak before my breaking voice. I should kiss my soul out on her lifted face. I should love her so, she should forgive me before I could so much as say, Forgive! and when I had her—to myself again—when these arms were sure of their own, and these lips of hers, when her precious breath was on this cheek again, and I could say:—

"Helen, Helen, Helen"—

and could say no more, for love and shame and sorrow, but only—

"Helen, Helen"—

"Yes," said the watchman's voice in the corridor. "It is all right, sir. Me and Inspector Drayton, we thought we heard a noise, last night, and we considered it safe to look about. We had a thorough search. We thought we'd better. But there wasn't nothing. It's all straight, sir."

It was morning, and Brake's clerk was coming in. It was very early, earlier than he usually came, perhaps; but I could not tell. He did not notice me at first, and, remembering Drayton's hypothesis, I shrank behind the tall desk, and instinctively kept out of sight for a few uncertain minutes, wondering what I had better do. The clerk called the janitor, and scolded a little about the fire, which he ordered lighted in the grate. It was a cold morning. He said the room would chill a corpse. He had the morning papers in his hand. He unfolded the "Herald," and laid it down upon his own desk, as if about to read it.

At that instant, the telegraph clicked, and he pushed the damp, fresh paper away from him, and went immediately to the wires. The young man listened to the message with an expression of great intentness, and wrote rapidly. Moved by some unaccountable impulse, I softly rose and glanced over his shoulder.

The dispatch was dated at midnight, and was addressed to Henry Brake. It said:

"Have you seen my husband, to-night?" and it was signed, *"Helen Thorne."*

Oh, poor Helen! . . .

Now, maniac with haste to get to her, it occurred to me that the moment while the clerk was occupied in recording this message was as good a time as I could ask for in which to escape unobserved, as I greatly wished to do. As quietly as I could—and I succeeded in doing it very quietly—I therefore moved to leave the broker's office. As I did so, my eye caught the heading, in large capitals, of the morning news in the open "Herald" which lay upon the desk behind the clerk. I stopped, and stooped, and read. This is what I read:—

SHOCKING ACCIDENT.

TERRIBLE TRAGEDY.

Runaway at the West End.

The eminent and popular physician,

Dr. Esmerald Thorne,

KILLED INSTANTLY.

7

At this moment, the broker entered the office.

With the "Herald" in my hand, I made haste to meet him.

"Brake!" I cried, "Mr. Brake! Thank Heaven, you have come! I have passed such a night—and look here! Have you seen this abominable canard? This is what has come of my being locked into your"—

The broker regarded me with a strange look; so strange, that for very amazement I stood still before it. He did not advance to meet me; neither his hand nor his eyes gave me the human sign of welcome; he looked over me, he looked through me, as a man does at one whose acquaintance he has no desire to recognize.

I thought:—

"Drayton has crammed him. He too believes that I was shut in here to sleep it off. The story will get out in two hours. I am doomed in this town henceforth for a drunken doctor. I'd better have been killed instantly, as this infernal paper says."

But I said,—

"Mr. Brake? You don't recognize me, I think. It is I, Dr. Thorne. I couldn't get here before two. I went to your house last evening. I got the impression you were here, so I came after you. I was locked in here by your confounded watchman. They have this minute let me free. I am in a great hurry to get home. Nice job this is going to be! Have you seen *that*?"

I put my shaking finger upon the "Herald's" fiery capitals, and held the column folded towards him.

"Jason," he said, after an instant's pause, "pick up the 'Herald,' will you? A gust of wind has blown it from the table. There must be a draught. Please shut the door."

To say that I know of no earthly language which can express the sensation that crawled over me as the broker uttered these words is to say little or nothing about it. I use the expression "crawled" with some faint effort to define the slowness and the repulsiveness with which the suspicion of that to which I dared not and did not give a name, made itself manifest to my mind.

"Excuse me, Brake," I said with some agitation, "you did not hear what I said. I was locked in. I am in a hurry to get home. Ask Drayton. Drayton let me in. I must get home at once. I shall sue the 'Herald' for that outrageous piece of work— What do you suppose my wife— Good God! She must have read it by this time! Let me by, Brake!"

"Jason," said the broker, "this is a terrible thing! I feel quite broken up about it."

"Brake!" I cried, "Henry Brake! Let me pass you! Let me home to my wife! You're in my way—don't you see? You're standing directly between me and the door. Let me pass!"

"There's a private dispatch come," said the clerk sadly. "It is for you, sir. It is from Mrs. Thorne herself."

"Brake!" I pleaded, "Brake, Brake!—Jason!—Mr. Brake! Don't you hear me?"

"Give me the message, Jason," said Brake, holding out his hand; he seated himself, as he did so, at the office table, where I had sat the night out; he looked troubled and pale; he handled the message reluctantly, as people do in the certainty of bad news.

"In the name of mercy, Henry Brake!" I cried, "what is the meaning of this? Don't you hear a word I say? Don't you feel me?— There!" I gripped the broker by the shoulder, and clinched both hands upon him with all my might. "Don't you *feel* me? God Almighty! don't you *see* me, Brake?"

"When did this dispatch come, Jason?" said the broker. He laid Helen's message gently down; he had tears in his eyes.

"Henry Brake," I pleaded brokenly, for my heart failed me with a mighty fear, "answer me, in human pity's name. Are you gone deaf and blind? Or am I struck dumb? Or am I"—

"It came ten minutes ago, sir," replied Jason. "It is dated, I see, at midnight. They delivered it as soon as anybody was likely to be stirring, here; a bit before, too; considering the nature of the message, I suppose, sir."

"It is a terrible affair!" repeated the broker nervously. "I have known the doctor a good many years. He had his peculiarities; but he was a good fellow. Say—Jason!"

"Yes, sir?"

"How does it happen that Mrs. Thorne—You say this message was dated at midnight?"

"At midnight, sir. 12.15."

"How is it she didn't *know* by that time? I pity the fellow who had to tell her. She's a very attractive woman. . . . The 'Herald' says—Where is that paper?"

"The 'Herald' says," answered Jason decorously, "that he was scooped into the buggy-top, and dragged, and dashed against— Here it is."

He handed his employer the paper, as I had done, or had thought I did, with his finger on the folded column. The broker took the paper, and slowly put on his glasses, and slowly read aloud:—

" 'Dr. Thorne was dragged for some little distance, it is thought, before the horse broke free. He must have hit the lamp-post, or the pavement. He was found in the top of the buggy, which was a wreck. The robe was over him, and his face was hidden. His medicine case lay beneath him; the phials were crushed to splinters. Life was extinct when he was discovered. His watch had stopped at five minutes past seven o'clock. It so happened that he was not immediately identified, though our reporter could not learn the reason of this extraordinary mischance. By some unpardonable blunder, the body of the distinguished and favorite physician was taken to the Morgue' "—

"That accounts for it," said Jason.

—" 'Was taken to the Morgue,' " read on Mr. Brake with agitated voice. " 'It was not until midnight that the mistake was discovered. A messenger was dispatched at twenty minutes after twelve o'clock to the elegant residence of the popular doctor, in Delight Street. The news was broken to the widow as agreeably as possible. Mrs. Thorne is a young and very beautiful woman, on whom this shocking blow falls with uncommon cruelty.

" 'The body was carried to Dr. Thorne's house at one o'clock. The time of the funeral is not yet appointed. The "Herald" will be informed as soon as a decision is reached.

" 'The death of Dr. Thorne is a loss to this community which it is

impossible to,'—hm—m—'his distinguished talents'—hm—m—
hm—m."

The broker laid down the paper, and sighed.

"I sent for him yesterday, to consult about his affairs," he observed
gently. "It is a pity for her to lose that Santa Ma. She will need it now.
I'm sorry for her. I don't know how he left her, exactly. He did a
tremendous business, but he spent as he went. He was a good fellow—I always liked the doctor! Terrible affair! Terrible affair! Jason!
Where is that advertisement of Grope County Iowa Mortgage? You
have filed it in the wrong place! Be more careful in future."

. . . *"Mr. Brake!"* I tried once more; and my voice was the voice of
mortal anguish to my own appalled and ringing ear.

"Do you not hear? Can you not see? Is there *no one* in this place
who hears? Or sees me, *either?"*

An early customer had strayed in; Drayton was there; and the
watchman had entered. The men (there were five in all) collected
by the broker's desk, around the morning papers, and spoke to each
other with the familiarity which bad news of any public interest
creates. They conversed in low tones. Their faces wore a shocked
expression. They spoke of me; they asked for more particulars of the
tragedy reported by the morning press; they mentioned my merits
and defects, but said more about merits than defects, in the merciful, foolish way of people who discuss the newly dead.

"I've known him ten years," said the broker.

"I've had the pleasure of the doctor's acquaintance myself a good
while," said the inspector politely.

"Wasn't he a quick-tempered man?" asked the customer.

"He cured a baby of mine of the croup," said the watchman. "It
was given up for dead. And he only charged me a dollar and a half.
He was very kind to the little chap."

"He set an ankle for me, once, after a football match," suggested
the clerk. "I wouldn't ask to be better treated. He wasn't a bit rough."

. . . "Gentlemen," I entreated, stretching out my hands toward the group, "there is some mistake—I must make it understood. I am here. It is I, Dr. Thorne; Dr. Esmerald Thorne. I am in this office. Gentlemen! Listen to me! Look at me! Look in this direction! For God's sake, *try* to see me—some of you!" . . .

"He drove too fast a horse," said the customer. "He always has."

"I must answer Mrs. Thorne's message," said the broker sadly, rising and pushing back the office chair.

. . . I shrank, and tried no more. I bowed my head, and said no other word. The truth, incredible and terrible though it were, the truth which neither flesh nor spirit can escape, had now forced itself upon my consciousness.

I looked across the broker's office at those five warm human beings as if I had looked across the width of the breathing world. Naught had I now to say to them; naught could they communicate to me. Language was not between us, nor speech, nor any sign. Need of mine could reach them not, nor any of their kind. For I was the dead, and they the living men.

. . . "Here is your dog, sir," said Jason. "He has followed you in. He is trying to speak to you, in his way."

The broker stooped and patted the dumb brute affectionately. "I understand, Lion," he said. "Yes, I understand you."

The dog looked lovingly up into his master's face, and whined for joy.

8

This incident, trifling as it was, I think, did more than anything which had preceded it to make me aware of the nature of that which had befallen me. The live brute could still communicate with the living man. Skill of scientist and philosopher was as naught to help the human spirit which had fled the body to make itself understood by one which occupied a body still. More blessed in that moment was Lion, the dog, than Esmerald Thorne, the dead man. I said to myself:—

"I am a desolate and an outcast creature. I am become a dumb thing in a deaf world."

I thrust my hands before me, and wrung them with a groan. It seemed incredible to me that I *could* die; that was more wonderful, even, than to know that I was already dead.

"It is all over," I moaned. "I have died. I am dead. I am what they call a dead man."

Now, at this instant, the dog turned his head. No human tympanum in the room vibrated to my cry. No human retina was recipient of my anguish. What fine, unclassified senses had the highly-organized animal by which he should become aware of me? The dog turned his noble head—he was a St. Bernard, with the moral qualities of the breed well marked upon his physiognomy; he lifted his eyes and solemnly regarded me.

After a moment's pause he gave vent to a long and mournful cry.

"Don't, Lion," I said. "Keep quiet, sir. This is dreadful!"

The dog ceased howling when I spoke to him; after a little hesitation he came slowly to the spot where I was standing, and looked earnestly into my face, as if he saw me. Whether he did, or how he did, or why he did, I knew not, and I know not now. The main business of this narrative will be the recording of facts. Explanations it is not mine to offer; and of speculations I have but few, either to give or to withhold.

A great wistfulness came into my soul, as I stood shut apart there from those living men, within reach of their hands, within range of their eyes, within the vibration of their human breath. I looked into the animal's eyes with the yearning of a sudden and an awful sense of desolation.

"Speak to me, Lion," I whispered. "Won't *you* speak to me?"

"What is that dog about?" asked the customer, staring. "He is standing in the middle of the room and wagging his tail as if he had met somebody."

The dog at this instant, with eager signs of pleasure or of pity—I could not, indeed, say which—put his beautiful face against my hand, and kissed, or seemed to kiss it, sympathetically.

"He has queer ways," observed Jason, the clerk, carelessly; "he knows more than most folks I know."

"True," said his master, laughing. "I don't feel that I am Lion's equal more than half the time, myself. He is a noble fellow. He has a very superior nature. My wife declares he is a poet, and that when he goes off by himself, and gazes into vacancy with that sort of look, he is composing verses."

Another customer had strolled in by this time; he laughed at the broker's easy wit; the rest joined in the laugh; some one said something which I did not understand, and Drayton threw back his head and guffawed heartily. I think their laughter made me feel more isolated from them than anything had yet done.

"Why!" exclaimed the broker sharply, "what is this? Jason! What does this mean?"

His face, as he turned it over his shoulder to address the clerk, had changed color; he was indeed really pale. He held his fingers on the great sheet of blue blotting-paper, to which he pointed, unsteadily.

"Upon my soul, sir," said Jason, flushing and then paling in his turn. "That *is* a queer thing! May I show it to Mr. Drayton?"

The inspector stepped forward, as the broker nodded; and examined the blotting-paper attentively.

"It is written over," he said in a professional tone, "from end to end. I see that. It is written with one name. It is the name of"—

"Helen!" interrupted the broker.

"Yes," replied the inspector. "Yes, it is: Helen; distinctly, Helen. Some one must have"—

But I stayed to hear no more. What some one must have done, I sprang and left the live men to decide—as live men do decide such things—among themselves. I sprang, and crying: "Helen! Helen!

Helen!" with one bound I brushed them by, and fled the room, and reached the outer air and sought for her.

As nearly as one can characterize the emotion of such a moment, I should say that it was one of mortal intensity; perhaps of what in living men we should call maniac intensity. Up to this moment I could not be said to have comprehended the effect of what had taken place upon my wife.

The full force of her terrible position now struck me like the edge of a weapon with whose sheath I had been idling.

Hot in the flame of my anger I had gone from her; and cold indeed had I returned. Her I had left dumb before my cruel tongue, but dumb was that which had come back to her in my name.

I was a dead man. But like any living of them all—oh, more than any living—I loved my wife. I loved her more because I had been cruel to her than if I had been kind. I loved her more because we had parted so bitterly than if we had parted lovingly. I loved her more because I had died than if I had lived. I must see my wife! I must find my wife! I must say to her—I must tell her— Why, who in all the world but me could do *anything* for Helen now?

Out into the morning air I rushed, and got the breeze in my face, and up the thronging street, as spirits do, unnoted and unknown of men, I passed; solitary in the throng, silent in the outcry, unsentient in the press.

The sun was strong. The day was cool. The dome of the sky hung over me, too, as over those who raised their breathing faces to its beauty. I, too, saw, as I fled on, that the day was fair. I heard the human voices say:

"What a morning!"

"It puts the soul into you!" said a burly stock speculator to a railroad treasurer; they stood upon the steps of the Exchange, laughing, as I brushed by.

"It makes life worth while," said a healthy elderly woman, merrily, making the crossing with the light foot that a light heart gives.

"It makes life possible," replied a pale young girl beside her, coming slowly after.

"Poor fellow!" sighed a stranger whom I hit in hurrying on. "It was an ugly way to die. Nice air, this morning!"

"He will be a loss to the community," replied this man's companion. "There isn't a doctor in town who has his luck with fevers. You can't convince my wife he didn't save her life last winter. Frost, last night, wasn't there? Very invigorating morning!"

Now, at the head of the street some ladies were standing, waiting for a car. I was delayed in passing them, and as I stepped back to change my course I saw that one of them was speaking earnestly and that her eyes showed signs of weeping.

"He wouldn't remember me," she said; "it was eleven years ago. But sick women don't forget their doctors. He was as *kind* to me"—

"Oh, *poor* Mrs. Thorne!" a soft voice answered, in the accented tone of an impulsive, tender-hearted woman. "It's bad enough to be a patient. But, oh, his *wife!*"

"Let me pass, ladies!" I cried, or tried to cry, forgetting, in the anguish which their words fanned to its fiercest, that I could not be heard and might not be seen. "There seems to be some obstruction. Let me by, for I am in mortal haste!"

Obstruction there was, alas! but it was not in them whom I would have entreated. Obstruction there was, but of what nature I could not and I cannot testify. While I had the words upon my lips, even as the group of women broke and left a space about me while they scattered on their ways, there on the corner of the thoroughfare, in the heart of the town, by an invisible force, by an inexplicable barrier, I, the dead man fleeing to my living wife, was beaten back.

Whence came that awful order? How came it? And wherefore? I knew no more than the November wind that passed me by, and went upon its errand as it listed.

I was thrust back by a blast of Power Incalculable; it was like the current of an unknown natural force of infinite capability. Set the will of soul and body as I would, I could not pass the head of the street.

₹9₹

Struggling to bear the fate which I had met, I turned as manfully as I might, and retraced my steps down the thronging street, within whose limits I now learned that my freedom was confined. It was a sickening discovery. I had been a man of will so developed and freedom so sufficient that helplessness came upon me like a change of temperament; it took the form of hopelessness almost at once.

What was death? The secret of life. What knew I of the system of things on which a blow upon the head had ushered me all unready, reluctant, and uninstructed as I was? No more than the ruddiest live stockbroker on the street, whose blood went bounding, that fresh morning, to the antics of the Santa Ma. I was not accustomed to be uninformed; my ignorance appalled me. Even in the deeps of my misery, I found space for a sense of humiliation; I felt profoundly mortified. In that spot, in that way, of all others, why was I withheld? Was it the custom of the black country called Death, which we mark "Unexplored" upon the map of life,—was it the habit to tie a man to the place where he had died? But this was not the spot where I had died. It was the spot where I had learned that I had died. It was the place where the consciousness of death had wrought itself, not upon the nerves of the body, but upon the faculties of the mind. I had been dead twelve hours before I found it out.

I looked up and down the street, where the living men scurried to and fro upon their little errands. These seemed immeasurably small. I looked upon them with disgust. Fettered to that pavement, like a convict to his ball-and-chain, I passed and repassed in wretchedness whose quality I cannot express, and would not if I could.

"I am punished," I said; "I am punished for that which I have done. This is my doom. I am imprisoned here."

Sometimes I broke into uncontrollable misery, crying upon my wife's dear name. Then I would hush the outbreak, lest some one overhear me; and then I would remember that no one could overhear. I looked into the faces of the people whom I met and passed, with such longings for one single sign of recognition as are not to be described. It even occurred to me that among them all one might be found of whom my love and grief and will might make a messenger to Helen. But I found none such, or I gained no such power; and, sick at heart, I turned away.

Suddenly, as I threaded the thick of the press, beating to and fro, and up and down, as dead leaves move before the wind, some one softly touched my hand.

It was the St. Bernard, the broker's dog. This time, as before, he looked into my face with signs of pleasure or of pity, or of both, and made as if he would caress me.

"Lion!" I cried, "*you* know me, don't you? Bless you, Lion!"

Now, at the dumb thing's recognition, I could have wept for pleasure. The dog, when I spoke to him, followed me; and for some time walked up and down and athwart the street, beside me. This was a comfort to me. At last his master came out upon the sidewalk and looked for him. Brake whistled merrily, and the dog, at the first call, went bounding in.

Ordinary writers upon usual topics, addressing readers of their own condition, have their share of difficulties; at best one conquers the art of expression as a General conquers an enemy. But the obstacles which present themselves to the recorder of this narrative are such as will be seen at once to have peculiar force. Almost at the outset they dishearten me. How shall I tell the story unless I be understood? And how should I be understood if I told the story? Were it for me, a man miserable and erring, gone to his doom as untrained for its consequences, or for the use of them, as a drayman for the use of hypnotism in surgery,—were it for me to play the interpreter between life and death? Were it for me to expect to be successful in that solemn effort which is as old as time, and as hopeless as the eyes of mourners?

What shall I say? It is willed that I shall speak. The angel said unto me: Write. How shall I obey, who am the most unworthy of any soul upon whom has been laid the burden of the higher utterance? Sacred be the task. Would that its sacredness could sanctify the unfitness of him who here fulfills it.

The experience which I have already narrated was followed by an indefinite period of great misery. How long I remained a prisoner in that unwelcome spot I cannot accurately tell.

What are called by dwellers in the body days and nights, and dawns and darks, succeeded each other, little remarked by my wretchedness, or by the sense of remoteness from these things which now began to grow upon me. The life of what we call a spirit had begun for me in the form of a moral dislocation. The wrench, the agony, the process of setting the nature under its new conditions, took place in due order, but with bitter laggardness. The accident of death did not heal in my soul by what surgeons call "the first intention." I retained for a long time the consciousness of being an injured creature.

As I paced and repaced the narrow street where the money-makers and money-lovers of the town jostled and thronged, a great disgust descended upon me. The place, the springs of conduct, wearied me, something in the manner that an educated person is wearied by low conversation. It seemed to be like this:—that the moral motives of the living created the atmosphere of the dead therein confined. It was as if I inhaled the coarse friction, the low aspiration, the feverishness, the selfishness, the dishonor, that the getting of gain, when it became the purpose of life, involved. I experienced a sense of being stifled, and breathed with difficulty; much as those live men would have done, if the gas-pipes had burst in the street.

It did not detract from this feeling of asphyxia that I was aware of having, to a certain extent, shared the set of moral compounds which I now found resolved to their elements, by the curious chemistry of death.

I had loved money and the getting of money, as men of the world, and of success in it, are apt to do. I was neither better nor worse than others of my sort. I had speculated with the profits of my profession, idly enough, but hotly, too, at times. I had told myself that I did this out of anxiety for the future of my family. I had viewed myself in the light of the model domestic man, who guards his household against an evil day. It had never occurred to me to classify myself with the mere money-changers, into whose atmosphere I had elected to put myself.

Now, as I glided in and out among them, unseen, unheard, unrecognized, a spirit among their flesh, there came upon me a humiliating sense of my true relation to them. Was it *thus,* I said, or *so?* Did I this or that? Was the balance of motives so disproportionate after all? Was there so little love of wife and child? So much of self and gain? Was the item of the true so small? The sum of the false so large? Had I been so much less that was noble, so much more that was low?

I mingled with the mass of haggard men at a large stock auction which half the street attended. The panic had spread. Sleeplessness and anxiety had carved the crowding faces with hard chisels. The shouts, the scramble, the oaths, the clinched hands, the pitiful pushing, affected me like a dismal spectacular play on some barbarian stage. How shall I express the sickening aspect of the scene to a man but newly dead?

The excitement waxed with the morning. The old and placid Santa Ma throbbed like any little road of yesterday. The stock had gained 32 points in ten minutes, and down again, and up again to Heaven knows what. Men ran from despair to elation, and behaved like maniacs in both. Men who were gentlemen at home turned savages here. Men who were honorable in society turned sharpers here. Madness had them, as I watched them. A kind of pity for them seized me. I glided in among them, and lifted my whole heart to stay them if I could. I stretched the hands that no one saw. I raised the voice that none could hear.

"Gentlemen!" I cried, "count me the market value of it—on the margin of two lives! By the bonds wherewith you bind yourselves you shall be bound! . . . . What is the sum of wealth represented within these walls to-day? Name it to me. . . . . The whole of it, for the power to leave this place! The whole of it, the whole of it, for one half-hour in a dead man's desolated home! A hundred-fold the whole of it for"—

But here I lost command of myself, and fleeing from the place where my presence and my misery and my entreaty alike were lost upon the attention of the living throng as were the elements of the air they breathed, I rushed into the outer world again; there to wander up and down the street, and hate the place, and hate myself for being there, and hate the greed of gain I used to love, and hate myself for having loved it; and yet to know that I was forced to act as if I loved it still, and to be the ghost before the ghost of a desire.

"It is my doom," I said. "I am punished. I am fastened to this worldly spot, and to this awful way of being dead."

Now, while I spoke these words, I came, in the stress of my wretchedness, fleeing to the head of the street; and there, I cannot tell you how, I cannot answer why, as the arrow springs from the bow, or the conduct from the heart, or the spirit from the flesh,—in one blessed instant I knew that I was free to leave the spot, and crying, "Helen, Helen!" broke from it.

$$\{10\}$$

But no. Alas, no, no! I was and was not free. All my soul turned toward her, but something stronger than my soul constrained me. It seemed to me that I longed for her with such longing as might have killed a live man, or might have made a dead one live again. This emotion added much to my suffering, but nothing to my power to turn one footstep toward her or to lift my helpless face in her direction. It was not permitted to me. It was not willed.

Now this, which might in another temperament have produced a sense of fear or of desire to placate the unknown Force which overruled me, created in me at first a stinging rage. This is the truth, and the truth I tell.

In my love and misery, and the shock of this disappointment—against the unknown opposition to my will, I turned and raved; even as when I was a man among men I should have raved at him who dared my purpose.

"You are playing with me!" I wailed. "You torture a miserable man. Who and what are you, that make of death a bitterer thing than life can guess? Show me what I have to fight, and let me wrestle for my liberty,—though I am a ghost, let me wrestle like a man! Let me to my wife! Give way, and let me seek her!"

Shocking and foreign as words like these must be to many of those who read these pages, it must be remembered that they were uttered by one to whom faith and the knowledge that comes by way of it were the leaves of an abandoned text-book. For so many years had the tenets of the Christian religion been put out of my practical life, even as I put aside the opinions of the laity concerning the treatment of disease, that I do not over-emphasize; I speak the simplest truth in saying that my first experience of death had not in any sense revived the vividness of lost belief to me. As the old life had ended had the new begun. Where the tree had fallen it did lie. What was habit before death was habit after. What was natural then was natural now. What I loved living I loved dead. That which interested Esmerald Thorne the man interested Esmerald Thorne the spirit. The incident of death had raised the temperature of intellect; it had, perhaps I may say, by this time quickened the pulse of conscience; but it had in no wise wrought any miracle upon me, nor created a religious believer out of a worldly and indifferent man of science. Dying had not forthwith made me a devout person. Incredible as it may seem, it is the truth that up to this time I had not, since the moment of dissolution, put to myself the solemn queries concerning my present state which occupy the imaginations of the living so much, while yet death is a fact remote from their experience.

It was the habit of long years with me, after the manner of my kind, to settle all hard questions by a few elastic phrases, which, once learned, are curiously pliable to the intellectual touch. "Phenomena," for instance,—how plastic to cover whatever one does not understand! "Law,"—how ready to explain away the inexplicable! Up to this point death had struck me as a most unfortunate phenomenon. Its personal disabilities I found it easy to attribute to some natural law with which my previous education had left me unfamiliar. Now, standing baffled there in that incredible manner, half of tragedy, half of the absurd,—even the petty element of the undignified in the position adding to my distress,—a houseless, homeless, outcast spirit, struck still in the heart of that great town, where in hundreds of homes was weeping for me, where I was beloved and honored and bemoaned, and where my own wife at that hour broke her heart with sorrow for me and for the manner of my parting from her,—then and there to be beaten back, and battered down, and tossed like an atom in some primeval flood, whithersoever I would not,—what a situation was this!

Now, indeed, I think for the first time, my soul lifted itself, as a sick man lifts himself upon his elbows, in his painful bed. Now, flashing straight back upon the outburst of my defiance and despair, like the reflex action of a strong muscle, there came into my mind, if not into my heart, these impulsive and entreating words:—

"What art Thou, who dost withstand me? I am a dead and helpless man. What wouldst Thou with me? Where gainest Thou Thy force upon me? Art Thou verily that ancient Myth which we were wont to call Almighty God?"

Simultaneously with the utterance of these words that blast of Will to which I have referred fell heavily upon me. A Power not myself overshadowed me and did environ me. Guided whithersoever I would not, I passed forth upon errands all unknown to me, rebelling and obeying as I went.

"I am become what we used to call a spirit," I thought, bitterly, "and this is what it means. Better might one become a molecule, for those, at least, obey the laws of the universe, and do not suffer."

Now, as I took my course, it being ordered on me, it led me past the door of a certain open church, whence the sound of singing issued. The finest choir in the city, famous far and near, were practicing for the Sunday service, and singing like the sons of God, indeed, as I passed by. With the love of the scientific temperament for harmony alert in me, I lingered to listen to the anthem which these singers were rendering in their customary great manner. With the instinct of the musically educated, I felt pleasure in this singing, and said:—

"Magnificently done!" as I went on. It was some moments before the words which the choir sang assumed any vividness in my mind. When they did I found that they were these:—

"For God is a Spirit. God is a Spirit; and they that worship Him must worship Him in spirit"—

Now it fell out that my steps were directed to the hospital; and to the hospital I straight-way went. I experienced some faint comfort at this improvement in my lot, and hurried up the avenue and up the steps and into the familiar wards with eagerness. All the impulses of the healer were alive in me. I felt it a mercy for my nature to be at its own again. I hastened in among my sick impetuously.

The hospital had been a favorite project of mine; from its start, unreasonably dear to me. Through the mounting difficulties which blockade such enterprises, I had hewn and hacked, I had fathered and doctored, I had trusteed and collected, I had subscribed and directed and persisted and prophesied and fulfilled, as one ardent person must in most humanitarian successes; and I had loved the success accordingly. I do not think it had ever once occurred to me to question myself as to the chemical proportions of my motives in this great and popular charity. Now, as I entered the familiar place, some query of this nature did indeed occupy my mind; it had the strangeness of all mental experiences consequent upon my new condition, and somewhat, if I remember, puzzled me.

The love of healing? The relief of suffering? Sympathy with the wretched? Chivalry for the helpless? Generosity to the poor? Friendship to the friendless? Were these the motives, all the motives, the *whole* motives, of him who had in my name ministered in that place so long? Even the love of science? Devotion to a therapeutic creed? Sacrifice for a surgical doctrine? Enthusiasm for an important professional cause? Did these, and only these, sources of conduct *explain* the great hospital? Or the surgeon who had created and sustained it?

Where did the motive deteriorate? Where did the alloy come in? How did the sensitiveness to self, the passion for fame, the joy of power, amalgamate with all that noble feeling? How much residuum was there in the solution of that absorption which (outside of my own home) I had thought the purest and highest of my interests in life?

For the first of all the uncounted times that I had entered the hospital for now these many years, I crossed the threshold questioning myself in this manner, and doubting of my fitness to be there, or to be what I had been held to be in that place. Life had carried me gayly and swiftly, as it carries successful men. I had found no time, or made none, to cross-question the sources of conduct. My success had been my religion.

I had the conviction of a prosperous person that the natural emotions of prosperity were about right. Added to this was something of the physician's respect for what was healthful in human life. Good luck, good looks, good nerves, a good income, an enviable reputation for professional skill, personal popularity, and private happiness,—these things had struck me as so wholesome that they must be admirable. Behind the painted screen which a useful and successful career sets before the souls of men I had been too busy or too light of heart to peer. Now it was as if, in the act or the fact of dying, I had moved a step or two, and looked over the edge of the bright shield.

Thoughts like these came to me so quietly and so naturally, now, that I wondered why I had not been familiar with them before; it even occurred to me that being very busy did not wholly excuse a live man for not thinking; and it was something in the softened spirit of this strange humility that I opened the noiseless door, and found myself among my old patients in the large ward.

Never before had I entered that sad place that the electric thrill of welcome, which only a physician knows, had not pulsated through it, preceding me, from end to end of the long room. The peculiar *lighting* of the ward that flashes with the presence of a favorite doctor; the sudden flexible smile on pain-pinched lips; the yearning motion of the dyes in some helpless body where only the eyes can stir; the swift stretching-out of wasted hands; the half-inaudible cry of welcome: "The doctor's come!" "Oh, there's the doctor!" "Why, it's the *doctor!*"—the loving murmur of my name; the low prayer of blessing on it,—oh, never before had I entered my hospital, and missed the least of these.

I thought I was prepared for this, but it was not without a shock that I stood among my old patients, mute and miserable, glancing piteously at them, as they had so often done at me; seeking for their recognition, which I might not have; longing for their welcome, which was not any more for me.

The moans of pain, the querulous replies to nurses, the weary cough or plethoric breathing, the feeble convalescent laughter,— these greeted me; and only these. Like the light that entered at the window, or the air that circulated through the ward, I passed unnoticed and unthanked. Some one called out petulantly that a door had got unfastened, and bade a nurse go shut it, for it blew on her. But when I came up to the bedside of this poor woman, I saw that she was crying.

"She's cried herself half-dead," a nurse said, complainingly. "Nobody can stop her. She's taking on so for Dr. Thorne."

"I don't blame her," said a little patient from a wheeled-chair. "Ev-

erybody knows what he did for her. She's got one of her attacks,—
and look at her! There *can't* anybody but him stop it. Whatever we're
going to do without the doctor"—

Her own lip quivered, though she was getting well.

"I don't see how the doctor *could* die!" moaned the very sick woman, weeping afresh, "when there's those that nobody but him can keep
alive. It hadn't oughter to be let to be. How are sick folks going to get
along with out their doctor? It ain't *right!*"

"Lord have mercy on ye, poor creetur," said an old lady from the
opposite cot. "Don't take on so. It don't *help* it any. It ain't agoing to
bring the doctor back!"

Sobs arose at this. I could hear them from more beds than I cared
to count. Sorrow sat heavily in the ward for my sake. It distressed
me to think of the effect of all this depression upon the nervous
systems of these poor people. I passed from case to case, and watched
the ill-effects of the general gloom with a sense of professional disappointment which only physicians will understand as coming uppermost in a man's mind under circumstances such as these.

My discomfort was increased by the evidences of what I considered mistakes in treatment on the part of my colleagues; some of
which had peculiarly disagreed with certain patients since my death
had thrown them into other hands. My helplessness before these facts
chafed me sorely.

I made no futile effort to make myself known to any of the hospital patients. I had learned too well the limitations of my new condition now. I had in no wise learned to bear them. In truth, I think
I bore them less well, for my knowledge that these poor creatures
did truly love me, and leaned on me, and mourned for me; I found
it hard. I think it even occurred to me that a dead man might not be
able to bear it to see his wife and child.

"Doctor!" said a low, sweet voice, "Doctor?"

My heart leaped within me, as I turned. Where was the highly organized one of all my patients, who had baffled death for love of me?

Who had the clairvoyance or clairaudience, or the wonderful *tip* in the scale of health and disease, which causes such phenomena?

With hungry eyes I gazed from cot to cot. No answering gaze returned to me. Craving their recognition more sorely than they had ever, in the old life, craved mine, in such need of their sympathy as never had the weakest of the whole of them for mine, I scanned them all. No—no. There was not a patient in the ward who knew me. No.

Stung with the disappointment, I sank into a chair beside the weeping woman's bed, and bowed my face upon my hands. At this instant I was touched upon the shoulder.

"Doctor? Why, Doctor!" said the voice again.

I sprang and caught the speaker by the hands. It was Mrs. Faith. She stood beside me, sweet and smiling.

"The carriage overturned," she said in her quiet way. "I was badly hurt. I only died an hour ago. I started out at once to find you. I want you to see Charley. Charley's still alive. Those doctors don't understand Charley. There's nobody I'd trust him to but you. *You* can save him. Come! You can't think how he asked for you, and cried for you. . . . I thought I should find you at the hospital. Come quickly, Doctor! Come!

⁅ *11* ⁆

Some homesick traveler in a foreign land, where he is known of none and can neither speak nor understand the language of the country; taken ill, let us say, at a remote inn, his strength and credit gone, and he, in pain and fever, hears, one blessed day, the voice of an old friend in the court below. Such a man may think he has—but I doubt if he have—some crude conception of the state of feeling in which I found myself, when recognized in this touching manner by my old patient.

My emotion was so great that I could not conceal it; and she, in her own quick and delicate way, perceiving this almost before I did, myself, made as if she saw it not, and lightly adding:

"Hurry, Doctor! I will go before you. Let us lose no time!" led me at once out of the hospital, and rapidly away.

In an incredibly, almost confusingly short space of time, we reached her house; this was done by some method of locomotion not hitherto experienced by me, and which I should, at that time, have found it difficult to describe, unless by saying that *she thought* us where we wished to be. Perhaps it would be more exact to say, *She felt us.* It was as if the great power of the mother's love in her, had become a new bodily faculty by which she was able, with extraordinary disregard of the laws of distance, to move herself and to draw another to the suffering child. I should say that I perceived at once, in the presence of this sweet woman, that there were possibilities and privileges in the state immediately succeeding death, which had been utterly denied to me, and were still unknown to me. It was easy to see that her personal experience in the new condition differed as much from mine as our lives had differed in the time preceding death. She had been a patient, unworldly, and devout sufferer; a chronic invalid, who bore her lot divinely. Her soul had been as full of trust and gentleness, of the forgetting of self and the service of others, of the scorn of pain, and of what she called trust in Heaven, as any woman's soul could be.

I had never seen the moment when I could withhold my respect from the devout nature of Mrs. Faith, any more than I could from her manner of enduring suffering; or, I might add, if I could expect the remark to be properly understood,—from her strong and intelligent trust in me. Physicians know what sturdy qualities it takes to make a good patient. Perhaps they are, to some extent, the same which go to make a good believer; but in this direction I am less informed.

During our passage from the hospital to the house, Mrs. Faith had not spoken to me; her whole being seemed, so nearly as I could understand it, to be absorbed in the process of getting there. It struck me that she was still unpracticed in the use of a new and remarkable faculty, which required strict attention from her, like any other as yet unlearned art.

"*You* are not turned out of your own home it seems!" I exclaimed impulsively, as we entered the house together.

"Oh, no, *no!*" she cried. "Who is? Who could be? Why, Doctor, are *you?*"

"Death is a terrible respecter of persons," I answered drearily. I could not further explain myself at that moment.

"I have been away from Charley a good while," she anxiously replied; "it is the first time I have left him since I died. But I had to find you, Doctor. Charley should not die—I can't have Charley die—for his poor father's sake. But I feel quite safe about him, now I have got you."

She said these words in her old bright, trustful way. The thought of my helplessness to justify such trust smote me sorely; but I said nothing then to undeceive her,—how could I?—and we made haste together to the bedside of the injured child.

I saw at a glance that the child was in a bad case. Halt was there, and Dr. Gazell; they were consulting gloomily. The father, haggard with his first bereavement, seemed to have accepted the second as a foregone conclusion; he sat with his face in his hands, beside the little fellow's bed. The boy called for his mother at intervals. A nurse hung about weeping. It was a dismal scene; there was not a spark of hope, or energy, or fight in the whole room. I cried out immoderately that it was enough to kill the well, and protested against the management of the case with the ardent conviction to which my old patient was so used, and in which she believed more thoroughly than I did myself. "They are giving the wrong remedy," I hotly said. "This surgical fever could be controlled,—the boy need not die. But he will! You may as well make up your mind to it, Mrs. Faith. Gazell doesn't understand the little fellow's constitution, and Halt doesn't understand anything."

Now it was that, as I had expected, the mother turned upon me with all a mother's hopeless and heart-breaking want of logic. Sure-ly, I, and only I, could save the boy. Why, I had always taken care of Charley! Was it possible that I could stand by and see Charley *die? She* should not have died herself if I had been there. She depended upon me to find some way—there must be a way. She never thought I was the kind of a man to be so changed by—by what had hap-pened.

I used to be so full of hope and vigor, and so inventive in a sick-room. It was not reasonable! It was not possible that, just because I was a spirit, I could not control the minds or bodies of those live men who were so inferior to me. Why, she thought I could control *any*body. She thought I could conquer *any*thing.

"I don't understand it, Doctor," she said, with something like re-proach. "You don't seem to be able to do as much—you don't even know as much as *I* do, now. And you know what a sick and helpless little woman I've always been,—how ignorant, beside you! I thought you were so wise, so strong, so great. Where has it all gone to, Doc-tor? What has become of your wisdom and your power? Can't you help me? Can't you"—

"I can do nothing," I interrupted her,—"nothing. I am shorn of it all. It has all gone from me, like the strength of Samson. Spare me, and torment me not. . . . I cannot heal your child. I am not like you. I was not prepared for—this condition of things. I did not expect to die. I never thought of becoming a spirit. I find myself extraordi-narily embarrassed by it. It is the most unnatural state I ever was in."

"Why, I find it as natural as life," she said more gently. She had now moved to the bedside, and taken the little fellow in her arms.

"You are not as I," I replied morosely. "We differed—and we dif-fer. Truly, I believe that if there is anything to be done for your boy, it rests with you, and not with me."

Halt and Gazell were now consulting in an undertone, touching the selection of a certain remedy; no one noticed them, and they droned on.

The mother crooned over the child, and caressed him, and breathed upon his sunken little face, and poured her soul out over him in precious floods and wastes of tenderness as mothers do.

"Live, my little son!" she whispered. "Live, live!"

But I, meanwhile, was watching the two physicians miserably. "There!" I said, "they have dropped the phial on the floor. See, that is the one they ought to have. It rolled away. They don't mean to take it. They will give him the wrong thing. Oh, how *can* they?"

But now the mother, when she heard me speak, swiftly and gently removed her arms from beneath the boy, and, advancing to the hesitating men, stood silently between them, and laid a hand upon the arm of each. While she stood there she had a rapt, high look of such sort that I could in no wise have addressed her.

"Are you *sure,* Dr. Gazell?" asked Halt.

"I *think* so," said Gazell.

He stooped, after a moment's hesitation, and picked up the phial from the floor, read its label; laid it down, looked at the child, and hesitated again.

The mother at this juncture sunk upon her knees and bowed her shining face. I thought she seemed to be at prayer. I too bowed my head; but it was for reverence at the sight of her. It was long since I had prayed. I did not find it natural to do so. A strange discontent, something almost like an inclination to prayer, came upon me. But that was all. I would rather have had the power to turn those two men out of the room, and pour the saving remedy upon my little patient's burning tongue with my own flesh-and-blood fingers, and a hearty objurgation on the professional blunder which I had come in time to rectify.

"Dr. Halt," said Dr. Gazell slowly, "with your approval I think I will change my mind. On the whole, the indications point to—this. I trust it is the appropriate remedy."

He removed the cork from the phial as he spoke, and, rising, passed quickly to the bedside of the child.

The mother had now arisen from her knees, and followed him, and got her arms about the boy again, and set her soul to brooding over him in the way that loving women have. I was of no further service to her, and I had vanished from her thought, which had no more room at that moment for anything except the child than the arms with which she clasped him.

It amazed me—I was going to say it appalled me—that no person in the room should seem to have consciousness of her presence. She was like an invisible star. How incredible that love like that, and the power of it, could be dependent upon the paltry senses of what are called live people for so much as the proofs of its existence.

"It is not scientific," I caught myself saying, as I turned away, "there is a flaw in the logic somewhere. There seems to be a snapped link between two sets of facts. There is no deficiency of data; the difficulty lies wholly in collating them."

How, indeed, should I—how did I but a few days since—myself regard such "data" as presumed to indicate the continuance of human life beyond the point of physical decay!

"After all," I thought, as I wandered from the house in which I felt myself forgotten and superfluous, and pursued my lonely way, I knew not whither and I knew not why,—"after all, there *is* another life. I really did not think it."

It seemed now to have been an extraordinary narrowness of intellect in me that I had not at least attached more weight to the universal human hypothesis. I did not precisely wonder from a personal point of view that I had not definitely believed it; but I wondered that I had not given the possibility the sort of attention which a view of so much dignity deserved. It really annoyed me that I had made that kind of mistake.

We, at least, were alive,—my old patient and I. Whether others, or how many, or of what sort, I could not tell; I had yet seen no other spirit. What was the life-force in this new condition of things? Where was the central cell? What *made* us go on living? Habit? Or selection? Thought? Emotion? Vigor? If the last, what species of vigor? What was that in the individual which gave it strength to stay? Whence came the reproductive power which was able to carry on the species under such terrible antagonism as the fact of death? If in the body, where was the common element between that attenuated invalid and my robust organization? If in the soul, between the suffering saint and the joyous man of the world, where again was our common moral protoplasm?

Nothing occurred to me at the time, at least, as offering any spiritual likeness between myself and Mrs. Faith, but the fact that we were both people of strong affections which had been highly cultivated. Might not a woman *love* herself into continued existence who felt for any creature what she did for that child?

And I—God knew, if there were a God, how it was with me. If I had never done anything, if I had never been anything, if I had never felt anything else in all my life, that was fit to *last,* I had loved one woman, and her only, and had thought high thoughts for her, and felt great emotions for her, and forgotten self for her sake, and thought it sweet to suffer for her, and been a better man for love of her. And I had loved her,—oh, I had so loved her, that I knew in my soul ten thousand deaths could not murder that living love.

And I had spoken to her—I had said to her—like any low and brutal fellow, any common wife-tormentor—I had gone from her dear presence to this mute life wherein there was neither speech nor language; where neither earth, nor heaven, nor my love, nor my remorse, nor all my anguish, nor my shame, could give my sealed lips the power to say, Forgive.

Now, while I was cast thus abroad upon the night,—for it was night,—sorely shaken and groaning in spirit, taking no care where my homeless feet should lead me, I lifted my eyes suddenly, and looked straight on before me, and behold! shining afar, fair and sweet and clear, I saw and recognized the lights of my own home.

I was still at some distance from the spot, and, beside myself with joy, I started to run unto it. With the swift motions which spirits make, and which I was beginning to master in a clumsy manner and low degree, I came, compassing the space between myself and all I loved or longed for, and so brought myself tumultuously into the street where the house stood; there, at a stone's throw from it, I felt myself suddenly stifled with my haste, or from some cause, and, pausing (as we used to say) to gather breath, I found that I was stricken back, and fettered to the ground.

There was no wind. The night was perfectly still. Not a leaf quivered on the top-most branch of the linden which tapped our chamber-window. Yet a Power like a mighty rushing blast gainsaid me and smote me where I was.

Not a step, though I writhed for it, not a breath nearer, though my heart should break for it, could I take or make to reach her. This was my doom. Almost within clasp of her dear arms, within sight of her sweet face,—for there! while I stood struggling, I saw a woman's shadow rise and stir upon the dimly lighted wall,—thus to be denied and bidden back from her seemed to me more than heart could bear.

While I stood, quite unmanned by what had happened, incredulous of my punishment, and yearning to her through the little distance, and stretching out my hands toward her, and brokenly babbling her dear name, she moved, and I saw her distinctly, even as I had seen her that last time. She stood midway between the unlighted parlor and the lighted library beyond. The drop-light with the scarlet shade blazed behind her.

I noticed that to-night, as on that other night, the baby was not with her; and I wondered why. She stood alone. She moved up and down the room; she had a weary step. Her dress, I saw, was black, dead black. Her white hands, clasped before her, shone with startling brilliancy upon the sombre stuff she wore. Her lovely head was bent a little, and she seemed to be gazing at me whom she could not see. Then I cried with such a cry, it seemed as if the very living must needs hear:—

"Helen! Helen! *Helen!*"

But she stood quite still; leaning her pale face toward me, like some listening creature that was stricken deaf.

The sight was more sorrowful than I could brave; for the first time since I had died I succumbed into something like a swoon, and lost my miserable consciousness in the street before her door.

₹12₹

When I came again to myself I found that what I should once have called a "phenomenon" had taken place. The city, the dim street, the familiar architecture of my home, the streams of light from the long windows, the leaves of the linden tapping on the glass, the woman's shadow on the wall, and the stirring toward me of the form and face I loved,—these had vanished.

I was in a strange place; and I was a stranger in it. It seemed rather a lonely place at first, though it was not unpleasing to me as I looked abroad. The scenery was mountainous and solemn, but it was therefore on a large scale and restful to the eye. It had more grandeur than beauty, to my first impression; but I remembered that I was not in a condition of mind to be receptive of the merely beautiful, which might exist for me without my perception of it, even as the life of the dead existed without the perception of the living. Death, if it had taught me less up to that time than it might have done to nobler men, had at least done so much as this: it had accustomed me to respect the unseen, and to regard its possible action upon the seen as a matter of import. As I looked forth upon the hills and skies, the plains and forests, and on to the distant signs of human habitation in the scenery about me, I thought:—

"I am in a world where it is probable that there exist a thousand things which I cannot understand to one which I can."

It seemed to me a very uncomfortable state of affairs, whatever it was. I felt estranged from this place, even before I was acquainted with it. Nothing in my nature responded to its atmosphere; or, if so, petulantly and with a kind of helpless antagonism, like the first cry of the new-born infant in the old life.

As I got myself languidly to my feet, and idly trod the path which lay before me, for lack of knowing any better thing to do, I began to perceive that others moved about the scene; that I was not, as I had thought, alone, but one of a company, each going on his errand as he would. I only seemed to have no errand; and I was at a great distance from these people, whose presence, however, though so remote, gave me something of the sense of companionship which one whose home is in a lonely spot upon a harbor coast has in watching the head-lights of anchored ships upon dark nights. Communication there is none, but desolation is less for knowing that there could be, or for fancying that there might.

Across the space between us, I looked upon my fellow-citizens in this new country, with a dull emotion not unlike gratitude for their existence; but I felt little curiosity about them. I was too unhappy to be so easily diverted. It seemed to me that the memory of my wife would become a mania to me, if I could in no way make known to her how utterly I loved her and how I scorned myself. I cannot say that I felt much definite interest in the novel circumstances surrounding me, except as possible resources for some escape from the situation, as it stood between herself and me. If I could compass any means of communicating with her, I believed that I could accept my doom, let it take me where it might or make of me what it would.

Walking thus drearily, alone, and not sorry to be alone in that unfamiliar company, lost in the fixed idea of my own misery, I suddenly heard light footsteps hurrying behind me. I thought:—

"There is another spirit; one more of the newly dead, come to this strange place."

But I did not find it worth my while to turn and greet him, being so wrapt in my own fate; and when a soft hand touched my arm, I moved from it with something like dismay.

"Why, Doctor!" said the gentle voice of Mrs. Faith, "did I startle you? I have been hunting for you everywhere," she added, laughing lightly. "I was afraid you would feel rather desolate. It is a pity. Now, I am as *happy!*"

"Did Charley live?" I asked immediately.

"Oh yes, Charley lived; what we used to call living, when we were there. Poor Charley! I keep thinking how he would enjoy everything if he were here with me. But his father needed him. It makes me so happy! I am very happy! Tell me, Doctor, what do you think of this place? How does it strike you?"

"It is a foreign country," I said sadly.

"Is it, Doctor? Poor Doctor! Why, I feel so much at *home!*"

She lifted a radiant face to me; it was touching to see her expression, and marvelous to behold the idealization of health on features for so many years adjusted to pain and patience.

"Dear Doctor!" she cried joyously, "you never thought to see me *well!* They call this death. Why, I never knew what it was to be *alive* before!"

"I must make you acquainted with some of the people who live here," she added, quickly recalling herself from her own interests to mine, with her natural unselfishness, "it is pitiful to come into this place—as you have done. You always knew so many people. You had such friends about you. I never saw you walk alone in all your life before."

"I wish to be alone," I answered moodily. "I care nothing for this place, or for the men who live here. It is all unfamiliar to me. I am not happy in it. I am afraid I have not been educated for it. It is the most unhomelike place I ever saw."

Her eyes filled; she did not answer me at once; when she did it was to say:

"It will be better. It will be better by and by. Have you seen"—

She stopped and hesitated.

"Have you seen the Lord?" she asked, in a low voice. She was wont, I remember, to use this word in a way peculiarly her own; as if she were referring to some personal acquaintance, near to her heart. I shook my head, looking drearily upon her.

"Don't you *want* to see Him?"

"I want to see my wife!"

"Oh, I am sorry for you," she said, with forbearing gentleness. "It is pretty hard. But I wish you *wanted* Him."

"I want to see my wife! I want to see my wife!" I interrupted bitterly. And with this I turned away from her and hid my face, for I could speak no more. When I lifted my eyes, she had gone from me, and I was again alone. When it was thus too late, it occurred to me that I had lost an opportunity which might not easily return to me, and I sought far and wide for Mrs. Faith. I did not find her, though I aroused myself to the point of accosting some of the inhabitants of the country, and making definite inquiries for her. I was answered with great courtesy and uncommon warmth of manner, as if it were the custom of this place to take a genuine interest in the affairs of strangers; but I was not able, by any effort on my part, to bring myself in proximity to her. This trifling disappointment added to my sense of helplessness in the new life on which I had entered; and I was still as incredulous of helplessness and as galled by it as I should have been by the very world of woe which had formed so irritating a dogma to me in the theology of my day on earth, and which I had regarded as I did the nightmares of a dyspeptic patient.

In this state of feeling, it was the greatest comfort to me when, at some period of time which I have no means of defining, but which could not have been long afterward, Mrs. Faith came suddenly again across my path. She radiated happiness and health and beauty, and when she held out both her hands to me in greeting they seemed to glitter, as if she had stepped from a bath of delight.

"Oh," she said joyously, "have you seen Him *yet?*" It embarrassed me to be forced to answer in the negative; it gave me a strange feeling, as if I had been a convict in the country, and denied the passport of honorable men. I therefore waived her question as well as I might, and proceeded to make known to her the thought which had been occupying me.

"*You* have the *entrée* of the dear earth," I said sadly. "They do not treat you in the—in the very singular manner with which I am treated. It is important beyond explanation that I get a message to my wife. A beggar in the street may be admitted to her charity,—I saw one at the door the night I stood there. I, only I, am forbidden to enter. Whatever may be the natural laws which are set in opposition to me, they have extraordinary force; I can do nothing against them. I suppose I do not understand them. If I had an opportunity to study them—but I have no opportunities at anything. It is a new experience to me to be so—so disregarded by the general scheme of things. I seem to be of no more consequence in this place than a bootblack was in the world; or a paralytic person. It seems useless for me to fly in the face of fate, since this is fate. I have no hope of being able to reach my wife. You have privileges in this condition which are evidently far superior to mine. I have been thinking that possibly you may be able—and willing—to approach her for me?"

"I don't think it would succeed, Doctor," replied my old patient quickly. "I'd *do* it! You know I would! But if I were Helen— She is a very reserved person; she never talks about her husband, as different women do; her feeling is of such a sort; I do not think she would *understand,* if another woman were to speak from you to her."

"Perhaps not," I sighed.

"I am afraid it would be the most hopeless experiment you could make," said Mrs. Faith. "She loves you too much for it," she added, with the divination of her sex. Comforted a little by Mrs. Faith, I quickly abandoned this project; indeed, I soon abandoned every other which concerned itself with Helen, and yielded myself with a kind of desperate lethargy, if I may be allowed the expression, to the fate which separated me from her. Of resignation I knew nothing. Peace was the coldest stranger in that strange land to me. I yielded because I could not help it, not because I would have willed it; and with that dull strength which grows into the sinews of the soul from necessity, sought to adjust myself in such fashion as I might to my new conditions. It occurred to me from time to time that it would have been an advantage if I had felt more interest in the conditions themselves; that it would even have spared me something if I had ever cultivated any familiarity with the possibilities of such a state of existence. I could not remember that I had in the old life satisfactorily proved that another *could* not follow it. It seemed to me that if I had only so much as exercised my imagination upon the possible course of events in case another *did,* it would have been of some practical service to me now. I was in the position of a man who is become the victim of a discovery whose rationality he has contemptuously denied. It was like being struck by a projectile while one is engaged in disproving the existence of gunpowder.

If a soul may properly be said to be stunned, mine, at this time, was that soul.

In this condition solitude was still so natural to me that I made no effort to approach the people of the place, and contented myself with observing them and their affairs from a distance. They seemed a very happy people. There could be no mistake about that. I did not see a clouded countenance; nor did I hear an accent of discomfort, or of pain. I wondered at their joyousness, which I found it as impossible to share as the sick find it impossible to share what has been called "the insolence of health." It did, indeed, appear to me as something almost impertinent, as possession always appears to denial. But I had never been denied before. I perceived, also, that the inhabitants of this country were a busy people. They came and went, they met and parted, with the eagerness of occupation; though there was a conspicuous absence of the fretful haste to which I had been used in the conduct of business. I looked upon the avocations of this strange land, and wondered at them. I could not see with what they were occupied, or why, or to what end. They affected me perhaps something as the concerns of the human race may affect the higher animals. I looked on with an unintelligent envy.

One day, as I was strolling miserably about, a child came up and spoke to me. He, like myself, was alone. He was a beautiful child,— a little boy; he seemed scarcely more than an infant. He appeared to be in search of some one or of something; his brilliant eyes roved everywhere; he had a noble little head, and carried himself courageously. He gave no evidence of fear or sadness at his isolated position, but ran right on,—for he was running when I saw him,—as if he had gone forth upon some happy, childish errand.

But at sight of me he paused; regarded me a moment with the piercing candor of childhood, as if he took my moral measure after some inexplicable personal scale of his own; then came directly and put his hand into my own.

I grasped it heartily,—who could have helped it?—and lifting the little fellow in my arms kissed him affectionately, as one does a pretty stranger child. This seemed to gratify him rather than to satisfy him; he nestled in my neck, but moved restlessly, slipping to the ground, and back again into my arms; jabbering incoherently and pleasantly; seeming to be diverted rather than comforted; ready to stay, but alert to go; in short, behaving like a baby on a visit. After awhile the child adjusted himself to the situation; grew quiet, and clung to me; and at last, putting both his arms about my neck, he gave the long, sweet sigh of healthy infant weariness, and babbling something to the general effect that Boy was tired, he dropped into a sound and happy sleep.

Here, indeed, was a situation! It drew from me the first smile which had crossed my lips since I had died. What, pray, was I, who seemed to be of no consequence whatever in this amazing country, and who had more than I knew how to do in looking after myself, under its mysterious conditions,—what was I to do with a spirit-baby gone to sleep upon my neck?

"I must go and find the Orphan Asylum," I thought; "doubtless they have them in this extraordinary civilization. I must take the little fellow to some women as soon as possible." At this juncture, my friend Mrs. Faith appeared, making a mock of being out of breath, and laughing heartily.

"He ran away from me," she merrily explained. "I had the care of him, and he ran on; he came straight to you. I couldn't hold him. What a comfort he will be to you! . . . Why Doctor! Do you mean to say you don't know who the child *is*?"

"It seems to me," she added, with a mother's sublime superiority,

"*I* should know my own baby! If I were so fortunate as to find one here!—How much less you know," she proceeded naively, "than I used to think you did!"

"Did the child *die?*" I asked, trembling so that I had to put the little fellow down lest he should fall from my startled arms, "did something really ail him that night when his mother—that miserable night?"

"The child died," she answered gravely. "Dear little Boy! Take him up again, Doctor. Don't you see? He is uneasy unless you hold him fast."

I took Boy up; I held him close; I kissed him, and I clung to him and melted into unintelligible cries above him, never minding Mrs. Faith, for I quite forgot her.

But what I felt was for my child's poor mother, and all my thought was for her, and my heart broke for her, that she should be so bereft.

"I should like to know if you supposed for one minute that she wouldn't *rather* you would have the little fellow, if he is the least bit of comfort to you in the world?"

Mrs. Faith said this; she spoke with a kind of lofty, feminine scorn.

"Why, Helen *loves* you!" she said, superbly.

13

"I believe," said my old patient, "I believe that was the highest moment of your life."

A man of my sort seldom comprehends a woman of hers. I did not understand her, and I told her so, looking at her across the clinging child.

"There was no self *in* it!" she answered eagerly.

"Oh," I said indifferently, "is that all?"

"It is everything," replied the wiser spirit, "in the place that we have come to. It is like a birth. Such a moment has to go on living. One is never the same after as one was before it. Changes follow. May the Lord be in them!"

"But stay!" I cried, as she made a signal of farewell, "are you not going to help me—is nobody going to help me take care of this child?"

She shook her head, smiling; then laughed outright at my perplexity; and with a merry air of enjoyment in my extraordinary position, she went her ways and left me.

There now began for me a singular life. Changes followed, as Mrs. Faith had said. The pains and the privileges of isolation were possible to me no longer. Action of some sort, communion of some kind with the world in which I lived, became one of the imperative necessities about which men do not philosophize. For there was the boy! Whatever my views about a spiritual state of existence, there always was the boy. No matter how I had demonstrated the unreasonableness of living after death, the child was alive. However I might personally object to my own share of immortality, I was a living father, with my motherless baby in my arms.

Up to this time I had lived in an indifferent fashion; in the old world, we should have called it "anyhow." Food I scarcely took, or if at all, it was to snatch at such wild fruits as grew directly before me, without regard to their fitness or palatableness; paying, in short, as little attention to the subject as possible. Home I had none. I wandered till I was weary of wandering, and rested till I could rest no more; seeking such shelter as the country afforded me in lonely and beautiful spots; discontented with what I had, but desiring nothing further; with my own miserable thoughts for housemates and for neighbors, and the absence of hope forbidding the presence of energy. Nothing that I could see interested me. Much or most that I took the trouble to observe, I should have been frankly obliged to admit that I did not understand.

The customs of the people bewildered me. Their evident happiness irritated me. Their activity produced in me only the desire to get out of sight of it. Their personal health and beauty—for they were a very comely people—gave me something the kind of nervous shrinking that I had so often witnessed in the sick, when some buoyant, inconsiderate, bubbling young creature burst into the room of pain. I felt in the presence of the universal blessedness about me like some hurt animal, who cares only to crawl in somewhere and be forgotten. If I drew near, as I had on several occasions done, to give some attention to the occupations of the inhabitants, all these feelings were accentuated so much that I was fain to withdraw before I had studied the subject.

Study there was in that country, and art and industry; even traffic, if traffic it might be called; it seemed to be an interchange of possessions, conducted upon principles of the purest consideration for the public, as opposed to personal welfare.

Homes there were, and the construction of them, and the happiest natural absorption in their arrangement and management. There were families and household devotion; parents, children, lovers, neighbors, friends. I saw schools and other resorts of learning, and what seemed to be institutions of benevolence and places of worship, a series of familiar and yet wholly unfamiliar sights. In them all existed a spirit, even as the spirit of man exists in his earthly body, which was and willed and acted as that does, and which, like that, defied analysis. I could perceive at the hastiest glance that these people conducted themselves upon a set of motives entirely strange to me. What they were doing—what they were doing it *for*—I simply did not know. A great central purpose controlled them, such as controls masses of men in battle or at public prayer; a powerful and universal Law had hold of them; they treated it as if they loved it. They seemed to feel affectionately toward the whole system of things. They loved, and thought, and wrought straight onward with it; no one put the impediment of a criticism against it,—no one that I could see or suspect, in all the place, except my isolated self. They had the air of those engaged in some sweet and solemn object, common to them all; an object, evidently set above rather than upon the general level.

Their faces shone with pleasure and with peace. Often they wore a high, devout look. They never showed an irritated expression, never an anxious nor that I could see a sad one. It was impossible to deny the marked nobility of their appearance.

"If this," I thought, "be what is called a spiritual life, I was not ready to become a spirit."

Now, when my child awakened and called me, as he had begun, in the dear old days on earth, to learn to do, and like any live human baby proceeded to give vent to a series of incoherent remarks bearing upon the fact that Boy would like his supper, I was fain to perceive that being a spirit did not materially change the relation of a man to the plainer human duties; and that, whether personally agreeable or no, I must needs bring myself into some sort of connection with the civilization about me. I might be a homesick fellow, but the baby was hungry. I might be at odds with the whole scheme of things, but the child must have a shelter. I might be a spiritual outcast, but what was to become of Boy? The heart of the father arose in me; and, gathering the little fellow to my breast, I set forth quickly to the nearest town.

Here, after some hesitation, I accosted a stranger, whose appearance pleased me, and besought his assistance in my perplexity. He was a man of lofty bearing; his countenance was strong and benign as the western wind; he had a gentle smile, but eyes which piercingly regarded me. He was of superior beauty, and conducted himself as one having authority. He was much occupied, and hastening upon some evidently important errand; but he stopped at once, and gave his attention to me with the hearty interest in others characteristic of the people.

"Are you a stranger in the country—but newly come to us?"

"A stranger, sir, but not newly arrived."

"And the child?"

"The child ran into my arms about an hour ago."

"Is the boy yours?"

"He is my only child."

"What do you desire for him?"

"I would fain provide for him those things which a father must desire. I seek food and shelter. I wish a home, and means of subsistence, and neighborhood, and the matters which are necessary to the care and comfort of an infant. Pray, counsel me. I do not understand the conditions of life in this remarkable place."

"I do not know that it is of consequence that I should," I added, less courteously, "but I cannot see the boy deprived. He must be made comfortable as speedily as possible. I shall be obliged to you for some suggestion in the matter."

"Come hither," replied the stranger, laconically. Forthwith, he led me, saying nothing further, and I followed, asking nothing more.

This embarrassed me somewhat, and it was with some discomfort that I entered the house of entertainment to which I was directed, and asked for those things which were needful for my child. These were at once and lavishly provided. It soon proved that I had come to a luxurious and hospitable place. The people were most sympathetic in their manner. Boy especially excited the kindest of attention; some women fondled him, and all the inmates of the house interested themselves in the little motherless spirit.

In spite of myself this touched me, and my heart warmed toward my entertainers.

"Tell me," I said, turning toward him who had brought me thither, "how shall I make compensation for my entertainment? What is the custom of the country? I—what we used to call property—you will understand that I necessarily left behind me. I am accustomed to the use of it. I hardly know what to do without it. I am accustomed to—some abundance. I wish to remunerate the people of this house."

"What *did* you bring with you?" asked my new acquaintance, with a half-sorrowful look, as if he would have helped me out of an unpleasant position if he could.

"Nothing," I replied, after some thought, "nothing but my misery. That does not seem to be a marketable commodity in this happy place. I could spare some, if it were."

"What had you?" pursued my questioner, without noticing my ill-timed satire. "What were your possessions in the life yonder?"

"Health. Love. Happiness. Home. Prosperity. Work. Fame. Wealth. Ambition." I numbered these things slowly and bitterly. "None of them did I bring with me. I have lost them all upon the way. They do not serve me in this differing civilization."

"Was there by chance nothing more?"

"Nothing more. Unless you count a little incidental usefulness."

"And that?" he queried eagerly.

I therefore explained to him that I had been a very busy doctor; that I used to think I took pleasure in relieving the misery of the sick, but that it seemed a mixed matter now, as I looked back upon it,—so much love of fame, love of power, love of love itself,—and that I did not put forth my life's work as of importance in his scale of value.

"That would not lessen its value," replied my friend. "I myself was a healer of the sick. Your case appeals to me. I was know as"—

He whispered a name which gave me a start of pleasure. It was a name famous in its day, and that a day long before my own; a name immortal in medical history. Few men in the world had done as much as this one to lessen the sum of human suffering. It excited me greatly to meet him.

"But you," I cried, "you were not like the rest of us or the most of us. *You* believed in these—invisible things. You were a man of what is called faith. I have often thought of that. I never laid down a bi-ography of you without wondering that a man of your intelligence should retain that superstitious element of character. I ought to beg your pardon for the adjective. I speak as I have been in the habit of speaking."

"Do you wonder now?" asked the great surgeon, smiling benign-ly. I shook my head. I wondered at nothing now.

But I felt myself incapable of discussing a set of subjects upon which, for the first time in my life, I now knew myself to be really uninformed.

I took the pains to explain to my new friend that in matters of what he would call spiritual import I was, for aught I knew to the contrary, the most ignorant person in the community. I added that I supposed he would expect me to feel humiliated by this.

"Do you?" he asked, abruptly.

"It makes me uncomfortable," I replied, candidly. "I don't know that I can say more than that. I find it embarrassing."

"That is straightforward," said the great physician. "There is at least no diseased casuistry about you. I do not regard the indications as unfavorable."

He said this with something of the professional matter; it amused me, and I smiled. "Take the case, Doctor, if you will," I humbly said. "I could not have happened on any person to whom I would have been so willing to intrust it."

"We will consider the question," he said gravely.

In this remarkable community, and under the guidance of this remarkable man, I now began a difficult and to me astonishing life. The first thing which happened was not calculated to soothe my personal feeling: this was no less than the discovery that I really had nothing wherewith to compensate the citizens who had provided for the comfort of my child and of myself; in short, that I was no more nor less than an object of charity at their hands. I writhed under this, as may be well imagined; and with more impatience than humility urged that I be permitted to perform some service which at least would bring me into relation with the commercial system of the country. I was silenced by being gently asked: What could I do?

"But have you no sick here?" I pleaded, "no hospitals or places of need? I am not without experience, I may say that I am even not without attainment, in my profession. Is there no use for it all, in this state of being which I have come to?"

"Sick we have," replied the surgeon, "and hospitals. I myself am much occupied in one of these. But the diseases that men bring here are not of the body. Our patients are chiefly from among the newly arrived, like yourself; they are those who are at odds with the spirit of the place; hence they suffer discomfort."

"They do not harmonize with the environment, I suppose," I interrupted eagerly. I was conscious of a wish to turn the great man's thought from a personal to a scientific direction. It occurred to me with dismay that I might be selected yet to become a patient under this extraordinary system of things. That would be horrible. I could think of nothing worse.

I proceeded to suggest that if anything could be found for me to do, in this superior art of healing, or if, indeed, I could study and perfect myself in it, I was more than willing to learn, or to perform.

"Canst thou heal a sick spirit?" inquired my friend, solemnly. "Canst thou administer holiness to a sinful soul?"

I bowed my head before him; for I had naught to say. Alas, what art had I, in that high science so far above me, that my earth-bound gaze had never reached unto it?

I was not like my friend, who seemed to have carried on the whole range of his great earthly attainments, by force of what I supposed would have to be called his spiritual education. Here in this world of spirits I was an unscientific, uninstructed fellow.

"Give me," I said brokenly, "but the lowliest chance to make an honorable provision for the comfort of my child in your community. I ask no more."

The boy ran chattering to me as I said these words; he sprang and clasped my knees, and clasped my neck, and put his little lips to mine, and rubbed his warm, moist curls across my cheek, and asked me where his mother was. And then he crooned my own name over and again, and kissed and kissed me, and did stroke me with such pretty excesses of his little tenderness that I took heart and held him fast, and loved him and blessed fate for him, as much as if I had not been a spirit; more than any but a lonely and remorseful spirit could.

ৼ14৾

In consequence, as I suspected, of some private influence on the part of my famous friend, whose importance in this strange world seemed scarcely below that which he held in the other,—a marked contrast to my own lot, which has been thus far in utter reversal of every law and every fact of my earthly life,—a humble position was found for me, connected with the great institution of healing which he superintended; and here, for an indefinite time, I worked and served. I found myself of scarcely more social importance than, let us say, the janitor or steward in my old hospital at home. This circumstance, however galling, could no longer surprise me. I had become familiar enough with the economy of my new surroundings now thoroughly to understand that I was destitute of the attainments which gave men eminence in them. I was conscious that I had become an obscure person; nay, more than this, that I had barely brought with me the requisites for being tolerated at all in the community. It had begun to be evident to me that I was fortunate in obtaining any kind of admission to citizenship. This alone was an experience so novel to me that it was an occupation in itself, for a time, to adjust myself to it.

I now established myself with my boy in such a home as could be made for us, under the circumstances. It was far inferior to most of the homes which I observed about me; but the child lacked no necessary comfort, and the luxuries of a spiritual civilization I did not personally crave; they had a foreign air to me, as the customs of the Tuileries might have had to Pocahontas.

With dull gratitude for such plain possessions as now were granted to me, I set myself to my daily tasks, and to the care and rearing of my child.

Work I found an unqualified mercy. It even occurred to me to be thankful for it, and to desire to express what I felt about it to the unknown Fate or Force which was controlling my history. I had been all my life such a busy man that the vacuity of my first experience after dying had chafed me terribly. To be of no consequence; not to be in demand; not to be depended upon by a thousand people, and for a thousand things; not to dash somewhere upon important errands; not to feel that a minute was a treasure, and that mine were valued as hid treasures; not to know that my services were superior; to feel the canker of idleness eat upon me like one of the diseases which I had considered impossible to my organization; to observe the hours, which had hitherto been invisible, like rear forces pushing me to the front; to watch the crippled moments, which had always flown past me like mocking-birds; to know to the full the absence of movement in life; to feel deficiency of purpose like paralysis stiffen me; to have no hope of anything better, and not to know what worse might be before me,—such had been my first experience of the new life. It had done as much as this for me: it had fitted me for the humblest form of activity which my qualifications made possible; it had taught me the elements of gratitude for an improved condition, as suffering, when it vibrates to the intermission of relief, teaches cheerfulness to the sick.

An appreciable sense of gratification, which, if it could not be called pleasure, was at least a diminution of pain, came to me from the society of my friend, the distinguished man and powerful spirit who had so befriended me. I admit that I was glad to have a man to deal with; though I did not therefore feel the less a loyalty to my dear and faithful patient, whose services to me had been so true and tender. I missed her. I needed her counsel about the child. I would fain have spoken to her of many little matters. I watched for her, and wondered that she came no more to us. Although so new a comer, Mrs. Faith proved to be a person of position in the place; her name was well and honorably known about the neighborhood; and I therefore easily learned that she was absent on a journey. It was understood that she had been called to her old home, where for some reason her husband and her child had need of her. It was her precious privilege to minister to them, I knew not how; it was left to me to imagine why. Bitterly I thought of Helen. Between herself and me the awful gates of death had shut; to pass them, though I would have died again for it,—to pass them, for one hour, for one moment, for love's sake, for grief's sake, or for shame's, or for pity's own,—I was forbidden.

I had confided the circumstances of my parting from my wife to no one of my new acquaintants. In the high order of character pervading these happy people, such a confession would have borne the proportions that a crime might in the world below. Bearing my secret in my own heart, I felt like a felon in this holier society. I cherished it guiltily and miserably, as solitary people do such things; it seemed to me like an ache which I should go on bearing forever. I remembered how men on earth used to trifle with a phrase called endless punishment. What worse punishment were there, verily, than the consciousness of having done the sort of deed that I had? It seemed to me, as I brooded over it, one of the saddest in the universe. I became what I should once have readily called "morbid" over this thought. There seemed to me nothing in the nature of remorse itself which should, if let alone, ever come to a visible end. My longing for the forgiveness of my wife gnawed upon me.

Sometimes I tried to remind myself that I was as sure of her love and of her mercy as the sun was of arising beyond the linden that tapped the chamber window in my dear lost home; that her unfathomable tenderness, so far passing the tenderness of women, leaned out, as ready to take me back to itself as her white arms used to be to take me to her heart, when I came later than usual, after a hard day's work, tired and weather-beaten, into the house, hurrying and calling to her.

"Helen? Helen?"

But the anguish of the thought blotted the comfort out of it, till, for very longing for her, I would fain almost have forgotten her; and then I would pray never to forget her before I had forgotten, for I loved her so that I would rather think of her and suffer because of her than not to think of her at all. In all this memorable and unhappy period, my boy was the solace of my soul. I gave myself to the care of him lovingly, and as nearly as I can recollect I did not chafe against the narrow limits of my lot in that respect.

It occurred to me sometimes that I should once have called this a humble service to be the visible boundary of a man's life. To what had all those old attainments come? Command of science? Developed skill? Public power? Extended fame? All those forms of personality which go with intellectual position and the use of it? Verily, I was brought to lowly tasks; we left them to women in the world below. But really, I think this troubled me less than it might have done; perhaps less than it should have done. I accepted the strange reversal of my fate as one accepts any turn of affairs which, he is convinced, is better than he might have expected. It had begun to be evident to me that it was better than I had deserved. If I am exceptional in being forced to admit that this consciousness was a novelty in my experience, the admission is none the less necessary for that. I had been in the habit of considering myself rather a good fellow, as a man with no vices in particular is apt to. I had possessed no standards of life below which my own fell to an embarrassing point. The situation to which I was now brought, was not unlike that of one who finds himself in a land where there are new and delicate instruments for indicating the state of the weather. I was aware, and knew that my neighbors were, of fluctuations in the moral atmosphere which had never before come under my attention. The whole subtle and tremendous force of public sentiment now bore upon me to make me uneasy before achievements with which I had hitherto been complacent. It had inconceivable effects to live in a community where spiritual character formed the sole scale of social position.

I, who had been always socially distinguished, found myself now exposed to incessant mortifications, such as spring from the fact that one is of no consequence.

I should say, however, that I felt this much less for myself than for my child; indeed, that it was because of Boy that I first felt the fact at all, or brooded over it after I had begun to feel it.

The little fellow developed rapidly, much faster than children of his age do in the human life; he ceased to be a baby, and was a little boy while I was yet wondering what I should do with him when he had outgrown his infancy. His intellect, his character, his physique, lifted themselves with a kind of luxuriance of growth, such as plants show in tropical countries; he blossomed as a thing does which has every advantage and no hindrance; nature moved magnificently to her ends in him; it was a delight to watch such vigorous processes; he was a rich, unthwarted little creature. With all a father's heart and a physician's sensibility, I was proud of him.

I was proud of him, alas! until I began to perceive that, as matters were working, the boy was morally certain to be ashamed of me. This was a hard discovery; and it went hard with me after I had made it. But nothing could reduce the poignancy of the inquiry with which I had first gathered him to my heart, in the solitudes where he had found me lurking: "If I were a spiritual outcast, what would become of Boy?"

As the child waxed in knowledge and in strength, questions like these dropped from his lips so frequently that they distressed me:—

"Papa, what is God?"

"Papa, who is worship?"

"Tell me how boys pray."

"Is it a kind of game?"

"What is Christ, papa? Is it people's Mother? What is it for?"

My friend, the eminent surgeon, left me much to myself in these perplexities; regarding my natural reserve, and trusting, I thought, to nature, or to some Power beyond nature, to assist me. But on one occasion, happening to be present when the child interrogated me in this manner, he bent a piercing gaze upon me.

"Why do you not answer the child, Esmerald Thorne?" he asked me in a voice of authority.

"Alas," I said, "I have no answer. I know nothing of these matters. They have been so foreign to my temperament, that—I"—

But here I faltered. I felt ashamed of my excuse, and of myself for offering it.

"It is a trying position for a man to be put in," I ventured to add, putting an arm about my boy; "naturally, I wish my child to develop in accordance with the social and educational system of the place."

"Naturally, I should suppose," replied he, dryly. He offered me no further suggestion on the subject, and with some severity of manner moved to leave me. Now it happened to be the vesper hour in the hospital, and my visitor was going to his patients, the "sick of soul," with whom he was wont to join in the evening chant which, at a certain hour, daily arose from every roof in the wide city, and waxed mightily to the skies. It was music of a high order, and I always enjoyed it; no person of any musical taste could have done otherwise.

"Listen!" said my friend, as he turned to depart from me. I had only to glance at his rapt and noble countenance to perceive the high acoustic laws which separated his sensibility to the vesper from my own. To him it was religious expression. To me it was classical music.

While I was thus thinking, from the great wards of the Home of Healing the prayer went up. The sinful, the sorely stricken, the ungodly, the ignorant of heavenly mercy, all the diseased of spirit who were gathered there in search of the soul's health, sang together: not as the morning-stars which shouted for joy, but like the living hearts that cried for purity; yea, like hearts that so desired it, they would have broken for it, and blessed God.

"God is a Spirit. God is a Spirit. We would worship Him. We would worship Him in spirit. Yea, in spirit. And in truth."

My little boy was playing in the garden, decking himself with the strange and beautiful flowers which luxuriated in the spot. I remember that he had tall white lilies and scarlet passion flowers, or something like them, held above one shoulder, and floating like a banner in the bright, white air. He was absorbed in his sport, and had the sweet intentness of expression between the eyes that his mother used to wear. When the vesper anthems sounded out, the child stopped, and turned his nobly moulded head toward the unseen singers. A puzzled and afterward a saddened look clouded his countenance; he listened for a moment, and then walked slowly to me, trailing the white and scarlet flowers in the grass behind him as he came.

"Father, teach me how to sing! The other children do. I'm the only little boy I know that can't sing that nice song. Teach me it!" he demanded.

"Alas, my son!" I answered, "how can I teach you that which I myself know not?"

"I thought boys' fathers knew everything," objected the child, bending his brows severely on me.

A certain constraint, a something not unlike distrust, a subtle barrier which one could not define, but which one felt the more uncomfortably for this very reason, after this incident, seemed to arise in the child's consciousness between himself and me. As docile, as dutiful, as beautiful as ever, as loving and as lovable, yet the little fellow would at times withdraw from me and stand off; as if he looked on at me, and criticised me, and kept his criticism to himself. Verily the child was growing. He had become a separate soul. In a world of souls, what was mine—miserable, ignorant, half-developed, wholly unfit—what was mine to do with his? How was I to foster him?

When I came face to face with the problem of Boy's general education, this question pressed upon me bitterly. Looking abroad upon the people and their principles of life, the more I studied them, the more did I stand perplexed before them. I was in the centre of a vast Theocracy. Plainly, our community was but one of who knew how many?—governed by an unseen Being, upon laws of which I knew nothing. The service of this invisible Monarch vied only with the universal affection for Him. So far as I could understand the spiritual life at all, it seemed to be the highest possible development and expression of love. What these people did that was noble, pure, and fine, they did, not because they must, but because they would. They believed because they chose. They were devout because they wished to be. They were unselfish and true, and what below we should have called "unworldly," because it was the most natural thing in the world. They seemed so happy, they had such content in life, that I could have envied them from my soul.

How, now, was I to compass this national kind of happiness for my son? Misery I could bear; I was sick and sore with it, but I was used to it. My child must never suffer. Passed beyond the old system of suffering, why should he? Joy was his birthright in this blessed place.

How was I, being at discord from it, to bring my child into harmony with it? I was at odds, to start on, with the whole system of education. The letters, art, science, industry, of the country were of a sort that I knew not. They were consecrated to ends with which I was unfamiliar. They were pursued in a spirit incomprehensible to me. They were dedicated to the interests of a Being, Himself a stranger to me. Proficiency, superiority, were rated on a scale quite out of my experience. To be distinguished was to possess high spiritual traits. Deep at the root of every public custom, of every private deed, there hid the seed of one universal emotion,—the love of a living soul for the Being who had created it.

I, who knew not of this feeling, I, who was as a savage among this intelligence, who was no more than an object of charity at the hands of this community,—what had I to offer to my son?

A father's personal position? Loving influence? Power to push the little fellow to the front? A chance to endow him with every social opportunity, every educational privilege, such as it is a father's pride to enrich his child wherewith?

Nay, verily. An obscure man ignorant of the learning of the land, destitute of its wealth, unacquainted among its magnates, and without a share in its public interests—nothing was I; nothing had I; nothing could I hope to do, or be, for which my motherless boy should live to bless his father's name. Stung by such thoughts as these, which rankled the more in me the longer I cherished them, I betook myself to brooding and to solitary strolling in quiet places, where I could ponder on my situation undisturbed.

I was in great intellectual and spiritual stress, less for myself than for the child; not more for him, than because of his mother. What would Helen say? How would she hold me to account for him? How should I meet her—if I ever saw her face again—to own myself scarcely other than a pauper in this spiritual kingdom; our child an untaught, unimportant little fellow, of no more consequence in this place than the *gamins* of the street before her door?

In these cold and solitary experiences which many a man has known before me, and many more will follow after me, the soul is like a skater, separated from his fellows upon a field of ice. Every movement that he makes seems to be bearing him farther from the society and the sympathy of his kind. Too benumbed, perhaps, to turn, he glides on, helpless as an ice-boat before the wind. Conscious of his mistake, of his danger, and knowing not how to retract the one or avoid the other, his helpless motions, seemingly guided by idleness, by madness, or by folly, lead him to the last place wither he would have led himself,—the weak spot in the ice.

Suddenly, he falls crashing, and sinks. Then lo! as he goes under, crying out that he is lost because no man is with him, hands are down-stretched, swimmers plunge, the crowd gathers, and it seems the whole world stoops to save him. The sympathy of his kind wanted nothing but a chance to reach him.

I cannot tell; no man can tell such things; I cannot explain how I came to do it, or even why I came to do it. But it was on this wise with me. Being alone one evening in a forest, at twilight, taking counsel with myself and pondering upon the mystery from which I could not gather light, these words came into my heart; and when I had cherished them in my heart for a certain time, I uttered them aloud:

"Thou great God! If there be a God. Reveal Thyself unto my immortal soul! If I have a soul immortal."

${15}$

My little boy came flying to me one fair day; he cried out that he had news for me, that great things were going on in the town. A visitor was expected, whose promised arrival had set the whole place astir with joy. The child knew nothing of what or whom he spoke, but I gathered the impression that some distinguished guest was about to reach us, to whom the honors of the city would be extended. The matter did not interest me; I had so little in common with the people; and I was about to dismiss it idly, when Boy posed me by demanding that I should personally conduct him through the events of the gala day. He was unusually insistent about this; for he was a docile little fellow, who seldom urged his will uncomfortably against my own. But in this case I could not compromise with him, and half reluctantly I yielded. I had no sooner done so than an urgent message to the same effect reached me from my friend the surgeon.

"Go with the current to-day," he wrote; "it sets strongly. Question it not. Resist it not. Follow and be swept."

Immediately upon this some neighbors came hurriedly in, and spoke with me of the same matter eagerly. They pleaded with me on no account to miss the event of the day, upon whose specific nature they were somewhat reticent. They evinced the warmest possible interest in my personal relation to it; as people do who possess a happy secret that they wish, but may not feel at liberty, fully to share with another.

They were excited, and overflowed with happiness. Their very presence raised my spirits. I could not remember when I had received precisely this sort of attention from my neighbors; and it was, somehow, a comfort to me. I should not have supposed that I should value being made of consequence in this trifling way; yet it warmed my heart. I felt less desolate than usual, when I took the hand of my happy boy, and set forth.

The whole vicinity was aroused. Everybody moved in one direction, like "a current," as my friend had said. Shining, solemn, and joyous faces filled the streets and fields. The voices of the people were subdued and sweet. There was no laughter, only smiles, and gentle expectation, and low consulting together, and some there were who mused apart. The "sick of soul" were present with the happier fold: these first had a wistful look, as one of those not certain of themselves or of their welcome; but I saw that they were tenderly regarded by the more fortunate. I myself was most gently treated; many persons spoke with me, and I heard expressions of pleasure at my presence. In the crowd, as we moved on, I began to recognize here and there a face; acquaintances, whom I had known in the lower life, became visible to me. Now and then, some one, hastening by, said:—

"Why, Doctor!" and then I would perceive some old patients; the look which only loving patients wear was on their faces, the old impulse of trust and gratitude; they would grasp me heartily by the hand; this touched me; I began to feel a stir of sympathy with the general excitement; I was glad that I had joined the people.

I pressed the hand of my little boy, who was running and leaping at my side. He looked confidingly up into my face, and asked me questions about the day's event; but these I could not answer.

"God knows, my child," I said. "Your father is not a learned man."

As we swept on, the crowd thickened visibly. The current from the city met streams from the fields, the hills, the forests; all the distance overflowed; the concourse began to become imposing. Here and there I observed still other faces that were not strange to me; flashes of recognition passed between us; some also of my own kin, dead years ago, I saw, far off, and I felt drawn to them. In the distance, not near enough to speak with her, shining and smiling, I thought that I perceived Mrs. Faith, once more. My boy threw kisses to her and laughed merrily; he was electric with the universal joy; he seemed to dance upon the air like a tuft of thistle-down; to be "light-hearted" was to be light-bodied; the little fellow's frame seemed to exist only as the expression of his soul. I thought:—

"If he is properly educated in this place, what a spirit he will make!"

I was amazed to see his capacity for happiness. I thought of his mother. I wished to be happy, too.

Now, as we moved on toward the plain, the sound of low chanting began to swell from the crowd. The strain gained in distinctness; power gathered on it; passion grew in it; prayer ascended from it. I could not help being moved by this billow of sweet sound. The forms and faces of the people melted together before my eyes; their outlines seemed to quiver in the flood of song; it was as if their manifold personalities blurred in the unity of their feeling; they seemed to me, as I regarded them, like the presence of one great, glad, loving human soul. This was their supplication. Thus arose the heavenly song:—

> "Thou that takest away
> The sins of the world!
> Whosoever believeth
> Shall have life.
> Whosoever believeth on Thee
> Shall have eternal life.
> Thou that takest away
> The sins of the world!
> And givest—and givest
> Eternal life!"

"I cannot sing that pretty song," said my boy sadly. "There is nobody to teach me. Father, I wish you *were* a learned man!"

Now, this smote me to the heart, so that I would even have lifted my voice and sought to join the chant, for the child's sake, and to comfort him; but when I would have done so, behold, I could not lift my soul; it resisted me like a weight too heavy for my lips; for, in this land, song never rises higher than the level of the soul; there are fine laws governing this fact whose nature I may not explain, and could not at that time even understand, but of the fact itself I testify.

"Alas, alas, my son!" I said, "would God I were!"

Now suddenly, while I was conversing with my child, I perceived a stir among the people, as if they moved to greet some person who was advancing toward them. I looked in the direction whither all eyes were turned; but I saw nothing to account for the excitement. While I stood gazing and wondering, at one movement, as if it were by one heart-beat, the great throng bowed their heads. Some object, some Presence of which I could not catch a glimpse, had entered among them. Whispers ran from lip to lip. I heard men say that He was here, that He was there, that He was yonder, that He had passed them, that He touched them.

"He blesseth me!" they murmured.

"And me! And me!"

"Oh, even me!"

I heard low cries of delight and sobs of moving tenderness. I heard strange, wistful words from the disabled of soul who were among us,—pleadings for I knew not what, offered to I knew not whom. I heard words of sorrow and words of utter love, and I saw signs of shame, and looks of rapture, and attitudes of peace and eager hope. I saw men kneeling in reverence. I saw them prostrate in petition. I saw them as if they were clinging affectionately to hands that they kissed and wept upon. I saw them bowed as one bows before the act of benediction.

These things I perceived, but alas, I could perceive no more. What went I out, with the heavenly, happy people, for to see?

Naught, God help me, worse than naught; for mine eyes were holden.

Dark amid that spiritual vision, I stood stricken. Alone in all that blessedness, was I bereft?

Whom, for very rapture, did they melt to welcome? Whom greeted they, with that great wave of love, so annihilating to their consciousness of themselves that I knew when I beheld it, I had never seen the face of Love before?

Among them all, I stood alone—blind, blind. Them I saw, and their blessedness, till I was filled with such a sacred envy of it that I would have suffered some new misery to share it. But He who did move among them thus royally and thus benignly, who passed from each man to each man, like the highest longing and the dearest wish of his own heart, who was to them one knew not whether the more of Master or of chosen Friend,—Him, alas, I saw not. To me He was denied. No spiritual optic nerve in me announced His presence. I was blind,—I was blind.

Overcome by this discovery, I did not notice that my boy had loosened his hold upon my hand until his little fingers were quite disengaged from my clasp; and then, turning to speak to him, I found that he had slipped from me in the crowd. This was so great and the absorption so universal that no one noticed the mishap; and grateful, indeed, at that miserable moment, to be unobserved, I went in search of him.

Now, I did not find the child, though I sought long and patiently; and when I was beginning to feel perplexed, and to wonder what chance could have befallen him, I turned, and behold, while I had been searching, the throng had dispersed.

Night was coming on. All the citizens were strolling to their homes. On street, and plain, and hill stirred the shadows of the departing people. They passed quietly. Every voice was hushed. All the world was as still as a heart is after prayer.

In the silent purple plain, only I was left alone. Moved by solitude, which is the soul's sincerity, I yielded myself to strange impulses, and turning to the spot, where He who was invisible had passed or seemed to pass, I sought to find upon the ground and in the dusk some chance imprint of His steps. To do this, it was necessary for me to stoop; and while I was bowed, searching for some least sign of Him, in the dew and dark, I knew not what wave of shame and sorrow came upon me, but I fell upon my knees. There was no creature to hear me, and I spoke aloud, and said:—

"*Thou departest from me, for I am a sinful man, O Lord!*" . . .

"*Lord,*" I said, "*that I may receive my sight!*"

I thought I had more to say than this, but when I had uttered these words no more did follow them. They seemed to fill my soul and flood it till it overflowed.

And when I had lifted up my eyes, the first sight which did meet them was the face of my own child. I saw at once that he was quite safe and happy. But I saw that he was not alone.

One towered above me, strange and dim, who held the little fellow in His arms. When I cried out to Him, He smiled. And He did give the child to me, and spoke with me.

${16}$

The natural step to knowledge is through faith. Even human science teaches as much as this. The faith of the scholar in the theoretic value of his facts precedes his intelligent use of them. Invention dreams before it does. Discovery believes before it finds. Creation imagines before it achieves.

Spiritual intelligence, when it came at last, to me, came with something of the jar of all abnormal processes. The wholesome movements of trust I had omitted from my soul's economy. The function of faith was a disused thing in me. Truth had to treat me as an undeveloped mind.

In the depth of my consciousness, I knew that, come what might, I had forever lost the chance to be a symmetrical, healthy human creature, whose spiritual faculties are exercised like his brain or muscle; who has lived upon the earth, and loved it, and gathered its wealth and sweetness and love of living into his being, as visible good whereby to create invisible stature; whose earthly experience has carried him on, as Nature carries growth,—unconsciously, powerfully, perfectly, into a diviner life. Forever it must remain with me that I had missed the natural step.

If I say that the realization of knowledge was the first thing to teach me the value of faith, I shall be understood by those who may have read this narrative with any sort of sympathy to the present point; and for the rest, some wiser, better man than I must write.

I do not address those who follow these pages as I myself should once have done. I do not hope to make myself intelligible to you, as I would to God I could! Personal misery is intelligible, and the shock of belated discovery. But the experience of another in matters of this kind has not a "scientific" character.

No one can know better than I how my story will be dismissed as something which is not "a fact."

In the times to be, it is my belief that there shall yet arise a soul, worthier of the sacred task than I, to which shall be given the perilous and precious commission of interpreter between the visible life and the life invisible. On this soul high privilege will be bestowed, and awful opportunity. Through it the deaf shall hear, the dumb shall speak. The bereaved shall bless it, and the faint of heart shall lean on it, and those who know not God shall listen to it, and the power of God shall be upon it. But mine is not that soul.

Even as One who was above man did elect to experience the earthly lot of man to save him; so one who is a man among men may yet be permitted to use the heavenly lot in such wise as to comfort them. The first mission called for superhuman power. The second may need only human purity.

I now enter upon a turn in my narrative, where my vehicle of communication begins to fail me. Human language, as employed upon the earth, has served me to some extent to express those phases of celestial fact upon which I still looked with earth-blind eyes. With spiritual vision comes the immediate need of a spiritual vocabulary. Like most men of my temperament and training, I have been accustomed to some caution in the use of words. I know not any, which would be intelligible to the readers of this record, that can serve to express my experiences onward from this point.

"A man becomes *terrestrialized* as he grows older," said an unbeliever of our day, once, to me.

It is at least true that the terrestrial intellect celestializes by the hardest; and it remains obvious, as it was written, that the things which are prepared may not enter into the heart of man.

This is only another way of saying that my life from the solemn hour which I have recorded underwent revolutions too profound for me to desire to utter them, and that most of my experiences were of a nature which I lack the means to report. My story draws to a stop, as a cry of anguish comes to a hush of peace. What word is there to say?

There is, indeed, one. With lips that tremble and praise God, I add it.

At a period not immediately following the event which I have described, yet not so far beyond it that the time, as I recall it, seemed wearisome to me, I received a summons to go upon an errand to a distant place. It was the first time that I had been intrusted with any business of a wider nature than the care of my own affairs or the immediate offices of neighborhood, and I was gratified thereby. I had, indeed, longed to be counted worthy to perform some special service at the will of Him who guided all our service, and had cherished in my secret heart some project of praying that I might be elected to a special task which had grown, from much musing, dear to me. I did most deeply desire to become worthy to wear the seal of a commission to the earth; but I had ceased to urge the selfish cry of my personal heart-break. I did not pray now for the precious right to visit my own home, nor weary the Will in which I had learned to confide with passionate demands for my beloved. I may rather say that I had come almost to feel that when I was worthy to see Helen I should be worthy of life eternal; and that I had dropped my love and my longings and my shame into the Hands of Infinite Love, and seen them close over these, as over a trust.

The special matter to which I refer was this: I desired to be permitted to visit human homes, and set myself, as well as I might, to the effort of cultivating their kindliness. I longed to cherish the sacred graces of human speech. I wished to emphasize the opportunity of those who love each other. I groaned within me, till I might teach the preciousness and the poignancy of *words*. It seemed to me that if I might but set the whole force of a man's experience and a spirit's power to make an irritable scene in loving homes held as degrading as a blow, that I could say what no man ever said before, and do what no spirit would ever do again.

If this be called an exaggerated view of a specific case, I can only say that every human life learns one lesson perfectly, and is qualified to teach that, and that alone, as no other can. This was mine.

When, therefore, I received the summons to which I have alluded, I inferred that the wish of my heart had been heard, and I set forth joyfully, expecting to be sent upon some service of the nature at which I have hinted. My soul was full of it, and I made haste to depart, putting no question in the way of my obedience. No information, indeed, was granted to me beyond the fact that I should follow a certain course until I came to its apparent end, and there await what should occur, and act as my heart prompted. The vagueness of this command stirred my curiosity a little, I confess; but that only added to the pleasure of the undertaking. It would be difficult to say how much relief I found in being occupied once again to some purpose, like a man. But it would be impossible to tell the solemn happiness I had in being counted fit humbly to fulfill the smallest trust placed in me by Him who was revealed, at this late, last moment, after all, to me, unworthy.

I set forth alone. The child was left behind me with a neighbor, for so I thought the way of wisdom in this matter. Following only the general directions which I had received, I found myself soon within the open country toward the region of the hills. As I advanced, the scenery became familiar to me, and I was not slow to recognize the path as the one which I myself has trodden on my first entrance to the city wherein of recent days I had found my home. I stopped to consider this fact, and to gather landmarks, gazing about me diligently and musing on my unknown course; for the ways divided before me as foot-paths do in fields, each looking like all and all like each. While I stood uncertain, and sensitively anxious to make no mistake, I heard the hit! hit! of light feet patting the grass behind me, and, turning, saw a little fellow coming like the morning wind across the plain. His bright hair blew straight before him, from his forehead. He ran sturdily. How beautiful he was!

He did not call me nor show the slightest fear lest he should fail to overtake me. He had already learned that love always overtakes the beloved in that blessed land.

"You forgot your little boy," he said reproachfully, and put his hand quietly within mine and walked on beside me, and forgot that he had been forgotten immediately, and looked upward at me radiantly.

Remembering the command to await what should occur, and do as my heart prompted, I accepted this accident as part of a purpose wiser than my own, and kissed the little fellow, and we traveled on together.

As we came into the hill country, our way grew wilder and more desolate. The last of the stray travelers whom we chanced to meet was now well behind us. In the wide spaces we were quite alone. Behind us, dim and distant, shimmering like an opal in the haze of fair half-tints, the city shone. On either side of us, the forest trees began to tread solemnly, like a vast procession which no man could number, keeping step to some inaudible march. Before us, the great crest of the mountains towered dark as death against the upper sky. As we drew near, the loneliness of these hills was to me as something of which I had never conceived before. Earth did not hold their likeness, and my heart had never held their meaning. I could almost have dreaded them, as we came nearer to them; but the deviation of the paths had long since ceased. In the desolate country which we were now crossing choice was removed from conduct. There was but one course for me to take; I took it unhesitatingly and without fear, which belongs wholly to the lower life.

As we advanced, the great mountain barrier rose high and higher before us, till it seemed to shut out the very sky from our sight, and to crush us apart from all the world,—nay, from either world or any, I could have thought, so desolate and so awful was the spot. But when we had entered the shadow formed by the mighty range, and had accustomed our eyes to it for a time, I perceived, not far ahead of me, but in fact quite near and sudden to the view, a long, dark, sharp defile cut far into the heart of the hills. The place had an unpleasant look, and I stopped before it to regard it. It was so grim of aspect and so assured of outline, like a trap for travelers which had hung there from all eternity, that I liked it not, and would not that the child should enter till I had first inspected it. Therefore, I bade him sit and rest upon a bed of crimson mosses which grew at the feet of a great rock, and to remain until he saw me turn to him again; and with many cautions and the most minute directions for his obedience and his comfort, I left him, and advanced alone.

My way had now grown quite or almost dark. The light of heaven and earth alike seemed banished from the dreadful spot. As it narrowed, the footing grew uncertain and slippery, and the air dense and damp. I had to remind myself that I was now become a being for whom physical danger had ceased forever.

"What a place," I thought, "for one less fortunate!"

As these words were in my mind, I lifted my eyes and looked, and saw that I was not alone in the dark defile. A figure was coming toward me, slight of build and delicate; yet it had a firm tread, and moved well-nigh the balance of a spirit over the rough and giddy way. As I watched it, I saw that it was a woman. Uncertain for the moment what to do, I remembered the command.

"Await what shall occur, and do as thy heart prompteth." And therefore—for my heart prompted me, as a man's must, to be of service to the woman—I hastened, and advanced, and midway of the place I met her.

It was now perfectly dark. I could not see her face. When I would have spoken with her, and given her good cheer, I could not find my voice. If she said aught to me, I could not hear her. But I gathered her hands, and held her, and led her on, and shielded her, and gave her such comfort as a man by strength and silence may give a woman when she has need of him; and, as I supported her and aided her, I thought of my dear wife, and prayed God that there might be found some soul of fire and snow—since to me it was denied— to do as much as this for her, in some hour of her unknown need.

But when I had led the woman out into the lighter space, and turned to look upon her, lo, it was none other. It was she herself. It was my wife. It was no man's beloved but my own. . . .

So, then, crying,

"Helen!"

And, "Forgive me, Helen!" till the dark place rang with her dear name, I bowed myself and sunk before her, and could not put forth my hand to touch her, for I thought of how we parted, and it seemed my heart would break.

But she said,

"Why, my dear Love! Oh, my poor Love! Did you think I would remember *that*?"

And I felt her sacred tears upon my face, and she crept to me,— oh, not royally, not royally, like a wife who was wronged, but like the sweetest woman in the world, who clung to me because she could not help it, and would not if she could. . . .

But when we turned our footsteps toward the light, and came out together, hand in hand, there was our little boy, at play upon the bed of crimson moss, and smiling like the face of joy eternal.

So his mother held out her arms, and the child ran into them. And when we came to ourselves, we blessed Almighty God.

Perceiving that inquiry will be raised touching the means by which I have been enabled to give this record to the living earth, I have this reply to make:

That is my secret. Let it remain such.

Typeset in 11/14 Bembo
with Bodoni display
Designed by Dennis Roberts
Composed by Celia Shapland
for the University of Illinois Press
Manufactured by Thomson-Shore, Inc.

University of Illinois Press
1325 South Oak Street
Champaign, IL 61820-6903
www.press.uillinois.edu